Floodtide

FRANK YERBY

Floodtide

Thorndike Press • Thorndike, Maine

Library of Congress Cataloging in Publication Data:

Yerby, Frank, 1916-
  Floodtide.

Reprint. Originally published: New York: Dial Press, 1950.
  I. Title.
PS3547.E65F5   1982   813'.54   81-21354
ISBN 0-89621-334-X   AACR2

Large Print edition available through arrangement with The Dial Press.

Cover design by David Freedman.

For Helen Strauss

Chapter 1

Ross Pary stood on the deck of the steamboat *Crescent City*, staring out over the Mississippi. He had his arms folded against his chest, and the fingers of one slender, white hand gripped the other arm with considerable force. One more bend, one more quiet sweep of broad, slow-flowing water, and then — home. He felt a queer tingle of emotion, just thinking of it.

Above his head, the whistle on one of the tall twin stacks spurted white steam, and cried out. There was a jangle of bells, and the *Crescent City* slowed, the cascade of muddy, yellow-white foam from her sternwheel thinning, her broad wake moving out behind her with a noticeable reduction of speed. Ross stiffened, staring hard in the direction of Natchez, his thin nostrils held tight against the outrush of his breath.

And it was there, again, that Morgan Brittany saw him. She came around the deck on her husband's arm, her frilled parasol dancing a little in the light breeze; then seeing Ross, she stopped.

"Let's wait here," she said. "This is a good enough place."

Lance Brittany looked toward Ross and glared. That affected young pup again, he thought; but Ross stood like a man of stone, unaware of their existence. Lance shrugged. He was fifty years old, and his bride of two months was twenty-five years younger than he, which did not help his naturally jealous disposition. Still, it was foolish to be afraid of every youngster they ran across, and this thin, delicate-appearing young fop was hardly the type of man to catch Morgan's roving eye.

"All right," he said, "we'll wait here."

Morgan glanced across the foredeck to the green and gold alluvial lowland of Louisiana, then carefully, little by little, she let her gaze stray back to where Ross stood.

He was, she saw, dressed in the height of fashion; he even exceeded the mode a bit, for that spring of 1850, the style of some of his clothes was not known in the United States. Morgan looked with approval upon his plum-colored frock coat, gathered tight at his slim waist, and flaring out as it fell almost to his knees. His waistcoat was of a soft, dazzling white, and his flowing cravat, gathered in a loose knot, was held to his starched and ruffled shirt by a great pearl stickpin. The collar of the frock coat was of maroon velvet, darker than the coat itself, and his plaid trousers, clinging to his well-turned legs, were strapped under the insteps of his polished black leather boots. The tall hat that sat so jauntily upon his shining blond hair was a soft dark brown, matching exactly one of the shades of the plaid. From under his folded arm, a slender gutta percha cane hung down, too short to be of much use, actually — a kind of swagger stick; but it became him.

There was, Morgan surmised, more to this Ross Pary than his fine plumage. His face, for instance, held her. Outlined against the morning light, it was as clean-cut as a medallion; not even the soft golden sideburns that curled down to the angle of his jaw, all the rest of his face being clean-shaven, were enough to blur that clearness of line. His nose was aquiline, almost Roman, high-bridged and thin-nostriled, and the set of his chin was firm and fine. Only his eyes betrayed him; somber and brooding, they gazed out over the muddy water in a way that made Morgan sorry for him, suddenly.

He has, she decided, a poet's face. And for once in her life, Morgan was very nearly right. Looking away from Ross's graceful slenderness to her husband's muscular frame, Morgan thought suddenly; he'd be much too easy — and smiled up at Lance.

Still, she could not dismiss Ross Pary that abruptly. She kept remembering that first night out of Memphis, when he had come down into the *Crescent City's* magnificently appointed saloon clad in an evening habit that had made every woman on the boat turn her head, and every man glare at him frostily and then glance self-consciously at his own attire as if to discover rusty spots. Very few of them could have worn those tight-fitting black trousers, buttoned above the ankle over the dove-gray spats. And none at all could have worn them with that completely unself-conscious grace. Yet, alone as he was, Ross had made no effort to push himself; he had merely acknowledged the self-introductions of those who proffered their cards, and murmured his name in return. His name, and nothing more.

Who the devil was he? Morgan wondered. He came from Natchez, which was Lance's home, and was now going to be hers — that much she had been able to worm out of the captain. Yet, when, with elaborate casualness, she had mentioned this fact to her husband, Lance had merely grunted. "Pary?" he said; "never heard of the family — so they can't be anything much."

As a member of one of Natchez' oldest and wealthiest families, Lance Brittany was indisputably in a position to know. Yet Ross Pary had the look of a gentleman about him. A gentleman and a poet, an aesthete and scholar, which after all, Morgan did not then realize, were not the attributes of the hard-riding, hard-drinking Southern gentry. A Southern gentleman might, as Ross had done aboard the *Crescent City,* swap quotations from Homer with Doctor Benbow in the original Greek; but no Southern gentleman would ever think of sitting down to the grand piano in a steamboat's saloon and entertaining the entire company with sweeping nocturnes played with matchless skill. "That," Lance had said brusquely, "was going too far."

Oblivious of Lance's frowning disapproval, she stared at Ross with such insistence that her gaze worked its curious alchemy inside his mind, and he turned and looked at her. She saw the slow flush steal upward along his untanned face, and suddenly she felt warm all over — warm and good. It was going to be nice living in Natchez. She was going to enjoy it.

11

Ross turned a troubled face back toward where the two-hundred-foot red-brown bluff on which the town of Natchez stood was coming into sight. It rose sheer out of the river, crowned with wild grapevines, and the splendid Magnolia Grandifloras, and towering giant oaks, between which the white Grecian columns of the planters' homes gleamed brightly, just barely visible amid the green shrubs and the explosive colors of flowers.

Now, he thought bitterly, she's going to find out. Now she's going to know. . . .

He was surprised to realize how important that was. There had been many women aboard the *Crescent City*, but only one Morgan. Even now, looking deliberately away from her, her face filled up his mind. It was a small, soft, creamy-white face, more heart-shaped than oval. It was, certainly, a pretty face; but not extraordinarily so. Even in the limited company of the steamboat's passengers, there had been prettier women. What was it, then, about Morgan? He stole a glance at her out of the corner of his eye. Then suddenly, absolutely, he knew. It was such a wicked face. It was the face of Cressid, of Iseult, of Morgan le Fay, for whom, doubtless, Morgan had been named.

It promised so much. It hinted of almost unimaginable delights all beyond the pale of society and its immutable laws. Did that old fossil Brittany believe the fact that he was married to Morgan insured his possession of her? If so, Ross decided, he was a fool. No man alive was going to watch that wine-red mouth, hovering forever between a pout and a smile, without being driven into some kind of action. Certainly not the impetuous sons of his native soil. You could look into Morgan's eyes and discover what blackness was, before light was, before time had begun, with the footsteps of God troubling the face of the waters. Beside them, even her hair seemed less than black. Yet Ross had seen her standing beside a raven-haired Creole from New Orleans, only yesterday, and the setting sun had raised rich highlights in the Creole girl's hair, rich brownish glints amid the blackness; but Morgan's hair had taken on a bluish sheen. It was, he thought, impossible for anything to be blacker than that. But her eyes – were.

And now, soon, he repeated with cold self-loathing, she's going to find out – she's going to know.

He hoped fervently that his brother Tom and his sister Annis would not meet him at the wharf. Tom was entirely too big and rugged and handsome, so that all his life Ross had paled into insignificance beside him; but it was

13

not that that troubled him now. It was rather that Tom was bluff and hearty, with an excess of animal spirits and an entire lack of either good taste or good manners. His clothes, Ross realized bitterly, would reveal their humble origin at once. And Annis, pretty as she was, was sure to look dowdy in the kind of things she wore.

At once Ross was ashamed of himself. They, his only living relatives, were the salt of the earth; and their clothes and manners could not be permitted to matter. His sojourn abroad, his Oxford education, had been, in a way, at their expense. Not that he had not earned the money himself; in fact, all the family's considerable advance in fortune had been entirely due to him. For Ross had what every other Pary since the beginning of time had lacked: ambition.

But, in a real sense, his going abroad had been at his brother's and his sister's expense; for it had meant that they had had to chain themselves to the lumber mill. But he could console himself with the thought that it was he who had bought into the mill in the first place, that when their saloon-keeping father had died, and left a considerable fortune to be divided among them, Ross alone had had the good sense to put every penny of his share into buying a partnership in old Peter Dalton's mill.

Afterwards Tom, reluctantly, had come in for a lesser share, with what money he had not gamed or wenched away.

Yet, even the memory of his success was a bitter one. It was his soft voice and almost instinctive good manners that had won so many building contracts for old Peter from the planters. He and old Peter, between them, had built half the imposing houses on the hill, chafing always under the direction of an imported architect.

Yes, Ross had built the houses, but he could not enter them. The planter aristocracy would never forget that he was born and raised and lived still in lusty, brawling Natchez under the Hill.

He looked up at the two hundred feet of bluff. Scarcely a ten-minute walk up Silver Street — but a lifetime journey for a man who wanted to move from the dirt and dives and squalor of the lower city, to the fair vista of upper Natchez — of Natchez on the Hill, where everybody who was anybody lived.

Ross was on the first leg of that journey. He meant to go up, come hell or high water. When there was money enough, he would go up. As a full-fledged architect, he could now command fat fees; fat enough, he reckoned, to build his own Greek Revival mansion in the upper city, to stretch out his own broad acres westward toward the setting sun, to become himself a planter, and hence a gentleman. It was not the smallest of all possible dreams.

The bells jangled once more, and the pilot backed water, reversing the great sternwheels so that the *Crescent City* slowed, came to a halt, then inch by slow inch started forward again. As they crept in toward the wharf, Ross saw Tom and Annis waiting there for him, and beside Tom, clinging to his arm, was Jennie Dalton.

Ross's heart turned over once, sharply, then settled down into a rapid drumroll. Jennie — his Jennie. No, not his, not ever his, not while his brother lived. And that, in one degree or another, was the story of his life. The younger brother. The second Pary boy. You know, the pale, quiet one. The one they always forgot. But no more. Damn it all to hell and tarnation, no more!

It was not alone that Tom was bigger than he, stronger than he, and far handsomer; but that he had that air of jaunty assurance that Ross had always lacked. Ross effaced himself, stepped out of the picture, blushed and stammered and hung his head. But in London and Oxford and in Paris, there had been girls of one sort or another who had found his shyness charming. The result was exactly what could have been expected. The shyness was rapidly vanishing. Abroad, it had vanished. But now, with the shores of his native Mississippi scant yards away, Ross Pary found to his pained astonishment that it had come back again.

He glanced once more at Morgan Brittany, and raced down to his cabin to get his valise. He was relieved to note that Tom had their Negro man, Simon, with him. Simon's brawny back and shoulders were certainly adequate to take care of his trunks. A few minutes later, he was wrapped in his brother's muscular arms.

"Ross!" Tom bellowed. "Well I'll be a cross between a razorback sow and a bull alligator! Lemme look at you! Great jumping Jehosaphat! What a swell!"

Annis kissed him tenderly, and Jennie brushed his cheek with her full, soft lips.

"You do look mighty fine, Ross," she said. "Don't reckon I've ever seen finer clothes."

"Thank you," Ross murmured. "And you look wonderful, too — all of you."

"Don't reckon this here town can hold you now," Tom beamed. "Hell, ain't a planter on the hill who can match your style. Hope you brought me some of them fancy English duds. I kind of got a hankering after style myself."

"I did," Ross said, and as he spoke, he was

17

aware that Morgan was coming down the gang-plank, and that she was surveying this gathering with feline care. Then her eyes rested upon Tom's massive form, and Ross could see them sparkle. God, he groaned inside his heart, not again!

Tom saw the glance and straightened up, looking back at Morgan in unfeigned admiration.

"Boy!" he breathed; "just who is that little queen?"

"Morgan Brittany," Ross said drily. "Lance Brittany's wife."

He could see Jennie's taut face slacken with relief at the word wife. Poor thing, she'd have a hard row to hoe if she married Tom — that is, if she hadn't done so already.

"Let's go," he said suddenly, with forced gaiety, "I'm aching to get home."

But before they could walk to Tom's surrey, Ross saw that Lance Brittany was staring at the half empty wharf, his face creased with frowning. With a murmured excuse to his relatives, Ross detached himself and walked over to him.

"Anything I can do, Mister Brittany?" he asked.

Lance stared at him, and the frown deepened. Then, he looked over to where Simon was putting the second of Ross's big trunks into the back of the surrey, and suddenly, unexpectedly, he smiled.

"Why yes, Pary," he said, "there is. You can lend me your nigger to take a message up to my house. I was expecting to be met, but apparently they didn't get my letter. Your man's reliable, isn't he?"

"Yes," Ross said shortly, "very." He was nettled at Lance Brittany's omission of the elementary courtesy of addressing him with a title. But he had committed himself already. Besides Morgan's black eyes, resting upon his face, were full of delicious invitation.

"Well then, call him over," Lance growled.

"Simon," Ross called. "Come here, won't you."

The Negro scurried over, his tattered cap in his hand.

"Yassir?" he said. "Yassir Marse Ross?"

"You're to take a message for this gentleman. You know the house called Buena Vista?"

"Yassir," Simon said.

"Well, run up there and tell them that Mister and Mistress Brittany are waiting at the wharf. Tell them to send the carriage down — at once. Now hop to it, Simon, don't tarry." He turned back to Lance. "That's it, isn't it, sir?"

The "sir" slipped out unwittingly, a part of the hard-learned courtesy that was in his very

19

marrow by now; but the moment he said it, he was sorry. It was beggarly to be polite to a man who refused courtesy in his turn.

"That's it," Lance said drily. "Thanks."

"You're entirely welcome," Ross said. "Sorry I can't offer you a lift, but as you see . . ."

"That's quite all right," Morgan said suddenly, amusement bubbling through her low, rich voice. "There are an awful lot of you, aren't there?"

"Enough," Ross smiled. "Well, good day to you both. Your servant, ma'am."

"Wait," Morgan said; "I've been dying to find out about you. Just what do you do, Mister Pary? Are you a planter? Or are you just a pianist?"

"Neither," Ross said. "I'm an architect."

"Oh, good!" Morgan said. "Maybe we can get him to build our new place — can't we, Lance?"

"Pary," Lance mused. "Now I remember — you folks are in partnership with Dalton in the lumber business. Built quite a few houses, as I recall. But I never heard tell of any of you being an architect before."

"We weren't," Ross said stiffly, "before. I studied it abroad — at Oxford and the École Polytechnique in Paris, and at the University of Barcelona in Spain. I plan to commence practicing my profession at once."

Lance studied him, dawning respect in his eyes.

"Drop by to see me," he said. "Tomorrow, if you can — maybe we can talk business at that."

"Thank you," Ross said. "I'll be happy to."

As he walked away, Morgan stared after him.

"What an extraordinary young man," she said in a low voice.

"In a way, he is," Lance admitted grudgingly. "First time I ever heard tell of anybody from under the Hill with enough grit in his craw to get himself a university education. That boy is likely to go far."

"Under the Hill?" Morgan echoed. "Just what is under the Hill, Lance?"

"This section. Nothing ever comes from down here except cutthroats and thieves and loose women."

Morgan stared at Jennie and Annis.

"Those girls," she whispered, "are they loose women?"

"Hardly. There are decent folks down here. The Parys are a rather good sort. None of them ever amounted to anything much, but they're a cut above the usual riffraff. Damn it, I hope that nigger of theirs doesn't forget. . . ."

Ross walked slowly toward the surrey. Here, by purest accident, opportunity had presented itself. Let him build a house, a fine house for

21

the Brittanys, and he was made. Half the planters of central Mississippi would beat a path to his door, demanding his services. A plantation of his own was not out of sight now.

But he never reached the surrey. While he was still ten yards away, the doors of a saloon, called, appropriately enough, The Dirty Spoon, opened, and half a dozen big ruffians came roaring out.

"Look at him!" one of them yelled. "Ain't he the cutest thing!"

"Well damn my eyes, if it ain't Ross Pary — all got up in them fancy duds!"

"Why Rossy, boy," another put in, "we're mighty glad to see you back in town. And don't let these boys plague you — ain't a thing wrong with them duds — 'cepting, maybe, they's a mite too clean."

The others lit upon this last suggestion with whoops of delight.

"Been away from ole Mississip' a long time, ain't you boy? Time you was gitting a little river mud in that pretty yaller hair!"

Ross stood his ground, white to the ears with rage and terror. Then as the first of the ruffians stretched out his grimy paws to seize him, Ross drew back the swagger stick and slashed him hard, across the face. The man fell back roaring. Then they fell upon Ross from all sides so

22

that his slender figure was borne to earth under their sweaty bulk. Ross felt the toe of a hob-nailed boot find his ribs and all the breath left his body. Then he saw the ruffians flying away from him in all directions, as Tom Pary sailed in, swinging his big fists. He managed to get to his feet, but at that it was still two against six. He saw Morgan Brittany looking at the fight, her face flushed with pure joy. Rage mounted up and beat about his ears. He picked up his cane again and started swinging it until it crashed into splinters against the thick skull of one of the ruffians. The man merely shook his head and bored in. A moment later, Ross found himself again flat on his back in a mudhole, convinced that his jaw was broken in at least three places.

The men ignored him then, and concentrated upon Tom. Tom sent one of them crashing into one of the slender pillars that supported the roof of The Dirty Spoon's gallery. It broke easily, being made of ancient, half rotted wood. Tom pulled the rest of it loose and used it as a flail, swinging it about him in a circle. At once the roof began to sag. One of the big men caught at another pillar, and tugged. It came loose, and he started swinging it in his turn. But Tom, with astonishing agility for a man of his size, avoided every blow.

Others began yanking at the slender posts. A minute later, the whole front end of The Dirty Spoon crashed into the street in a pile of rubble. The noise attracted the attention of the denizens of The Bucket of Blood, another dive across the street. They came out, bellowing like delighted bulls, and joined the fray. What the fight was about, they hadn't the slightest idea. They didn't need an idea; to the rivermen who lived under the hill any fight was its own justification.

In the renewed uproar, Tom managed to slip away and pick his slender younger brother up in his arms. He put Ross in the surrey, and took the reins. But before they were out of Silver Street, both saloons had been torn to the ground and the rivermen were going happily to work on a third.

Lying with his head pillowed in Jennie's lap, Ross looked back at the carnage. His face was swollen so badly that he could not open his mouth, and his fine, London-tailored clothes were in muddy tatters. Behind him, the rivermen were working bloody mayhem upon one another, with knives, broken whiskey bottles, and pieces of the demolished taverns.

But, even above the din of battle, Ross could hear Morgan's clear, delighted laughter. He felt sick suddenly, acutely, physically ill. Jennie

24

put out her soft white hand and stroked his bloody face. And Ross Pary, a man grown, a scholar and a gentleman, buried his face in the palms of his hands and cried like a child.

Such was his homecoming.

Chapter 2

Ross sat before the ancient, battered piano, and flexed his long fingers. He let the tips of them rest lightly upon the keys, then drew them back again, and sat there, frowning moodily at the piano. He was clad in a dark green silk robe, and a muffler of heavy white silk was wound about his slender throat. Above the robe, the right side of his face was grotesquely swollen, and his eyes looked out from under his fair brows, brooding and sad.

He leaned forward again, and caught himself suddenly, a brief grimace of pain crossing his face. His chest was tightly bandaged under the robe: Doctor Benbow, whom Tom had called, had found a slightly fractured rib. But he ignored the sharp stab, and putting his hands once more on the yellowed keys, began to play.

The piece was a gay mazurka, and Ross hammered the keys, almost forcing the triple time, accenting the third beat; but it didn't suit his mood, and he stopped it abruptly in the middle of a chord. He hesitated another moment, then almost fiercely he launched into the Appassionata Sonata. He played it all the way through, wincing at the flat notes from the badly out of tune piano, and afterwards he felt better. Music had always been a kind of release for him. Old Hans Humboldt, who had eked out his exiled life in Natchez by giving lessons to the planters' daughters, had taught Ross to play as a child, glorying in and wondering at the boy's talent. Herr Humboldt had wanted to make a concert pianist out of him, but Ross had other ideas. His music was to be his joy and his salvation – not his profession.

And now, with the strong Beethoven music some of the tension and the anguish had gone out of him. So when he started to play again, it was the Fantasie Impromptu he chose. The music soared up, lilting and fine despite the inadequacy of this battered wreck of a piano that had once stood in old Tom Pary's saloon. It was covered with whiskey stains, and Bowie knife scars, and here and there a bullet had crashed through it; but Ross Pary loved it. A new piano, of course – that would be one of the first things. But this old wreck would be preserved along with a sign that had stood above it: "Don't shoot the piano player. He's doing his best."

But they had shot him, Ross remembered. Accidentally of course, in the midst of one of those endless fracases that so enlivened life under the Hill. And his father, in desperation, because the flatboatmen were forever demanding music, had called upon Ross to play. He had been then no more than seven or eight years old; but already he could play well by ear. His father kept him at it for more than a year, during which time old Hans Humboldt, seeking a moment's solace from the planter families whom he hated, had wandered down the Hill and into the saloon. It was then that Ross's musical education had begun.

My music, and my life, he thought, because it had been the fat, slovenly Heidelberg graduate who had opened his eyes to what life could be, who had given him that thirst after knowledge that had carried him finally halfway across the world. And unfitted me forever for the world I must live in, Ross added bitterly to himself. I should have learned to use my fist and a gun. That's the kind of education that counts here. And not only here. On the Hill, too. Only they do their brawling more politely up there. A slap in the face, and cards exchanged. Then pistols for two. But it adds up to the same thing. The victim's just as dead.

His fingers lingered lovingly over the keys, the sweet, sighing music drifting until he became aware at last that someone else was in the room, standing there listening with rapt attention. He turned on the stool and saw Jennie.

"Oh no!" she breathed. "Don't stop, Ross — it's beautiful. . . ."

Ross looked at her a moment, seeing the soft, light-brown curls gathered in bunches back of her ears, and the blue eyes that were always filled with so much light and intelligence and spirit that they completely dominated her face; then he turned back to the piano and played the Fantasie through again, adding a little extra flourish.

He turned back to her, smiling, though it hurt his face to smile.

"It's new, isn't it?" Jennie asked. "I never heard you play that before. Who wrote it?"

"A man named Chopin. A very great composer. One of the greatest, I think. I used to hear him often in Paris. But, as he only died last year, we'll have to wait a hundred years before the world decides that he was as great as I think he is."

"That isn't fair," Jennie said gravely.

The hurt, brooding look returned to Ross's eyes.

"What is fair, in this world, Jen?" he demanded.

"Nothing, I suppose. I was thinking about you this morning. It's a crying shame that you have to live down here with all these rough-necks. A real gentleman like you. You ought to live on the Hill — not under it."

Ross's mouth tightened into a determined line.

"I'm going to live up there," he said. "And sooner than you think. Only," and he looked at Jennie with his heart in his eyes, "what good is it — now?"

Jennie's face softened with pity.

"I'm sorry, Ross," she said. "Sometimes I wish it were — different. But maybe it's good that it isn't. You really aren't my sort, Ross. When you go up in life, a woman like me would only be a millstone around your neck. You're much too fine for me. I'm just a plain girl, suited for a plain man — like Tom."

"Like Tom," Ross echoed bitterly. "You know, Jen — I've come close to hating Tom at times. Everything I've ever wanted, he got. Without half trying, without even wanting them very badly. . . ."

"You," Jennie pointed out, "have your music

and your education and your beautiful manners."

"Yes," Ross said; "but only because Tom didn't want them. Don't get me wrong, Jen; I'm not complaining of Tom. A man couldn't ask for a better brother. It's just that he's a little too much for me. I get along very well until people meet him. Then they forget me. I don't blame them — Tom is really something."

"They won't forget you now," Jennie said. "You're something, too, now — something special. We've got enough men in Natchez with big fists and copper-lined bellies. Reckon we could use a few men of refinement and taste. We won't always be uncivilized."

Ross got up from the piano.

"You're right, Jen," he said, excitement moving in his voice. "The town's changing. Right now it has some of the finest houses in the South, finer even than the Delta planters' homes. And it's going to have more. I'm going to build them!"

"You love houses, don't you?" Jennie observed.

"Yes. Come here, Jen — I want to show you something." He put his hand atop the piano and brought down two large rolls of paper. Carefully he unrolled the first of them, and Jennie drew in her breath sharply. It was a pencil sketch of a house — a house of breathtaking magnificence. It towered up amid moss-draped oaks, slim-columned and tall, with great galleries sweeping all around it on two levels, and on its top a little balustrade-enclosed platform commanded a view of the river. At the bottom of the sketch, Ross had written the single word, *Finiterre*.

"This," he said, "is the Brittanys' house. It's going to stand on a bluff in their north section, overlooking the river — far way from everything. That's why I called it Finiterre."

"Finiterre?" Jennie echoed blankly.

"It means Land's End. Do you like it, Jennie?"

"It — it's overpowering," Jennie said. "I would like very much to see it when it's done; but I don't think I'd like to live in a house like that."

"Nor would I. That's why I drew this one."

He unrolled the other sketch. It showed a simple Greek temple, almost severe in its plainness, but having such singing harmony of line, that Jennie could not tear her gaze away from it. The scroll-like ironwork had been reduced to a minimum; simple Doric columns held up the gallery, instead of the vine-leaf-encrusted ornamentation of the Corinthian columns he had drawn for Finiterre. Instead of the two massive galleries, one above the other so usual in the typical Greek Revival house, it had only the lower one, and the columns soared up unbroken to support the roof, which added immensely to their sweeping look of height. Above the single gallery, however, there was a tiny balcony, opening from an immense, fanlighted window on the second story. It was sheltered by the same roof that covered the gallery far below, and its ironwork balustrade was as delicate and fine as old lace. Jennie's gaze crept down the paper until she came to the name he had given it.

"Moonrise," she murmured. "That's lovely. But why Moonrise, Ross?"

"There's a place out on the old Merrill Plantation where you can see the moon come up. It looks like it rises out of the river. I'm going to build this house there, Jen — as soon as I get the money. The Merrills are all dead or moved away, and the land has reverted to the county. I can buy it for a song. And every night I'll stand on the balcony and watch the moon silver the water. There'll be white roses planted all around the gallery — nothing but white ones, Jen — so that when the moonlight touches them, they'll blaze like silver, and the moss in the trees will be silver, too — out there in the stillness." He looked at her, his pale face working.

"Only," he said softly, "I had always dreamed of standing there — with you."

"Ross, please!" Jennie said. "I don't think you're being very fair to Tom — or to me. Be good, won't you?"

"All right," Ross said quietly. "But Moonrise is going to be a legend one of these days. They'll point it out to strangers and they'll say: 'This is the house that Ross Pary built for the girl he couldn't have. And he lived in it until he died, and there was never a woman in it because of that.' "

"Now," Jenny said tartly, "you're being a fool."

"That," Ross said, "is nothing new. When haven't I been?"

"Oh, you!" Jennie sighed. Then she changed the subject. "Tell me, Ross," she said, "have the Brittanys approved of your plan?"

"They haven't seen it."

"They haven't seen it? Why, Ross? This is your big chance. You were supposed to go up to Buena Vista day before yesterday, and . . ."

"I know. But I could hardly go up there looking like this, Jen. I sent Simon up with a note expressing my regrets, and asking a postponement. Lance Brittany wrote back telling me to come when I can. It appears his wife is pressing him to build the house. She doesn't

34

like Buena Vista."

"And I don't like her," Jennie said.

"Nobody asked you to," the cool, amused voice came from the doorway. "Besides, you're only a woman, and I've never cared whether women like me or not."

They turned, both of them at the same instant, and stared at Morgan. She was wearing a black riding habit that Ross recognized instantly as a Paris creation. It was fitted very closely about her exquisite figure from the waist to the shoulders, but below the waist it flared out into an enormous bell shape over fine wire hoops. Her collar and undersleeves were of the finest white Belgian lace, and her outermost petticoat, part of which plainly showed, because she had the tail of her riding skirt looped over her left arm in the approved French fashion to keep it out of the way while riding, was white muslin with lace inserts and tucks. She wore the sauciest little black velvet hat in the world atop the high piled mass of her midnight hair; though, after a moment, Jennie saw that only the crown was velvet, the brim being of yellow straw, matching exactly the shade of her kid gloves. There was a jaunty ostrich-tip plume stuck in its band, and from the front of the brim a mauve veil trailed down, or would have, if Morgan had not that moment

35

tossed it back to reveal her perfect, beautifully wicked little face.

"Do you," Jennie raged, "usually walk into people's houses without knocking?"

Morgan smiled at her. It was, Ross decided, the most enticing, and at the same time absolutely the cruelest smile in the world.

"This is a house?" she drawled. "Forgive me, I didn't know. . . ."

"Why, you . . . you . . ." Jennie gasped. There must be a word for Morgan. But Jennie didn't know it. Old Peter Dalton had reared her much too strictly for her to know such words.

Morgan laughed easily. It was pure, rippling laughter — as clear and as musical as spring water. Issuing from those lips, it was doubly startling.

"Now really, my dear," she said; "you don't mean to tell me that a girl from under the Hill doesn't know the words?"

"No," Jennie said, "I don't. But right now I sure Lord wish I did!"

"I'll come around sometime and teach you," Morgan said, "when I have nothing more interesting to do. But right now I have something more interesting — much more interesting. Leave us, won't you? I want to talk to Ross."

"I will not!" Jennie spat.

"Possessive little thing, aren't you?" Morgan

said. Then she smiled up at Ross, so that the waves of color mounted in his face and all his flesh tingled.

"Ross," she murmured, "tell her to go, won't you? I'd really much rather talk to you alone."

Ross stiffened.

"Sorry, ma'am," he said quietly; "but I couldn't do that. After all, she has as much right here as you do."

"That's right, isn't it?" Morgan smiled. "Neither of us has any right to be here alone and unchaperoned in a man's room. Perhaps I interrupted something. Do forgive me, my dear, if I did. I do so love romances — especially clandestine ones."

"Oh!" Jennie gasped. "How perfectly disgusting! What kind of a woman are you anyhow?"

"A rather complete one, I've been told," Morgan drawled. "Oh dear, how tiresome! Ross, darling, why didn't you come to see me as you promised?"

That word "darling" was a little too much for Jennie. She clapped both her hands to her face, and turning, fled the house. Morgan threw back her head and laughed merrily.

"I knew that would get her," she said. "Now she probably thinks we're having an affair." She stopped suddenly, looking at Ross with pure deviltry in her black eyes. "You know," and her voice dropped down to a husky whisper, "that wouldn't be a half bad idea at all, come to think of it. . . ."

"Good God!" Ross said.

"I shocked you," Morgan sighed. The sigh, Ross knew, was as false as her laughter. "I'm sorry. It was wicked of me. But I do so like to shock people. Tell me, Ross — why didn't you come?"

"It's obvious, I think," Ross said icily. "I was in no condition to. You saw what happened to me. In fact, you seemed to be enjoying it."

"I was," Morgan said. "There's nothing better than a good fight between a score of primitive brutes. But," she mocked him, "you aren't a brute, are you? You certainly acquitted yourself rather poorly in that affair."

"There are other ways," Ross said, "of making one's mark in the world besides beating out a man's brains."

"True," Morgan sighed. "It's a pity, though — isn't it? Right now, I can't think of any half as interesting."

"You are a savage creature," Ross snapped, "aren't you?"

"Yes," Morgan said, the deviltry back in her eyes. She walked over to where he was, standing so close to him that he could smell the rich, heady perfume in her hair. "Yes," she whispered, "I am. Want to find out just how savage, Ross?"

"Heaven forbid!" Ross said.

"Still," Morgan mused, "it might be fun, at that. You might even have a little blood in your veins. . . ."

"And what," Ross said harshly, thoroughly angry now, "do you think I have?"

"Ice water," Morgan said, "and lamb's milk. What else?"

Ross took a half step forward, and caught her by both her arms; but before he had even reached her, Morgan's head went back a little, her black eyes closing, and Ross could see her warm red mouth softening and parting inches below his own.

He stopped dead. Then abruptly he released her and stepped back again.

"Oh, damn!" Morgan said.

"What's wrong?" Ross said.

"You. That was your cue to crush me in your arms, and prove to me that your blood beats warm as any other man's. Don't you ever take a hint?"

"Rarely," Ross said drily. "Still, if you want to be kissed, I reckon it's kind of ungentlemanly of me not to oblige. . . ."

He put out his arms and drew her to him.

Then he kissed her a long, long time and very thoroughly. When at last he drew away his face, Morgan's long, black lashes fluttered open very slowly, and in her eyes was the dawning of a new respect.

"Did they teach you," she said huskily, "to kiss like that — in France?"

"No," Ross smiled, "in Spain. The climate's warmer there — and so are the girls. I went for a month's vacation, and stayed a year. Someday I'm going back."

"Hang Spain!" Morgan said fiercely. "You're wasting time, Ross. I really don't have very much longer."

Ross stared at her in astonishment.

"You mean you want me to go on kissing you?" he demanded.

"Well," she said, her black eyes dancing with mischief, "you can start from there. Something might come to you. You might get an interesting idea, though at the moment I doubt it."

Ross put his arms about her and stood there looking at her as though considering the matter.

"You are still wasting time, darling," Morgan said softly.

Ross kissed her then, hotly, angrily, trying to hurt her; but she clung to him, shivering as though she were cold, caressing his mouth with her own with wonderful expertness, going up on tiptoe, and clinging, digging her finger tips into the soft silk of his robe, and at last, opening her mouth a little upon his, so that he was reminded of the odor of the figs of Valencia, hot under the Spanish sun, and the roaring of his own blood in his ears was like the noise of the crowds in the Plaza of bulls on a Sunday afternoon.

"Mighty pretty!" Tom Pary said. "Yessir, mighty pretty! Congrats, Ross — didn't know you had it in you."

Morgan whirled away from him and faced Tom. The motion was beautifully and superbly feline — all catlike grace. Then slowly, with deliberation, she smiled up at Tom.

"The other Mister Pary," she said. "The big Mister Pary. The big, beautiful Mister Pary, who can kill a man with his fists."

Tom put up his hand and pushed a lock of his dark, deepcurling hair out of his face. Then he grinned at her.

"You sure lay it on thick, ma'am. No wonder you had Ross going."

"I came to see your brother," Morgan said easily, "on business."

"That," Ross said miserably, "is the truth. Look, Tom, I —"

"No explanations, boy," Tom said gruffly.

41

"You don't need to explain a thing like this to me. There's only one thing I'd like to ask the lady, though. Pardon me, ma'am — I don't mean no offense; but just where is your husband right now?"

"Over in Louisiana, looking over his plantation," Morgan said. "Do you think I'd be here if he weren't?"

"I don't know," Tom said honestly. " 'Pears to me there ain't much you wouldn't do. And I hope that business of yours with my brother is finished, 'cause, even though it don't sound right polite, I reckon I'm going to have to ask you to leave."

"Why?" Morgan said.

"Your husband is a big man in these parts, ma'am. Also he's got a reputation for a bad temper and the marksmanship to back it up. Ross, here, is a good boy. He ain't used to such things."

"And you are used to them, Tom?"

"Considerable. But I don't hold with killing if I can avoid it. Look, ma'am, let's face it: we ain't quality, we Parys. But we're going up. Ross, now, I expect to see him master of a plantation before the year is out. Don't reckon we can afford a scandal right now. So leave Ross alone, won't you?"

"Yes," Morgan said quietly, "I'll leave him

alone. But on one condition. . . ."

Tom stared at her, his big, ruggedly handsome face frowning and puzzled.

"And what might that be, ma'am?" he asked.

"That you ride home with me. It will be dark in a little while, and I don't like riding alone."

Tom shot a glance at his brother.

"All right," Ross said miserably, "ride her home, Tom."

"Thank you," Morgan said. Then she turned once more to Ross. "Show me that drawing that girl was looking at when I came in," she said. "The one of the house you're going to build for me."

Silently Ross unrolled the sketch of Finiterre. Morgan studied it, her eyes widening as they took in the details of its splendor.

"Yes," she said; "yes, yes! You'll build it all right. This is the house for me. Oh, you'll build it — I'll see to that!" She snatched up the drawing, then very slowly she put it down again.

"No," she said, half to herself, "that wouldn't be wise, would it. You come tomorrow, and show it to my husband yourself. He'll be back early tomorrow morning. 'Bye, Ross." Then turning, she put her small hand through the crook of Tom's arm.

"Come on," she said, "Big Tom. Big, handsome Tom, who looks like a pagan god, and preaches me sermons like a backcountry Presbyterian divine. Come ride with me. It will be quite a ride, I promise you."

After they had gone, Ross slumped down before the piano, but for the life of him he could not play. He sat there a long time without moving, without even daring to think, until his sister Annis came in and put her soft white hands on his shoulders.

"Ross," she said gently, "what's the matter. Jennie told me that woman was here. Did she . . .?"

"Did she what?" Ross said curtly.

"Hurt your feelings. Jennie said she was awfully rude."

Ross stared at his sister, seeing her pale blonde, blue-eyed, wonderfully like himself, except that in Annis even his refinement of feature had been exceeded, had been softened into real beauty.

"No," he said shortly, "she didn't offend me, Annis. She merely came on business. I'm to build her house."

"Oh, Ross," Annis said, "how nice!"

"Yes," Ross said wearily, "it is, isn't it?" He got up stiffly from where he sat. "Excuse me, Sis," he said; "but I think I'd better lie down — I'm very tired."

"Here," Annis said, "let me fix your bed."

She busied herself smoothing back the covers, and pounding the pillows into plumpness; then she kissed her brother gently and left the room.

Ross drew off the robe and stretched himself out on the bed. He lay there a long time, and finally, though he had not thought it possible, he slept. He woke up hours later in the darkness, filled with an aching, terrible sense of loss. Groping on the night table beside his bed he found the sulphur matches and lit the lamp. Then he looked at the big clock on the mantel. It was four o'clock in the morning. Somewhere, far off and sad, a dog howled, just once and was still. In the oak grove on the top of the bluff the whippoorwills were crying. Slowly, inch by inch, entirely against his will, Ross Pary turned his bruised body over and looked toward his brother's bed.

It lay there in the light of the lamp, white and unrumpled, just as Annis had made it. Tom Pary had not come home.

Chapter 3

Ross came out of the county land office, and stood on the walk blinking up at the sunlight that was shredding itself through the festoons of Spanish moss on the oaks. The street was very quiet, so that he could hear his own heartbeats. I'm a landowner, he told himself in quiet astonishment. I own a plantation.

But just shaping words in the darkness of his mind, did not help much. It was too immense a thing to be grasped so easily. He started toward his mare, standing so quietly at the hitching rail before the office. He'd have to ride out to his new place. He'd have to see the land, let the rich black earth run through his fingers, before he could believe it was his.

His. Two hundred and fifty acres of rich cotton lands, bought for a song, all because of people's superstitions. Ross knew the history of the Merrill place. Yellow fever had swept off the entire Merrill family, except Mrs. Merrill, in one night and afterwards she had gone mad of grief and loneliness. Then the house itself had burned — a fire set, most people believed, by the madwoman herself. And Mrs. Merrill had died in the flames.

The Merrills had been a tragic folk, granted. Young Roger had died in Mexico in the War; and Sophie had run off with a Yankee overseer, who left her destitute with three small children in an Ohio town. She had come back at last with her brood, just in time for them all to get Yellow Jack and die with the rest of the Merrills.

Still, what had that to do with him? What fault was that of the rich, gently rolling lands? Yet the county clerk had looked at him as though he was out of his mind when he expressed his intention of buying the Merrill place. Ross had finally put an impatient end to his warnings, but not before the clerk had volunteered the information that the folks who had owned the land before the Merrills had had hard luck too. . . .

Maybe he was right, Ross mused, maybe I am out of my mind; but not for the reasons he thinks. That took all of my savings. Now I don't even have the money to buy Negroes, let alone build my house. I'm a fool, all right. Why didn't I wait? A year or two wouldn't have made any difference, and I would have been ready then. . . .

But he knew the answer to that one. Morgan. He'd never be able to forget her careless drawl: "This is a house?" Well, there would be a house now — and such a house that even she would have to respect. He knew well enough that her contemptuous remark about the home in which the Parys had lived so long was grossly unfair; but that made little difference. Actually the lovely Greek Revival mansions that Yankees believed typical of the South were even in this year of Our Lord, 1850, extremely rare. The Louisiana sugar planters had a few, and the cotton planters of the Delta and the Natchez section a few more. There were others scattered throughout the length and breadth of the South; but, Ross knew, even so there were not very many. How could there be when of the one and one quarter million white people who lived in the section, less than two thousand owned more than one hundred slaves apiece?

The typical planter's house was more like his own home, a low rambling structure, one cut above a dogtrot cabin, with saddles and harnesses piled up on the front porch, and the implements of agriculture cluttering up the front yard. The average cotton planter and often even the great landowners were rough and ready country squires, having neither the time nor the inclination to acquire anything like the culture that Ross himself possessed. Even their sons, from whom the older generation demanded a university education, usually whiled away their time at college with dog and horse races, gaming, wenching, and other such diversions, to return at last with a gentleman's passing grade, and but little more knowledge than they had possessed before they left home.

Still, he had to show Morgan. Morgan — and himself. A house such as he had dreamed of building would erase the last of the scars that life under the Hill had left upon his much too sensitive soul. When he had at last become one of the planter gentry, he could stand up tall and proud and look any man in the eye, his humble beginnings forgotten.

Slowly, dreamily, he untied Nancy from the rail, and was on the point of putting one booted foot into the stirrup when he saw his brother coming toward him. Ross stopped still and waited.

"Jennie told me I'd find you up here," Tom said sheepishly. "Look, Ross, it ain't the way you think. I didn't . . ."

But Ross stopped him with a lifted hand.

"No explanations, Tom," he said quietly. "They aren't necessary between us. You said that yourself, yesterday. I'm not going to quarrel with you — not over a woman like Morgan Brittany. I was making a fool of myself yesterday. Maybe you made a bigger fool of yourself last night. I don't know, and I don't even want to know. Appears to me the point for both of us to remember is that that little witch can't belong to either of us. And if she could, I think that the way for the one who lost to take it would be like a losing poker hand. So let's forget Morgan, shall we?"

"All right," Tom said. "God, but she's a funny kind of a girl!"

"Funny, how?" Ross said.

Tom looked away from him off down the street, and his big face was frowning and puzzled.

"She's cold," he said. "Never would think it to look at her, but my guess is she's as cold as ice."

"Cold?" Ross snorted. "Her!"

"Yes, her. That's a mighty good act she pulls, playing up to a man thataway. But it's just an act. When the chips are down, she freezes up quicker'n a wink. Now, you take last night. . . ."

50

"No," Ross said tartly; "I won't take it, Tom. I don't want any part of it."

"Sorry," Tom said, then his crooked, engaging grin spread over his face. "Just kind of reckoned it would relieve your mind to know. . . ."

"Just what would I know, Tom," Ross said evenly; "that she actually pushed you off, which is possible; or that you're a gallant enough liar to say she did even if she didn't, which is just as possible? Let's drop it, shall we?"

"Kerplunk!" Tom laughed. "There it lies — leastways unless you want to pick it up."

"Let it lie," Ross said. Then he looked up at his brother, and a slow smile lighted his thin face. "Well, Tom," he said; "I've done it. I've bought the Merrill place."

"Jehosaphat!" Tom bellowed and swinging down from his horse, seized his smaller younger brother in a bear hug so tight that Ross cried out with pain.

"Gosh, I'm sorry!" he said at once. "I plumb forgot about your busted rib. Ross, this is great! When do we start aplantin'?"

"We don't," Ross said sadly; "not for a year or two at any rate. It took every red copper I had left to buy the land. And it takes more than land, Tom."

"Don't I know it," Tom said. "That time I was overseer for the Quitmans, I used to lay out their money like water for supplies. And niggers are plumb downright dear these days. . . ." He looked at Ross, and a slow light began to dawn in his eyes.

"Say, boy —" he almost whispered, "how about letting me come in with you? I've got a little over ten thousand dollars put away — we could buy quite a few niggers with that, and enough supplies to work part of the place anyhow. . . . I don't mean to push myself in on your idea, but seeing as how we've mostly always been together in everything . . ."

"I was hoping you'd say that," Ross said.

"Were you, now?" Tom said wonderingly. "I never figured myself in on this thing, 'cause I knew what it meant to you. You've got a hankering after high society and rich living, and I ain't — leaseways, not much. Having me around would be like having a boarhog in the parlor."

"Come along and root away," Ross laughed. "Besides, you'll change," he added seriously. "In two years you'll be smoking Cuban cigars with Governor Quitman up at Monmouth, and matching him yarn for yarn."

"Ain't he a great old boy, though!" Tom laughed. "You should have been here on inauguration day. Cannons abooming so'd you of thought a war was on, and wimmen all in white throwing flowers down in his path, and asinging 'Hail to the Chief!' And him in his Mexican War uniform ariding on a milk white hoss. I tell you, Ross, boy — that was something. Sure is full of ole Nick, all right. Right now he's fair set to get the country in a war with Spain over this Cuban business. Him and some greaser named Lopez is thick as thieves at a lawyer's funeral. Hear tell they're planning an expedition to set Cuba free."

"Cuba should be free," Ross said; "but I sure don't hold with him on this secession business. Appears to me he's going a mite too far. I saw in the paper that those hotheads in South Carolina are toasting him as the coming President of 'our Southern Republic.' He and Rhett are two of a kind. This Compromise that Henry Clay introduced in the Senate week before last is good enough for now. We got much the better of the bargain — a fugitive slave law that actually works, and at least an even chance that Utah and New Mexico will come in as slave states."

"But they got California," Tom reminded him.

"True enough; but how many of us give a fig about moving to California and taking our slaves? It's so much talk, Tom — that's all; and John Quitman's been spoiling for a fight all his life. You know he organized that old Fencibles military company here. Even the Mexican War wasn't enough for him, now he has to take Cuba — and not to set it free, either. As a new territory it could form five new slave states with ten new Senators — that's what our Governor is aiming for. You'd never dream that he was a Yankee bred and born, would you?"

"Turncoats always shout the loudest," Tom said. "But, Ross, coming back to the subject of our new plantation, why don't you speak to old Paw Dalton? He's been piling up money since afore we was born, and all he can do with it is to leave it to Jennie, so it's only going to be mine anyhow — though that ain't why I'm marrying Jennie, as you well know. Maybe you can pry him loose from some of it — enough to build your house anyhow."

"Building a plantation house doesn't cost anything," Ross said. "Why right there on the place is timber enough to build it, and clay enough for all the bricks we'll need. It's furnishing it that costs, and buying Negroes who have some skill as carpenters and artisans. But I can't approach old Peter. He's done so much for us already. . . ."

"Have it your own way," Tom said. "Planning to ride out and look over the place?"

"I was, but it's too late now. I have to ride up to Buena Vista and talk business with the Brittanys."

"Well, that's right on the way. I'll wait outside for you. I ain't got no hankering to get tangled up with that black-eyed little witch again — 'specially with that fire-eating husband of hers around."

"All right," Ross said; "but first I have to go change my clothes."

"What's wrong with the duds you've got on now?" Tom asked wonderingly.

"They're not good enough," Ross said. "I don't intend being treated like a tradesman. I've got to make an impression somehow."

"To heck with it, then," Tom said cheerfully. "I'll ride out with you tomorrow instead. Tell you what — this afternoon I'll scout around and see if any likely niggers are going to be put up for sale tomorrow. That'll be the first thing."

"Good," Ross said. "Going home now?"

"Nope — not for a few minutes, anyhow. Got to buy a little present for Jennie. She's right pert riled up at me. Seems that Annis told her I went riding with Morgan. Oh, well, she'll get over it."

"I hope so," Ross said.

An hour later, he had just finished dressing, and was carefully fitting his tall black hat at precisely the right angle upon his head when he heard a knocking on his door. He crossed the bedroom in two strides and opened it. Jennie stood there, her young face strained and sad.

"Oh, Ross," she said; "how fine you look! You always dress so well."

Ross glanced self-consciously at his clothing. He had put on garments he had never worn before, a cloth brown cutaway, with a white waistcoat, pale gray trousers, with dark gray, black-piped braid down the sides, a spotted green cravat, tied in a loose, flowing bow, yellow chamois gloves, and black Paris-made boots that glowed like polished ebony. He lifted his hand to take off his hat, but Jennie stopped him.

"No, don't," she said. "It's on just right." She looked at him a long moment and then added softly. "They mean something to you — don't they? Your clothes I mean. They kind of make up for something, don't they, Ross?"

"Yes," Ross said harshly, "they help me forget I was born under the Hill."

"I think," Jennie said, "that where a man dies is more important than where he was born. You won't die under the Hill, Ross. I just saw Tom, and he told me you've bought your

Moonrise. Maybe you'll finish your life there — when you're an old man, with your children and grandchildren around you. Or maybe not even there. In Jackson, perhaps — or even in Washington. It's been done before."

"Thanks, Jen," Ross said.

"You're going to see her, aren't you? That woman I mean. Aren't you, Ross?"

"Yes," Ross said; "but only on business, Jen."

"I wish you didn't have to have dealings with her. 'Cause she won't let it stay like that. You're very attractive, Ross; though I don't think it would make much difference to her if you were old and crippled and ugly."

"Jen!" Ross said.

"It's the truth. You wear trousers. You're a man. To women like her, any man will do — for a while. But it always has to be a new man — somebody else's man. Her own doesn't interest her."

"Don't be bitter, Jennie," Ross said. "I asked Tom to see her home last night."

"I know. And nothing happened between them. Not yet. But something will happen between her and Tom, and her and you, and between her and any other man whom she can get alone for five minutes. I hate her. She's like one of those spiders who eats up her mates. . . ."

"Rather a beautiful spider, don't you think?" Ross teased.

"Yes. Too beautiful. I can even see what a man sees when he looks at her. Skin as white as snow. Hair as black as night. And eyes blacker than that – as black as her evil heart."

"Now you are being bitter, Jen," Ross said quietly.

"I know. I can't help it. I'm sick with jealousy. And with fear, too. I love Tom. I love you, too – in a different way – like a brother, really. And that kind of a woman destroys men. Oh – not literally. She leaves them alive, after a fashion. They can walk and breathe, and move about. But they aren't men any more. They're – they're things without souls."

"What a terrible thing to say."

"The truth is sometimes terrible," Jennie murmured. "But I won't bother you any more. Go on and see her. It's your big chance. Just try to keep out of her clutches. And, by the way, Father wants to see you. That's why I came."

"Thanks, Jen," Ross said; "I'll run over right now."

Jennie waited until he picked up his riding crop, then the two of them crossed the little yard that separated the two houses. It had been a long time since Peter Dalton had been able to move about, and now the sight of him shocked

Ross profoundly.

The old man was dying. Death was there in his face, hovering just behind his wonderful old gray eyes, but they were not afraid.

"How are you, sir?" Ross began uncertainly.

"You don't need to ask that," old Peter said. "You've got eyes. You can see. I'm dying, lad. That's why I sent for you. I've been about this business of passing on to my reward for two years. It's getting tiresome."

"I think you're wrong, sir," Ross began with false cheerfulness; "you look a little tired, but hardly —"

"Poppycock!" Peter Dalton snorted. "I'm an old man. I've lived my life, and it's been a good one. I've come a long way, son, since I left the old country. And you're going even further. You're doing what I've wanted to ever since I came to Mississippi. Only I never had the courage — or the good sense. You're a good boy, Ross; I'm proud of you."

"Thank you, sir." Ross was deeply touched.

"Don't thank me. Thank God. Thank Him you've got the brains and the courage and the ambition. But I didn't haul you over here to pass out compliments. I was going to leave all my worldly goods to Jennie, who's always been a good and dutiful daughter to me. But when Tom told us about your plantation, I got a bet-

59

ter idea. I'm going to give you part of that money — right now."

"But, sir —" Ross began.

"Don't gainsay me, lad! If I leave it all to Jennie, it'll only pass into the hands of that worthless brother of yours. Oh, I know — Tom's a good enough boy. Only there's nothing between his ears. He'll run through the money like a shot. I can't stop Jennie from marrying him, since women, bless 'em, will have their way in such matters. And most of them will mistake brawn and good looks for character. Yep, Ross, I'm going to give you outright the sum of twenty-five thousand dollars — with a few strings attached to it. . . ."

Ross waited. There was, at the moment, not a thing he could think of to say.

"The strings are very simple and they won't hurt you any. I want you to get that plantation going — right now, at once. And I want you to provide a place for Jennie and Tom to live on it. You'll have to put Tom to work. He knows considerable about planting, and nobody can deny he's a good worker. That way, Jennie will always have a home, no matter how big a fool Tom makes of himself."

"Papa!" Jennie began.

"Hush, child. I know what I'm talking about. You see, Ross, I'm not being so generous after all. Jennie and Tom will get three times what I'm giving you. But I've got more faith in your good sense than in either of theirs. In a few years, you're going to be rich. And in a few years they're going to be down to their last copper, and are going to need you. Those are the strings. Want to take my offer under those conditions?"

"Yes," Ross said without hesitation. "That's the only way I could take it, sir – with the idea that I was doing something for you in return. But Mr. Dalton, I ought to tell you that Tom's decided to come in with me already, and what's more, he's putting ten thousand dollars into the plantation that he's saved."

"Money that Jennie took away from him and saved for him," Peter Dalton said dourly. "Blood's thicker than water, but I know Tom. However, you don't need to defend him, Ross. If I didn't think he was a good enough sort, I'd send Jennie packing back to my brother in Scotland. He's a good boy, brave as they come, and generous to a fault; it ain't his fault that he was born without brains."

"Oh, papa, hush!" Jennie said.

"I've written out a draft on my account up at the bank. Here it is. Tomorrow you can go up and draw on it as much as you need – up to twenty-five thousand, of course. That ought to be enough to get you started."

"More than enough, sir," Ross said. "You're being wonderfully kind."

"I'm being smart! From the moment you came to me with your paw's money to buy into the mill, I knew you were a good one. First year you were with me, you got me twice as much business as I'd ever had before. Another thing — you know that building I own near the corner of Main and Canal Streets? Funny thing," the old man mused, gazing away from Ross out the window; "I own so much property up on the Hill, and I've never tried to live there — I never dared. . . ."

"Yes, Mister Dalton," Ross said; "I know the place."

"Open yourself an office in that building. Put up some elevation sketches in the windows. With your ideas, and your touch with the pencil, you'll make half the people in Natchez dissatisfied with the houses they now have."

"Really, sir," Ross began; "you're being much too kind. I couldn't —"

"Don't be finicky, lad. You can pay me rent if it'll make you feel any better. Now get out of here, boy — time's awasting!"

Riding up Silver Street toward the Hill, Ross Pary was troubled. It had all been much too easy. He had his plantation, and money to build his house, and buy his slaves and put in his first crop. On top of that he was making a fair start in his chosen profession. The years of struggle and privation were behind him; but not so far behind that he did not remember them. He had had to labor and fight, and go without sleep, and often without food as a youth to put himself through the academy, with occasional, haphazard, and always grudging aid from his father, and cheerful, generous, but deuced infrequent aid from Tom. All that was behind him now, that and the years that he had worked after his father had died, and left him and Tom, amazingly, five thousand dollars apiece. Buying in with old Peter Dalton had been a logical step. Besides his own family, the Daltons had been just about the only decent family under the Hill, all the rest being, individually and collectively, thieves, footpads, drunkards, and prostitutes.

But now, after all the labor and preparation, to have the doors swing wide just when he was girding up his loins to mount furious assault upon the citadel of his dreams, was, to say the least, disconcerting. Things that came too easily went just as easily, or turned to ashes and dust in a man's open hand. Even at twenty-eight, Ross Pary knew that. The life he had lived had made him wise beyond his years.

Riding through Natchez, his eye was caught by a series of placards. "A Free Cuba!" they shouted. "Down with the Tyrant, Spain! Monster Mass Meeting on the Esplanade tonight! Come hear our Honorable Governor, John A. Quitman, speak on this timely subject! Hear the sorrows of the Cuban people from the lips of General Narciso López, and his valiant aid, the Señor Eduardo Izquierdo! Our destiny lies to the South — Come strike a blow in behalf of our friends!"

Reading them, Ross frowned. This Cuban business was really getting bad. There was no doubt that the Cuba of 1850 was one gigantic prison camp in which the Spaniards practiced hideous cruelties. But, even if this filibustering expedition of López succeeded, how much freedom would the Cubans gain thereby? Quitman, Mississippi's New York born Governor, was a fire-eater, an imperialist, and a believer in the doctrine of America's "manifest destiny."

No, not America's, Ross corrected himself, the South's manifest destiny, which to John Quitman meant more land into which to expand the South's "peculiar institution." Was this man López a fool? Couldn't he see that by enlisting the aid of the most outspoken proslavery advocate in the land next to Robert Barnwell Rhett of South Carolina, he would only end by changing masters for the mass of the Cuban people? Or was López really interested in freedom? Men stung with the subtle poison of lust for power sometimes embrace the most unlikely causes. . . .

He shook his head and rode on. As soon as Buena Vista came in sight, he realized why Lance Brittany wanted a new house. Buena Vista was a good house, a good, solid, old-fashioned house, of the type in which more than any other, the vast majority of the planters lived. It was one and a half stories high, with dormer windows projecting from the peaked roof, and slim, cypress columns, no bigger around than the masts of a small schooner, supporting the roof of the gallery. It sprawled low and wide over the landscape, having many rooms and an air of serene comfort; but it lacked the white magnificence of the Greek Revival houses that since the eighteen thirties had excited the imagination of the wealthier planters These tall, gracefully-columned houses were already becoming a symbol, and like most of the South's symbols they represented something that existed only for the tiniest of minorities.

Practically everything the Northerners believe about us isn't so, Ross reflected; and nine-tenths of what we believe about ourselves. . . .

He had been nettled during his brief stopover in New York on his way home to find out that the Yankees believed that all Southerners were rich, lived in white-porticoed mansions and owned slaves. He had listened to their almost pointless abolitionist cant until he had been angered enough to look up the figures. Three hundred and forty-seven thousand slave-owning families out of one and one quarter million white families in the South. Out of every twelve Southerners, nine owned no slaves at all. And of the slave owners, five-sevenths owned less than ten Negroes each, most of them like Tom and himself having only one. There were eight thousand planters who owned fifty or more hands, and only eighteen hundred who had more than one hundred — eighteen hundred out of more than a million Southerners. Certainly the South's "peculiar institution" was peculiar to damned few people!

He dismounted and passed Nancy's reins over to the little Negro boy who seemed to appear out of thin air, and climbed the three low steps to the gallery. At once the doors swung open as the Negro butler bowed him into the hall. After a minute, he saw Morgan coming toward him, one hand cordially outstretched, and again it was necessary for his mind to correct his heart's impression that she was the most beautiful woman he had ever known. Seeing her there, smiling, radiant, her cheeks flushed with color, her warm, inviting lips parted a little in a slow smile, he recalled once more his brother's words: "She's cold. When the chips are down, she freezes up like ice." Cold! Ross thought. Tom must be mad!

"So you finally came," Morgan laughed. "Oh, Ross, I'm so glad! I was beginning to despair. And you brought the sketch. Marvelous! Come on, Lance is in his study. Now all we've got to do is convince him that this is the house."

"We'll convince him," Ross said, with a conviction he was far from feeling.

Morgan caught his hand and led him almost at a run toward the door of the study. She's so gay, Ross thought. How could any one believe that she's evil? Of course, she has a wild, wicked way of talking; but it's mostly a game to her, I reckon.

Morgan knocked on the door hard and threw it open almost before Lance's rumbling bass had called, "Come in."

Lance Brittany got up from behind his desk where he had been busy totaling accounts. He was, Ross saw at once, in good humor. The results of his arithmetic had made him so.

"Pary," he said. "Glad to see you. You

brought your sketch, eh? Well, then let's have a look at it."

Wordlessly Ross unrolled the sketch on the desk top in front of Lance. The planter studied it with minute care. His face was still and carefully controlled, but Ross could see the glow brightening in his dark eyes. Finally he straightened up.

"All right, Pary," he said gruffly; "you've got yourself a job."

"You darling!" Morgan cried and throwing both arms about his neck, kissed him, hard.

"What was that for?" Lance asked in mock severity; "because you're pleased with the idea of the house, or because Mister Pary is a pleasant young man?"

"Both," Morgan said merrily. "Oh, Lance — it's finer than D'Evereux or Monmouth!"

But Lance was studying the sketch once more.

"Finiterre," he muttered. "So you've even named it for me, Pary. But why Finiterre?"

"There's a high bluff on your land, Mr. Brittany, near the boundary between it and the old Merrill place. The view from there is beyond comparison: the river far below, and the sweep of land stretching out for miles on the other three sides — why I can almost see now how it'll look from your captain's walk. . . ."

Lance stared at him speculatively.

"You've got a persuasive tongue in your head, Pary," he said. "You have a horse with you, haven't you?"

"Yes," Ross said. "You want me to show you the spot?"

"Naturally. I'll admit I hadn't made up my mind just where I wanted the house built; but I'll have to see this location before I'll know whether it suits me."

"I'm coming too!" Morgan said, clapping her small hands gleefully like a child.

"All right," Lance said; "but don't be long in changing. . . ."

After Morgan had gone up to her room, Lance sauntered over to the bell cord and gave it a pull.

"Well," he said, "what will it be, Pary? Port, sherry, Madeira — or just plain bourbon?"

"Bourbon is rich enough for my taste," Ross said easily. So the great Lance Brittany begins to thaw, he thought. Wonder how he'll take the news that we're going to be neighbors?

Lance gave the order to the Negro who came in answer to the bell and turned back to Ross.

"Finiterre," he said. "Land's End, eh? Way and begone out on the end of nowhere. Damn my soul, Pary, if I don't like the idea! Adds a little mystery to the thing. The big house sitting out there under the trees, with just a touch of aloofness about it. . . ."

He picked up the decanter of bourbon from the tray the Negro had brought, and poured two brimming glasses with a steady hand.

"To Finiterre," he said.

"To Finiterre," Ross murmured, "and may those that dwell therein know only happiness."

"Thank you, Pary," Lance Brittany said, and drained his glass. He stood there, holding it in his big hand, and stared at Ross with frank curiosity.

"You may come from under the Hill," he said at last; "but I'll lay odds that you'll never end up there."

"I don't intend to," Ross said.

Riding out to Finiterre, for to Ross at least, the place already had that name, none of them said much. They were each of them lost in his or her private world, through which the slow clopping of the horse's hoofs came but dimly. Once or twice Ross was aware that Morgan was looking at him. She had dropped a little behind the two men, and her gaze was upon him steadily for whole minutes at a time. He had the warming impression that it was not lacking in interest. Interest and something more. Yet Tom had said that she was cold. Could it not be, Ross thought, with the natural egotism that has always been the downfall of the male of the species, that Tom's clumsiness and lack of finesse were responsible for the "freezing up"? Casting a quick backward glance over his shoulder at the evening sunlight pouring illumination into that exquisite, heart-shaped face under the intense blackness of her hair, Ross Pary was sure of it. Had I been presented with such an opportunity, he thought, I'd have made much better use of it. . . .

They came at last to the high bluff and sat upon their mounts gazing silently out over the river. Far away and dim the Louisiana bank lay green and gold in the waning sun, and below them the great river flowed quietly, muddy golden in the sunlight, and blue silver in the shadows. The bluff on which they were was crowned with ancient, towering oaks, all richly festooned with hanging moss. A little breeze stirred the delicate, feathery mass, and when the sunlight caught in it, it blazed.

"Oh yes, Lance!" Morgan said eagerly. "Yes, yes, yes!"

"Finiterre," Lance growled. "Land's end. Damn my soul, Pary — you're right!"

"Thank you, sir," Ross said.

"When can you begin?" Lance demanded.

"Whenever you're ready, sir. Of course, it seems a shame to have to buy timber when your place is so heavily wooded. But it would take better than two years to season the lumber properly, and you'd need brick. . . ."

Lance grinned at him, triumphantly.

"Come with me," he said.

They rode down the bluff and back down the road for a distance of two miles. Then Lance turned his horse off the road into a smaller wagon trail. It came out on a clearing, and Lance pointed with his crop. In the middle of the clearing stood a magnificent kiln, capable of burning enough brick for ten houses.

"I've been planning to build for some time, Pary," Lance said. "Now take a look at the trees around this clearing."

Ross looked and saw to his astonishment that they were all bare and dead, though beyond them the woodland was green with spring. Riding closer, he saw the reason. The giant, perfect oaks, and lower down in the marshy places, the hoary gray cypresses, had all been ringed with a deep cut, some years before, killing them, and allowing them to season where they stood.

He came back to where the Brittanys waited and made Lance a little bow.

"It's going to be a pleasure to work for a man with such foresight," he said. Then he sat there on his mare staring at the kiln.

"What's the matter?" Morgan asked, "is anything wrong?"

"No," Ross said slowly; then he turned once more to Lance. "I wonder if I could presume upon your generosity, sir," he said. "I'm going to need brick for my own place. Could I send my people over with a few wagon loads of clay to burn brick in your kiln? It would save me months, and I'd be mightily indebted to you, sir."

"Your own place?" Lance boomed. "What the devil do you mean, Pary?"

"The old Merrill place," Ross said evenly. "I'm going to be a neighbor of yours. I — bought it this morning."

"Well I'll be damned!" Lance said helplessly. "You're the first man I've ever met that I couldn't figure. So you're going to be a planter, eh?"

"Yes," Ross said, "on a small scale."

"Two hundred and fifty acres isn't a small scale," Lance said gruffly. Then suddenly, surprisingly, he put out his big hand. "Congratulations, Pary!" he said. "Damned if you aren't the right sort!"

"Thank you, sir," Ross said.

"Oh, Ross, how perfectly marvelous!" Morgan said. "We couldn't ask for a nicer neighbor — could we, dear?"

"Reckon we couldn't," Lance said. "It's a great thing you've done, boy. People have been calling us Southerners autocratic and despotic for years. Now you're going to find out we aren't. We aren't even aristocratic in the hereditary sense. We took a bunch of French pirates, the Surgets, and established one of our greatest lines; we let a dry goods clerk like David Hunt become one of our largest land-owners. And we took a Yankee ex-school-teacher turned lawyer like John Quitman, and made him Governor of the State. But I don't know anybody who's ever climbed the Hill, before. There were two families, the Littles and the Lows, who did it once, but neither of them left descendants. That's going to make it harder for you. It's easy to forget a man's origins when you don't know them any too well. Lots of people are going to call you an upstart, Ross; but, hell, boy, you've got a better education and better manners than any of them. It's my guess that you'll make out fine."

"He will," Morgan said. "I know he will — and we're going to help. Know what Lance? We're going to invite him to that party you're giving for Governor Quitman and General López tonight!"

"Now really," Ross began, "I wouldn't dare presume. . . ."

"No presumption at all, Ross," Lance laughed. "Hell, it'll be fun! It's going to be damned fine sport just watching the faces of some of our older and stuffier gentry when I introduce the new owner of Merrill!"

Ross stared at them, so moved that he found it difficult to speak.

"I don't know what to say," he said helplessly.

"Don't say anything," Lance said. "You've done it all yourself. All we're doing is speeding up the process a bit. And about those bricks — you're welcome to them, and all the timber you can cart away."

"Thanks," Ross said, his voice trembling in spite of all his efforts to control it. "Thank you both — I'll be indebted to you the rest of my life. . . ."

"Think nothing of it," Lance began; but Morgan interrupted him. She held in her hand the little watch she had pinned to the front of her riding habit.

"Oh, Lance," she wailed; "we're going to be late to the mass meeting!"

Lance consulted his own timepiece.

"Not if we hurry," he said. "Coming, Ross?"

"Yes," Ross heard his own voice saying to his own surprise. "Why yes, I am."

Ross now — no more just Pary, spoken carelessly. A little later it would be Ross Pary of Moonrise. And still later — who knew? He felt warm inside, warm and good. He was now, after all the troubled years, a man who had arrived.

An hour later, standing next to Lance and Morgan under the oaks on the broad sweep of the Esplanade, Ross discovered that there was more to this business of Cuba than he had suspected. Governor Quitman mouthed grandiloquent phrases, hinting at the great destiny of the South which lay ever southward. That destiny, Ross well knew, to John A. Quitman meant only the expansion of slavery below the Rio Grande, and into all Central and South America as well as the islands of the Caribbean. Slavery no longer existed in any of those lands, except in Cuba and the other small islands held by Spain, and the great state of Brazil. And Ross, whose sojourn in Spain had made him minutely acquainted with these matters, knew that even in those countries it was being gradually abolished. Beyond that, Quitman and Southerners of his type, meant to expand their peculiar institution to the south at the expense of the independence of those nations — which they clearly looked upon as future colonies, which could be made into territories, whose climate and type of agriculture would almost automatically, under Southern leadership, demand a slave economy. The territories in a short time would become States, with a terrible preponderance of power of the ballot over the abolitionist North.

Thinking about it, listening to the subtle trend of the Governor's oratory, Ross Pary was troubled. He accepted slavery, regarding it as a necessary evil; but to him it was a far from holy cause, and the wisdom of spreading it was at least questionable.

At his side, Morgan was frowning. Seeing his glance, she went up on tiptoe and whispered quickly into his ear:

"I hate slavery. I'd like to see all the Negroes freed!"

Ross stared at her, but after a moment's reflection, it came to him that her attitude was hardly surprising. Morgan was New York born and bred, and abolitionist sentiments were to be expected of her.

He turned back to the platform under the torchlights, where after a flowery introduction by Governor Quitman, General Narciso López was bowing to the crowd. A handsome, white-haired Venezuelan, General López made an imposing figure, but Ross, who alone of those present knew his record, studied him with cool contempt. López had fought for Spain against his native land, and had been forced to flee the country when Venezuela won her independence. In Spain he had served in the first Carlist War, rising to the rank of Major General, and being appointed Governor of the province of Valencia. Then in 1841 he had appeared in Cuba along with Don Jerónimo Valdes, and had risen rapidly in power and influence. It was, Ross thought angrily, a mighty funny thing that López hadn't been interested in Cuban independence then. Nothing like that. He was interested in the same thing that interests him now: power and money for Narciso López. Before I'll work up any concern over poor abused Cuba, he'll have to explain to me why it wasn't until Don Leopold O'Donnell relieved him of his offices and commands in 1843 that he got interested in Revolution. No nation will ever win her independence at the hands of a man who twice in his life has already changed sides. . . .

López made a masterly speech. Even Ross had to admit that. He convinced his hearers that the Cuban Junta favored annexation by the United States. But what Ross Pary wanted to know was why.

He could see Lance Brittany, frowning and thoughtful, taking it all in. Throughout the crowd were old men of the highest rank in

Natchez, but the bulk of those present were made up of young blades spoiling for a fight — any fight so long as it promised adventure and glory.

A moment later, Ross had his answer. General López introduced Eduardo Izquierdo, and asked him to tell the crowd his experiences with the despotic government of Spain. Unfortunately, López explained, Señor Izquierdo could speak no English, so he would have to serve as translator.

Ross watched Señor Izquierdo coming forward, an old and broken man, hobbling to the front of the rostrum as though every step cost him painful effort. Then Izquierdo began to speak, and his voice was a musical instrument of compelling depth and power, the lovely Castilian rippling from his tongue. At first, Ross, who after a year in Spain and being blessed by nature with a natural gift for languages spoke fluent Spanish, paid no attention to the translation. Then it caught him. López was at best paraphrasing — at worst, he was distorting and more. Often he was simply lying.

Izquierdo told a moving story. He had been a member of the mulatto poet Plácido's original Revolutionary band in 1844. He had seen Plácido lashed almost to death, and afterwards he had seen him die along with the Negro musician Pimienta, and the rest of the brave liberated Negroes who died that their less fortunate brethren might be free.

This, to Ross's angry astonishment, López translated as merely that Señor Izquierdo had early associated himself with the Revolutionary movement. And it was then that he got López' drift. The Venezuelan could scarcely permit the citizens of Natchez to learn that the Cuban Revolution had begun as an anti-slavery campaign.

Izquierdo told of his capture by the Spaniards, and the details of the hellish torture that had made him the crippled wreck they saw. López' translation of this part was fluent and exact, and many women in the crowd wept.

Looking at Morgan, Ross saw a half smile lighted her face. With each added detail, the expression of interest, even of – of pleasure, Ross realized with horror, grew. Morgan Brittany looked as if this recital of sickening brutality was the most enjoyable thing she had ever heard. Staring at her, Ross realized that he had seen this expression upon her face previously, and after a moment, he remembered where and when. The day he had been set upon by the river ruffians, Morgan had looked like this. Gazing at her now, Ross felt cold and sick, so he turned his attention once more to the speaker.

"When I think," Eduardo Izquierdo said tensely, "about my years of struggle — of the terrible times when I was a guerrilla leader, I am moved to quote the words of the immortal Hidalgo of Mexico, written in his confession, to make of it my own *grito de dolores* — my cry of sorrows. I need only substitute the word 'Cuban' for 'Mexican,' and it becomes mine, and I will say it now: 'Who will give water for my brow and fountains of tears for my eyes? Would that I might shed from the pores of my body the blood which flows through my veins in order that I might mourn night and day for the Cubans who have died, and that I may bless the never-ending mercy of the Lord.' But I must omit here his words of repentance for I have not repented. I sorrow only for the brave and hopeless dead, or to return to Padre Hidalgo's words, 'I exhale each moment a portion of my soul. . . . Ah, America! Ah, Americans, my compatriots. And Europeans, my progenitors! . . .' " The old man paused, fighting for breath.

In the stillness, Morgan could hear Ross's rich baritone, murmuring the words, completing the part that Izquierdo had begun:

" 'Have pity, have pity on me! I see the

destruction of the soil which I have wrought; the ruins of the fortunes which have been lost; the infinity of orphans I have made; the blood which in such abundance and temerity has been shed; and — this I cannot say without fainting — the multitude of souls which dwell in the abyss because they followed me. . . ."

"Why!" Morgan whispered; "you understood him! And you speak it, too — so beautifully. . . . Tell me, Ross what does it mean?"

"Later," Ross said. "Listen to him now."

"It cannot be permitted," Izquierdo concluded in the same exalted vein, "that Cubans remain slaves — that any man remain a slave! With your help my sorrows will be ended; with your aid and that of Almighty God — all men shall be free!"

He turned then and hobbled back to his chair, his tired old eyes dimmed with tears.

"Señor Izquierdo said," López finished smoothly, "that Cuba counts upon your fullest aid to free her from despotic Spain and join her with a more beneficent power. . . ."

"Well I'll be damned!" Ross said.

After the cheering had died down and the rush of the younger men to sign up for the expedition had begun, Morgan turned to him.

"He didn't say it right, did he, Ross?" she demanded. "That old man kept saying *los esclavos*

— and that means slaves; and *los negros*, and that means the same thing it does in English. And this López never said a word about either Negroes or slavery!"

"Careful, Morgan!" Lance warned, for several of the people in the crowd had turned to stare at her. But Morgan made no attempt to lower her voice.

"He did mistranslate it, Lance — and on purpose, too! Now didn't he, Ross?"

"Yes," Ross said softly; "he did. I'll tell you what Señor Izquierdo said, tonight. . . ."

"Oh, tonight! I had almost forgotten that! Lance, darling, we'd better hurry home — there's so much to do. And Ross, you'll meet Señor Izquierdo tonight, and his daughter. She's a lovely creature — I only wish I could talk to her. General López will be there, too — and Governor Quitman. It'll be quite a party. Well, 'bye now. See you at eight."

Ross bowed.

"I'll be there," he said.

When, at nine o'clock that same night, Ross stepped inside the great salon at Buena Vista, the Negro butler hesitated a barely perceptible fraction of a second. There were, Ross knew, no greater snobs on earth than black house servants. Cato, the Brittanys' butler, knew

83

everybody who was anybody in Natchez. That he did not know Ross, made him instantly suspicious.

"What did you say your name was, sah?" he muttered.

"I didn't," Ross said, and passed him over his tall evening hat, and loosened the cords which held the white silk-lined opera cape that swung jauntily from his shoulders.

Cato was nonplussed. This young man in the sparkling new evening habit looked like a young prince. His richly ruffled dress shirt was quite the finest the old Negro had ever seen, and the studs were real pearls, too — Cato could tell that at a glance. His small white linen bow cravat encircled his high winged collar, and had been tied by a practiced hand; and his white waistcoat was of the softest, finest white silk, embossed with off-white figures. Even his white broadcloth gloves were the best, and the buttons that fastened the black evening trousers that fitted his well-turned legs like a second skin about the ankles, were pearls, too. Shiny pumps with the smallest possible black cloth bows. . . . Cato didn't know this man, but he was by long odds the finest gentleman present.

"Yassuh," Cato said apologetically; "didn't mean no offense, sah, but I'm 'bliged to announce you."

"Pary," Ross said, "Ross Pary."

"Mistuh Ross Pary!" Cato bellowed.

The chatter of the guests died, and one by one they turned to stare toward the doorway. In varying degrees their reactions matched Cato's; but those few who had known Ross before, for whom in the past he had built houses, stared at him thunderstruck. After a moment Morgan came toward him, and as she did so, Ross caught his breath sharply.

She had on an evening gown of white silk, cut in extreme décolletage, that fitted her breasts and waist like a sheath and flared out below into a great bell shape over the hoops. With that hair and those eyes as points of contrast, the dress, on Morgan, was electrifying. She wore a diamond tiara in her high-piled hair, and against the little bunches of jet curls behind her ears, her long, emerald-cut diamond pendant earrings glistened like white liquid fire. A necklace in the form of a spray of diamonds lay along the soft rise of her breasts; and against the creamy whiteness of her flesh they looked like droplets of some magic fluid, scattered there by an enchanter's hand.

"Ross!" she cried gaily; "I'm so glad! I was beginning to believe you weren't coming. I would have been desolate. . . ."

At her words, those who knew Ross Pary and

85

his origin, reached a state bordering upon apoplexy. But Lance Brittany excused himself smoothly from the little group around Governor Quitman and came forward with outstretched hand.

"Glad to see you, Ross," he said. "You don't know most of the people, do you? Very well, I'll introduce you."

Then, taking Ross firmly by the elbow, he led him from group to group, murmuring after each introduction, the words which became Ross's "open Sesame!" into this new world: "Mister Pary is our youngest planter. He's just purchased the old Merrill place."

Ross could see their faces change as they heard it. Astonished wrath faded into comprehension, and, among the young ladies and their devoted mamas at least, after one quick appaisal of the quiet splendor of his attire, into quick acceptance. The men were slower. With the natural conservatism of the masculine sex, it would take them time to get used to the idea; but the ice was broken; and since, in social matters, the women by diplomacy, guile, or sheer dominance of personality ruled their households, Ross Pary had won.

He moved through an avenue of soft feminine smiles and quickly downcast eyes toward the group around the Governor. He was only a few feet away, when he saw her. And involuntarily he stopped dead. But Lance was urging him forward, and as he moved the room and the crowds and the renewed chatter faded away out of time and mind and there was no one else in the world but this tall willow-slender girl with golden skin, dark-brown hair with red-gold lights in it, and eyes as green as a southern sea.

"Your Honor," Lance was saying, "may I present my new neighbor, Ross Pary of Merrill. He has just bought the place, and plans to put in his first crop this season. . . ."

"Then he has his nerve," John Quitman boomed. "Nobody else ever made a go of that wilderness. Glad to meet you, Mister Pary."

"I'm honored, sir," Ross said.

"Meet General López," Quitman said. "General – Ross Pary."

Ross bowed.

"I have," he murmured in flawless Castilian, "much pleasure to know you, your Excellency. Your secure servitor, sir."

The little group around Governor Quitman froze. The Governor recovered first.

"Well, I'll be damned!" he boomed. "Brittany, you've been holding out on me! We've got to have this man. He'd be invaluable!"

General López put out his hand with a suave smile.

"Castilian," he said, "even to the lisp. I take it then, that you enjoyed Señor Izquierdo's eloquence rather better than most."

Ross looked him straight in the eye.

"I did, Señor," he said. "And much, much better than your translation of it."

Narciso López did not waver.

"The reasons for such a translation must have been obvious to you, Señor Pary," he said. "Señor Izquierdo is an old man and – well – unrealistic. But you must meet him. Eduardo, meet the marvel of the age – a young *Americano rubio* who speaks perfect Spanish!"

Izquierdo smiled gently up at Ross, and put out a wasted hand.

"I am honored, Señor," Ross said, "to meet a patriot and a brave man."

"Much thanks, young man," Eduardo Izquierdo said gently. "It is good to hear Spanish again, and for you to have taken the trouble to learn it is a great compliment. And now – my daughter. *Muñeca mia*, may I present the Señor Pary? Señor Pary, my daughter the Señorita Conchita Izquierdo, the last of my treasures. . . ."

"And the greatest, without doubt," Ross said, "with twin emeralds for eyes, and all the gold of

El Dorado for coloring, and pigeon-blood rubies for lips." Then he bent with continental grace and kissed her hand.

"What did you say to her, Ross?" Morgan demanded a little crossly. "What does '*Labios rojos de los rubis como la sangre de las palomas*' mean?"

"It means," General López laughed, "that the young caballero is practiced in the arts of love. He said that Señorita Izquierdo has ruby lips the color of the blood of doves. . . ."

"How poetic!" Morgan said. "You've never said anything so pretty to me, Ross."

"Hardly," Ross said drily. "I value your husband's friendship enough to want to keep it."

". . . and also in diplomacy," Narciso López said.

Conchita Izquierdo looked at Ross, and a slow wave of color climbed her exquisitely modeled cheekbones.

"I have not the words," she said; "but I think the Señor is being more than kind."

"Only just," Ross answered; "perhaps not even that. I shall see you again? A little later, maybe?"

"*Tal vez, quizás,*" Conchita murmured. "How do you say it in English?"

"Perhaps," López supplied.

"I prefer certainly to perhaps," Ross said;

"but that will have to do for now. . . ."

"Oh, come on!" Morgan said. "You still have lots of people to meet."

"You sound like a jealous woman, Morgan," Lance said curtly.

"I am," Morgan laughed. "I have great plans for Ross — though I haven't picked out a girl for him yet. But, when I do, she won't be a sunburned Cuban wench."

"I'll do my own picking thank you," Ross laughed; "and that sunburned Cuban wench will do very nicely, as far as I'm concerned."

"Damned right she will," Lance said. "Half the young blades here decided that already, but the lingo's got them stopped. If I had time I'd have you give me lessons, Ross. If the women of Cuba are like that one, I vote we annex it at once!"

"Oh, you men!" Morgan said.

A little later, the people of Natchez were relieved of any lingering doubts that they might have entertained as to just where Ross Pary stood. For when Lance Brittany led the procession into the dining room with Eliza Quitman on his arm, followed by the Governor, escorting Morgan, only that romantic adventurer, Narciso López, flanked by two smiling Natchez belles, separated Ross Pary from the guest of honor himself.

Conchita Izquierdo's hand rested on his left arm so lightly that he had to look to see that it was there, and his right gave strong support to the tottering steps of her father. And behind them trooped the rest of the guests.

Ross had to check himself to keep from staring at the bounty that was piled on the long tables. There, under the soft glow of the candles, were already platters of several varieties of meats, vegetables, pickles, preserves and jellies. As soon as they had seated themselves, relays of servants sprang into action. No glass of port or sherry was ever allowed to diminish one inch. As soon as Ross put his down, a black hand appeared on his left, ready with the decanter.

It was, he decided, much wiser not to drink it; for with Lance's indefatigable servants in attendance, a man courted quick intoxication. The lines of Negroes criss-crossed each other coming and going with the magnificent silver service. The rolls and biscuits were almost too hot to be lifted with the bare fingers, and they remained so throughout the course of the meal, for the Negroes replaced them at the slightest hint of cooling. In addition to chicken fried, roasted, and cooked in dumplings, there were platters of whole suckling pigs, and game in abundance: venison, wild turkey, rabbits, doves, quail and wild duck. In the center of the table, the piéce de resistance, a glazed boar's head complete to the candied apple in his mouth, glared at Ross so balefully that that unaccustomed young man almost lost his appetite.

His eyes wandered over the serving platters seeing lettuce, tomatoes, and cucumbers made into a salad, every conceivable type of greens, beans, squash, white potatoes, turnips, okra, asparagus, artichokes and beets. Surrounding the giant glazed hams, their surfaces coated with brown sugar and dotted with whole cloves, were dishes of candied sweet potatoes, and still others held ears of green corn, swimming in butter.

He saw suddenly that Conchita was looking at him, her green eyes wide with astonishment.

"One is not expected," she said wonderingly, "to eat all this?"

"Heaven forbid!" Ross answered.

He spent the rest of the time talking to her, drawing her out carefully, for he knew well the conservatism of people reared under Spanish customs. But, by the time the Negroes came with pound cakes, raisin cake, chocolate layer, devil and angel food cakes, three varieties of berry pies, apple pies, and both pumpkin and sweet potato pie, she was chatting with him freely, even smiling a little.

"No," she said, "you wrong the General, a little, I think. Even when he first came to Cuba, he refused to give the oath to abjure liberalism; and that is why, when his friend Don Jerónimo was replaced by Don Leopold O'Donnell, he was stripped of his powers. As for his fighting for Spain, he first fought against her — he held Valencia with the utmost gallantry for Bolívar. It was only after he believed that the cause was lost that he went over to Spain — after Bolívar had fled, his forces scattered. . . ."

"A braver man," Ross said, "would have died for what he believed — lost or not."

Conchita smiled at him with grave commiseration.

"Wars are won by wise men, Señor," she said, "not necessarily by brave ones. A man who surrenders now, lives on to finally win. And it is the winning that is important when liberty is at stake, not any man's glory, or his heroism."

That, Ross had to admit, was true. He reflected on how he would possibly have conducted himself, given such a choice, and even the thought made him shudder.

"I would never make a soldier," he said a little sadly.

"Who knows?" Her green eyes were warm

now, with a little smiling light in them. "I have seen academicians with soft white hands accustomed only to the pen die like heroes. In our fight even the priests, like good Padre Hidalgo of Mexico, have taken up the sword. The more intelligent the man, the better. Because intellect, real intellect — is always ethical. And an ethical man can make choices, and among the choices are the things he cannot do. . . ."

"Such as?" Ross said.

"Such as living like a beast when he can die like a man. Such as giving up his honor and his dignity. When he is asked to do that, this of the dying becomes easy. He will be afraid. Many times he will be afraid. Only the stupid are fearless." She looked away from him, off into space, and Ross could see old, remembered terror in her eyes. "I have been afraid many times," she said softly; "my father has been afraid. But when the time comes, the fear does not matter. The choice becomes no choice. One dies, because the dying is infinitely preferable to the living, and the only thought one gives is to how one shall manage the act of the dying. That is of the greatest importance. . . ."

Ross listened to her, frozen into a statue of attention by this girl, not, he guessed, out of her teens, who talked so calmly of dying.

"The ones who cannot do it," Conchita said,

"the ones who have left only the kind of fear that is holy fear, that they cannot manage the courage to refuse the blindfold, or to walk steadily to the wall, or shout *'Viva la Libertad!'* or who believe they might sicken and faint at the sight of the twisting screw of the garrote, we always manage to aid. They find the little knife sharp enough to shave with, baked into their bread, so sharp that the quick little slash downward and forward back of the left ear does not hurt at all, and thus we, their friends, grant them a good death. Because always this of the dying must be managed well for the people are very impressionable, and the life of a *Cuba libre* must be watered with the blood of her martyrs. . . ."

Ross put out his hand and took hers, forgetting absolutely the rest of the guests.

"I think," he said, "that you could be the Jeanne d'Arc of your people."

"No," Conchita said, and even her voice shuddered; "I never want to go back to Cuba again!"

"Why not?" Ross asked.

"There are some things, Señor, that have not words. At least not such words as I could say to you."

"And what words could you say?" Ross's voice was low.

Conchita looked him full in the face, and her green eyes were filled with light.

"Later," she said softly. "It is not yet time. . . ."

As Ross turned a little away from her, he was aware that Morgan was staring at him, and that she must have been doing so for some time. There was black, sulphuric fire in her eyes.

She leaned forward across the table to say something to him, but whatever it was never came out, for at that moment Lance Brittany stood up with the announcement that coffee and brandy would be served to the men in the drawing room with their cigars, while those of the ladies who cared to, could have an anisette with Mistress Brittany in the little parlor.

Ross walked along with the men, inwardly cursing this time-honored custom. There had been so much he had wanted to say to Conchita Izquierdo, and with López' expedition nearing readiness, there was so little time. . . .

In the drawing room, the men savored their cigars long and quietly, each apparently waiting for the other to speak. Then George Metcalfe broke the ice. For the benefit of General López, and other strangers who didn't already know it, he drawled, he'd like to tell the story of how Captain Russell got back the preacher's money. Ross, who knew the story, had to admit that George told it well. Even the Cubans, whose history had included more than one raffish priest, could see the humor of the fledgling preacher's losing the total funds of the delegation of ministers in an under the Hill gambling hall. When George reached the climax, how Captain Russell, being refused the return of the money by the gamblers, tied his hawser to the pilings upon which the building stood, and started to drag it into the river with his steamboat, even men well acquainted with Natchez under the Hill, roared.

Then George's brother, Henry, countered with the story of Jim No-Ribs Girty, and Marie Dufour. But when he reached the end of his story, no one laughed.

"They started shooting," Henry said; "and when the smoke cleared, it turned out that Jim had ribs after all instead of the natural breastplate of bone the rivermen swore he had. He lay on the floor with the blood seeping out from under his beard. And Marie took one look, then put her gun in her mouth and blew the back of her head off. That night, all the dives under the Hill closed for the first and last time in their history — out of respect for Jim and Marie."

Others took up the endless saga of Natchez under the Hill, each with his long tale of endless carnage, of ears and noses bitten off, of eyes gouged out, or — in snickering whispers — of the imported "French" girls, who danced "mother-naked" on the tops of tables.

Ross had the feeling that they were doing it for his benefit — that he was being subtly but unmercifully ridden. I'm being too sensitive, he told himself, but his face kept growing paler during the recitals of the hellish doings of the place where he had been born.

"We have places like that in Havana, too," General López laughed, and Lance Brittany caught sight of Ross's face. For all his gruff exterior, Lance was a kindly man. Instantly, but smoothly, he changed the subject.

"About the question of nullification — or secession, if you prefer, what do you think the attitude of the great powers would be toward a Southern Republic, Governor?" he said to Governor Quitman.

"Delight," Quitman said instantly. "It would mean an end to high tariffs, and England, particularly, would be pleased, since she'd be able to get all our cotton at reasonable rates. After all, Lance, cotton is king!"

"Well, now," Lance drawled, "there's some difference of opinion about that. . . . Mister Pary, here, has just returned from a six years sojourn abroad, four of them I understand in

England – at Oxford, and the other two in France and Spain. . . . Well, Ross, from first hand observation, what do you think England's attitude would be – particularly if our relationships with the North deteriorated to the point of hostilities – which could happen?"

Then men stared at Ross, their thoughts written all over their faces. This upstart – this under-the-Hiller, had been to Oxford! Wonders never ceased. Still, and this too, Ross could see, you had to respect a man who'd done that, and since he now owned Merrill, what the hell. . . . Many among them, too, Northerners and Westerners, had come from beginnings as humble, though they guarded their secrets jealously, secure in the knowledge that Natchez had no way of ferreting out their blacksmith father, their illiterate, steerage passenger immigrant mother, their Uncle Ned who had been hanged for stealing horses in the Missouri Territory. . . .

"England would be divided," Ross said clearly. "The upper classes, particularly the mill owners, would be for us. But there's tremendous anti-slavery sentiment among the masses. Some of our leading abolitionists have even spoken over there. In the end, I think, she'd remain neutral. You must not forget, gentlemen, that England is a limited, constitutional monarchy, and the people, after all, hold the balance of power. I'm sorry, Governor, if what I'm saying is contrary to what you want to hear. But that is my opinion — merely that of a private individual, though I tried to keep in close touch. . . ."

Many of the men were nodding in sage agreement, and Ross knew he was not alone in his sentiments. Natchez, as a whole, had never been in favor of secession. Too many of her leading citizens hailed originally from the North and East.

"What about France?" Quitman shot at him.

"She would be pleased, but for no reason that we'd like. Her rulers cherish expansionist sentiments in the Western hemisphere, and they'd welcome any split, any diminution of power of the United States that would make them feasible. As our good Governor has often said, our destiny lies to the South, in lands whose climate and agriculture would lend themselves to the expansion of our system, thus setting up an effective check to the ambitions of the North. If we secede, and if war should come — we'd find France directly across our path, and hostile in the bargain."

"And Spain?" Narciso López demanded.

"Has scant reason to love us," Ross smiled, "since we've given asylum to so many, whom, like yourself, General, she regards as her bitterest enemies. Besides, we've made no bones of our interest in seeing that the remainder of her possessions in this hemisphere are freed of her yoke."

As soon as he had closed his mouth an excited babble broke out among the men. They fired questions at him, which he did his best to answer. A quarter-hour later, he was pleased to note every lingering trace of hostility toward him had vanished. For this, he knew, he had Lance Brittany to thank. Lance in his way, had the makings of a diplomat.

The talk turned now on the proposed Compromise suggested by Henry Clay. The discussion grew heated. The carefully preserved balance between slave states and free was being broken, with the free states gaining. Of course, Utah and New Mexico might eventually decide to come into the Union as slave states, but with California so determinedly free soil in sentiment, it would take both of the new territories to even things up. And Utah, lying as far to the North as it did, was doubtful, though Governor Quitman and the other rabid slavery men regarded New Mexico as a certainty.

But, as Lance drawlingly pointed out, California extended even further south than New Mexico, and her climate was similar — yet she had overwhelmingly gone free soil in her plebiscite; what reason had they, then, to hope that New Mexico would not do likewise?

As for the new fugitive slave law, Ross told them, it was hardly a gain. Its only effect would be to crystallize abolitionist sentiment against the South. Already, while he was in New York, men were talking of resisting Federal agents who sought runaway slaves by force of arms. The South's future, to him, looked dark. . . .

Governor Quitman, fire-eater that he was, hero of the Mexican War, leaped up with his classic, unanswerable argument that one Southern gentleman was the equal of any six money-grubbing Yankees, and elaborated his point with so much fury, that Lance was moved to glance at his watch.

"Time we rejoined the ladies," he said. "I'm attending the Nashville Convention in June, Governor, which I believe you and the Governor of South Carolina were instrumental in calling — 'to devise some mode of resistance to Northern aggression'— I believe those were your words. But I'll lay you odds that whatever means of resistance the delegates advance, it won't be secession. Well, gentlemen, shall we go?"

On the way out of the drawing room, more than one man paused to shake Ross's hand. He found himself the recipient of numerous invitations, to dine — to have a drink at this or that saloon, so that "we can talk about this thing further. . . ." As many as he could, he accepted. This was to be his new world.

Almost immediately, Ross saw Conchita coming toward him. Her lovely face, with just enough recent Indian or *Mestizo* heritage to give it spirit, was troubled.

Ross took her arm.

"What passes?" he asked her, using the ancient Castilian expression. "Where is your father?"

"Gone upstairs to bed. We're to spend the night here, as he is far from well, and the riding would weary him. For that, now, I have much sorrow. . . ."

"Why?" Ross demanded.

"La Señora Brittany. I did not tell you before, Señor — but my father and I have been in New York for two years now. I speak the English — badly, but I speak it. I understand it even better. This of the comprehension is a thing I do not often admit, because I am then saved from much tiresome and impertinent questioning."

"What did Morgan do?" Ross asked grimly.

"She took advantage of my supposed ignorance of English to make sport of me. She said that my coloring clearly revealed that I had a touch of the tarbrush. What signifies that, Señor?"

"That you have Negro blood!" Ross raged. "Where is she? Just wait until I see her. I'll . . ."

"This of the blood of the blacks is then an insult?" Conchita asked wonderingly. "Why?"

"The Negroes are an inferior race," Ross began patiently, but Conchita flashed her eyes at him.

"What nonsense!" she said. "Plácido was a mulatto, and he was a great poet, and a great man. And Pimienta was as black as — as black as her hair. I knew them both as a child. They were friends of my father. It so happens that I have not the blood of the blacks, but only Spanish and *Indio,* a little. But many of my best friends are mulattas, and my tutor, a graduate of the University and the most brilliant man I've ever known, was a black. My father freed his slaves because of them — that's what started all the trouble. I'm afraid, Señor, that you *Norteamericanos* are not very civilized!"

"And I," Ross sighed, "am afraid you're right. . . ."

"Come dance with me," Conchita laughed, all good humor again. "There is going to be music — inferior music, without doubt, since it is going to be played by your inferior blacks. But we must not stamp our feet too hard, or this inferior house will fall down, since the same inferior hands clearly built it, and by tomorrow we shall all be dead of eating the inferior food that they cooked, and . . ."

"Let us leave this of the inferiority," Ross grinned, "shall we?"

"It has departed," Conchita said, and veiled her green eyes with her dull-golden lashes. "You know, Señor, you are a very handsome man."

"Your father," Ross observed, "should have gone to bed hours ago. His absence improves you!"

Then they both laughed together.

Dancing with Conchita, Ross soon discovered, even in the formal patterns of the *Contre danse*, corrupted by then in Natchez and elsewhere into "Country Dance" though it was anything but rural, was an indescribable sensation. Conchita floated, weightless; the music bore her up, her feet moved on air, she was a poem of loveliness, of grace, and before the evening was half over, Ross Pary had forgotten his crazy desire for Morgan, his lifelong love for Jennie Dalton. He had, in fact, forever lost his heart.

"Come walk with me in the garden," he

whispered, half aware that Morgan's gaze, black and baleful, was upon him as she swept by on John Quitman's arm.

"You go too fast, Señor," but there was no reproach in her tone. "Unfortunately, I was forced to leave my *dueña* in Cuba, so . . . "

"Hang your *dueña!*" Ross said, "Come on!"

"After a while," Conchita murmured. "First I must go see after my father, who sleeps badly in strange houses. You, Señor —"

"No, not Señor," Ross said. "This of Señor and Señorita is now ended. Ross."

"You, Ross," Conchita said, a little glow showing in her eyes, "should stroll into the garden for a cigar. Afterwards I shall join you. To leave together would be indiscreet, no?"

"It would be indiscreet, yes," Ross laughed; "but delightful. Don't keep me waiting long, *muñeca mía* — I'm not a very patient man."

Conchita stared at him.

"Muñeca Mía," she whispered, "that's what Father calls me — his little doll. I like being called that, though I am neither little — nor a doll."

"To God, thanks," Ross said fervently, "for that!"

In the Brittanys' garden, the moonlight washed the moss-draped oaks with silver, and the magnolias threw back the light in a soft blaze. Even the edges of the camellias were silvered, and the white roses looked like giant gems from a master jeweler's hand.

Ross drew in on his slim Cuban cigar so that the end of it glowed in the shadows. And as he did so, a cloud swept across the face of the moon and the wash of silver was swallowed up in darkness. He heard the rustle of silk on the path and threw the cigar out and away from him, its trajectory making a red arc in the night. Then he turned and to his vast astonishment, the girl slipped without any protests whatsoever easily into his arms.

He pressed her to him holding her close, and the cloud moved past the moon's disk.

Ross Pary drew a helpless breath. For the liquid-fire blaze of a diamond tiara flashed in his eyes, set in deep curling midnight, and the low throaty laughter rippled devilishly about his ears. And before he could close his mouth to say anything, to protest, Morgan went up on tiptoe and kissed him. She clung her mouth to his endlessly, achingly, the soft underflesh of lip and tongue-tip, hotly, wetly, sweetly, adhesive, diabolically expert at their play, so that in spite of himself, he kissed her in return with real enthusiasm, and at the last, as he tried to draw his head back and away from her, he was conscious suddenly, of a blindingly sharp pain.

He freed himself and raised his hand to his mouth. It came away dark with his own blood, where Morgan had caught his underlip in her white teeth and bitten it through.

"Now," she laughed, "now, I've set my brand on you. Tell that to your Cuban wench! Explain those marks if you can." Then she turned and ran away from him toward the house. Ross started after her, fury pounding through all his veins. He stopped short, for Conchita stood there in the path, swaying a little; then she, too, turned and walked back toward the door, willow-slender, graceful, slow-moving, with all the dignity in the world in her walk. But Ross Pary did not follow her for he had seen, the instant before she turned, clear on her cheeks in the moonlight, the bright silver tracks of her tears. . . .

Chapter 4

"You sure look like hell" Tom Pary grinned.

"Oh, shut up!" Ross said.

"My little brother. My good little brother. How was she, Ross? Brother! From the looks of you, she must have been something!"

"Tom, for God's sake . . ."

"Only the good ones bite," Tom said. "The real, honest to pete, vinegar mean ones. The she-cat ones — who go ahowling and screeching like they was scairt to death then crouch down ten feet ahead and wait. . . ."

"Look, Tom —" Ross began.

"I'm alooking. And damn my soul, Ross, boy — I kind of like what I see. Never knew you had it in you. Used to worry about that. I see now I didn't have a thing to worry about. Nary a thing! Reckon I was wrong about her being cold after all. Yessir, looks like little Morgan's got her share of bitch'n' bitters just like the next gal. . .."

"How," Ross asked coldly, "do you know it was Morgan?"

"Now don't try to put me off. You ain't that smart. Tell me, boy — how was she? What else can she do beside bite?"

"Oh, come on!" Ross said crossly. "All the likely niggers will be sold before we get there."

"No, they won't. Most of the planters hereabouts are pretty well stocked up. By the way, Ross, Paw Dalton sent seven or eight wagons full of clapboards up to our place, and some mighty good square jousts and other timber. Soon as we get the niggers up there, we get the 'quarters' set up anyhow. What about having them knock together a shack for us to stay in 'til we get the house built?"

"All right," Ross said; "but I won't be up there too much. I've got to get the Brittanys' place going and . . . "

"And that ain't all you've got going!" Tom laughed.

"Will you drop that, Tom?" Russ said sullenly.

"Oh, don't take it so serious. 'Pears to me the only thing what ought to bother you is the chance of having Lance Brittany call you out.

That would make one hell of a mess — 'specially since you can't shoot worth a damn."

"That does bother me," Ross said gravely. "Especially since there is really nothing between Morgan and me, and Lance has been so damned kind."

"Reckon I'd better take you out and give you a few lessons, so in case you do have to defend yourself . . . "

"All right," Ross said. "Some other time, though. Right now, we've business to attend to."

They rode out on the old Natchez Trace until they came to D'Evereux, and there Ross reined in his mare. Tom pulled up beside him and the two of them sat there looking at the house.

"Our place going to look like that?" Tom asked.

"Yes — very much. Only it'll be simpler, and a little plainer but with nicer lines."

A worried frown crossed Tom's big, handsome face.

"Don't know how I'm agonna fit in a house like that," he mused. "Jennie's been after me to mend my ways and my manners; but I ain't never paid her no real attention. But looks like I'll have to now. We're going to be real folks, now — ain't we, Ross? Real, big planters!"

"Hardly big," Ross said drily, "when you consider the fact that Lance Brittany has more than eleven hundred acres divided into three plantations — a small one here, and two big ones in Louisiana. Our two hundred and fifty acres won't amount to very much, Tom."

"We'll have more!" Tom said. "Just you wait, boy, we'll have more!"

So, Ross thought to himself, the bug has bitten Tom, too. Well, ambition isn't the worst disease a man could have. He dug his heels into Nancy's flanks, and the mare started out again at a trot.

They came a few minutes later to the slave block, which lay less than a quarter of a mile past D'Evereux on the Trace. Off to the left they could see the sprawling building called the Barracks, where slaves just smuggled in from Africa were clothed, rested and fed, and taught to speak a few words. Of course, with the government's cutters keeping such a close watch, the brute Africans were few these days; the majority of slaves being those who were sent down from the exhausted lands of Maryland and Virginia, with a sprinkling from Georgia.

Tom had been right, Ross saw. There were very few people standing before the block. The auctioneer went through his motions without spirit, bringing the blacks forth, flexing their muscles, opening their mouths to show their teeth, but sales were few.

The most spirited bidding was over a pretty mulatto girl with skin like yellowed ivory, and dark red hair with only a slight kink to it. Her usefulness as a ladies' maid which the auctioneer extolled, had slight bearing, Ross knew, on the interest she aroused.

"Think I'll put in a bid for that wench myself," Tom grinned, but Ross laid a restraining hand upon his arm.

"No, you don't!" he said. "We've got precious little money to spend for good hands. I don't mean to see it wasted upon a yellow wench to warm your bed. Besides you and Jen will be getting married soon, and things like that don't help matters any."

"Damned right," Tom said. "Jennie ain't no bloodless planter's lady. She'd probably whip that wench off the place and break my fool head in the bargain. Well boy, they've got some prime hands here. We ought to do all right."

By midafternoon he and Tom had bought nearly fifty good hands, both men and women. Ross was especially pleased to acquire five young Negroes who had had some training in carpentry. They were about to quit the scene when Ross noticed a stir of interest pass through the crowd. The auctioneer, pleased by the Parys' steady buying, had whispered a word to his assistant, and the man had hurried off toward the barracks. Now he was back, leading a huge Negro. This black was quite the finest physical specimen that Ross had ever seen. He stood, Ross judged, fully two inches taller than Tom, and Tom was six foot two. In his bare arms the muscles knotted and corded, thicker than a ship's hawser, and his chest was bigger around than a fair-sized oak. He had great, sloping shoulders, from which loose muscles slanted down into a narrow waist, ribbed with rock-hard sinews. He reared his great head upon his bull-like neck, and stared at the whites out of yellowish, bloodshot eyes.

"A noble brute, if I ever saw one," Tom whispered. "Hell, boy, I'm going to buy him!"

"I give you Brutus!" the auctioneer cried. "Thirty-two years of age, two hundred and forty-five pounds of solid muscle! Trained as a blacksmith, but he knows planting too. Gentlemen, this is the finest of the lot! I'll listen to a bid of two thousand for this prime hand! What am I bid. . . . "

"I'll give you twelve hundred," a little lawyer in the front row called. "Not a cent more — that nigger looks dangerous to me."

This, Ross reflected, was the truth. Brutus'

face was frowning and still, filled with a massive dignity, almost with contempt. There was pride there, and spirit. This black would surely prove difficult.

Tom hesitated.

"That little lawyer ain't far wrong," he muttered. "That nigger looks like a killer. . . . "

"Wait," Ross said.

"Surely, gentlemen," the auctioneer said, "you'll give me a better offer. This man is skilled in the finest iron work. He's strong — and a good worker and . . ."

There was a grudging offer of thirteen hundred from a man beside them. The auctioneer frowned. This was not going at all the way he'd planned.

There was the sound of hoofbeats on the Trace, and they all turned to see two carriages approaching. The auctioneer waited, hoping that among the newcomers someone might make him a better offer.

As the carriages drew up, Ross saw that one of them belonged to the Montcliffes; but the other one he did not know. The coachmen got down and opened the doors, and the gentlemen stepped to the ground. The ladies, however, remained seated in the coaches. Ross stiffened suddenly, his face paling. For there, between the Montcliffe girls, sat Conchita Izquierdo.

He turned his face resolutely back to the auctioneer.

That's finished, he thought bitterly, finished before it got started, and all because of that black-hearted little witch! What difference did it make to her? She's not really in love with me – or with Lance or with any other man. She merely can't bear the thought of any other woman's having any happiness. . . .

He was aware, after a moment, of the cackle of black laughter. The two coachmen, apparently recognizing each other, were making crude jokes at the expense of the miserable herd of newly sold slaves.

"Look at that nigger," one of them guffawed; "ain't nothing under that wool but water! Betcha he ain't brung no more'n two hundred dollar!"

"Whole lot of 'em look awful sad to me," the Montcliffe's coachman replied. "Buy 'em all for what my master paid for me."

"And what was that?" the other liveried black asked slyly. "Six hundred?"

"Nawsuh! I'd have you know Marse Thomas paid seven hundred dollars to git hisself a fine hand at the reins."

"Now do tell!" the other coachman said, elevating his broad nostrils. "Didn't know I was lowing myself so – 'sociating with no seven hundred dollar nigger. Marse Henry paid one thousand dollars for me, and was glad to git me so cheap!"

Ross listened to this display of human vanity on its most elementary level with amusement, but, when he looked up, he was aware that the Negro, Brutus, was trembling with fury. Suddenly, before anyone knew what he was about, he stepped down from the block and caught both gaily clad coachmen in each of his powerful hands; then slowly, without apparent effort, he lifted them up until their boot toes alone trailed in the dust.

"Slave niggers!" he boomed. "Bragging 'bout what you cost! Can't buy a man! Ain't no price set on a man. Buy things like you, buy fool beast niggers like you, but not no man. I been slave, I slave now, but my heart free. Don't nobody own that but God! One of these days He's agonna sot the rest of me free, too! You — you dressed up dirt!" With that he brought his big hands together with tremendous force so that the heads of the coachmen crashing one against the other made a sound like hollow drums. Then he opened his big hands, letting them crumple soundlessly into the dust. Instantly the auctioneer's assistant was upon him, swinging his loaded nine-foot whip. It whined through the air, and sang and bit, and with every blow it drew blood.

Still Brutus did not move. Inside the coach, Conchita covered her face with her hands. Ross felt sick watching it. Never before in his life had he seen anything quite as moving and noble as that black man.

"I withdraw my offer!" the man who had bid thirteen hundred dollars cried.

"And I, also!" the little lawyer yelped; "that nigger's dangerous!"

"Git back up there, you big, murderous ape!" the slave driver roared. "Git up there, I tell you!" And every word he spoke was punctuated by the whining, ugly whistle of the lash.

"Wait!" Ross was surprised to hear his own voice calling; "I'll give you fifteen hundred dollars for that man!"

Everybody turned to stare at him. The auctioneer recovered first.

"Sold!" he roared. "I'm glad to be rid of him!"

"You put down that whip," Ross said to the driver with icy calm. "I won't have him marked."

The driver shrugged.

"Your risk, Mister," he said.

"I'll take it," Ross snapped. Then, turning to the Negro, he said very quietly. "Brutus, come here."

The black man hesitated, then step by slow

step, he walked over to where Ross stood. Ross was not a short man, standing five foot ten and one-half inches in his socks, but the giant Negro dwarfed him. Beside him, Tom stiffened, and his hand went towards his shoulder holster.

"Take your hand off your gun, Tom," Ross said calmly. "Brutus won't harm me. Will you, Brutus?"

The Negro looked at him wonderingly. Here, he dimly sensed, was a new kind of white man.

"Were you badly treated before?" Ross asked him.

"Yassuh," Brutus said. "Them Georgia folks treat a man something awful!"

"Well," Ross said, "you won't be now. You're going to be my lead hand, and my blacksmith. And you won't be beaten. I'm going to trust you, Brutus. You look like a man who can be trusted."

The slave driver was coming forward now, with the chains and manacles in his hands.

"Better let me chain 'em up, sir," he said; "especially that big nigger. He might make a break for it."

Ross looked at him coldly.

"My people are not to be chained," he said. "Tom, take them away. Brutus, you lead the line."

Suddenly, amazingly, Brutus smiled. It transformed his whole face, making him almost handsome.

"Yassuh!" he boomed, "You a good man, boss. You'n' me gwine to git along."

"I hope so," Ross said. "All right, Tom."

But before Tom could move off, they both heard the swift rustle of silk, as Conchita came flying from the coach and took Ross's arm.

"Now I have much shame for last night," she whispered and the tears were there, bright in her green eyes. "You are what I thought you, a man of much goodness, and of immense heart, and of an enormity of kindness. But Ross — Ross — why did you kiss her?"

"It was dark," Ross said bluntly. "I thought she was you!"

Conchita looked at him a long moment, then suddenly she began to laugh. Her fingers tightened on his arm, and going up on tiptoe she whispered: "And I have formidable sorrow that it was not!"

"That will be remedied," Ross smiled. "Later. . . ."

"Bro — ther!" Tom said in an undertone. "So it wasn't Morgan, after all! Ross, I beg your pardon. I sure Lord underrated you. Who is she? And I always laughed at you for wanting an education. Right now I'd give my right arm to be able to savvy Spic!"

"Conchita," Ross said in English, "may I present my brother, Thomas Pary? Tom, this is the Señorita Conchita Izquierdo."

"Mighty proud to make your acquaintance, ma'am," Tom said, sweeping off his big hat. "And I sure Lord wish that I had seen you first."

"That," Conchita laughed, "would have made the small difference, Señor — though you are very handsome, too." She clung shamelessly to Ross's arm. "It is," she said to Tom, "that your brother here is also so nice, and so — so gentle. I have for him a great fondness. . . ."

It was the first time that Ross had heard her speak English, and her fluency surprised him. Then he reflected that he shouldn't have been surprised. Anyone as intelligent as Conchita would find little difficulty in mastering a foreign tongue.

"Fondness," Tom teased, "is hardly the word. You mean you love him, don't you."

Conchita turned and smiled up at Ross.

"Yes, yes!" she laughed; "I love him, I adore him. I am going to take him home with me in my little handbag, no?"

"Take the Negroes home," Ross said, "and see that they are fed. Don't work them today. Buy a couple of pigs and give them a barbecue.

Then, tomorrow, they'll work like blazes."

"Right," Tom said. "So long, Señorita. You don't know it, but you're getting yourself an awfully nice brother-in-law!"

Ross could feel Conchita stiffen.

"What's the matter?" he asked.

"Nothing," she whispered. "Walk me back to my friends, Ross."

"May I," Ross asked, "see you — tonight?"

"Yes — but first you must ask the permission of the Señor Montcliffe with whom we are staying. Then, afterwards, I'll ask my father."

"Oh, damn!" Ross exploded.

"Do not preoccupy yourself, my Ross. Father likes you very much. He will not refuse."

"I hope not," Ross said.

When they were close to the carriage, Ross bowed to the Montcliffes.

"I'm sorry about your coachman," he said to Henry Montcliffe. "If my man has injured him in any way, I'll be glad to incur the medical expenses. . . ."

"Don't worry about it, Mister Pary," Henry Montcliffe said. "You can't hurt a nigger by banging him on his head. Besides technically speaking, your big black hurt my man before he belonged to you. So actually I have no legitimate claim."

"Just the same . . ." Ross began.

"Forget it!" Henry Montcliffe laughed. "Here comes Scipio now!"

Turning Ross saw the coachman limping along in all his bedraggled finery. He winced at every step, his black face twisted into a grossly exaggerated grimace of pain.

"He'll be whining for a week," Montcliffe said. "Serves him right. House niggers get spoiled something awful."

"Mister Montcliffe," Conchita said suddenly, "Mister Pary wishes to call upon me tonight. May he?"

"Wish I could prevent him, honey," Henry Montcliffe smiled. "I'd like to keep you for myself. But after that demonstration you just gave us, I reckon I'd better just retire as gracefully as possible. Of course, Mister Pary, you're welcome to call at any time at all. By the way, I want to thank you for standing up to Governor Quitman the way you did last night. It's time some one presented him with a few facts. . . ."

"To a man who believes a thing as strongly as our Governor," Ross said; "facts don't matter much."

"True," Henry Montcliffe said sadly. "Still . . ."

"Oh, bother!" Ellen, the older of the two Montcliffe girls said. "Mister Pary has been in

123

Paris recently. I want to talk to him about fashions. All you men think about is politics."

"Not always, Ellen," her younger sister Jane put in. "I think Mister Pary must have quite a lot to think of. Mister Pary, I don't mean to be rude, but would you mind telling me what happened to your mouth?"

Involuntarily Ross stiffened, and put the fingers of his right hand to his torn mouth. Then he recovered. He smiled steadily at Jane and murmured:

"I'm sorry, Miss Montcliffe; but, as a matter of fact, I do mind. You'll forgive me, won't you?"

"Well put, Pary!" Henry laughed. "Time somebody was giving my meddlesome sister her comeuppance."

But both Jane and Ellen were staring at Conchita with wide-eyed awe, mingled, Ross was sure, with not a little admiration.

"Conchita, you naughty girl!" Jane murmured. "Did you do that?"

Conchita pouted prettily.

"No," she said; "but I know who did. Tell me, Señor Montcliffe, is it permitted for ladies to fight duels in Mississippi?"

"No!" Henry roared. "What an idea!"

"Then I shall have to assassinate her," Conchita said calmly. "I shall stick her with my little knife so, and she will fall down and her blood will be all over everything. Or perhaps I will tie her up and torture her a little first and then . . ."

"Conchita!" the Montcliffe sisters chorused.

"Darlings," Conchita laughed. "I make the big joke, no?"

But looking at them, Ross could see that they were not at all sure.

"Who was she, Conchita?" Jane breathed. "We're just dying to know?"

Conchita shrugged.

"That," she said, "is entirely the affair of the Señor Pary, who has various loves. *Mi alma,* will you try to be good until tonight so that I will not have to shoot *all* the ladies of Natchez?"

"I'll try," Ross said, and bowed to them all. "Good day, ladies," he murmured. Then to Henry, "Your servant, sir."

"Pary," Henry Montcliffe observed, as Ross swung himself gracefully into the saddle, "is much too polite."

"I think he's the handsomest thing!" Ellen said.

"And to think," Jane said tartly, "that he comes from a family of river rats from under the Hill!"

"That man," her sister replied, "is a gentleman; I don't care where he came from!"

"Conchita," Henry laughed, "add Ellen to your list!"

When Ross left the slave market, he rode back into Natchez and sought the building that his elderly partner Peter Dalton owned. He found it in a good state of repair, though somewhat in need of painting. And in addition to the office on the ground floor, the rooms above were now also vacant.

Ross walked through them, his mind busy with plans. It would be months, maybe even a year, before he could build Moonrise. In the meantime, he didn't relish the idea of either occupying a shack out on the plantation, or his old home under the Hill. He had made too many friends; the prestige which was so important to him would suffer in either case. But here, in these rooms, he had the solution. In a matter of days, they could be transformed into neat, even smart, bachelor's quarters. Why, he thought excitedly, I could even entertain here!

He inspected the walls carefully. They were dirty and had many cracks. But the floors were good. Ross went back down the stairs and rode to a nearby supply store. Here he purchased plaster, rolls of wallpaper and paint. The storekeeper's Negro followed him back to his new rooms and laid the supplies carefully upon the floor.

Ross stood there, staring at them. Obviously he could not do the job himself, though from long practice under Peter Dalton's direction he was quite skilled at all the techniques involved. Yet it had to be done. And since his reconciliation with Conchita, it had to be done at once.

He walked down the stairs slowly, his face frowning and thoughtful. As he reached the street, an idea struck him. He and Tom had to hire an overseer, anyway. Planters did not drive their own slaves. That was one of the most formidable of the taboos. Why not hire the man now, and put him to work here?

No sooner had the idea come to him than he acted upon it. There was on the outskirts of Natchez a family named Martin, various members of which had worked for Ross and Peter in the mill. David Martin, the eldest son would be just the man. Not only was he a kindly fellow, but he was both a good carpenter and a good planter, having worked as an overseer for several planters during off-seasons at the mill.

Ross mounted his mare and rode rapidly out to the Martins' house. David was at home and greeted him with evident pleasure.

"Why yessir, Mister Pary," he said cheerfully, "I'll be glad to work for you. When do I start?"

"Right now," Ross said. "Get your things and come with me."

He took David back to his new abode and went over with him the things that needed to be done. Then he gave him a note to take to Tom out on the plantation. Tom was to let David have one of the Negroes trained as carpenters and five of the smaller, less muscular hands.

"Bring them here at once." Ross directed. "Keep them working late — all night if necessary. I want this place finished upstairs and down by tomorrow night. Can you do it?"

"Why sure," David said. "With six men I'll have it done long before then. There ain't really so much work."

"Good," Ross said. "Get at it, then. I still have things to do."

He spent the rest of the evening buying furniture for the place. He was surprised at the number of things he needed: A dining room table and chairs, a serving buffet; a bed, chair, night table and highboy for his bedroom, and also a washstand. A large room to the rear he converted into a kitchen, but, as it still had space left after the small black-iron range would be put in, he bought a slipper-shaped bathtub, and a mirrored cabinet for his razors and toilet articles. The fourth room, a large one which swept all the way across the front, would be his parlor. Here he would place the sofa and delicate Louis XIV chairs, the little tables, and the lamps with the hand-painted shades. Still — something was missing. . . .

Then, as he moved through the furniture store, he saw it: a piano — a magnificent grand piano, much too large for the end of the room he would have left. Yet he had to have it. Even if the room would look crowded, he had to. Later, of course, after he had built Moonrise, the piano and the better pieces of the furniture would be moved up there. When he left the store, he had the pleased realization that he was going to be master of one of the most fashionable bachelor establishments in Natchez, if not in the whole South. . . .

That night, walking with Conchita in the gardens of Camellia Hill, the Montcliffes' place, he was filled with too much happiness, even to speak. Life stretched out before him, a long vista of golden days, filled with promise. Tomorrow he would begin both Moonrise and Finiterre. With Tom and David taking care of the planting, he was free to concentrate on the building. In a year or two, with the white beauty of Moonrise filling their gaze, people would forget he came from under the Hill. He would move securely and with confidence among the great of Mississippi. And with a wife as charming, as exotic, as Conchita, what heights might he not reach?

"You are silent, *mi alma*," Conchita said softly. "Why are you so still?"

Mi alma — my soul. And Conchita said it so prettily. . . .

"You said you'd never go back to Cuba," he said. "Then what are your plans, Conchita? Does your father mean to return to New York?"

"No. The climate up there is too fierce. He is going to practice law with a countryman of ours in New Orleans. José Méndez speaks English, but my father knows much more law. And there are many people of our tongue in New Orleans. They are thinking, too, of establishing a Spanish newspaper in the city. Naturally I shall go with him."

Ross frowned.

"This Méndez," he said morosely; "is he young?"

"Yes — and very handsome. Are you jealous, my Ross?"

"Yes. But then, I don't think you'll go to New Orleans. I think you're going to stay here — with me."

"With you?" Conchita breathed; "how is that, my Ross?"

"Does not a wife," Ross said gently, "usually stay with her husband?"

Conchita turned her face away from him suddenly, and Ross saw her shoulders shake.

"Conchita!" he said. "*Muñeca mía* — what's wrong?"

"Nothing that I can explain," she sobbed. "Oh, Ross — Ross, I was so hoping that you would not ask me — that."

Ross stared at her in pure amazement.

"Why not?" Then slowly, laboriously, he got it out: "Is there — someone else?"

"Oh, no! No one in this world but you. I love you, Ross. So very much do I love you! But — I cannot marry you. . . ."

"Why?" Ross demanded. "Why not, Conchita *mía?*"

"That," she whispered, "is a thing you must not even ask. But believe me, Ross, it is only because I cannot — no other reason. . . ."

"There's a reason, all right," Ross said grimly. "A very simple reason. . . ."

"And that is?" Conchita murmured.

"You don't love me," Ross said bitterly.

"I don't love you!" Conchita exclaimed. "I, who cried all night after I saw her in your arms! I, who've thought of nothing, of no one but you, from the moment I first saw you! Where is he now? I ask myself. What is he doing? Oh, Ross, Ross . . ." She bent down her head and gave way to a wild torrent of sobs.

Ross put out his arms and drew her to him.

"Don't cry, *muñeca mía,*" he murmured. "Don't cry over me. I'm not worth it. And whatever this thing is that prevents you from marrying me, we'll find a way around it — because you've got to be mine."

"I am yours," Conchita wept; "in my heart I am yours. But I cannot come to you, my Ross. I have not the deceit — nor the dishonesty. . . ."

"Now you're talking foolishness. You're an angel, Conchita, and angels can never be deceitful or dishonest."

"I can," Conchita said. "I have been — even with you."

"Rubbish," Ross said. "No more tears now." Then gently he bent and kissed her mouth.

Conchita kissed him back with haunting passionate tenderness, kissing him even after he had attempted to draw away, then swinging at last against the circle of his arms, her green eyes bright with tears.

"Now," she whispered, "now you must go. This of the kissing is too much — too much. I have much shame for the way I feel now. . . ."

"I — I'll see you again?" Ross asked.

"If you do not," Conchita said, "I think that I will die!"

"And yet," Ross said wonderingly, "you will not marry me. . . ."

"I cannot marry you," Conchita corrected. "Now kiss me quickly, and go — while I can still bear it. . . ."

There was probably no more confused and puzzled young man in the whole state of Mississippi than the man who guided the mare Nancy away from the towering oaks of Camellia Hill.

The next night, Ross Pary rode away from Finiterre, slumped far over in his saddle from weariness. Even he was surprised at the immense amount of work that had been accomplished. The underpinnings, hand-hewn from native cypress, were already in place, and the massive timbers were beginning to rise. Within a week, the framework of Finiterre would be in place. There was no doubt that by fall, Finiterre would be completed.

So sure was Lance Brittany of this that he had already ordered the rarest materials from France, England, and Italy. From the ancient craftsmen of Europe would come the marble mantels which would adorn every room, the delicate glass for the side and fanlights of the doors, the crystal chandeliers, and the bronze ones with their hand-etched blown glass globes, the gay Brussels carpets, the hand-blocked wallpaper, the tall tier mirrors with gold-leaf frames, the silver knobs and other fittings for the doors, the gold window cornices, the elaborately carved and richly upholstered mahogany and rosewood furniture, the heavy brocade draperies, the exquisite hand-woven lace curtains, the bronzes, the marble pieces of sculpture, the books that would fill the library shelves, the silver plate that would gleam from handsome sideboards, and the delicate china and crystal that would grace the banquet tables. It had cost, literally, a fortune.

Ross, in his turn had ordered considerable materials for his own place, cutting corners wherever he could to save expense. His silver for instance had been ordered from Kirk of Baltimore, and the bulk of his furniture from small shops in New Orleans. It was being made to his own sketches, and though it would be quite as handsome as the Brittanys', it would cost only a fraction as much as theirs did. Then, since Moonrise, with its fifteen rooms would be only half the size of the massive Finiterre, his expenses were considerably less to start with.

In one thing only did Lance Brittany have

the advantage: labor. He could afford to detach a large number of slaves from the fields and keep them working in shifts on his new house until it was too dark to see. Even though Moonrise was much smaller and less elaborate, Ross doubted that he could have it done before Christmas.

Oh well, he thought, I'll have comfortable enough lodgings. Wonder how David is coming along? Shame to keep Tom out in that miserable shack the Negroes threw together for him, and it not even finished yet. But he seems to enjoy it. Tom always was a hardy soul. . . .

He was surprised, when he came to his new dwelling place, to see the lamps on the second floor glowing out of curtained windows. He tied Nancy to the hitching post and went up the stairs. He opened the door and stood still.

"Surprise!" Jennie and Annis chorused.

The rooms were finished. They smelled of paint, and everything was in place. And they were so clean that they shone. They looked lovely, Ross had to admit. There were even flowers in the vases, and all the furniture had been rubbed and polished. Of course, David and the Negroes had done their work well, with plaster and paint and wallpaper, but the arrangement of the pieces, the lacy bows upon the curtains, the flowers and countless other delicate details bespoke the touch of feminine hands.

"Thanks, girls," Ross said. "It sure does look nice. . . ."

"Nice!" Annis said; "it's lovely. Oh, Ross, why didn't you save a room for me?"

"You'll have a room," Ross said, "at Moonrise — before Christmas, too. And you and Tom, Jen, will have a whole apartment."

"Maybe," Jennie said, and the bitterness in her voice caused Ross to look at her. Jennie's face, he saw, was terribly strained, and the corners of her mouth were trembling.

"What's the matter, Jen?" he asked. "Anything wrong?"

Jennie shot a rapid, sidelong glance at Annis; then, with impressive control she turned and smiled at Ross's sixteen-year-old sister.

"Annis, dear," she said, "how about making some coffee? Ross looks like he needs refreshment."

"I do," Ross groaned. "Lord, I'm tired!"

Annis ran off toward the kitchen, happy to be of service.

"Now, Jen?" Ross said.

"I rode out to Moonrise," Jennie said despondently, fighting against her tears. "I wanted to see the place. I wanted to see Tom. And the place is lovely, Ross. Tom has done

136

well. It's unbelievable how much of it he already has plowed. . . ."

"But you didn't see Tom," Ross surmised; "and therefore you think. . . ."

"No, Ross. I did see him — and I know. *She* was there, sitting on that black mare she calls Satana, dressed in one of those riding habits that manage to look positively indecent on her even though they do cover her up."

"So she was there," Ross said crossly; "maybe she was looking for me."

"No, Ross. Though, if she had found you instead, it would have made little difference to her. And Ross —" Jennie's voice dropped down into near silence, "she sidled that horse up to Tom's while I was watching, and put up her arms to him. He — he kissed her — hard. Oh, Ross, I —"

"Now, Jen," Ross said comfortingly, "don't take on so over that. Morgan's a tempting little witch, and Tom is a bit of a devil. Still . . ."

"I didn't stay to see what went on after that," Jennie said. "I should have, though. I should have waited. Then I should have taken my crop and —"

"Jennie!"

"Sorry. I hate her. She's evil. There's no limit to the things she'll do. And married to a fine man like Mister Brittany. Don't you see, Ross

— that somebody's going to die for her adulteries? And I don't want it to be Tom?"

"I will have to look into this," Ross said grimly. "Don't worry, Jen, I'll straighten Tom out."

"Don't get tangled up in her web yourself," Jennie said, her voice flat, toneless, terrible. "I should hate to have you both destroyed because of her."

"Coffee's ready!" Annis sang out from the kitchen. "Come and get it!"

The last days of March flew by, then all of April, and Finiterre had reached a recognizable shape. It was the talk of Natchez; people rode out to see it, and sat in the carriages to watch the work. Ross took advantage of this interest to display in the window of his office a large drawing of how the house would look when completed and immediately the orders began pouring in. Ross found himself so busy that he had to hire three assistant draftsmen, and still the work on Moonrise suffered.

He was, at this time, much too busy to be really unhappy; but his life existed in a kind of noisy vacuum. Conchita refused absolutely to become his wife, and Tom, when questioned about Morgan, told him flatly to attend to his own damned business. The trouble was, Ross knew, that with the bulk of his land lying on the Louisiana side of the river, Lance Brittany was away from home far too much of the time. Ross was sure that Tom rode up to Buena Vista to see Morgan, but he had neither the time nor the inclination to do anything about it.

If only Moonrise were finished! Then he could make Tom see the wisdom of marrying Jennie at once. As it was, he could only wait. And late in June, Conchita and her father were to leave for New Orleans.

Of course, New Orleans was not very far away. He could manage to get down there to see her. But still there was José Méndez who had already been up to Natchez to call upon her. Ross was sick with worry, thinking about it. So as a remedy, he threw himself into his work. Now, Moonrise, too, was beginning to take shape, and the foundations had been laid for five other great houses. These years were times of unrivaled prosperity for the cotton planters, and the money from commissions poured in.

Out on the Brittany place, the kiln roared day and night burning brick, and a small steam-driven sawmill, which Ross had borrowed from his own lumber mill, sawed the seasoned timber into planks. The slaves cut tongues and grooves by hand, and labored long, carving the delicate leaf and vine motifs on the Corinthian columns with chisel and maul. The out-buildings rose quickly around it; the stables, the barn, the tool sheds, the smoke house, the slave quarters, even the delicately latticed garden house. . . .

Moonrise grew more slowly, but it rose with such exquisite purity of line that soon the carriages were stopping before it too. And Ross Pary knew no sleep from one week end to the next.

Then, late in May, Natchez and New Orleans alike went wild with excitement. Early in the month, a little flotilla of three ships: the brig *Susan Loud,* commanded by Colonel Robert Wheat of New Orleans; the barge *Georgina,* and the steamer *Creole,* under the command of General Narcisco López, with Colonel Bunch and Lieutenant-Colonel Smith, both of Mississippi, as his seconds, had sailed from New Orleans toward their rendezvous at the islands of Murgeres and Contoy, off the coast of Yucatan. They had six hundred well armed men aboard, and made the islands without difficulty. There they had landed, and had begun their practice drill.

But now, the news that poured into Natchez from Cuba was all bad. Forty men mutinied and were left behind on Contoy Island. López herded all the rest into the *Creole* and sailed for the port of Cardenas, where the *Creole* promptly went aground in the harbor.

The impetuous filibusterers decided upon an attack in spite of this unforeseen accident. But the Spanish had had time. López took the barracks and the railroad station by storm but lost more than half his company, including Colonel Wheat and Colonel O'Hara of Kentucky, both of whom were seriously wounded. And the Spanish armies were on the march.

López pulled the remainder of the troops off, refloated the *Creole,* and sailed for eastern Cuba. But on the way, he met the mighty battleship *Pizzaro,* and had to run his gunless steamer toward the Florida Keys. He made Key West by the skin of his teeth.

But the forty men left on Contoy were now in the dungeon of Morro Castle in Havana, and the Spaniards had announced their intention of hanging them. The American Minister to Spain, Daniel M. Barringer of North Carolina, was working day and night to save their lives, and the whole South was screaming for war with Spain.

Conchita could not even talk about the Contoy prisoners without crying.

"You do not know the Spanish," she told Ross. "Those men will not know an hour free from torture! And to think they went to set us free. . . ."

There were Natchez men among the prisoners, Ross knew; but despite his love for Conchita, Ross shared Lance Brittany's much greater concern about the outcome of the convention to be held by the slaveholding states in Nashville in June. Many of the delegates, he knew, were set to propose secession. And secession meant war.

War with Spain, a foreign power, was one thing. But war with the North, with men of the same heritage, often of blood kinship, who spoke the same language, was a thing too terrible to contemplate. Most of Natchez felt the same way as he did about it.

In the little informal parties that Ross gave at his lodgings, the talk was sharp and explosive. Tempers frayed rapidly under the tension. Many times only Ross's diplomacy prevented an exchange of cards.

"This is a lovely place you have here," Morgan said, as she sipped her sherry. Lance nodded in agreement.

"Yes, very," he said.

Morgan looked at Conchita, sitting gracefully in one of the gilt chairs, and her black eyes narrowed even as her lips smiled.

"You like it, don't you?" she said. "Oh, I know you speak English. Jane Montcliffe told me."

"Yes," Conchita said simply, "I like it very much."

"But then," Morgan drawled, looking around at the other guests, "you must have been here many times before — under less crowded circumstances. . . ."

"Morgan!" Lance began; but Conchita waved a small, graceful hand.

"Perhaps I have, Señora," she said evenly; "perhaps, even as you've said — many times. But you'll agree that our host is a very charming man — in crowds, or — alone."

"Expecially alone," Morgan smiled. "I should think that he could be most attentive when he did not have to divide his hospitality among so many."

Conchita looked her full in the face, then very slowly she smiled.

"The possibility exists, does it not, Señora — that you could be very right?"

Lance Brittany threw back his head and roared.

"Bested by God!" he said. "That'll teach you, Morgan, to study your foe more carefully before you measure his steel. Now you've found out exactly nothing, and had your suspicions increased. Be good, won't you?"

"I could find out," Morgan said sullenly, "if I wanted to. The matter really doesn't interest me."

"I'm leaving for Nashville, tomorrow," Lance said heavily. "I only hope I can get a few of those fire-eating fools to listen to me. This slavery question can be solved. We've existed a long time slave and free. Don't see why we can't go on like that."

"Because slavery is unjust," Morgan said tartly. "You have no right to own a man, like a horse!"

"My dear little abolitionist," Lance mocked; "you have no right to own a man like a slave. And don't tell me you don't want to. You'd like nothing better than to see me grovel at your feet."

Ross lifted the decanter of sherry.

"Let's drop this business of slavery, shall we?" he said. "I don't know anything about politics or slavery or any such weighty matters. All I know is houses. Well, Lance, what do you think of Finiterre, now?"

"It's going to be beautiful," Lance said. "I'm growing impatient, Ross. Right now, it looks like it'll take forever."

"You'll live in it by September," Ross told him. "Now, if you'll excuse me, I'd better go stir Wallace up."

Wallace was a young mulatto whom Ross had bought as his valet and house servant. Apart from a certain slowness, he was a very good man.

A week later, Conchita rode out to Finiterre, and told Ross in Morgan's presence, that she and her father were leaving for New Orleans in forty-eight hours.

"You must spend them with me, *mi alma,*" she whispered, speaking very rapidly in Spanish; "you must not leave me for an instant!"

"Yes," Ross said. "I'll spend them with you — them and many more. Because whenever I can, I'll come to New Orleans. I'll keep on coming until you forget this foolishness about not marrying me. . . ."

Then he bent down and kissed her.

Morgan laughed.

"How touching!" she said. "Really, Ross, you've become a man of parts. What did she say?"

"That I am leaving, Señora," Conchita said quietly; "that you have no longer any hindrance to your designs." Then she brought her crop down upon her horse's flank, and bounded off, across the fields.

As he looked at himself in the mirror that last

night, adjusting the black cravat with the gold fleur de lis embroidered in it, Ross Pary's face was bleak. Nothing he had said, no persuasion, no entreaties, had been able to sway Conchita one iota from her consistent refusals to marry him. Nor had he been able to discover the reasons for it.

Conchita was the most complete woman he had ever known, gay and sad by turns, mocking and tender, and always, even in her most tender moments, astonishingly intelligent. Her judgment of people, Ross had discovered, was devastatingly exact. And when she joined Jennie in her condemnation of Morgan Brittany, Ross, who rather liked Morgan despite her ways, was more than a little swayed by it.

Ross gave the black cravat a final touch, and picked up his hat. He was about to go down the stairs when Wallace came into the room.

"Man downstairs want to see you, sir," he said. "Colored man off the Brittany place."

"Send him up," Ross said. Damn it all, he thought, what did Morgan want now?

The Negro who entered the room a moment later, was dressed in the fine livery of a Brittany house servant. He stood there, hat in hand, looking at Ross.

"Well," Ross said harshly, "speak up, man! What is it?"

"Miz Morgan says you come right now," the man got out. "Say there's trouble. Say she need your help!"

"Oh, damn!" Ross groaned. "Tell her —" Then he thought the better of it. Maybe Morgan was in some kind of trouble. He wouldn't put it past her. Very slowly he turned to Wallace.

"Ride out to Camellia Hill," he said, "and tell Miss Izquierdo that I'm going to be delayed. Tell her not to worry, I'll be there a little later."

Then he put on his tall hat and marched down the stairs. It was only a few minutes' ride to Buena Vista, which stood scarcely a mile beyond Natchez itself. A Negro appeared and took the reins, but Ross told him to wait there with Nancy, as he'd be out in a few minutes. The little groom smiled. He apparently had his doubts.

Cato opened the door for Ross and bowed deeply.

"Missy say you come right on upstairs, Marse Ross," he said. "She 'specting you."

Ross gave the butler his hat and started up the broad stairway, frowning. Lance was still in Nashville, and he didn't like this. Damn it, he didn't like it at all. He had reached the upper hall, when he heard a piercing shriek, and a Negro girl came dashing out of one of the

147

doors, holding a hand from which blood gushed from a hideous wound.

"That you, Ross?" Morgan's voice sounded pleasantly. "Come in, won't you?"

Ross walked slowly through the doorway, but just inside he stopped. Morgan was seated before her mirror clad in a gown of black lace. She was brushing out her long black hair, and her reflection smiled at him out of the mirror. The gown, Ross decided, was intended for sleeping — or seduction, his mind added bitterly. For the black lace was devastatingly transparent, or just as devastatingly opaque, depending upon where you looked, or how Morgan moved, or what she intended to conceal, or what to display.

"Come here, darling," she drawled. "You've kept me waiting so long."

Ross walked very slowly over to where she sat. When he was close, he looked down at her dressing table and saw a large pair of scissors, bloodied half the length of their blades.

"You did that! You — stabbed that girl!"

"The wench annoyed me," Morgan said easily. "I don't like being annoyed. Incidentally you've annoyed me a great deal yourself of late, parading that off color Cuban wench around before my eyes!"

"That," Ross said flatly, "is none of your

damned business, Morgan. What did you want? Your man said you were in trouble?"

"Trouble?" Morgan said. "Oh, yes — I was troubled. I was lonely, Ross, darling. That's why I wanted you here."

"Well, I'll be a —" Ross got out, and whirled to leave the room. But Morgan sprang up as graceful as a slim cat, and caught his arms.

"Don't go, Ross," she breathed, something like terror in her eyes. "I can't stay alone! I hate being alone — I — I hear things!"

"Rubbish!" Ross snapped.

"It's not rubbish! It's true, I tell you — it's true!" Her voice rose to such a despairing wail that Ross looked at her closely. Either Morgan was a consummate actress, or she was telling the truth. There was terror in the depths of her black eyes, now, naked and terrible.

"Don't you have something you could take?" he asked. "Something to make you sleep?"

"Brandy helps a little," Morgan said. "But there is one thing that never fails."

"What's that?" Ross demanded.

"I'll tell you later," Morgan whispered. "First have a brandy with me. . . ."

"All right," Ross growled; "but I can only stay a little while. I'm expected. . . ."

"Conchita," Morgan said. "Conchita of the sea green eyes and the sultry, tropic walk.

Cochita, whose father is too ancient and too feeble to guard her properly, or even to keep her out of the very chic rooms of one Ross Pary."

"That's enough of that, Morgan." Ross said.

"Yes, it is. I'm sick of her. Even talking about her makes me sick." She turned away from him, swirling the midnight mist of her gown and pulled the bell cord. "Bring a decanter of brandy," she said to the Negro who appeared, "then see that we are not disturbed — not for anybody."

Ross watched her slim fingers, a few minutes later, pouring the brandy, and wondered at the force of her enchantment. She had played a trick on him but for the life of him, he could not hate her. Nobody could hate that slim curving grace, showing now and again like new snow with dawn flush upon it, caught up in that magic net.

But when she gave him the brandy, he stared at it. Morgan had filled two great, bell-shaped goblets to the brim. People Ross knew, usually drank such potent stuff out of thimble-sized goblets. He looked at her.

"What's the matter?" she taunted, "afraid?"

Ross Pary was afraid, mortally afraid, and he knew it. But all his life he had been cursed with pride. So he lifted the goblet and drained it, and Morgan matched him, putting her goblet down empty beside his own.

"Another?" she said easily; but Ross shook his head.

"No!" he got out on a strangled breath, "for the love of God, no!"

But in an incredibly short time he could feel the subtle poison of the brandy creeping along all his veins. He watched in growing astonishment while Morgan downed two more without blinking. Then, very slowly, she stood up.

"Come here, Ross," she said.

And I, Ross thought, am flesh and blood, not stone. Conchita's waiting. I have to go. . . . Unsteadily he got to his feet; but, before he could move, Morgan was against him, twisting her mouth into his. Ross brought his hands up to break her grip, but they refused to work that way. Instead they crept around her waist and tightened, while she clung her mouth to his and moaned somewhere deep in her throat like a feline she-thing, and the thunders awoke in his blood.

He broke free finally, and Morgan leaned back against the circle of his arms and smiled up at him. Then she put her mouth to his again and strained against him, and one of her hands went away from him, and came back again and Ross felt something pressing into his side —

something hard. He tore his mouth away from hers and looked down.

Morgan had a little pistol in her hand. Both of its hammers were cocked and her finger lay on the trigger, trembling a little.

"What the devil —" Ross began.

"Now," Morgan said, "you will not go to her. You'll stay here with me, tonight. All night. And there won't be any noises in the dark. . . ."

Ross stared at her. He could feel the anger rising in him. He tightened his grip on her and swept her up into his arms, ignoring the little pistol. Then he walked over to the great four-poster bed and put her down upon it, and knelt beside it, looking at her.

"This is what you want of me?" he said brusquely.

Morgan looked at him, holding the little pistol very steadily pointed at his heart. Then suddenly, wildly, she began to laugh.

"No!" she said. "Not of you nor of any other man. Why, you conceited little beast!" Then, just as abruptly, her mood changed.

"Come here, Ross," she whispered, and lifting her free hand, drew him down to her, raising her mouth to his, tormenting his lips with aching tenderness, her left hand holding hard about his waist, her nails digging in so that he could feel them even through his clothing, while the muzzle of the little pistol bruised his flesh.

"God!" Ross groaned, "merciful God!"

He had to end it somehow, and then, suddenly, Conchita's words came back to him. An ethical man has choices. He can decide, for instance, when the shame of living outweighs the indignity of dying. He can make the decision. And he can never be any woman's creature, any woman's toy. . . .

He hurled himself up and away from her, but Morgan did not fire. Instead, as though she had forgotten him, she rose from the bed and began to dance. Ross lay there, propped up on one elbow, watching her. Then, after a while, the rhythm of that dance came over to him. He could hear the notes of it, printing themselves out in the air before his eyes. It had no melodic line; it was crashing, savage, atonal. The music that Morgan danced to, the savage, silent music was there, inside his mind; and he could hear it almost physically in his ears like a far-off accompaniment. He saw her whirl, the black gown swirling out , waist high, so that her flesh beneath it was dazzlingly white against that mist of darkness.

He stared at her, etching the notes into the tissues of his brain, then in frantic haste he sprang up from the bed, less in fear of Morgan, or of dying, than that he should forget before he could reach home, before he could get to the piano. He had to put it down, before it could be lost. Morgan's music — this wild, enchanted strain.

He started across the room, and she fell against him, sobbing with exhaustion, and found his mouth again in the half darkness and again bewildered his blood, and clung to him and wept so that her mouth quivered upon his, and her body, slow-writhing, working against his, and all his senses drowning again in the surf pounding of his blood, his arms tightening around her in quick, ferocious jerks until the breath was gone from her and the resistance and the will; and lifting the little pistol, she shot him.

Ross felt the bullet tear through low on his left side and far out so that it merely creased his flesh, making a wound that was ugly, in appearance, but not dangerous. He swayed back away from her and moved out of the room, and Morgan stood there looking after him, holding the little pistol still smoking in her hands and making a sound in her throat that started out like low, wild laughter and ended in crying.

He went out of the room and all the way down the stairs he could hear in his mind the sound of that music.

The little Negro brought his mare and helped him to mount, looking at him in wonder and fear. Ross sat in the saddle, trying to hold himself upright; but he reeled drunkenly, and gave Nancy her head, knowing that she would take him home. He put his right hand out against the pommel of the saddle and fingered the notes, humming them to himself, but he found it impossible to carry the strain, because the music lacked both melody and harmony. All it had was rhythm, pulsating and wild, almost monotonously repetitious, with an infinity of accented, staccato beats; but the music itself was wildly exciting – as electrifying as Morgan herself.

He got down painfully from the mare in front of his lodgings, and letting the reins trail untied over the hitching post, lurched up the stairway. He had to stop three times to rest, but doggedly he persisted in his climb. The lamps were on in the parlor, and he half turned to call Wallace to prepare the hot water and the bandages that would stop the slow seeping of his blood; but, as he did so, he saw Conchita. She was stretched out upon the blue sofa, fast asleep.

Ross stared at her a long moment, then moved over to the piano and sat down. He flexed his long fingers, feeling for the notes; then, after a little stumbling, he had them. He played the music very softly, pausing now and again to write the notes he had played, and the music took hold of him so that he played it with verve and fury, hammering the chords, accenting the beats until Morgan's music filled the whole room.

He felt in the midst of it the soft hands upon his shoulders, but the music would not let him go. He continued to hammer at the keys drunk with brandy and the rhythm of the music until Conchita reached over his shoulder and snatched the score away from him, crying:

"No, no! It's her music! Hers!"

Then as he turned with drunken gravity upon the stool, she tore it very slowly and neatly and with ceremonious care into little bits and scattered them over the floor.

"It's hers, my Ross," she said. "As evil as she is. Terrible like her. You must not give it to the world."

Ross stood up, reeling upon his feet, more from the brandy than from the wound, which had stopped its bleeding. He took a step toward Conchita, his arms outstretched. Then slowly and with great dignity, he bowed to her, but at the end of it, he could not straighten up, but continued downward, hearing through the darkness, Conchita's high, hysterical cry:

"Ross! Ross! *Jesu y María Santíssima,* he is killed!"

He lay on the floor in the pit of the sick whirlpool, trying to speak to her, trying to say, "I'm not hurt, it's only brandy, I'm not—" but he couldn't get the words out, and Conchita knelt beside him staring at the little dark splotch of blood upon his clothes and wailing:

"*Mi alma* — my soul, do not leave me where is it the pistol tell me where, oh *corazón, mío,* where, that I may use it that I may go with thee Oh where . . . "

Then she fell across him in a shuddering heap and he went out softly on the ebb of darkness.

Chapter 5

"Conchita," Ross said, "it is nothing. One does not preoccupy oneself over such a scratch."

"I did not know it was so small. And now I have a great annoyance with you for frightening me so. I thought you were dead. I was screaming like a demented one when Wallace came in and took you up. I was searching for a pistol with which to blow out my brains. Fortunately, I did not encounter one. When Wallace showed me you lived, I felt such a fool!"

Ross put out his hand and caught hers, holding it gently. He looked at her with grave tenderness.

"You would have died because of me?" he said.

"Yes. But then I am one crazy little bird, no?"

"Yes. Crazy. Mad. Insane. You wanted to kill yourself because you thought I was dead; but you will not bring me happiness while I live."

Conchita looked away from him out of the window.

"Always you use the wrong words, my heart. Not 'will not'; but can not. The difference is immense."

Ross's long fingers tightened about her hand.

"Why can't you, *muñecita?*" he said.

"That is a little history. And it is part of the big history of Cuba. Someday I will tell you. Someday when I am strong enough not to die when you scorn me."

Ross raised himself up on one elbow and stared at her.

"When I scorn you?" he said. "Now I know you are mad!"

"Perhaps," She bent down then and kissed his mouth, the touch of her lips so delicate that the sensation was more imagined than felt. "Ross, why did she shoot you?"

"She had three great *copas* of brandy, this big. And brandy whispers strange things into the mind. For instance, it told her to dance. That is where I got the idea for that music."

"Yes. It was very like her. Wild and hideous – like her heart. But she is beautiful, herself; disgracefully beautiful. Tell me, Ross –

does she dance well?"

"Sufficiently. I don't know. I'm not a good judge of those things."

"It is strange that she should dance for you, and I should not. For I am a dancer. That's why we left New York."

"Riddles again," Ross groaned. "You left New York because you are a dancer?"

"Yes. We have very little money, and I wanted to go on the stage as a dancer. There was a great impresario who saw me dance the flamenco and made me an offer. Father was horrified. Then there was this of Narciso López, and at the same time a letter from José Méndez, so father decided to bring me South. The rest you know. . . . Shall I dance for you?"

"No. Later, perhaps. Now I'd rather you sat here and held my hand." He started suddenly, an expression of concern in his eyes. "Conchita!" he said; "you should not be here! You were supposed to be in New Orleans today with your father. . . ."

"I know," she said simply. "But I am not in New Orleans with my father. I am here with you, which is nicer. Ever so much nicer."

"But your father —"

"Received this morning before you awakened a note from me, telling him that you have been gravely injured — in my behalf, and that I was

160

attending you together with your sister. He wrote back that he would await me in New Orleans, but that I must be careful of my reputation."

"But Conchita, almost none of that is true!"

"You would have me be so unkind as to worry him?" Conchita asked. "Kindness is sometimes better than truth."

Ross looked at her, shaking his head.

"I don't understand you," he said. "I don't understand you at all."

"Don't try to," Conchita said tremulously. "Just love me. That is sufficient."

"But what are you going to say if my sister or Jennie should come? Or even some stranger? I assure you that a scandal of formidable size would arm itself!"

"If they should come, they would not enter. Wallace has been instructed to say that you have gone to New Orleans – with me. So, my Ross, you are now my prisoner. And I shall devise tortures for you – such as having to kiss me a thousand times. . . ."

"What a little liar you are!" Ross laughed. "Well, shall we commence the torture?"

"I have not lied to you," Conchita said seriously. "I cannot. If I could, I should be your Señora by now. As for the torture – let us wait until you are a little stronger, and it is a little darker. . . ."

Wallace came in then with a bowl of steaming soup. Conchita took it from him and began to feed Ross carefully, tenderly, as though he were a child.

"Marse Ross," Wallace said. "There was a lady downstairs."

Ross sat up.

"What lady, Wallace?" he demanded.

"That black haired lady — Miz Brittany. I told her you wasn't here, that you gone to Newawleans; but she wouldn't believe me. Said you couldn't. Said you was hurt too bad. Had to do some tall talking, 'cause she kind of took me by surprise, I mean her knowing that you was hurt. . . ."

"So?" Ross said.

"So I told her that Miss Conchita took you away in a carriage, with a doctor, and I didn't know when you'd be back."

"Good!" Conchita laughed. "Wallace has also the talent for falsehoods, does he not, Ross?"

"Show me a Negro who doesn't," Ross grinned. "Go on, Wallace."

"That's all, suh. Except that she swore something awful, and got back on that black horse of hers and hit it with her crop so hard it screamed. Then she rode off real fast, and that was the last I seen of her."

"Thank God," Ross breathed.

"I wish," Conchita said grimly, "that I had answered the door, so that I could have taken the crop away from her and beat her and beat her and beat her!"

"Conchita!"

"She shot you, did she not? For that not even a beating would be enough. I should like to scratch out both her eyes!"

Ross looked at Wallace, standing there with his mouth hanging open.

"You may go now, Wallace," he said quietly; "and you haven't heard Mrs. Brittany's name mentioned, you understand? You haven't see her in weeks."

Wallace stared at him a moment, then he grinned.

"Yassuh, Marse Ross," he said; "from now on I'm deaf, dumb, and blind!" Then, still chuckling, he left the room.

Conchita took up the spoon again and fed Ross the rest of the soup. The light slanted into the window at an acute angle, and Ross realized that it must be late, evening, that he must have slept most of the day. His side ached dully, but his mind was clear. And, now, after eating the soup, he felt much stronger. Still, he made no attempt to get up, but stretched out lazily, smiling up at Conchita.

"Tell me about Cuba," he said.

Conchita put the empty bowl on the table, and coming around to the other side of the bed, lay down beside him, pillowing her head on his shoulder. For a moment Ross felt a sense of shock, but he dismissed it. Conchita was fully clothed, and such actions apparently had no significance to her.

"It is beautiful," she said, closing her eyes; "so beautiful. When first you see it the beaches are very white, and the water that sweeps them is like emerald and also like milk upon its edges. And the great ceibas are huge and dark green and under them it is so cool, even in the heat of the day. There are bamboos, very slim and tall, with fine leaves but growing so close together that you cannot see the sun through them, and mangoes, too, with little pinkish yellow blossoms and afterwards the fruit like all the sweetness in the world.

"We have there oranges, and many *vegas* of tobacco, and cocoa, and coconut palms, and wine palms, and bunches of *plátanos* – the fruit that you call bananas, and the coffee shrub, and papayas so big that it seems always that they will break the little stems that hold them to the trees. And whole seas of cane with the *ingenios*, the mills, flaunting banners of smoke, like great ships tied down in the midst

164

of earth. And the old, old cities, Habana and Trinidad, and Matanzas and Camagüey, with the old buildings that are poems frozen into stone, and the *casas grandes* of the rich with their patios, and flowers and fountains; and the *bohíos* of the poor, which are nothing but bamboos tied together with thatched roofs over them, and chickens and pigs and naked children in the yards, and the bougainvillaea all over everything like clouds of heavy purple, and the church bells ringing the call to mass in the morning, and all the people moving in the streets — poets, countrymen, priests, soldiers, scoundrels, harlots and great ladies — and that is Cuba. . . ."

"You loved it, didn't you?" Ross said.

"Like I love you. As fiercely. As tenderly. With all my heart." Then burying her face against his throat she began to cry.

"Don't, Conchita, don't!" Ross groaned; "please don't cry. . . ."

But she cried very softly for a long time, and then her breathing smoothed and quieted and Ross saw that she was asleep. He kept very still so as not to disturb her until his whole body ached from keeping the same position, and outside the window the light spilled out of the sky and one star hung in the sky above his window and winked at him.

Finally, she stirred, and Ross bent down and kissed her, and she did not open her eyes but kissed him back, slowly, tenderly, endlessly until they knew both of them that the kissing was not enough.

"Ross," she breathed, "my Ross. . . ."

"You wish it?" he whispered.

"Yes. And thou?"

She had long since given over saying "you" to Ross, slipping easily and tenderly into the intimate "thee" and "thou," which in Spanish establishes the closeness of a relationship once and for all.

"I, also," Ross groaned; "but it is wrong — very wrong."

"Between us there can be no wrong. Only right. Now have done with the words, my own, for this of the waiting is a thing insupportable. . . ."

"Oh, God — Conchita. I —" Ross began, but she came up hard on both elbows and stopped his mouth.

"Are you happy, my Ross?" Conchita whispered.

"Terribly. And you?"

"Insupportably. We are *macho y hembra,* no? Man and his mate. The primitive ones — the fierce ones — the tender."

"Conchita . . ."

"Kiss me, my Ross, for in a little while it will be light, and I must go before then."

"Why? Why must you go, Conchita *mía?*"

"That you do not see me. I have much shame of your seeing me. . . ."

"Why? Mother of God, why?"

"Because I am ugly. My body is ugly. I could not bear you looking at me. . . ."

Instead of answering, Ross put out his hand to the night table, and groped until he found the box of sulphur matches. He lit one, holding it high. Instantly Conchita snatched at the coverlet, drawing it up to her chin. Ross bent over to the lamp and lit it, adjusting the wick. The yellow glow spread softly through the room.

"No, Ross!" Conchita wept; "Oh, no, no, no!"

But he put his hand on the coverlet and drew it down, and looked at her, seeing her slim, soft-curving, utterly lovely, except the hard, white circle of scars, that started upon the perfect, soft golden hillock of her left breast and traveled at intervals across her body, and down to a little below her waist. They were, he saw, the type of scars that a saber would make, or a broad bladed dagger. There were seven of them.

"This," he said with gruff tenderness, "is of the little history that is part of the greater history of Cuba, isn't it?"

"Yes," Conchita sobbed.

"And these are also the reasons you could not marry me?"

"Yes."

"Then," Ross said softly, "the reason is dead. For these are badges of honor. These are holy scars. . . ." Then bending down his head he kissed them every one.

"Oh, no, Ross!" she cried. "You do not understand. Oh, no – please no!"

"Tell me about it," he said.

She was crying so hard she could not speak, but he gathered her into his arms, and stroked the red-brown hair and kissed her mouth over and over again and after a while she quieted.

"All right," she said brokenly. "It is better that you know. For now, even though it will be ended, I will have had happiness a little. . . . It goes back a long time – six years ago, when I was thirteen. . . .

"There was a man. A dark man, a mulatto. He was called Diego Gabriel de la Concepcíon Váldez, but he took the name Plácido. His life was sad, for not only was he of the blood of the blacks, but he was illegitimate, and his only love died of the cholera. . . . By trade he was a maker of combs, and thus traveled much throughout the island. And little by little he could not support the sight of slavery. So he wrote poems about it, wonderful poems. In one of them he made his oath to be always the foe of the Spaniards, to stain his hands always with their blood, and then to die in front of their rifles and be free.

"And he kept this oath of his. He was a friend of my father's. I saw him often. My father was, you understand, in the first place, before he was a lawyer, an *hacendado* – a planter, you call it. And we had many slaves. But always this of the slaves was a thing that troubled my father, and he listened very carefully to Plácido and also to Pimienta, and others of the free Negroes who had obtained an education. Izquierdo, they used to say, is one white man who is a friend of the blacks. Often they met at my father's *finca*, which in Cuba is a place more like what you call a farm than a plantation, for we grew many things there, not just cane. . . .

"It was near Matanzas, Plácido's home, so we saw him most of all. Father was always kind to his blacks; but little by little he came to see that even kindness was not enough. It is good to be kind, of course; but kindness does not make up for the monstrous blasphemy of keeping and driving like beasts souls made in the image of Our Father, God. Father would have freed his blacks long ago, but he dared not. Men have been killed in Cuba for less than that. And Father was still a young man and loved life. But finally the Spaniards closed in upon this noble friend of ours. They arrested him in Santa Clara once, but could prove nothing. And then again in Trinidad, and finally in Matanzas, as one of the Conspirators of the Stairway, though actually they had nothing to do with a stairway except that after they were caught, the Spaniards swung all twenty-eight of them head down from beneath a staircase and beat them with whips until the blood ran down their faces and dripped on the floor. . . ."

"Good God!"

"I have heard many tales," Conchita said, "of men who died under torture with their lips still sealed. They remain just that – tales. Give a Spaniard time enough, and a sufficiency of his favorite toys: the whip, the boot, the rack, the thumbscrew – and he'll extract a confession from the Holy Ghost. . . . Plácido confessed. Pimienta confessed – he who used to play for me to dance by when I was a child. And on one of those days that are so beautiful in Matanzas, with a clear blue sky and a plenitude of sun, they marched them tottering and weak and burdened down with chains, through a crowd of twenty thousand persons come from all of Cuba to see them die. . . .

"I was there — and I saw it. I could not turn away my eyes. And I learned then that nothing becomes a noble life better than the way of taking leave of it. They died well — all of them, refusing the blindfold and shouting *'Viva la Libertad!'* and standing up tall and proud, those black and brown and yellow men, and *Cuba libre* was conceived that day, though it kicks still in the womb of tomorrow, waiting to be born. . . .'"

"But the scars?" Ross asked.

"I am coming to that. Father wept like a child as his friends died. He decided to free his blacks at once; but we were under the rule of Captain-General Leopold O'Donnell, whose records show he put to death the ones he felt like counting, and does not include the hundreds of Cubans of other complexions he killed. It was impossible. So father waited, but all over the island the blacks kept rising, and a man named José Antonio Saco wrote a history of slavery that father read over and over again until he wore it out. And every month people were being beaten to death, and shot, and hanged and strangled until father could stand it no longer. So, three years after Plácido's death, he freed his slaves. This, under the law, he could do. But that did not stop our black-hearted Spanish Governor with the Irish name from declaring him a traitor, and confiscating our *finca*. . . ."

She looked up at Ross, and her green eyes misted over with tears.

"Must I," she begged, "tell you the rest of it?"

"Yes," Ross said. "It's better told."

"At your orders, Señor! But first you must kiss me, for I think that no more after this will you kiss me, or think of me without shame. . . ."

"And I think," Ross said, "that never again as long as I live will I be able to think of you without reverence, without worship, without. . . ."

"Hush," Conchita said; "do not say these words of me!"

Ross drew her to him and kissed her very tenderly, and the white scars upon her body glowed sharp and ugly in the lamplight.

"Now," she said, "now I will tell you. They drove us from the *finca*, the soldiers; but before we had gone many miles, others of them — the soldiers of Captain Juan Costa — waylaid us. He is a strange man, that Don Juan Costa — he tortures people to death for pleasure, but he has to have violins to play him to sleep. He is of an enormity of fat, and of many strange practices, he will do anything for a daub of a

painter, or a bad musician; but anyone else —
he kills. He calls himself the patron of the arts;
but the art of murder is his chief concern. . . .

"And his soldiers are like him in some ways.
They — they beat my poor father into un-
consciousness, and then seven of them, seven
great smelly, drunken beasts, dragged me down
from my horse and away into a thicket of bamboo. Then — I cannot say it, Ross! I cannot!
How does one become clean again, *mi alma?*
What way exists of scraping off such filth from
the lining of one's soul?"

She looked at him, and the tears cascaded
down her cheeks.

"You made me tell you, Ross," she sobbed;
"it was not enough that I lay all night naked in
your arms; I had to bare my heart as well; I had
to strip my soul!"

Ross put both his arms about her shoulders,
shaking now with sobbing, and crushed her to
him, kissing her eyes, her mouth, her throat.

"Have no shame for this, *chiquita mia,*" he
murmured. "The sin was not yours, and
already you are free of it. Now it is gone, all
gone, and you can stand up beside me before
the priest, and wear your bridal white and none
can gainsay you. I love you, Conchita, and that
is enough. That is more than enough — that is
all we need. . . ."

Conchita looked up at him, wonderingly.

"You'd marry me still," she whispered, "knowing this?"

"Try and stop me!"

She lay very still in his arms and after a time she put up one hand and let the fingers of it stray lightly over his face as though she could outline the image of it, as though the tactile sense would somehow sharpen the memory of him.

"Now," she said gently, "I cannot stop you; but it cannot be for a long time yet. I cannot leave my father, Ross. He'd die without my care."

"Bring him with you. There will be room at Moonrise for us all."

"That is only the first thing. The second is that you are not a Catholic, which is not insurmountable, because you could become one. Would you? It is much to ask."

"It is nothing and less than nothing. Let us leave the objections, shall we?"

"No. There is still one more, and it is the greatest of them all. I — I could not marry a man who kept slaves. And without the slaves there is no Moonrise. But my father has given the years of his youth, his life, truly, to the cause of freedom. I cannot turn my back on that. . . ."

"And you," Ross said, "have given your blood. . . ."

"And my honor. So, my Ross, it still cannot be. Not yet. But someday when things have changed . . ."

"And in the meantime?" Ross groaned.

"We go on like this. In dishonor. In shame. I have much sorrow because of this, but how else could it be? Without you, I would die."

Ross looked at her, his face creased with frowning. I could free them, he thought. I could turn the blacks loose. But they are more Tom's than mine, and some of them were bought with Peter Dalton's money, and then the law makes it difficult. Why is it that what is right is never simple as it appears, and all of life is one long hell of complications that wrings a man's heart dry of tears?

"Do not preoccupy yourself, my Ross. You've worked hard for the place you've gained, and I would have great shame if you destroyed it all because of me."

"The choice isn't even mine, Conchita," he said slowly. "I don't own the plantation alone, nor even the Negroes. Still, I'll work out something. . . ."

He touched the scars lightly with his finger tips, and Conchita looked at him.

"I did not tell you about them, did I?" she said.

"No," Ross said, "you didn't."

"Afterwards, after they had done with me, they had fear because I was after all a Criolla, of good family, which made it different from having sport of a mulatta or a Negress. So they decided that I must die, and six of them rode off, leaving one who had lost in the drawing of the straws to do it. But this man was a coward, and additionally suffered from that sickness of cruelty that I think your Morgan has. . . ."

"Not *my* Morgan!" Ross said emphatically.

"One thrust of the bayonet would have been enough. One good clean thrust. I prayed to him to do it; I begged him; I wept. Instead he did this — the little thrusts one after another all over so that I was covered entirely with my own blood, and an agony of hurting, but not enough to die. He would have kept it up I think, until at last I did die, but some of the Negroes my father had freed came up and found him there and killed him, horribly. They had only *machetes* and clubs against his rifle, but when they were finished it was unnecessary to bury him. There was not a sufficiency of him left for burial. Then they took me to their little *bohío*, hidden in the brush, and their women nursed me back to health and my father also, for they had brought him in, too. And, finally, they took us across to Florida in a little fishing boat, and since all Southerners without exception hate Spain and want to annex Cuba, they allowed us to stay and were very kind until my father's Cuban friends in New York sent us the money to come there. And that is all of my sad little history that is part of the big history of Cuba. . . ."

She looked at him, smiling a little through her tears.

"Now I must go, my Ross. My father awaits me."

"No," Ross said, "not yet. It is not yet morning."

Conchita looked past him out the window where the darkness was beginning to thin a little.

"No," she whispered, "it is not, is it?" Then once more she put her mouth to his.

Chapter 6

From where he sat on the piano stool, Ross could hear the booming of the cannon. The noise rolled in the windows, slow, belly-deep, heavy. Every time the guns crashed, the whole building shook. Ross put both hands to his head, digging his fingers into the shaggy mass of his thick blond hair. Damn them all! Would they never have done with their shooting?

He got up and stood by the window, the red and yellow glare of the torches passing below in the street on the way to the Esplanade making flickering shadows on his face. Fools, fools! he groaned; don't they know where men like Quitman are leading them?

He hadn't gone to the torchlight ceremonial in honor of Mississippi's intrepid Governor, because more and more everything men like

John Quitman stood for was beginning to sicken in his throat. He, for one, was heartily glad that Quitman had resigned the Governor's chair. That was something to celebrate; but not for the reasons that the citizens of Natchez were celebrating it.

Those reasons, to a man of Ross's temperament, were well-nigh incredible. Several weeks ago, a Federal Grand Jury sitting in New Orleans had indicted López, Quitman and an associate named Henderson for violating the neutrality laws of 1818, in connection with the ill-fated López affair; but Quitman, from the bastion of the Governor's chair, had screamed his defiance of the Federal Government and all its works.

The Federal Government, he roared, had no power over the Governor of Mississippi! The State of Mississippi was a sovereign state, he argued; the Government in Washington had no more right to arrest him than had the government of China. If, under the law, he could not send the members of the State Militia to arrest the President of the United States, he'd be double damned and pickled in brine before he'd allow the President to arrest him! There had been too much interference already with the individual rights of the States. If, on top of telling the people of the South that they couldn't move where they pleased and take their slaves with them, the Federal Government was now going to try the head of a government affiliated with it only voluntarily, for a violation of one of its stupid laws, he, John Quitman would resist to the death!

Half the young blades in the State had already assured the Governor of their support, Ross knew. Orators had advised him to surround himself with militiamen and tell the United States to go to hell. Maybe the rest of the South had knuckled down to the fear of Federal might in Nashville, but the sovereign State of Mississippi was prepared to wage war singlehandedly for her rights. Ross had looked upon this piece of monumental folly with speechless amazement. Perhaps, as Governor Quitman had obviously hoped, the rest of the South would have been drawn into the conflict; but the end of it had been plain to anyone with eyes to see, even before it could begin. The South of 1850, without one powder works within its borders; without a single factory for the manufacture of arms, without one-tenth the wealth, or one-fourth the manpower of the North, would be crushed in a matter of weeks. But now, apparently, John Quitman had seen the light. Only yesterday he had resigned the office of Governor, and agreed to submit to the

Court's jurisdiction as a private citizen, in order to save Mississippi the humiliation of being invaded by a foreign power, the Government of the United States. He would, he told cheering throngs in New Orleans, sponsor a move to abolish the Federal Courts in the States.

Much of the gunfire and applause down there now, Ross knew, grew out of a sense of relief. Every halfway intelligent citizen knew how much chance Mississippi stood against the United States.

The thunder of cannon fire slammed against Ross's eardrums, leaving him deafened and sick with fury. On the Esplanade they had already fired fifteen rounds in honor of John Quitman, and fifteen for the Southern States. Now they were launching into another fifteen for mankind in general. The noise tore at Ross's nerves. He had been busy with a new interest of his, before the uproar had made it impossible. Since the discovery forced upon him by Morgan's wild dance, that his musical talents perhaps included composing, Ross had been obsessed with the desire to do a piece for Conchita. He remembered the songs of Spain: the swift fiery gypsy music of Andalusia; the haunting love songs of Sevilla. Something like that — only different! Something that had Conchita in it: her fire, her spirit, her intelligence, her honesty, her beauty, even her passion. But it was difficult – damnably difficult.

That troubled him. Morgan's music had come to him easily, almost without conscious effort. Was it that Morgan, then, possessed a greater hold over him than his beloved Conchita? He hoped not. Yet, there was something about Morgan. . . . Thank God Lance was home again. Now all the whispering behind fans on the shaded galleries would come to an end. He was sick of the whispers: Morgan riding at midnight with Henry Montcliffe – going God knows where; Morgan walking brazenly through the streets of Natchez, clinging affectionately to Tom Pary's arm – and Jennie crying and crying over the nights she spent watching from the bedroom window of her house for a light in the Parys' home across the street, for the sound of Tom's horse's hoofs – a sound that many nights did not come at all. Other men, and other whispers. Good God, was there no end to the number of cavaliers that Morgan needed to make her content?

Well, there was no use staying here in the apartment. Clearly he would get nothing done tonight – neither the music nor the sketches he had promised the Whitneys, his newest clients. As he put on his tall hat, he had the feeling that he'd be glad when the plantation was operating on a paying basis. Then, although he had no intention of giving up architecture, he'd certainly practice it in a much more leisurely fashion.

Outside in the street, he paused a moment considering the matter of where he should go. Not to the mass meeting, certainly. He had heard entirely too much windy bombast in the last few weeks. If those fire-eaters on the Esplanade wanted to fight both Spain and the Federal Government, let them. He didn't want to fight anybody. All he wanted was peace.

He turned Nancy's head toward Moonrise, his own beautiful house that he could never find time to complete. Out there he would be able to think, reach some decisions: what to do about Conchita, what about Jennie and Tom — what, in fact, to do about Morgan. For it wasn't true that he didn't have to do anything about Morgan. That was a delusion — a dangerous delusion. For not only was she endangering the Parys' future with her continued flirtation with Tom — Ross was convinced that it was nothing more; but her poison was in his system too. Why else, if he were really free of Morgan, could he still play her music from memory, feeling it in his veins like bitter fire?

He rode slowly out of town, away from the noise and the shouting, until he came out on one of those roads that were like tunnels of green lace, so thickly had the branches of the oaks interwoven above them. Even there he did not urge Nancy to a faster pace, but continued to clop along slowly, bent forward in the saddle, his face frowning and thoughtful.

But about two miles beyond the city he became aware of a movement in the underbrush and, turning in the saddle, made out the dim forms of two horses, tethered side by side just off the road. He shrugged, and was about to ride on, when he realized that one of the horses was gray.

Tom Pary rode a big, gray gelding. And the smaller animal nuzzling contentedly beside the taller horse was black. Even in the moonlight its coat glistened like black satin. There are other black horses in Natchez, he told himself angrily; but all the same he was sure. The gray was Tom's big gelding. And the black was Satana, Morgan's fiery mare.

He felt cold, suddenly. Ice-cold and sick. The underbrush was very thick, and beyond the road the moonlight could not penetrate the branches of the oaks. He felt something like fury stir in him, and the big veins at his temples stood up and beat with his blood. He realized that he was trembling, shaking in his boots like a man palsied. Then he laughed. It was bitter laughter, directed at himself.

So Tom tumbles her in the brush like a nigger wench, he thought; what concern is that of mine? Why all the heat, Ross Pary? Is it because in your heart of hearts you've always thought of her as yours that you feel yourself the cuckolded one instead of Lance?

Lance! Ross stiffened in the saddle. Lance was home again. Always a man quick to take offense, he had already fought three successful duels over matters which compared to this had been less than trifles. For this, Tom Pary could die. Good marksman as Tom was, he was no match for Lance Brittany's almost unbelievable skill with a pistol. And if it came to swordsmanship, about that Tom knew nothing, while Lance handled a rapier or a saber with the same sure hand. . . .

Ross sat still upon his mare, but his brain raced. Where was Lance now? Wherever that was, he'd have to find him and keep him there, at least until Morgan had had a reasonable chance to get home again. God, he groaned, when a man is a slave to the fever in his loins, what follies would he not commit!

But, before he could decide in which direction to start his search — whether toward Buena Vista, or out to Finiterre, or even back to the mass meeting, Morgan came out from under the trees, her arm linked through the crook of Tom's elbow, her face filled with laughter. Her clothing, Ross could see, was disheveled. The two of them walked toward their horses.

Ross sat there, not knowing whether to move or stay still. Then, attracted by the movement of the two horses, Nancy whinnied. Tom whirled in his saddle, his hand going toward his left armpit where his gun was; then very slowly it came away empty, but his face was black with fury.

Morgan stared at Ross a long moment. Then she laughed.

"Ross!" she said scornfully. "Good little Ross! Good, busy little Ross — whose endless activities also include spying."

Tom reined in the gelding, dancing him over to where Ross sat.

"You dirty little sneak," he began. "I've got a good mind to . . ."

"To do what, Tom?" Ross said.

"To break your gawddamned neck!" Tom roared.

Ross smiled at him. He was filled with a curious, icy calm. He wasn't afraid. It was a good feeling not to be afraid.

"If you try it," he said quietly, "I'll kill you. Brother or not, I'll kill you. You think I've worked all these years to have you tear it down because you're a slave to your swinging gut? Under the circumstances it would be a pleasure to put a bullet through your stupid carcass. . . ."

Tom stared at him in pure disbelief.

"Well, I'll be damned!" he muttered.

"It would at least save Lance the trouble of doing it later. By the way, you'd better ask that married tart of yours where her husband is right now."

"I know where he is," Tom grunted. "In Nashville. And now I am going to learn you — using such language about her!"

"Language?" Ross said. "Oh, yes — I called her a tart. I apologize. She isn't a tart, is she? After all, tarts do get paid."

"Why you —" Tom snarled, and lunged forward; but Morgan stopped him.

"No," she said, "No, Tom — I find this highly diverting! Go on, Ross — what other bad qualities do I have?"

"I wouldn't know," Ross said. "It doesn't interest me. All I care about right now is why you told this poor, stupid ox of a brother of mine that Lance was still in Nashville when he's been back in Natchez for more than a week? Do you want a killing?"

"It might be fun," Morgan said easily.

Tom stared at her.

"Where is he?" Ross said. "Where is Lance right now, Morgan?"

"At the mass meeting. But that won't be over for hours. . . ."

"It was almost over when I left," Ross said. "Tom, you take her home. I'll try to detain Lance. And you'd better pray that I succeed."

"Gosh, boy," Tom said huskily. "Reckon I kind of had you figured all wrong. . . ."

"Don't figure," Ross said; "just ride — ride like hell!" Then he whirled Nancy around and started off at a hard gallop back towards town.

Tom looked at Morgan, his eyes hostile.

"You lied to me," he said.

"Of course," Morgan laughed. "I always do. Ross is right — you are a big, stupid ox. Come on, now — let's ride."

Ross saw the little group of riders coming up the road toward Buena Vista, and pulled up Nancy, hard. It wouldn't do to approach them at a gallop. The less curiosity he aroused — the better. As he rode toward them, he was relieved to see that all the other riders turned off into another road, leaving Lance Brittany to ride home alone.

Ross rode up to him with elaborate casualness.

"Howdy, Lance," he said; "I was looking for you."

Lance studied him.

"And in a great hurry, too," he said, "from the looks of that horse. She's been ridden damn near to death. What's the matter, Ross? Anything wrong?"

"No — nothing," Ross said, trying to keep his voice calm. "I just wanted to discuss something with you — a detail change for Finiterre . . ."

"And you abused a fine piece of horseflesh like that mare for that? You know, boy, I sometimes think you're crazy. . . ."

"You're right," Ross smiled; "I am. I wasn't in a hurry, actually. It was just such a fine night that I felt like riding like blazes — so I did. Now about this change, if you'll ride down to my diggings . . ."

"Why?" Lance drawled. "Buena Vista is much closer. Can't we discuss it there?"

"No," Ross said hastily; "there're some sketches and they're up at my place."

"Do we have to discuss it tonight?" Lance said tiredly.

"I'm afraid so — you see, I'd like to get your Negroes started on it the first thing tomorrow. Besides you can rest there all you like, and Wallace will whip you up the finest julep you ever tasted."

"All right," Lance said, and Ross knew that he had won. But, actually, his troubles were only beginning. He had no idea for changing any important detail of Finiterre. And the sketches he had mentioned were quite nonexistent. He'd have to stall desperately for time, matching his wits against a man who was nobody's fool. Damn Tom anyhow! Tom and Morgan. He had enough troubles of his own. . . .

As soon as he was safely inside the rooms with Lance, he called Wallace and ordered him to make mint juleps.

"Yassuh," Wallace grinned. "Right away suh!" His mint juleps were a source of great pride to Wallace.

"Well, Lance," Ross began, "what do you think of your friend Quitman now?"

"I still think he's a smart man, but he tries to go too fast. He's no fool, though. As soon as he saw he'd gone too far, he pulled in his horns. Nobody wants a war, and Mississippi sure Lord couldn't whip the whole damned Union. . . ."

"Two wars," Ross said. "He's almost started two full-sized wars in one year. Quite an accomplishment for one man."

"I don't get you," Lance said. "What two wars, Ross?"

"With the United States — and with Spain. He was largely behind this Cuban business you know. . . ."

"That's true," Lance said thoughtfully.

"Funny thing — in a way that was Jeff Davis' fault. When López first came to the States, he was looking for a prominent American to lead his expedition. So he went to Jefferson Davis first of all, and Davis sent him to Major Lee — you know, Robert E. Lee of the Virginia Lees; but Lee declined, and López came back to Jeff Davis for another suggestion. Naturally, as a native of Mississippi, Davis knew Quitman well — so he told López to see him. John backed López fully, but as Governor, he couldn't see his way clear to take an active part. It was John who suggested Wheat and O'Hara. . . ."

Wallace came in then with the juleps, the glasses frosted all over, and the sprig of mint floating jauntily from the top.

Lance took his up and looked at it. Then he sipped it slowly.

"Hummmn," he said. "Good. This is damned good, Wallace — you've got the touch. I'll have to send my man over so that you can teach him the secret."

Wallace's grin almost split his tan face.

"Be glad to, suh!" he beamed. "Any time at all. . . ."

"I heard," Lance said, "that both Wheat and O'Hara were badly wounded in the landing, and several other good men were killed. Hell of a thing, that — to die in an obscure filibustering foray. . . ."

"Hardly obscure," Ross murmured, "since it almost got us into a war. . . ." He was at ease now. By this time Morgan should be at home, safely in bed, and Tom halfway back to Moonrise.

"I don't agree," Lance said. "What could we have fought Spain about? We did violate her neutrality — we did open fire upon her colonial soil. . . ."

"The Contoy prisoners," Ross put in quickly. "If Barringer hadn't succeeded in getting them released, there'd have been a war. Remember, Lance, not one of those men set foot on Cuban soil. They mutinied against the leaders of the expedition, and wouldn't go on. The Spaniards took them off Contoy in warships. . . ."

"Contoy is a Spanish island, remember. That in itself made them guilty of invasion."

"But they committed no hostile act. They even surrendered without a fight. To have hanged them would have been pushing a thing too far. There are too many people spoiling for a fight with Spain now for that not to have been seized upon."

"That's possible. Call your man back, Ross. I could use another of these things."

Ross pulled the bell cord.

"Two more juleps," he said to Wallace. Then

turned back to Lance. "Tell me about the Nashville Convention," he said.

"There's nothing to tell," Lance said. "Rhett made the keynote address. Urged secession, as everybody expected him to. But nobody else wanted to secede or to fight a war, or to do anything except hold the present line as closely as possible. So the whole thing degenerated into a burst of high-sounding oratory and windy platitudes. . . . The South's still in the Union, and all the resolutions they passed in Nashville won't hide the fact that she's there to stay. . . . Now, Ross, what about those sketches?"

"Of course," Ross said easily, and pulled the bell cord. When Wallace put his head in the door, Ross said: "As soon as you finish the juleps, bring me my portfolio. . . ."

Wallace, usually so slow to complete anything he was asked to do, was this time, of course, disgustingly prompt. He appeared almost at once with the mint juleps on a tray, and the portfolio under one arm.

Ross took the portfolio from him and made a great show of looking through it.

"That's funny," he said, "I could have sworn. . . ." Then he glared up at Wallace.

"Wallace, you black rascal," he said, "have you been pawing through my papers again?"

"Nosuh!" Wallace gasped, more in astonishment than fear. "Nosuh, Marse Ross — you knows I never touches your things!"

Lance looked at Ross, his gaze level and calm.

"Were there ever really any sketches?" he said.

Ross stared at him.

"Of course," he said. "Why else would I have brought you up here?"

"Morgan," Lance said.

Ross's throat constricted. He could not breathe. There must be some way out of this thing, but at the moment he couldn't think of any.

"What," he got out at last, "has Morgan to do with this?"

"I don't know," Lance said. "You tell me."

"Look, Lance," Ross said, "I brought you up here because I'd worked out a series of connecting breezeways between the house and the kitchen, and also the outhouses. In rainy weather, they'd be very useful. Besides, I thought I could make them beautiful as well — the roofs supported by miniature copies of the gallery's columns. . . ."

"What is Morgan up to now?" Lance said wearily.

"Lance, for God's sake —"

"No, not for God's, boy. For Morgan's. She takes hold, doesn't she? Got you, hasn't she? Wait, I'm not accusing you of anything. You're far too decent a sort, and I kind of flatter myself that you value my friendship."

"I do," Ross said.

"Thanks. You're a good boy and I like you. What I figure is that Morgan's been up to something, and you're trying to be gallant about the whole affair. Keep me from getting hurt — maybe keep me from taking a rawhide to Morgan and killing whatever poor devil's she's mixed up with now."

"Lance, I swear. . . ."

"Don't swear. I'm old enough to know a lie when I hear one. There was some mighty damned good reason why I shouldn't get home just then. That poor mare of yours was all in a lather, you had ridden her so hard. And you didn't do that because you felt like riding like blazes. You may be a fool, but you're not cruel. And you couldn't show me those sketches because there weren't any. Still, in a way, it was all mighty decent of you." He sipped his julep in calm appreciation. "Damned good stuff, this," he said.

"You're wrong, Lance," Ross began; "I didn't —"

"I'm not wrong, and you did. Don't worry,

boy, I'm not going to say a word to Morgan."
He looked at Ross steadily. "Do me a favor,
boy. Tell this other man to be careful. Tell him
I'm on to him. I won't ask you who he is. You
wouldn't tell me, and I don't want to know. At
fifty, a man sort of loses the hankering to go out
and shoot somebody."

"Lance," Ross said; "why did you marry
her?"

"Her father and I were friends. We were at
Harvard together. He was considerably older
than I, and already married. He was, even then,
a queer sort. I was the only friend he had. . . ."

Ross waited.

"His name was Page — Morgan Page. I think
he wanted a son — so when Morgan was born
he gave her that mannish name. And I don't
think he ever forgave her for being a girl. I
don't know what went on in that house.
Morgan has never said. But whatever it was, it
left its mark upon her. Even now she's got to be
admired — the more admirers, the better. But,"
he looked at Ross gravely, "I don't think she's
ever been actually unfaithful to me. I don't
think she could be. . . ."

"Why?" Ross said, remembering the moonlight on that road, and the shadows in the
brush, black and thick.

"Because, basically, she hates men. She married me because she had to, and because of all the men she knows, she dislikes me least. You see when Page died, quite literally in the arms of his latest paramour, he left Morgan and her mother penniless. Faith, Morgan's mother, survived her worthless husband less than four weeks. It was, I believe as nearly an authentic case of a woman's dying of a broken heart as I've ever heard of."

"You said he was worthless," Ross said; "but you also said he was your friend. Why, Lance?"

"Morgan Page was one of the most charming fellows you'd ever want to meet. Mind you, Ross, the Pages were old-line New York aristocrats, with generations of wealth and breeding behind them. But it took Morg, as we used to call him, less than twenty years to run through all that money. He had a cruel streak in him, too. I think now that he was mad. And Morgan's just like him. That's why I'm so careful of her."

"You — you think the sickness is in the blood?"

"I don't know. I just try to be patient and gentle. All I do know is that Morgan has never forgiven him for what he did to her mother. He could, I understand, be quite barbaric. Even that devilish charm of his was a kind of a symptom. It was too flashy — too brilliant. And he could turn it off and on like a faucet."

"Lance," Ross said, "suppose you're wrong. Suppose Morgan could – turn to another man, what then?"

Lance stared at him, and Ross didn't like his eyes. They were terrible.

"I'd kill him," Lance said quietly, "and afterwards I'd kill her. Because Morgan could never be forced or persuaded. It would be her idea, Ross – conceived entirely by her long before."

"But – if she inherited her father's weakness . . ."

"How do I know? All I know is she's mine. And she's going to stay mine, if I have to kill every man in the State of Mississippi. 'Night, Ross."

"Good night, Lance," Ross said. "I'll see you tomorrow. . . ."

It was, he reflected as he closed the door behind Lance, one mighty pretty kettle of fish. Then he crossed over into his bedroom, taking a half full decanter of bourbon with him. But he had emptied it before he fell asleep.

The next day, out at Finiterre, he pushed his broad straw hat back off his forehead, and mopped his brow. It was hot. The black men working on the house were glistening with sweat; but they worked steadily, with a certain unconscious rhythm. Finiterre was almost finished. All that remained was to install the windows, and stain and polish the floors. The outside would be painted white, but that would be done later. All the outbuildings were complete. The Negroes working on the house were now living in the neat, whitewashed quarters some distance away. It was, Ross mused, remarkable how many other buildings were necessary to the existence of a plantation manor. There were the stables, the chicken coops, the smoke houses, the spring house in which perishables were kept, the tool house for the agricultural implements, the barn for the cattle, the pigpen, the garden house of cool lattice work for the mistress of the establishment to escape the heat, the smithy where the iron work was done, and the kitchen. The kitchen was built a reasonable distance from the big house, because in the country effective firefighting companies were non-existent; and it was much easier to replace the simple kitchen house when a careless cook started a blaze than the expensive manor itself. In the kitchen the iron pots hung on wrought iron legs over an open fire in the huge fireplace; but there was also a beehive-shaped clay oven for the baking. Ross, wiping the back of his neck and feeling it raw from the pitiless midsummer sun, wondered how much of the hearty eating habits of the South were due to the impossibility of preserving anything in the summertime. The spring house, carefully shaded, and located over fresh, cool flowing water, helped; but it was the house servants that solved the problem by the simple expedient of devouring everything left upon their masters' tables. . . .

Satisfied with the house, Ross rode out a few yards to watch the men who were busy laying out Morgan's formal garden. So far she had not taken the slightest interest in her garden, but Ross had insisted that there must be one – so fine a house as Finiterre demanded it. Lance, who took great pride in everything connected with his new home, agreed, so the work was being pushed forward. Of course, it was much too hot to plant anything now, but the brick walks were being laid, and the slaves had dammed up the little spring that flowed behind the house and diverted its course so that it filled up a shallow depression, making a delightful little pond set in the lawn.

The garden, Ross had planned, would be bordered and shaded by varnished lauria mundi; there would be cape jasmine, slender altheas, and dark green arbor vitae, lined with trim boxwood hedges, accented by cones of the same plant. In the little beds would be fragrant amaryllis, purple magnolia, Arabian and night-blooming jessamines, lemon verbena, aloe, snow-drops, caco, and sweet shrub. Over the walls of the garden house honeysuckle would climb, and the humble outhouses, built, because it pleased some ironic vein in Lance's nature, in the shape of Greek temples, would be covered by Cherokee roses and the trailing vines of wisteria.

Finiterre, Ross knew, would be beautiful. But he doubted that anyone would find happiness there.

As he turned Nancy to ride back in the direction of Moonrise, he saw Morgan coming down the stairs of the nearly finished house. She was dressed all in white, and her face, under the lace-edged parasol, had all the sweet innocence of a child's.

Maybe Lance's history of her background and her past explained Morgan, but at the moment Ross doubted it. You couldn't explain a person, really. There was always something missing. The vital part. The living, breathing part. The tangled mixture of love and hate, dream and thought, of what was known, and what was merely hoped for — and the lines between those things were always unclear. As unclear, perhaps, as the borders between good and evil. That line, Ross thought, is meaningless to Morgan.

She came toward him, small, demure, smiling. Last night didn't exist for Morgan, Ross realized with a sense of shock. With her what was done was done. She would forget faithlessness, deceit — even, Ross realized suddenly with absolute conviction, murder, if it suited her purpose at the moment. And there would be no remorse. Morgan was neither Venus nor Aphrodite, but Astarte, the dark Chaldean goddess. And goddesses are above man-made laws. Morgan could, if it pleased her, return with her husband to the very scene of her adulteries, and nothing in the surroundings would move or remind her.

Looking at her, Ross felt cold suddenly, despite the heat. There was something in the very pleasantness of her expression that was terrible. He found himself repeating the lines from *Hamlet*: "That one may smile, and smile, and be a villian . . ."; and it was only when Morgan looked up at him quizzically that he realized that he had said them aloud.

"You hate me, don't you, Ross?"

"No," Ross said shortly; "I just don't understand you, that's all."

"But you do dislike me. You think I'm no good. You're right."

"Look, Morgan. . . ."

"You're nice, Ross. You're sensitive and

talented and fine. There are times when I love you very much."

"Morgan, for the love of God!"

"I do. I've never known a man before I could love. Most men are such beasts."

"Lance isn't a beast," Ross said.

"Oh, yes, he is. He's a very intelligent beast – but still, a beast. He thinks he can solve everything with a whip – or a gun. And nothing can be solved that way – nothing at all."

Ross stared at her in wonder.

"What can be solved," he said quietly, "with one man after another?"

"Nothing. But that has nothing to do with solutions. It's just that things pile up inside of me. . . ."

"What things?" Ross demanded.

"Things like being afraid of the dark. Things like hearing noises. Things like hating and wanting to hurt – even to be hurt. Then the man is the door. It bursts open and all those things flood out and I'm free. Poor Lance – it's a wonder I haven't killed him by now. . . ."

"Or poor Tom," Ross said bitterly, "or poor Henry – or who else? How many more, Morgan?"

"No," Morgan said, "just poor Lance. The others I just torment. It's easy to reduce a man to panting idiocy, Ross. One whiff of womans-flesh and they're baying the moon. . . ." She looked back at the house. "It's very lovely, Ross," she said, "I'm going to be happy there."

"Will you?" Ross said moodily; "I doubt it."

"Oh, yes. I'm never unhappy. It's only the people who have to live with me that are. Like Lance."

Ross leaned down toward her.

"He knows," he said soberly.

"Of course. Every time I've been out with a man he knows it, because I always come home and stick my nails into his back, and bite his throat till the blood runs down. He's fifty now, Ross. What will I do when he's too old?"

"Get yourself another," Ross said.

"No." She shuddered suddenly, her expression filled with loathing. "I couldn't. Only a mindless brute would have the strength I need, the bottomless appetites. And I'd torture him. Stupidity always affects me that way. Or, if I took someone like you — someone with sensitivity and real intelligence, I'd hunt and hunt until I found all the secret, festering little hurts — all the things he's trying to hide, or deny, all the self-doubts, all the delusions, all the lies he's told himself to keep fast hold on his dignity and his pride. And I'd tear at them, until they were visible and raw, until he'd bleed to death inside his heart. He'd die terribly, raving mad, thinking himself unworthy of life. . . . No, Ross — after Lance, there won't be anyone else."

"You're mad," Ross said; "you really are mad!"

"Or sane," Morgan smiled, "and living in a lunatic world. Who knows?"

Then she turned and left him, walking back towards the empty house, her footsteps lost in the sound of hammering.

Chapter 7

That summer and fall of 1850 were quiet — a time of waiting. In Washington, Zachary Taylor, President of the United States went out in a broiling sun to witness the laying of a cornerstone. The day was July Fourth, Independence Day, and above that cornerstone the workmen were going to build a spire of stone, pointed like a needle at the top in honor of George Washington. Five days later, Zachary Taylor was dead of sunstroke, and Millard Fillmore sat in the White House.

In Mississippi, Judge John Isaac Guion, President of the Senate, took John A. Quitman's place in the Governor's chair, and a jury in New Orleans found Quitman and Henderson, and López not guilty of violating the neutrality laws of 1818 in connection with their attempt to set Cuba free of Spain.

Henry Clay's Compromise of 1850 became law; California entered the Union as a free State and the territories of New Mexico and Utah were given self-determination on the question of slavery. Fillmore, the first "Dough-face" President, as John Randolph called Northern pro-slavery men, ordered a stern prosecution of the new Fugitive Slave Law, provided for in the Compromise, and twenty thousand escaped slaves, living quietly in the North, started a wild stampede for Canada. No more slaves could be bought or sold in the District of Columbia, but a man living there, might keep the ones he already owned.

In New York, Narciso López quietly began raising funds and recruiting men for his second expedition against Cuba; and near Natchez, Mississippi, one Ross Pary, architect, completed the building of Finiterre. . . .

When it was done, Ross had a feeling of emptiness. The rest of it, the arranging of the elaborate furnishings that had already reposed for weeks in a warehouse in New Orleans before the completion, was a matter of the owner's individual tastes, though Ross could and did make suggestions. Lance usually accepted these suggestions and followed them; but Morgan argued endlessly on every detail;

and in the end, always got her way.

Yet the results were pleasing; four times out of five, Morgan's feminine instinct was at least as good as Ross's trained taste. Finally he gave it up, telling Morgan: "Do as you please. You're only going to, anyhow, and I've other things to do."

The other things were the five houses he was building for other clients; his own house, Moonrise; and Conchita Izquierdo. The bulk of the work on the other houses he passed on to his assistants. Finiterre had made him; it was the most talked about house in the State. Ross Pary now, could rough out a plan, sketch his beautiful elevations showing how the completed house would look, pocket his fee, and exercise only a nominal amount of supervision over his draftsmen and engineers. For the whole of the summer and part of the fall, he supported his new plantation. Tom came to him constantly for more money for needed supplies.

But, with the harvest, Moonrise came into its own. Whatever Tom Pary's faults were, nobody could sneer at his abilities as a planter. By mid-October, the Parys were independently wealthy men. The wagons rolled endlessly down to the landing, loaded with the bales of cotton; in New Orleans, the cotton factors gave one look at the fine, long staple fiber, and placed it among their very top grades.

Ross had the feeling that he could do no wrong, make no mistakes. Everything he touched turned to gold. So, feeling ever more sure of himself, he delegated more and more of his tasks to his assistants, and plunged into the completion of Moonrise. He took his sketches out to the forge and stood beside Brutus as the big black hammered the slender rods of iron into the intricate wrought iron balustrade for the small balcony. He was surprised at how fast Brutus learned; his hands seemed to have knowledge of iron embedded in their very sinews.

Ross sat on a sawhorse a little way from the forge, watching the iron glowing red as Brutus pumped the bellows, the shower of sparks flying out as he struck it, bending it around the cone of the anvil to the exact shape desired, then plunging it hissing into the water.

Yet Brutus never smiled. And that was a strange thing. The Negroes of Moonrise were well treated, and better fed than most of the blacks on the surrounding plantations. In the quarters under the chinaberry trees, there was a chapel, and a hospital; and David Martin, the overseer, was a kindly man, very seldom given to the use of the whip. When he did use it, it was mostly to threaten. Sometimes, a lazy black, caught sleeping under the shade of an oak, might receive one sharp crack across the buttocks to galvanize him into action. But David knew that Ross would question sternly any extended lashing of his people; that and his own easygoing nature prevented any really harsh punishment. The result was that the Moonrise blacks were fat and laughing. They sang all the time, and planters coming through Natchez under the Hill from the steamboat landing, could easily point out the Pary Negroes to strangers on Saturdays when the slaves were given a free day to visit town.

"Don't know how he does it," more than one grumbled. "His niggers work like blazes for him, and he never has the slightest trouble. . . ."

But Brutus' face, heavy in the red glow of the forge was lined and sad.

"Brutus," Ross said, "I heard you were planning to run away the first chance you get. What I want to know is — why? I don't think you've been badly treated."

Brutus put down the heavy hammer and leaned on it, the whites of his eyes red in the firelight.

"Nosir," he said; "I been treated real good. Think maybe you'n' Marse Tom just about the best white folks in the world."

"Well?" Ross demanded.

"It's my wife, sir. Can't stand being without her. Can't stand not seeing my little boy. . . ."

"Your wife?" Ross said; "I didn't know you had one!"

"Yassir. Over there in Georgia — at the old place. Her'n' me was married proper — in the church. Then old marse died and his boy took over. That there young Marse Linton was meaner'n dirt. Took a whip to my Rachel, and I hit him. That's how come I was sold."

"I see," Ross said. "But Brutus, there're an awful lot of good looking young women on the place. A fine-looking man like you could take his pick. . . ."

Brutus stared at him.

"Marse Ross, Marse Ross," he said, shaking his massive head. "I'm plumb downright shamed of you. S'posin' you had a wife and you had to go away from her for a while. A real good wife, sweet to you, lovin'. . . . You look around and pick yourself out somebody else? Would you, Marse Ross?"

"No," Ross said; "I don't reckon I would."

"Me neither," Brutus said.

Ross looked at Brutus. He had the planters' usual feeling that all Negroes were children; but how did you explain a man like Brutus?

And what could you do about him once you had him explained?

"Where is the Linton place, Brutus?" he asked quietly.

"Down near Savannah. Marse Ross, you don't mean —"

"Yes, Brutus," Ross said; "I'm going to try to buy your Rachel and the boy. I don't promise you I'll succeed; but I'm going to try."

"Thank you, boss!" Brutus said huskily. "You good man, Marse Ross. God gwine to bless you — sure. . . ."

Looking at him, Ross saw to his own vast astonishment, that the huge black's eyes were filled with tears.

"I hope so," he said drily; "I could use a few blessings. Now finish that balustrade for me, Brutus. There's so much to be done. . . ."

He sat down that same night and wrote the letter, making an offer for Rachel and the child. Now, he thought, Brutus and I will have to wait. But that's all life is — waiting. . . .

He put on his hat and went down the stairs. Time to have it out with Tom. Time to get him to see the light of reason. But, Ross thought bitterly, how can I convince him, when she bewitches me, too? He swung up into the saddle, and paused long enough to adjust the pistol that hung under his left armpit.

Never before this year had he carried a gun. In an age and in a section where a man felt undressed without his swordcane and pocket pistol, Ross Pary had never borne arms in his life. The thought of shooting a human being made him ill. But now he carried a pistol, and the answer to that was the answer to so much of what was wrong with his life: Morgan.

Any time the whim moved her, Morgan could put Tom in such a position that Lance would feel honor bound to kill him. Ross meant to prevent that — at gunpoint if need be. If a duel occurred, Lance would most likely kill Tom, which to Ross was unthinkable. But, if by some accident, Tom were to win the fight, Ross found that he wouldn't like that either. Lance Brittany had been his friend — a brave, generous man who deserved the best of life. So, on that November morning, Ross had made up his mind. The inevitable had to be turned aside; the tragedy had to be prevented. By diplomacy, if possible; by guile, if diplomacy failed. Even, if no other road were left open — by force.

He came, after his ride, out into the broad fields of Moonrise. He could hear the Negroes' singing far off and faint, and turned Nancy's head toward the sound. That was where Tom would be. He rode through a wooded section and came out upon a broad sweep of fields. The sight of it moved him. Black, rich and gently rolling, the land stretched out before his eyes to the rim of the world, and above them the clouds piled up, fleecy white and great-domed with feathery silver edges, and all between them was blue. He could see the blacks moving down the rows in lines between the plants, the sacks slung over their shoulders, their fingers stretching out, grasping the white bolls, tearing them loose, and plunging with them into the great sacks, in time to the lead hand's singing.

Beside them, he saw the two horsemen, David Martin, and Tom, his brother, for whom he didn't mean to weep. So he urged Nancy forward until he came up to them, and both of them turned at his approach.

"Howdy, Mister Pary," David said; "what brings you out here this fine day?"

"Business," Ross said; "I've got to have a word with Tom."

He could see the guarded look come into his brother's eyes as he spoke. Tom knew. It was going to be difficult — damned difficult. . . .

Tom straightened his hulking form in the saddle and looked at Ross.

"Speak your piece, boy," he said truculently.

"No," Ross said. "Ride back with me a bit,

Tom. It's a private matter. . . ."

"All right," Tom said. "Dave, take 'em down into the south section, next. I shan't be gone long."

They rode together in silence until they came to the wooded place. Tom pulled the gelding up.

"This is far enough," he said. "Well, Ross?"

"You know what's on my mind, so I'll skip the preliminaries," Ross said. "Tom, when are you going to marry Jen?"

The red stole up out of the open collar of Tom's shirt, and climbed to the rim of his ears.

"When I get Goddamned good and ready to," he said.

"Moonrise will be finished by Christmas," Ross said quietly. "It would be damned nice to open it with a wedding."

"Look," Tom said hotly; "when I get hitched is my business. Let's leave it mine, boy. There's enough bad blood between us already."

"You're right," Ross said. "But there's one thing that isn't your business, Tom. And that's what bothers me. Aside from the fact that it hurts me to see Jennie eating her heart out over you, I want to see you married to her to put a stop to that."

"To what?" Tom demanded.

"You and Morgan — as if you didn't know.

Morgan damned sure isn't your business; and keeping that up is going to lead to killing. Drop her, Tom. Don't you see you can't win?"

"You're mighty interested in me'n' Morg, ain't you?" Tom growled. "Why, boy? 'Cause you've got an itch in that direction yourself?"

"Oh, damn!" Ross said; "you know better than that."

"Do I? The second time I saw Morgan she was in your arms — in your room to boot. And where'd you get that gunshot wound Doc Benbow had to patch up. Don't tell me Lance was just target practicing. . . ."

"That," Ross said, "is none of your damned business, Tom."

"Then this ain't none of yourn. Another thing — it was Morg who bit your mouth, not that Cuban girl. It's one of her tricks. Don't ask me how I know, 'cause I just might tell you."

"Forget it," Ross said wearily; "there just isn't any reasoning with you. For the record, I'd like to say one thing: You've been one hell of a fine brother to me — up till now. You've saved my hide from being beaten to rags many a time. You've even saved my life. There were times, when I was in the Academy, that you went without shoes and proper clothing to see that I had money. That's the way it was, Tom. And that's the way I'd like to see it again. But since that black-haired witch came to Natchez, we've done nothing but quarrel. I don't like quarreling with you, Tom. It's no damned fun. I'd like to see you free of her, so we can be brothers again. And much as you get me riled, I haven't the slightest hankering to put flowers on your grave."

" 'Scairt of that, eh? Well, Ross, boy — let me tell you one thing: I hope to God Lance Brittany does find out. Because, if we was to take that trip over to the sandbar, I'd bring a woman home to Moonrise — and it damned sure wouldn't be Jennie!"

Ross looked at him.

"You're mad," he said at last.

"Maybe. But I'm right smart handy with a gun myself. And I'm going to have Morg. Ain't never been a woman born what could get me so heated up and keep me that way. Can't eat from thinking about her. Try to sleep, and she's in my dreams. All right she's a devil; but I ain't no angel, neither. . . ." He stared past Ross toward where the Spanish moss on the oaks was shredding the sunlight. "The night she's finally mine, I'm going to mash her mouth bloody — make her cry and pant and beg!"

Ross stared.

"You mean she hasn't been — yet?" he asked.

"No," Tom said miserably. "You know Morg

better'n that, Ross."

"I reckon I do," Ross said, and pulled Nancy's head half around.

"Where're you going?" Tom said.

"To see — her," Ross said. "Maybe I can talk some sense into her head. I give you up. You're bewitched."

"You ain't so far wrong at that," Tom drawled.

At Finiterre, Ross climbed the curving steps slowly, savoring his own handiwork, and finding it good. He hoped that Lance was not at home, though, in fact, there was small likelihood of that, since the Louisiana plantations occupied so much of his time.

"Well, Cato," he said to the Brittanys' butler, as he passed over his hat, gloves and crop, "how do you like your new home?"

"Just grand, Marse Ross," Cato beamed. "You shore know how to build 'em. Been washing Aeneas' face, you know — he the butler out at Camellia Hill — with this house ever' time I see him!"

"That's not very kind of you, Cato," Ross laughed; "but keep it up; maybe you'll get me some more business."

Although he spoke in jest, there was more than a little truth in what Ross said. The planters were influenced by their Negroes more than they cared to admit, or even knew. Nearly every great house was ruled over, actually, by a middle-aged black nurse, who could and did tell everybody from the planter on down just what she thought. Generations of Southern whites were schooled by her in the basic arts of living; kindliness and that real courtesy that has nothing to do with artificiality. Similarly, house servants such as Cato, by talking to themselves when they were sure they'd be overheard, put many an idea into their master's head. It was not beyond the realm of possibility that Cato's friend, Aeneas, if he complained enough, might set the Montcliffes thinking of building a new home. . . .

"Your master at home?" Ross asked.

"Nosir," Cato said. "He cross the river at Tideland. But Mis Morgan here."

"Very well," Ross said; "I'll talk to her then, if she's not busy."

Cato walked to the foot of the stairs and called:

"Bessie! Come down here!"

The maidservant came tripping lightly down the stairs. She was, Ross saw, a pretty mulatto girl, with still, sullen features. Something about her seemed familiar. Ross glanced down at her right hand. On the back of it was a large, ugly scar, grayish white against the coppery brown of her skin. Yes, it was the same one — the one who had annoyed Morgan to the point of getting the blade of a scissors through her hand for her pains. Ross wondered just how great the provocation had actually been. Knowing Morgan, he guessed that it had been slight.

"Yessir?" Bessie said.

"Tell your mistress," Ross said, "that I'd like to have a word with her."

"Yessir," Bessie said; "but who must I say. . . ."

"Mister Pary," Ross said. He had forgotten that Morgan's upstairs maid did not know him, that in fact, she had seen him but once before in her life, and on that day she had been too badly hurt to pay much attention to anybody.

"Pary?" Bessie said, and Ross could see the bewilderment in her eyes; "but —"

"There's two Mister Parys," Cato told her. "This is Marse Tom's brother."

"Oh, I see," Bessie said. "Yessir, Mister Pary, right away, sir." Then she went back up the stairs.

So Tom has been here, Ross thought, in the house. Funny none of the blacks have gotten around to putting a bee in Lance's bonnet. There's nothing house Negroes love better than a juicy bit of scandal. But the moment he thought about it, he realized why they hadn't:

Morgan. By now, he thought, they're probably more afraid of her than of death. . . .

But, before he had more time to think about it, Bessie leaned over the balustrade and called down:

"Miz Morgan say you come right on up here."

"No thanks," Ross said. "Tell her if it isn't too inconvenient, I'd rather talk to her down here. . . ."

Bessie disappeared in the direction of the bedroom; but this time, instead of the maidservant, Morgan, herself, leaned over the sweeping curve that Ross had designed.

"What's the matter, Ross," she laughed; "afraid of me?"

She had on a soft blue dressing gown, Ross saw; and her hair was combed loose so that it hung down about her shoulders. And again her face had that expression of sweet innocence, almost of naivete that was contradicted by the mockery in her eyes.

"Yes," Ross said; "I am afraid of you, Morgan. Come down, won't you?"

"Oh, bother!" Morgan said, but she came down all the same. When she was close she put out her hand to Ross.

"We'll go in the little parlor," she said. "Cato, bring us some brandy."

"No," Ross said; "no brandy for me, Cato. A little bourbon and branch water will do quite nicely, thank you."

Morgan stared at him.

"You are afraid of me!" she said somberly. "Don't be, Ross. I like you. You're the only person on this filthy earth I do like. I wouldn't harm you. . . ."

Ross cast a glance at Cato's retreating back. Then he put his finger lightly on the tiny crescent-shaped scar on his lower lip.

"Oh, that!" Morgan laughed. "It becomes you — it's a nice little beauty mark, really."

"And the bullet hole in my side?" Ross said tartly.

Morgan stopped laughing.

"I am sorry, Ross," she said. "I only meant to frighten you. But then you frightened me — your devilish charm, you know. You were about to accomplish what no one else ever has. Was it bad?"

"Bad enough," Ross said. "But that's ancient history. Let's forget it, shall we?"

They had come by this time into the little parlor. Ross had designed it for the practical purpose of receiving one or two guests, thus making it unnecessary to use the big salon, which could be reserved for parties and banquets, when the guests would be numbered in scores.

"Let me see!" Morgan said. "Scars fascinate me. I've never seen the mark of a bullet wound." Then she put out her hand and began to unfasten the buttons of his waistcoat.

Ross drew back.

"Morgan, for the love of God!" he said.

"Don't be such an old woman," Morgan said; "I know what a man looks like. After all I have been married for a year, now."

"If you don't mind, Morgan," Ross said stiffly, "I'd rather not put on an exhibition. I came on a more important errand."

"Your brother, Tom," Morgan said. "He is a nuisance!"

Ross opened his mouth to say something, but Cato knocked on the door. Morgan called out to him to come in, and the old black brought the tray with the glasses, and the two decanters. He had brought also a pitcher of ice water for Ross. Ross noticed that Cato avoided looking at Morgan. Her behavior, Ross guessed, must be shocking to the strictly trained house servants.

Morgan poured the great bell-shaped goblet full of brandy, but Ross took only the smallest portion of bourbon.

"Must you drink so much?" he said.

"Yes," Morgan said; "yes, yes, yes! It exhilarates me. It makes me live."

"You have plenty of life now," Ross said.

"I know. But I want more, much more. Life should sing, and bubble, and dance, like this brandy. Around here, it limps." She lifted the goblet and drained it, then put it down on the table.

"That was to us," she said. "To you, Ross. And to me. . . . And what about that great, hulking oaf Tom? Have I broken his stupid heart?"

"Yes," Ross said, "you have."

"I tried hard enough. He has the one trait that maddens me most in a man: simple, unquestioning egotism. He's big and very good-looking. Up till now, he's probably never had the slightest difficulty tumbling whatever wench he wanted in the hay. And he persists in following me about, because the idea can never penetrate his thick cranium that there might be a woman who doesn't want him. But there is. I don't."

"I know," Ross said. "Why don't you send him packing?"

"He amuses me. I have so little diversion, Ross. Look, I'm going to teach you about women. A woman can stand anything — except being bored. Men never realize that. They never realize that the creatures that they've created in their curious, twisted minds, just don't exist. I've learned a lot since I've been here. For

224

instance, you Southerners justify your endless production of little mulattoes on the grounds that if you hadn't the Negresses as an outlet, the purity of Southern womanhood might be endangered by your base passions. . . ."

"Well," Ross said, "isn't that so?"

"Of course not! No woman's chastity has ever been endangered by a man's base passions. Quite the contrary. It is only put in jeopardy by her own."

"My God!" Ross said.

"Listen to teacher, darling. Where you men got the idea that a good woman hasn't any carnal emotions is more than I can see. Or that there is such a thing as a good woman. . . ."

"Now really, Morgan. . . ."

"Please, Ross, what I'm telling you will do you a world of good, if you'll only listen and try to understand. There are no good women, in the sense that you Southerners think. There are women who lack opportunity to be as promiscuous as they'd like to be; there are women who are afraid, and there are women who are cold. That's all. And even the cold ones are that way because their men are stupid and clumsy and lack finesse. . . ."

"You are talking utter nonsense!" Ross said.

"Am I? Your little Conchita is a good girl, isn't she? But I'll wager she isn't cold; and I'll also wager that your wedding night — if it ever comes — will merely be a legalization of something that has been going on for a long time."

"That's enough, Morgan," Ross said.

Morgan laughed. "One more lesson, and I'm through. In a way it's the most important of all. Women, my dear Ross, simply do not think like men. They have a fine, instinctive contempt for logic. A woman — any woman — can watch some poor, bedraggled daughter of joy being ridden out of town on a rail with complete vindictive satisfaction, and commit adultery the next night with the same complete satisfaction and absolute self-justification because her husband has committed the most heinous of all crimes — that is, he has bored her to tears."

"Morgan," Ross said, "you are mad!"

"I'm not. I'm very sane really. That's what makes me seem mad. The thing that you men forget, especially such men as your brother, is that no woman has the slightest interest in the act of love itself. That may seem contradictory, but it's so — and it explains a lot of things. At any wedding, watch the groom. He's suffering the tortures of the damned, trying to conceal his impatience. All he can think about is how it'll be when he finally gets his little Belle alone. But the bride? Ha! She's thinking about how lovely her wedding gown looks, and how nice the flowers are, and savoring the look of envy upon the faces of her unmarried friends. But don't mistake me, Ross — she may not find physical love repugnant — though often she may, depending upon the boorishness of her mate. She may enjoy it hugely. The point is that it is, with the woman, always something that just happens as the result of something else, something else she's much more interested in. . . ."

"And what's that?" Ross demanded.

"There's no word for it, though you might call it romance. The scene, the moonlight, the music, the tender flattery, the little attentions, which to a man are the preliminaries, necessary but irksome, to be dispensed with whenever possible, to the main show. But to a woman they are the main event. What happens afterwards occurs because she may have been drawn in emotionally to the extent that she also wants completion, but much more often simply because she likes him and is grateful to him for making her feel wanted and needed and important, and therefore complies."

Ross stared at her. Much of this, he had to admit, made sense. It fitted in with so many things that he himself had observed.

"That's why," Morgan said, a little mocking smile lurking about the corners of her mouth, "no woman in her heart of hearts gives a fig about feminine fidelity, or chastity or any of the other nonsensical ideas you men dreamed up to protect your jealous interests. She knows what she does with her body isn't important, so long as she's smart enough to avoid the consequences. And it certainly doesn't help her mental reservations about the role you've called upon her to play when she observes that all of you without notable exception feel quite free to do anything you damned well please, while holding your women in bondage. I've heard the planters' ladies talk. Two brandies and they talk quite freely. You know what they say, Ross? And with real regret, too?"

"No, what?" Ross said.

"That the only free things in the South are a colored woman — and a white man."

"Morgan, please!"

"I've finished," Morgan said, and poured herself another brandy. "Now what about Tom?"

"He's in love with you, Morgan."

"I know that. It's funny."

"No, not funny — pathetic. You know Jennie Dalton?"

"Yes. The little washed out one with the big blue eyes. The one who hates me."

"And with good reason. She and Tom have

been engaged for years."

"So?"

"Turn him loose, Morgan," Ross begged. "Send him packing. Jennie's father is dying. He may not last out the month. She'll be all alone then, and she'll need Tom. Tom needs her. They're so right for each other. . . ."

Morgan measured him with her black eyes.

"What concern is that of mine?" she said.

"It's only elementary decency," Ross said angrily. "Would you wreck two lives because of a whim?"

"Yes," Morgan said. "Why not?"

"You are a devil!" Ross spat.

Morgan shrugged.

"I've told you that," she said. "Don't be tiresome, Ross. Tom amuses me. When he ceases to amuse me, I'll send him packing — but not before. I'm surprised at how little you know me — or else you wouldn't have come here with your silly, sentimental arguments about Jennie's happiness, or her needs. I don't give a fig whether she's happy or not, or whether she's destitute. All that concerns me is my happiness, my needs. I need to be amused. And as long as big Tom is sufficiently diverting, Jennie can go hang. Another bourbon, darling?"

"Damn!" Ross said. He sat there looking at

her, holding the glass in his hand. Then he leaned forward.

"What about Lance, Morgan?" he said. "He's nobody's fool. You can't keep him in the dark forever. And, when he finds out, he'll kill Tom."

"So?" Morgan murmured, and took up the decanter again.

"You don't care!" Ross raged. "That would amuse you, too, wouldn't it? That would be the greatest thrill of all, wouldn't it? To have a man shot down in his blood because of you! That would really put a delicious tingle in your little, pink guts!"

"How well you put it!" Morgan laughed. "As a matter of fact, it would."

Ross looked at her, his face very white and still.

"You said a lot about the different kinds of women," he said slowly. "What kind are you, Morgan? I really want to know."

"The different kind. The one the rules weren't made for. The one who always holds the whip hand."

"Not always," Ross said. "Your day will come."

"I doubt it. Not as long as men are men. The mistake that most women make is that they grow fond of the creatures. I don't; therefore I always win."

She looked at him, smiling peacefully.

"Remember what I said about women getting dragged into the game? About their getting emotionally involved to the point that they imagine that what the man wants is also what they want? I don't Ross — not ever. I have a nice body; but then many women have nice bodies. What they never realize is what a wonderful weapon it is! Oh, I go along — I kiss them, and allow them to caress me, and caress them back until they're senseless with desire. Then — no more. You should see their fine male egos disintegrate, Ross; you should see them cry, and grovel and beg. . . ."

"Suppose," Ross said, "one of them used force?"

"I'd kill him. And not a jury in the South would convict a woman on the charge of defending her honor. The funny part about it is they can always tell I'm capable of killing. They take one look at my eyes — and draw back."

Ross stood up.

"I'm wasting time," he said. "But I'd better tell you one thing, Morgan. You get Tom killed, and I'll kill you. You're a menace. I'd be doing society a favor. I don't care what the consequences would be. Knowing that I'd be hanged, I'd do it. So now you know."

"I don't know," Morgan said easily, and got up. "Because you wouldn't kill me, Ross. You couldn't."

Ross stared at her.

"Why not?" he finally said.

"Because you're really very gentle. You have one of the kindest hearts in the world. When it were put to the test, you couldn't do it. I know that."

"Don't provoke me, Morgan. Don't push me too far."

Morgan smiled at him, and the old, mocking light was back in her eyes.

"There's another reason why you couldn't do it, darling," she said.

"What's that?" Ross demanded.

"Because," Morgan said softly, "because you're a man."

She started toward him then, walking very slowly, smiling up at him. When she was close, she put up her arms, letting her hands rest lightly upon his shoulders.

Ross moved quickly, his own hands coming up, seizing her wrists, forcing them down and out away from him. Then he stood back.

"No," he said. "After the lecture, the demonstration is unnecessary."

Morgan threw back her head and laughed. Then she made a half turn away from him.

Ross turned too, thinking, it's finished, there's nothing more I can do here damn her to hell and back again for a lovely witch and me for an utter fool because on top of it all I want her. . . . But Morgan's face blurred under his eyes as she whirled on the heel of one slipper, and hurled herself against him, her mouth meeting his, and her long nails piercing the flesh on the back of his neck so that the blood welled up around each polished semicircle, and her body moving up into his, slow-writhing, so close that he felt scalded through his clothing, and the rage inside of him black and bottomless, and the little feathery wave of terror there too, now inside the rage, feeling himself lost, hating that feeling until finally the hating was strong enough so that he tore himself free of her and slapped her hard across the mouth.

Morgan went down in a crumpled heap in a corner. Then she pulled herself up on one elbow and lay there looking at him, the red marks of his fingers clear upon her face, her mouth bruised, and a slow, dark trickle beginning to pencil a ragged line downward from one of its corners.

Ross looked at her, seeing her face framed in the wild tangle of her hair, her eyes searching his, her body slim, soft-curving, perfect beneath the blue robe, and one of her long legs curled under her, and the other thrust out white and blinding against the dark stuff of the rug, the whole of her having so absolutely the look of complete felinity, of the mating tigress waiting for the second, loved yet hated, assault, that he brought his closed fists up and thrust them over his eyes.

"Ross," she whispered, her voice low, harsh, trembling. "Ross. . . ."

But terror mounted up in him and beat about his head like hidden wings. He whirled then and fled from the room; but, before he reached the doorway, he heard her laughing. He stopped still, jerked to a halt by the invisible cords of that sound. But the terror was in him, the mortal fear, and he could hear Jennie's voice once more in his ears: "That kind of woman destroys men. Oh — not literally. She leaves them alive after a fashion. But they aren't men any more. They're — things without souls. . . ." He started off again, and all the way out into the open, the sound of that laughter followed him.

He had, as he flung himself into the saddle, the curious certainty that he would never be free of it.

Chapter 8

Ross Pary sat at the table in his dining room. He had a glass of bourbon in his hand, but he had scarcely tasted it. Across the room in the gilt-framed mirror he could see the reflection of his face. It looked haunted and old.

He lifted the glass of whiskey and tasted it, then put it down with a grimace. Drunkenness wouldn't help. Nothing would help. He got up from where he sat and walked to the window. Outside it was raining. The street was empty except for a lone cart drawn by two desolate mules, putting their hoofs down tiredly into the sticky black mud, the rain dripping from the tips of their drooping ears. The Negro who drove them sat hunched over too, his broad-brimmed straw hat sodden and flopping down so that it hid his face. And the mud swallowed up the sound of their passing.

God, Ross thought, God — if Conchita were only here. . . .

It was no day on which to be alone. In the grate the fire had burned down to a few embers, but he made no move to replenish it. If Conchita were here, they could sit before the fire — the two of them, and read the warm, coming years in the flickering light. But without her, the fire would be a mockery. Ross was afraid of what he might see in it.

He rubbed his hands together and stared at the piano. But that was no good either. He had tried playing it already, and all that had come out was Morgan's music. Damn Morgan anyhow! Why was she like that? Vengefulness, Lance had suggested, for the cruelties of a father, translated into a hatred for all men. But that was much too simple, too pat. And, Ross reflected, it didn't really explain Morgan. Morgan was anything but simple. Morgan was intricate, many-surfaced, endlessly complicated. It didn't even explain her to say that she was mad. The idea, applied to Morgan, was meaningless.

If making her own rules and living by them was madness, then Morgan was mad. But who did not make his own rules? That most people made them in conformity with what they thought was expected of them might mean that most people were sane, or it might mean that most men are cowards. And, considering the regularity with which people broke the rules, self-made or otherwise, when given an opportunity, Ross was inclined toward the latter view.

Morgan was beautiful. Morgan was cruel. Day is day and night is night. Children are cruel. Savages are cruel. Nature itself is absolutely pitiless. Remember the hurricane of 1840? Half Natchez had been smashed. The shacks of squatters. The mansions of the great. Babies had died — and old men.

Maybe, Ross thought, kindness is itself a sickness — part of the effeteness of civilization. Certainly people afflicted with it, like me, don't stand much of a chance when they're confronted with these dawn-age ones, these absolutely certain ones, people like Morgan who are very clear and direct and terrible. While I'm thinking about the why's, people like Morgan act. They don't have to ask themselves whether it's good or bad, only "Do I want to?" And when the answer is "yes" they strike very hard and all at once and their victim dies or lives on bleeding out his life from wounds that are incurable because they don't show. . . .

He moved over to the table and took out a

cigar. He put it in the corner of his mouth and lit it and the smoke climbed up and veiled his head.

The trouble is I want her. It's wrong to want Morgan because she's somebody else's and because wanting her is a thing that a man can die of. It's a bad thing because I don't love her I hate her really she's the most completely evil thing I've ever encountered and no good could ever come of wanting her and all these things don't mean a thing because knowing them I want her still. I love Conchita — not Morgan. I shall marry Conchita and settle down to a life of peace and happiness yet at the same time I'll go on wanting Morgan until one of the two of us is dead.

God, he groaned, God, kind merciful God!

There was at the very bottom of all this an idea. It was a very small idea, almost hidden, but Ross didn't want to bring it out where he could examine it. I'm mad, he kept telling himself, stark, raving crazy!

But he was not, and he knew it. He was simply afraid. Bring out that idea, and he was damned. Because the idea that he was trying to keep buried in the back part of his brain was different from all the other ideas he had had in his life. The difference was that it could not exist as an abstraction. Once considered, it had to be acted upon. And the consequences of acting upon it were unimaginable.

He went back to the table and picked up the glass of bourbon. Then he took the cigar out of his mouth and drank the bourbon down all at once without pausing for breath and afterwards he felt better. Whiskey, he thought, has its uses. He poured himself another, but before he could drink it, Wallace came in with his hat and gloves and riding crop.

Ross stared at them.

"Man from the Brittany place brung these," Wallace said. "Brung this note, too."

Ross took the envelope from Wallace and held it in his hand looking at it. Then he picked up a paper knife from his desk and slit it open. The paper was tinted and richly perfumed. He remembered that scent. He had smelled it many times in Morgan's hair.

"Darling," he read. "It was most injudicious of you to leave these things. If Cato had given them to my husband, there might have been trouble. I'm sorry I laughed. But it was myself I was laughing at – not at you. Come to me, my darling. For you know – you know!" The note was not signed.

Ross sank very slowly into a chair, his face graying.

"Going to send an answer, Marse Ross?" Wallace asked.

"No," Ross said hoarsely. "No, Wallace — no answer."

Come to me, my darling. For you know — you know! The idea was out now. It had been clothed in certainty. It was a terrible idea, and like most terrible ideas, it was very simple: if he, Ross Pary, wanted Morgan Brittany, he could have her. He, alone, of all the men that panted after her.

If Ross had had one shred of real vanity he could have doubted it, even now. But his humility was very real. Even those things in him which looked like pride were not: his fine clothing, and fine horse, and the lovely house he was building. In another man those would have meant, look at me! Behold how fine I am. But in Ross they had always been props to support his failing assurance. They were not meant for other eyes. Rather, he could look at them and tell himself, "I can do it, too. I can dress well and own land and live in a fine house. I also belong. . . ." A man of pride, of vanity, more often than not wanted to lead men, wanted to take his world between his two hands and change it — or break it. Ross did not. He merely wanted to join the men he considered his superiors; he wanted to become one of the leisurely, the graceful, the sure. He didn't want to change anything, break anything. All he wanted was quietly and completely to belong.

Knowing himself, he could not attribute the idea that Morgan was his to any excess of natural vanity. He could not look in the mirror and say, "Of course, why not? Any woman would!" Because any woman wouldn't. He knew that. Conchita would, because she loved him. And Morgan would — why?

Because she loved him? Poppycock. Morgan could watch him die and her only interest would be in the prolongation of his sufferings. Then why on earth? Why? Why? Why?

He sat down at the piano and began to play her music, deliberately this time, as though searching for something. The music hammered through the rooms, tearing at his senses. Then in the middle of a chord, he stopped. He knew.

Morgan lived for domination. For mastery. And he had rejected her. He had struck her down in anger. He — the gentle one, the pale slender one, who looked like the artist he was, like the musician, like the poet. Lance Brittany was gentle with his wife. Fearing an inherited weakness, he was careful. Tom Pary and Henry Montcliffe and the other men in her life, fearing her, without knowing that they feared her, quaking before that terrible directness, that blinding clarity of hers, had begged her, had implored her favors.

But you didn't beg a woman like Morgan. You matched force with force — cruelty with pain. What Morgan could master, she despised. What she couldn't — she wanted. It was as simple as that.

He got up from the piano and called Wallace.

"Saddle Nancy," he said; "I'm going out."

Then he dressed himself with even more than his usual care. Over his figured blue foulard suit, with its white waistcoat with pale pink embossings, he put on a MacFarlan coat, really a kind of cape, which, instead of having sleeves, had two smaller capes attached to the shoulders hiding the sleeves of the sack coat beneath when a man was in repose. It had a certain flair to it, an élan. It became Ross. Its dark blue tones increased the pallor of his thin face, added new somberness to his brooding eyes. A woman seeing him in it, might dream up histories for him, tales of hidden loss, and manfully borne sorrow. But Ross was not thinking about that. He was remembering Morgan lying prone in the corner where he had struck her down, her bruised mouth like a great, dark flower crushed against her face, and the whiteness of her body like a cry. . . .

Wallace put his head in the door to tell him that the mare was ready.

"Wait," Ross called out to him, "saddle that nag of yours, too. You're going with me."

"Me, Marse Ross?" Wallace said.

"Yes. You have to bring Nancy home again, from the steamboat landing. I'm going to New Orleans for a few days."

"Yessir," Wallace said. "Right away, sir."

He had done right, Ross knew. This was wise. But, looking back over the muddy white wake that spread out behind the boat toward Natchez, he wondered how it might have been.

He got off the steamboat at the foot of Toulouse Street, and hailing a cabriolet, directed the driver to take him to the Saint Louis Hotel. As the cab stopped before the great, copper-plated dome, Ross, despite all his worries and his anxiety to see Conchita at once, had a real feeling of pleasure. This was another of the things he had always wanted to do. For the Saint Louis was the home of the great.

He looked at the building with professional interest, for it was the work of two of the greatest Creole architects, the de Pouillys. The dome alone weighed one hundred tons, and was constructed of earthen pots like a medieval European church. As he crossed the rotunda, a vast circle some sixty-six feet in diameter, and paved with varicolored marble in a geometric pattern, a Negro rushed forward and took his bag. Ross followed him to the desk, pausing momentarily to gaze at the raised dais behind its railing from which slaves were auctioned, and the lovely murals on the wall from the hand of Dominique Canova.

The clerk greeted him with marked respect, for which, Ross knew, he had his clothes to thank. He had also, although he did not know that, a certain air about him, born of his studies and his travels. Whatever it was, Ross found himself established in one of the hotel's finest rooms.

From his window, he could look down on the river and on both Saint Louis and Royale Streets. He loved New Orleans. It was France in America; it was cosmopolitan, cultured, old. . . .

When he came down again, he was dressed for the evening. The doorman engaged a cab for him at once, and he settled back against the cushions, after giving the driver the address on Dauphine Street where Conchita lived with her father. He wondered how she'd greet him. Her letters had been warm, even ardent. But what had been between them was a thing that had happened too quickly, and which might prove quite as fragile as many another newborn thing. . . .

The house where the Izquierdos lived had an air of genteel decay. There was a greengrocer's store on the ground floor, and beside it a fruitmonger's stall. But on the second floor, the warm, yellow light of the lamps flooded out between the latticed blinds, etching the lacy ironwork of the upper gallery against the darkness.

Ross got down, paid the driver, and knocked. After uncomfortable moments of waiting, a Negress opened the door.

"Yes?" she said; "who you wants to see, M'sieu?"

"Mademoiselle Izquierdo," Ross told her. "Is she at home?"

"Yessir, she at home, her. But she got company. Who I'm going to tell her want to see her, sir?"

"Pary," Ross said. "Ross Pary — she'll know."

"You wait right here, sir," the girl said. "I go git her directly."

Company, Ross mused. That's bad. This fellow, now — what's his name? — Méndez, that's it, José Méndez. Conchita said he was very handsome. Oh, damn it! It would be just my luck to . . .

But he never finished the thought, for the door burst open and Conchita flew out straight into his arms. Afterwards, long afterwards,

245

when it was possible to speak, Ross found he could not. He caught her by her shoulders, hard, and held her away from him so that he could look at her.

He could see the great tears brimming over her long lashes, and shook his head.

"Don't cry, Conchita *mía*," he said tenderly; "there is nothing to weep over. . . ."

"Nothing but happiness," she said. "Oh, Ross, *mi alma*, if you had not come soon I would have died!"

Then she kissed him again, clinging her mouth to his endlessly, achingly in the stillness until he was getting the feeling that life always had a way of being a little too much for him at the wrong times and in the wrong places when she broke away from him, laughing gaily, and took his arm.

"Come," she said. "My father is above, and José. It is better that you speak to them."

"José," Ross said in a disgruntled tone. "He calls upon you?"

"Yes. It is the wish of my father that I marry José. But it is not my wish. He is a good boy, very handsome and nice, but —"

"But what?" Ross said.

"He is not you."

"Thank God!" Ross said.

They came up the stairs into a dark hallway,

and Conchita turned to him, and put her arms up and drew his head down until the hammers started once more in his blood.

"No!" he whispered; "no more! How can I meet them with my face like fire?"

"It is so nice – the darkness," Conchita said. "Once before there was darkness. Do you remember, my Ross?"

"Can I forget to breathe?" Ross said. "It would be easier than forgetting – that."

"Come!" she laughed. "We must see them and then we must plan our escape. . . ."

At the doorway, she paused, and Ross could hear the voices.

"It's madness, I tell you," a voice he did not know was saying, "the people will never rise! They are too beaten down, too cowed. Why should they rise, Señor Izquierdo, when they know that a revolt can only mean a terrible death?"

"Liberty for one's children, José," Eduardo Izquierdo said, "is worth a terrible death."

"But this of the dying does not serve! It is the living and the winning that count. And we cannot win now. We have not the arms, the supplies, the –"

"We have the will. That is sufficient. And with men like my esteemed and honored friend Joaquín de Aguero to lead the people, all Cuba

247

will flame with revolt from one end to the other."

"But —" José began, and Conchita pushed open the door.

Eduardo Izquierdo turned in his chair, leaning forward on his cane.

"The Señor Pary," he said. "You have cost me much worry, young man."

"Good evening, sir," Ross murmured. "If I have caused you worry, I have much sorrow, Señor. Nothing was further from my intention."

At the sound of Ross's courtly Spanish, José Méndez stared. This one, he thought, is more than formidable. Usually these Americanos have not the brains to master another tongue. . . .

"Yet you have," Señor Iquierdo continued; "but first, may I present the Señor José Méndez, my partner in the newspaper *La Unión* and also my good friend."

"I have much pleasure to know you, Señor," Ross said; "your secure servitor, sir."

"Much pleasure!" José snapped.

"Sit down," Izquierdo said. "*Muñeca mia,* find the gentleman a chair."

Conchita pushed one forward, and Ross sank into it, while Conchita stood behind it leaning her folded arms on its back.

"This of the preoccupation," Ross began; "of what consists it, sir?"

"Of my little *muñecita's* interest in you. However honorable your intentions, the differences in background and training are insurmountable. . . ."

"Hardly that, Señor Izquierdo," Ross said. "I received a considerable part of my education in Spain. I know and sympathize with your customs. As for my intentions, they are very simple: With your permission, Señor, and with hers, I mean to make Conchita my wife."

He could see young Méndez bristle, but Izquierdo's eyes held no surprise, only sadness.

"My daughter," he said with grave dignity, "has always been given every freedom. I do not believe in slavery — not even in enslaving my children. But I must ask that both of you wait for a while. Possibly one or both of you may change. . . ."

"Never," Ross said.

"Ah, youth," the old man sighed. "Still, a year will not be insupportable. Thereafter, we will see. . . ."

"I bow to your decision, Señor," Ross said.

"Father," Conchita said suddenly, "have I your permission to accompany Señor Pary to the theatre? He has come a long way and . . ."

"Without a *deuña*?" José snapped; "Conchita,

249

what's gotten into you?"

"She has often accompanied you to the theatre without a *deuña*," Eduardo Izquierdo pointed out. "And the Señor Pary is Caballero of much wisdom and taste. I have heard him speak on several matters in the house of the Señores Brittany. Of course, my dear; but do not stay out late."

"Thank you, Father," Conchita said, and kissed him. Then she made a face at José, and skipped from the room, pausing long enough in the doorway to say to Ross: "Be tranquil, my soul, I shall not be long. . . ."

José stared at Ross.

"What is your profession, Señor?" he demanded.

"I am a planter, and an architect," Ross told him calmly.

"Then you are, doubtless, the owner of slaves?"

"I am," Ross said.

"We are firmly opposed to slavery," José said. "In a free Cuba, there will be no slaves."

"That," Ross said, "is noble of you, Señor Méndez."

"You surprise me," José sneered; "I expected you to defend slavery with much heat."

"Slavery," Ross said, "is a moral wrong. At my death, or, if possible, before it, all my people shall be freed."

"Good!" Eduardo Izquierdo said.

"Why good?" José demanded. "At his death he will free them, after he has spent a lifetime growing fat from their labors. Then the sacrifice is slight."

Ross looked at him thinking: I must not lose my temper. He can win only if I let myself get angry and act badly and what's to be gained is worth a little forbearance.

"You are right, Señor Méndez," he said easily; "to free them at my death would scarcely be a true demonstration of my sentiments. But you forget my words. I said, *or before, if possible. . . .*"

"Why should it not be possible?" José said. "A stroke of the pen, and it is done. It seems to me a thing of great facility, even of simplicity."

"It's not, though," Ross said. "In the State of Mississippi there is a law which prohibits their manumission within the borders of the State. I should have to fight the matter through the courts which would take years, and cost a fortune. Or, I should have to sell them out of the State to a trusted friend, who would follow my instructions to free them. Even though I provided such a one with purchase money, where could I find such a man? What guarantee would I have that the temptation of having his hands upon a group of trained Negroes worth a fortune, would not prove too much for him? It is not simple, Señor Méndez. Nothing in life ever really is. . . ."

"True," Izquierdo sighed. "It is not simple. I freed my own blacks and I know. There would be, additionally, the repercussions from your slaveholding neighbors, who might be moved even to reprisals."

"I have thought of that, but I do not preoccupy myself with it," Ross said. "There are other difficulties. The blacks on my place were bought jointly by me, my brother, and the Señor Dalton, the father of my brother's affianced. I do not rightly know which of them I own, and which are the property of my partners. Besides, Caballeros, you have seen the lot of the freed blacks here in the South. I am fond of my people. I wish to prevent their having such a fate."

"How could you prevent it?" José asked. He was, Ross could see by his tone, considerably mollified.

"By spending years educating my people before freeing them. That, likewise, is against the law in my State; but I could do it. But to send them out unlettered and helpless would be scarcely kind. . . ."

"And my Ross is the soul of kindness," Conchita said, as she came through the door. "Come on, my own, or we shall be late."

She brushed her father's cheek lightly with her lips, and put out her hand to José.

"Conchita —" José whispered, and Ross could hear the pain in his voice.

Poor devil, he thought, it isn't an easy thing, is it?

"Be tranquil," Conchita murmured; "You, *amigo mío*, are escaping a hard fate. It is my Ross who is to be pitied — not you."

Then Ross took her arm and they went very fast through the dark hall and down the stairs. They walked up Dauphine to Conti, and Ross signaled a cabriolet with his cane. The driver drew his ancient nag to a stop. They got in, and the driver opened his little trap door and said:

"Where to, sir?"

Ross looked at Conchita.

"This theatre to which I am taking you," he said; "where is it, my Conchita?"

Conchita stared at him, then, suddenly she started to laugh.

"Ross, Ross!" she said in Spanish. "You are, like all men, of a formidable stupidity! I had to tell my father something. . . ."

Ross frowned.

"Then where shall I take you?" he said. "We can't ride around all night."

Conchita leaned against him and buried her face in his cape.

"I must say it!" she whispered; "I − not you! Oh, Ross − must you always shame me so?"

"But, Conchita . . ."

"Take me," she said fiercely, "to wherever you are staying, to wherever there is darkness and an absence of people! . . . Oh, Ross!"

"Conchita," Ross murmured, "I am staying at the Saint Louis Hotel, which is a hotel that is of great size and well known. To enter it with you would not only arm a scandal, but would be simply impossible. . . ."

Conchita straightened up and looked at him.

"Then," she said, "take me somewhere else."

Good God, Ross thought, what an imbecile I am!

"*Muñecita mía,* little doll," he told her, "I know but little of New Orleans, and absolutely nowhere I could take you where there is darkness and an emptiness of people. Do you −?"

Conchita's green eyes widened in the darkness.

"No," she said tartly, "but now I wish terribly that I did. For two reasons: first because now that I have become both wicked and shameless, I want to be alone with you; and secondly it would divert me much to explain to you how I came to know such a thing!"

"I'll be damned!" Ross said helplessly.

"Tell him to drive down to Jackson Square," Conchita said. "Perhaps I shall think of something. . . ."

The ancient nag moved off, slow-clopping in the darkness. The ancient streets of the Vieux Carré inched backward behind them, and only the dimmest light came from between the shutters of the window.

Ross put out his arm and drew Conchita to him. He kissed her a long time but without force. But, when he released her, she put up both her hands and cradled his face between them.

"I love you, my Ross. So very much I love thee. Enormously, terribly – with all my heart. There are times when you are not here that I think I will die of wanting you. I have not very much the patience. I think about how it will be when we are together finally in our own little house with the children – Ross! You wish children, do you not? You have never said. . . ."

"At least a dozen," Ross smiled, "all of them like you."

"And I, equally; but they must be like you with fair hair and blue eyes and none of my obscurity of coloring. Gentle like you, patient. Oh, *corazón mío*, heart of my heart, I wish we could commence them now!"

"That would be a grave thing," Ross said. He peered at her. "Conchita," he whispered, "I have much fear of that."

"Be tranquil. I had for a nurse a Negress of the brush, who was very wise. She taught me many things. That danger does not exist. . . ."

"Thank God!" Ross said fervently.

"I wish it did!" Conchita said fiercely. "It would solve so many things. My father would have to consent then and —"

"Conchita!"

"Sorry. I am one crazy little bird, no?"

"Yes. But we must be careful."

"Jackson Square," the driver said.

Ross looked at Conchita.

"Pay him and let's get out," Conchita said, "at least I can walk with you in the darkness."

They got down from the cab and started to walk around the square. But in November in New Orleans the nights are damp with the beginning of the winter's chill, and after a time, it started to rain.

"Oh, damn!" Ross said.

"Equally," Conchita said. "I have thought and thought and nothing exists within this head of mine. So now I have to walk here in the darkness and the wet, when I want to be safe and warm somewhere in your arms. . . ."

"I am a fool!" Ross said bitterly.

"No — just good. Such things do not come easily to the good. But do not preoccupy yourself, *mi alma*. Stop there in the shadow of the Cabildo, or in the Alley of the Pirates and kiss me very much. That will warm our blood."

She was, Ross discovered to his sorrow, quite right. They stood in each other's arms in the doorway of the old building that the Spaniards had erected in the days when Louisiana was a province of Spain. Conchita lay heavily against him, her face buried in the hollow of his throat, crying so hard she could not speak.

"Little one," Ross whispered, "my tender little one, do not weep. . . ."

"I cannot help it," she sobbed; "I thought that I would have so much joy of your coming, and it has become now a thing of sorrows, a kind of torture, because having you I cannot have you, and loving you we cannot love. . . ." She looked up at him suddenly.

"You might ask one of the drivers of the little cabs," she whispered, "whether there is not a place to which we could go. . . ."

"No!" Ross said; "no, Conchita — no!"

"Why not?" she said.

"Because — Oh I can't explain it really, I have not the words. But, my own, it cannot be like that. We cannot go to a place of shame because what lies between us is not shameful. What happened between us happened without plan, without scheming and hiding and being afraid. It is a thing very beautiful and very fine that neither of us can cheapen. Someday again without thinking, without planning, it will happen. And then finally there will be the church and the priest and the sanctity of God upon it. . . . I am sorry; I have said it badly. . . ."

"No — well. And you have much right, my Ross. Now you must take me home again, and you must go back to Natchez. Because with you here, near me, the refraining will be a thing insupportable." She looked up at him tenderly. "I will come to you," she said. "I do not know when or how, but I will come. And then we shall have such joy of each other that the Angels shall envy us! Come now — let us go. . . ."

That next night, as the steamboat slid into the landing at Natchez, Ross Pary felt the sickness rise in him. It was going to be a good thing, a fine thing, he thought, and I ruined it. By not thinking, by not realizing how hard it would be. . . . He walked out toward the foredeck, and stared at the low, dim light of Natchez Under the Hill, remembering the last time he had stood like that looking upon the world he meant to conquer. Well, he had conquered it now; he had climbed the Hill, and what good was it?

He had his house, Moonrise, nearly completed, his lands, and his slaves. And he was ashamed now of gaining his bread from the sweat of other men's brows, and just beyond Moonrise lay Finiterre, Land's End, the place of his desolation. Before, standing here, there had also been — Morgan. Over there in that darkness, among those lights slow-sliding toward him, would there also be Morgan? He could feel the terror moving in him at the thought.

If there had been Conchita last night in New Orleans, he would have been armed; Conchita would have brought him peace, stilled the tumult in his blood. It would have been a new beginning, a new dedication, against which all the hosts of hell might have hurled themselves in vain. But now he felt weak, and lost and unsure with the small voices of fear wailing within his heart.

I could, he realized with horrified certainty, betray Lance, my friend, and Conchita, my love — even betray myself and that is the worst of it. Because of Morgan I could silence my dignity, make sport of honor, sell myself into a kind of slavery whose degradation has no limits, and whose term has no end. . . .

He straightened up, as though by the act of stiffening his body, he could stiffen his will. I may not escape her, he thought; but it won't be because I haven't tried. . . .

As he came down the gangplank to the wharf, he saw the woman waiting below. He stopped dead, his heart beating a drumroll in his throat. Oh, God, no! he thought; not now, not already, I need time — time —

But there was no escaping it, so he came on down the gangplank and straight toward the woman who waited. And when he was close, joy awoke, for the woman waiting there was Jennie Dalton.

"Jen!" he said gaily, "what on earth are you doing —" But then he saw her face. The joy drained out of him all at once, and coming up to her he took her hand. She was not crying. She hadn't been. And she should have. It would have been better had she cried.

"Jen," Ross whispered, "Jen . . ."

"Father," she said clearly. "Ten o'clock this morning, Ross. I tried to find Tom, but I couldn't. I — I think *she* has him. No matter, you're here. I always could depend upon you. Wallace told me you were in New Orleans. I — I met all the boats. Thank God you came. . . ."

"I — I'm sorry, Jen," Ross said gently.

"I know. Father always doted on you. He always said I was a fool to choose Tom when you are so much the better man. He was right. I was a fool. I am still. . . ."

"Please, Jen . . ."

"I'm alone now. I have no way to turn. I shall never live at Moonrise because Tom will never be free of her."

"Come and live there anyway," Ross began, but Jennie stopped him.

"No, Ross. That's impossible. A single woman cannot live in the house of a single man. Not in Natchez, Mississippi; not in this year of Our Lord, 1850. And I can't marry you for two good reasons: You no longer love me, because of this Cuban girl. She's lovely, Ross, and really very nice. I think you'll be very happy. And the second reason is still the same: much as I admire you, I couldn't come to you still loving Tom. And I love him still — God help me, I do!"

"He loves you, too," Ross said urgently. "Believe me, Jennie, I know. Morgan has bewitched him, now — but he'll come out of it, and then. . . ."

But Jennie shook her head.

"No, Ross," she said, "he won't — not ever. Come on now, I need you."

The arrangements were soon made, and Peter Dalton lay in the little cemetery under the Hill where all his life he had lived well and bravely. Throughout the funeral Tom Pary sat with his red face somber and still, listening to Jennie's gentle weeping. Then, after it was done, he mounted his horse and rode away.

The weeks that followed were for Ross one of the bad times. He worked endlessly, pushing Moonrise toward completion. By the first of December, he knew he had won. He would live in his house by Christmas. But the victory was a hollow one. He'd live there with little Annis, and his brother Tom, and no woman of his choosing would sit at the foot of the table. A year would soon pass, but there remained the question of the slaves because Conchita would never consent to be mistress of a slaveholding establishment.

And there remained also — Morgan. Try as he would, Ross could not avoid seeing her occasionally. He could feel her great black eyes upon him, burning into his calmness, his pretenses. What he could do, he did: he never saw her alone, and gave Wallace strict orders that she was never to be admitted to his rooms without her husband. But the strain of it told upon his nerves.

He seldom played the piano any more,

because sooner or later, Morgan's music would rise up in him, demanding to be played. He rode the dark roads at midnight, unable to find sleep. And he drank much more heavily than had been his custom, and grew thinner and paler until his somber, dark blue eyes seemed too big for his face.

He sat out at Finiterre one evening upon Nancy, watching Lance Brittany jump his new hunter over the high barred gate. The horse was a magnificent dappled gray stallion, and he soared over the gate as effortlessly as though he had wings. No other horse in the county, perhaps even in the State, Ross knew, could make that jump. And Lance rode him like a centaur, the man and beast almost one flesh.

Lance came riding up to him, his dark face flushed with happiness, so that he looked almost boyish despite the white wings at his temples, and the fine threads of white that showed in his dark hair.

"Some nag, eh Ross?" he grinned.

"Yes," Ross said; "that animal is absolutely all horse. What do you call him, Lance?"

"Prince. I'm going to try to get a mare of the strain. That way I'll always have the best horses in the State. You're staying for dinner, aren't you, boy?"

"Well —" Ross began.

"Stay," Lance said. "You've been shunning us here of late. And Finiterre ought to be your second home. . . ."

"All right," Ross said. "Lance, how high is that gate?"

"Don't rightly know. It has twelve bars. I've been thinking of adding another, but it might be dangerous. You saw Prince jump. Tell me, how far does he clear the top?"

"By inches. Another bar and his left foreleg would catch, sure. . . ."

"What," Morgan asked, "would happen then?"

Lance turned to her, frowning.

"I thought you were up at the house," he said.

"I was. I just came out. What would happen, Lance, if his foreleg hooked the top bar?"

"He'd take a header," Lance said grimly. "Break both his forelegs and neck. And I'd be killed."

"Couldn't you jump free?" Morgan whispered.

"No," Lance said flatly; "I'd be killed."

"Then don't add another bar, darling," Morgan said sweetly. "Come in, dinner is almost ready."

She was grave and thoughtful throughout that meal. Ross didn't like that. She was attentive and courteous — even kind. Not once during that dinner did she loose the barbed shafts of her wit. Ross could see Lance relaxing under the influence of the good wines and the food and Morgan's kindness. But he sat very stiffly in his chair, alert and watchful.

This was a Morgan he had never seen before. And Morgan playing the role of a good wife and gracious hostess was something. Everything she does, Ross thought, she heightens — raises it out of the commonplace. . . . And once more he was reminded of how impossible it was to actually comprehend Morgan. More than any other woman he had ever met, she was endlessly complicated. Yet, he had had at times the feeling that Morgan was quite simple and direct. Looking at her, he tried to resolve the contradiction. Is it, he mused, because in her all the dreadful complexities of our civilization exist, but are controlled by her will so that they express themselves in a kind of terrible simplicity?

"You look so puzzled, Ross," Morgan said. "What's the matter?"

"You," Ross said boldly; "I don't understand you, Morgan."

"Don't try, boy," Lance said. "Things less difficult than that have driven men mad."

"If I were in your shoes, Lance," Ross said

drily, "I probably would be mad by now."

"Who says I'm sane?" Lance quipped.

"The difference is, Ross, dear," Morgan said calmly, "that Lance trusts me. He knows he can. You don't, do you?"

"No," Ross said; "I don't."

Morgan turned to Lance with a smile.

"Ross thinks I'm capable of infinite wickedness," she said. "He's been listening to gossip. Darling," she said to Ross, "why don't you just tell Lance the things you've heard. Wouldn't that relieve your mind?"

Lance glared at her.

"That's enough, Morgan," he said. "For the record, I'd better tell you that I've talked with Ross numerous times, and he has yet to utter an unkind remark about you. I think that sometimes he's even lied in your behalf."

"How sweet!" Morgan laughed.

"The point is, my dear," Lance said heavily, "that there are two dozen people who would delight in giving me a detailed account of your activities on the many occasions that I am away from home. I've had to shut some of them up before they could get started. At fifty, a man wants peace. I don't want to be put in a position where I'd have to kill someone. . . ."

"That," Morgan mocked, "is kind of you, dear."

Lance ignored the interruption.

"In a way, I do trust you," he said. "I think you're daring and reckless and a fool. I don't think you're either wicked or faithless. But don't ever let me find out that I'm wrong. If I ever should have to change my opinion — God help you." He turned back to Ross. "Sorry," he said; "this was no time for such talk. Reckon the conversation got a little out of hand. . . ."

"It's all right, Lance," Ross said.

He put out his hand to take up his demitasse, but he did not drink it, for he saw Cato coming through the door, his eyes wide with excitement.

Lance looked at him.

"What's the matter, Cato?" he growled. "Something wrong?"

"Yassuh!" Cato said. "Marse Ross, your man Simon's outside. He say you come right now! Say there's trouble down at Miss Jennie's!"

"Trouble?" Ross said. "What kind of trouble, Cato?"

"I dunno, suh. You have to ask Simon that. . . ."

Ross stood up, nodding to Morgan.

"You'll excuse me?" he said politely.

"I'll come with you, if you don't mind," Lance said. "Maybe you'll need help."

"Do," Ross said. "I might at that."

They found Simon in the hall, shivering with fright.

"What ails you, Simon?" Ross demanded. "What's happened to Miss Jennie?"

"Nothing yet, boss — I hope," Simon quavered. "Ever since old Marse Dalton died them fellows down there been picking at her. Told her I was going to tell you or Marse Tom, but she wouldn't let me. Said Marse Tom didn't care, and she didn't want to bother you. . . ."

"Get to the point, man!" Ross snapped.

"They — they drunk, Marse Ross! Six of 'em! They been hanging around the house all evening — just waiting for dark. And Miss Jennie there all by herself. . . . Thought I better come tell you. Them fellows might . . ."

"Thanks, Simon," Ross said quietly. "Cato, get me my things. And give Simon a drink. I think he needs it."

"Get my things too, Cato," Lance said.

"Lance," Ross said, "there's no need. . . ."

"Six of those river rats against you alone? Don't be a fool, Ross. Are you armed?"

"Yes," Ross told him, "I have a gun."

"Good! Come into the study a minute, won't you?"

Ross followed him into the study. Lance caught hold of a broad door set into the paneling and opened it. Behind it, on the wall, the rows of guns gleamed dully. Lance took down a frontier model Colt, almost as big as a small cannon, and stuffed it into his belt. Then from the center of the panel, he brought down something that looked like a thick coil of rope. Looking at it, Ross saw that it was a loaded muleskinner's whip. It was fourteen feet long.

Lance, Morgan had said, believed everything could be solved with a gun or a whip. This time, Ross thought, maybe he'll be right. In the hands of an expert, a muleskinner's whip was a terrible weapon. Of the two weapons, Ross would much rather have faced the gun.

"Now," Lance said grimly, "I'm ready."

Nancy was a fast horse, but compared to Lance's Prince, she might as well be standing still. Lance held the big stallion back, both to allow Ross to keep up with him, and to save the animal; because it was a long ride down to Natchez Under the Hill. To Ross the ride seemed to last forever.

But finally they were thundering down Silver Street. Just before they reached the house, they heard Jennie scream. Ross threw himself down from the mare, and hit the dirt running. He went through the smashed door, hanging crazily upon its hinges, with Lance on his heels. The rivermen did not hear him coming.

They were much too busy.

They had thrown Jennie across the bed, and four of them were holding her arms and legs, while the other two tore at her clothing.

I'm in time, Ross breathed, thank God, I'm in time. Then he lifted the pistol and shot the biggest of the rivermen in the belly. The man sat down at once with a surprised grunt, holding his belly with both hands and staring stupidly at blood that oozed out between his fingers. All the others made a break for the door with Lance Brittany just behind them, swinging the long lash the moment he was in the open and had space enough to use it. It sang and whined and bit, and Ross could heard the river rats' agonized howling.

But Ross did not follow them. He bent down and picked up a blanket and used it to cover Jennie's nakedness. She nestled in his arms crying:

"You came, didn't you, Ross? You always come when I need you. You — not Tom. . . ."

Ross didn't answer her. He was looking at the big man who sat in the corner holding his punctured abdomen, and staring at the never-ending flow of his blood. He sat there, like that, until he died.

I've killed a man, Ross thought. I — who never before carried a gun or wanted to hurt any living creature. He felt sick, the hot nausea rising in his throat.

"Come on," he said to Jennie, "let's get out of here."

They met Lance coming back, coiling the big whip about his shoulders. His dark, handsome face bore a grin of complete satisfaction.

"I took a square yard off each of their hides," he said. "You all right, Miss Jennie?"

"Yes," Jennie whispered, "thanks to you two. . . ."

"Don't mention it," Lance said. "It was a pleasure. Tell you what, Miss Jennie. You go get some clothes on, and then you come stay out at Finiterre for a while. Mrs. Brittany would be glad to have you, I'm sure. . . ." He stopped suddenly, halted by the horror in Jennie's eyes. "Why, what's the matter, Miss?" he asked kindly.

"No!" Jennie got out, her voice harsh, low, strained. "Never!"

Lance stared at her, then looked at Ross.

"Jennie is among those," Ross said quietly, "who — don't admire Morgan. . . ."

"I see," Lance murmured. "Big Tom, too — eh? So that was the reason for those non-existent sketches, eh, Ross? You were protecting your brother's hide."

"Let's not discuss it now, Lance," Ross said.

"Jennie, you'd better get dressed."

"I can't go back in there with — him," Jennie whispered.

"With whom?" Lance demanded.

"The man I shot," Ross said. "He — he's dead, Lance."

"Good!" Lance said grimly. "He had it coming. You wait here, Miss Jennie. Ross and I will drag him out."

They went back into the house, and Lance unceremoniously caught hold of the big man by one of his arms and pulled him over. He fell with a sickening looseness, his eyes wide open and staring.

"Grab his other arm, Ross," Lance said brusquely.

There had never been anything in all his life that Ross had wanted less to do than to touch that dead man. But Lance was staring at him.

"Don't be squeamish," he said. "You had guts enough to kill him — which he richly deserved — now have guts enough to drag him out. That girl will freeze out there."

Ross caught hold of the left arm and the two of them dragged him out of the room down the hall, and out back of the house.

"Reckon we'd better notify the authorities," Lance said.

Ross leaned weakly against the side of the house.

"What authorities?" he said. "The sheriff doesn't even come down here. You don't know Under the Hill, Lance."

"Won't there be trouble?" Lance asked.

"No. His friends will get drunk and forget him. And down here the law doesn't exist."

Lance looked at Ross pityingly.

"No wonder you wanted to leave," he said.

"I hated it!" Ross said.

"The thing for you to do," Lance said, "is to get this girl out of here — sever all connections with your past. Everybody else has forgotten it; it's time you did, too."

"Right," Ross said, almost inaudibly.

"What'll we do with him?" Lance said. "He can't stay here."

"Roll him over the bluff — let the river take him. . . ."

"All right," Lance said, "come on."

They dragged the dead man the few short yards to the river, and gave him a shove. He rolled down the incline with that curious look of bonelessness that only the dead have, and went into the water with a mighty splash. Ross stared down at him, sinking slowly beneath the surface, then he turned his head and was quietly sick upon the ground.

"You're a curious cuss," Lance observed; "as tender as a woman, yet you always do what you have to, don't you? Only in you it takes a kind of courage that, come to think of it, is mighty fine. You've got sense enough to be scared, but you would have ridden down here and taken those six hoodlums on alone. And you have no stomach for violence, yet you'd fight like seven cornered devils when there's no other choice. Damn my soul, Ross, I like you; I really do!"

"Thanks," Ross said.

They went back around the house to where Jennie waited, shivering and blue with the December cold.

"It's all right, Jen," Ross said. "You can go in, now."

Jennie moved hesitantly into the house.

Lance turned to Ross.

"What are you going to do with her? She's your brother's fiancée, I understand, so she can't stay out at Moonrise. People would talk. She won't come to Finiterre — and she can't stay here. Quite a problem, Ross."

"I'm going to give her my rooms," Ross said, "and move to that temporary house of Tom's. My sister, Annis, is out there now. I'll have her come in and stay with Jen. That'll fix it. . . ."

"Damned inconvenient, if you ask me," Lance said.

"It is. But I'll be in my new house by Christmas. Three more weeks won't hurt me any."

"Ross," Lance said, "what's this about Morgan — and Tom?"

"Please, Lance," Ross began; but the thunder of hoofbeats stopped him. They both looked up and saw Tom's great gelding pounding down Silver Street. Tom pulled the animal up so hard it reared. Then he hurled himself from the saddle, his face as white as a sheet.

"Jen —" he gasped. "Where is she, boy? Is she all right?"

"In the house," Ross said. "Yes, she's all right, Tom."

"Thanks!" Tom said, and was off, pounding through the door.

He was inside a long, long time.

Lance looked at Ross with a sly grin.

"Better unlimber that shooting iron, boy," he said; "looks like Miss Jennie needs some more rescuing."

"No," Ross said, "here they come now."

Tom came out of the house with his big arms around Jennie's waist. Jennie's face was glowing with happiness, and tears clung to her lashes.

"Gentlemen," Tom said, "I want to thank you. I'm mighty grateful. Jennie told me what you done. So you got one of the bastards, eh, Ross? Good boy! I'm proud of you."

"If you had been keeping up with Jennie like you should have —" Ross said angrily.

"I know," Tom said. "You're damned right, Ross. I've been a fool." He smiled down at Jennie with clumsy tenderness, then he looked back at Ross. "All right, boy," he said; "you got your wish. There's going to be a wedding at Moonrise — come Christmas time. . . ."

Ross stared at him.

"Well I'll be damned!" he said.

"I'm taking Jennie up to your place," Tom said. "She'll have to stay there, boy. There ain't no place else. . . ."

"Right," Ross said.

Tom lifted Jennie up on the gray gelding, then climbed up in front of her.

"So long, gentlemen," he said, "and many thanks. . . ."

Ross turned back to Lance, but the older man clapped him on the shoulder hard, a smile lighting his dark face.

"That crow I was going to pick with you is dead, Ross," he said. "Reckon it never was anything much, knowing Morgan as I do. Let's leave it buried, shall we?"

"Right," Ross said. "I'll play a requiem over its grave. . . ."

Chapter 9

The rain wept through the branches of the oaks and the long streamers of moss hung down, unstirred by any wind. Ross Pary, wrapped in an oilskin poncho, leaned against the dripping bark of an oak and looked at his house. He wore no hat, and his thick curling blond hair lay soaked and plastered against his forehead. But he lay back against the trunk of the oak, unmoving.

Before him, the house, Moonrise, stood filling up his eyes. His Negroes had made a clearing in the oak grove, but the trees they had left, framed the house, so that a guest coming up the winding drive always saw it through a screen of gnarled bough, and thick green and gray silver moss. It was not a great house like Staunton, or Monmouth, or Laurel Hill; but those who saw it afterwards recalled it as a little gem, though, actually, it was not small.

All its lines had been designed to give the illusion of height. By having only one gallery, instead of two, and letting the Doric columns soar up to the roof, the illusion was increased; and the small balcony, with its wrought iron balustrade that hung under the same roof at the height of the second story, added a Creole touch which somehow harmonized with the whole.

His house. With his own two hands he had done it. For this thing he had climbed the Hill. And the woman he had dreamed of would this day become mistress of it, but as his brother's wife, not his. He had given up that dream, of course. But, standing there in the rain, he wondered if his resignation had not been too ready; if his second, fairer dream might not turn to ashes, too, in its turn.

Tom's marriage to Jennie was only going to increase his difficulties; for how, once Moonrise had become the dwelling place of a family, would he ever be able to fulfill his pledge to Conchita to free the slaves? And with Tom removed from the list of those who provided her with diversions, what was to prevent Morgan Brittany from hurling even greater temptations at his well-nigh defenseless head?

Ross groaned, thinking of it. The weather suited his mood. He got a crazy kind of comfort out of standing there, bareheaded in the rain, as if the lowering skies were the visible symbols of his confusion and his grief.

He heard a noise in the brush, so slight that at first he thought he had imagined it; but, when he turned, Brutus stood there beside him.

"Marse Ross, Marse Ross," Brutus said. "You's going to catch your death!"

Ross looked at Brutus' giant frame, already soaked to the skin, and entirely unprotected.

"What about you, Brutus?" he smiled. "You're wetter than I am."

"Sure thing, boss," Brutus laughed; "but I'm a bigger man than you is and a whole lot tougher."

"Come for your Christmas gift, Brutus?" Ross asked. "You're early, aren't you?"

"Nawsuh, Marse Ross — didn't come for that. Just come to ask you if you done heard anything from Marse Harry. . . ."

"Marse Harry?" Ross began, then he recognized the name. "Oh, you mean Mister Linton," he said. "As a matter of fact, Brutus, I did."

He could see Brutus' body stiffen, as the big man held his breath. He means it, Ross thought, this Rachel of his is as important to him as Conchita is to me. And why not? I suspect that under that black hide beats a heart as true as any other man's.

"What did he say, Marse Ross?" Brutus was tense.

"He's willing to make the sale," Ross said; "but he hasn't anyone to send Rachel and the boy over here with. I reckon I'll have to send after them —" Ross stopped suddenly, and light showed in his blue eyes. After the wedding, he was in for a long siege of idleness. Most of the houses he had designed were finished, or nearly so. And the plantation needed little attention until planting time. He had dreaded those empty days. Too much time then for thinking — for regrets. Too many hours to conjure up Morgan's baleful beauty in the imagination, or see it in the flesh. A trip like this would be good for him. It would get his mind off things, perhaps would even give him a fresh point of view.

"You know, Brutus," he said; "I think I'll go over there myself next month and get them."

"Would you, boss?" Brutus said. "That sure be mighty kind of you. It's a mighty heap of trouble for you to go to just for me. . . ."

"Not just for you," Ross told him. "I need to get away from here for a while."

"Trip be good for you," Brutus nodded sagely. "You been looking right pert peaky here of late. If you do go, boss, be sure and give Miss Cathy my regards. . . ."

"Miss Cathy?" Ross said. "Mister Linton's wife?"

"Nawsuh — his sister. She as good as gold. She was always takin' up for us."

"I'll do that," Ross said, and straightened up; for the sound of carriage wheels sounded clearly on the drive. But when the vehicle itself came in sight, he saw that it was only a hired hack. A moment later, he moved toward it, smiling, for he had seen the glint of brown hair with red-gold lights in it, and the small, well shaped head leaning forward as Conchita stared at his house.

"You came!" Ross said, and put out his hand to Eduardo Izquierdo; then, involuntarily he stiffened, for sitting on the other side of Conchita was José Méndez.

"I took the liberty of accompanying my friends," José said stiffly; "in my reportorial capacity, of course. I hope that you do not mind, too much, Señor Pary."

"No, not at all," Ross lied politely; "though I cannot imagine what interest a Mississippi wedding would have for the readers of *La Unión*."

"Not the wedding," José said. "Plantation life — the institution of slavery. Those things are of great interest, Señor. . . ."

"I see," Ross said; then: "Well, Conchita — aren't you even going to talk to me?"

"I have not the breath," Conchita laughed, "after seeing your house! Oh Ross, it is superb, and of all beauty, and of enormous grace. I envy much your sister-in-law who will live in it."

"That," Ross said drily, "is an envy that you could soon rid yourself of — if you only would. . . ."

"Someday," Conchita whispered, and touched his hand.

Ross walked alongside the carriage in the rain until they came to the stairs of the gallery. There the servants came rushing out, bearing umbrellas, so that the guests reached the shelter of the gallery without getting wet. Ross tossed his oilskin to Simon, now elevated to the post of butler, and took Señor Izquierdo's arm. In the smaller parlor, a fire roared in the grate, and decanters and glasses stood ready at hand.

"Truly a *casa grande* — a regal house," Eduardo Izquierdo said, as he sipped his Madeira. "It's a pity that such a house must be a fruit of human bondage. . . ."

"How else," Ross said mildly, "could such a house be built?"

"There are in the North," José Méndez put

in, "many great houses, and up there slavery does not exist."

"Not our kind of slavery," Ross said; "but something less kind. The great houses of New York and Massachusetts, Señor Méndez, are built by men who employ child labor, and the labor of women — white labor, though you may tell me that is beside the point."

"Let us," Conchita said impatiently, "leave this of slaves and slavery, Caballeros. I should very much like to see the rest of this house, my Ross — if you would be so kind. . . ."

"With pleasure," Ross said, and offered her his arm. José took Señor Izquierdo's arm and followed them. They moved through the house, with Conchita exclaiming over the quiet elegance of its furnishings.

"You will note," Eduardo Izquierdo said, "that they have here the same problems that we have in our South American countries — heat and humidity; and in many ways the solutions have been the same — high ceilings to permit the heat to rise away from the floors, long hallways open at both ends to let the breeze through, and the use of white and pale colors to reflect the sunlight instead of absorbing it."

"But no tiles," José observed, "which are cooler than wood — no patios, and insufficient shutters for the windows. I like our solution better, Señor. . . ."

"We have colder winters," Ross pointed out. "For that reason alone, your Spanish *casas* would not serve. Then, too, we have much more rainfall."

"It's beautiful," Conchita said. "It is enormously and immensely beautiful. I would not have it other than the way it is."

"Thank you," Ross said. "This apartment we cannot enter, because Miss Dalton and her friends are busy with the preparations for the wedding — though Conchita can, if she wants to."

"May I?" Conchita said. "That interests me vastly — the preparations. And perhaps I could even be of service."

"Of course," Ross said; "if you'll promise to come back to us as soon as you can."

"I promise," Conchita said, and went through the door.

"Your brother," José Méndez asked, "where is he now? Surely he has also the preparations?"

"There is a little house about a mile from here where he lived while this house was being built. Tom is there with certain of his friends taking a rather jovial leave of bachelorhood. I suggest that we join them — as the time grows short before the guests are to arrive. . . ."

"If you'll forgive me," Conchita's father said, "I'd prefer to remain in the little room beside the fire. To go out once more into the rain is little to my liking. But you young men would doubtless enjoy the festivities. . . ."

"I think I would, at that," José said, "with your permission, Señor. . . ."

Ross gave orders to the servants to have a small landau brought around front, and he and José were driven in it down to the smaller house. Upon entering it, Ross was surprised to find Henry Montcliffe, George and Henry Metcalfe, Charles Dahlgren, and Doctor Benbow among the group who were toasting Tom's last hours of freedom. He needn't have been, he reflected a moment later, for his big, good-looking brother was just the type of man to get along well with Natchez' wildest young blades, Dahlgren, banker that he was, could count half a dozen bullet, rapier, and bowie knife scars upon his body from both formal and informal encounters, and the escapades of the others would have filled a good many folio volumes. They had sensed at once that Tom Pary was their kind of man. If his education was rather inferior to their own, his robust charm more than made up for the lack. Ross's polish and brillance awed them; most of the rough and ready country gentry felt ill at ease in his presence; but with Tom, they were completely at home.

The celebration waxed hilarious; the usual crude and more than a little off-color jokes were bandied about, and the bourbon disappeared with amazing speed. Before any of them thought it possible, a Negro appeared to summon them up to the big house to greet the arriving guests and commence the festivities.

Many of the people of Natchez had thought twice about attending this wedding. The Parys were "new" people; the older families were still uncertain as to how much acceptance should be granted them. But feminine curiosity prevailed. People who had seen Moonrise from the outside whispered about its splendor; the mothers of unmarried daughters heard via the grapevine of what a figure the younger Pary had cut at the Brittanys' party for General López. They argued realistically that it wasn't where a man had come from, but where he was going that counted; and Ross Pary was evidently going somewhere — fast.

So it was that when Ross and the other younger men reached the house, they found the drive choked with the carriages of the very finest families. The great salon, big as it was, was filled to overflowing. Ross could hear the babble of excited talk:

"Such a lovely house! I do declare, Martha, I don't believe I've ever seen finer furniture. . . ."

"And the flowers! December, no less — why they must have been shipped all the way from Florida or Cuba at ruinous expense. . . ."

"Did you see the livery on the niggers? Silk! Why half the people hereabouts can't afford to dress themselves so fine, let alone their niggers. . . ."

"Have you noticed, my dear, that Morgan Brittany isn't here? I wonder why. After all she was the one who introduced the Parys to polite society. . . ."

No, Ross thought miserably, Morgan isn't here. In a way that's a good thing, but in another, it isn't; because I'm afraid Lance isn't going to understand. What could I do? Jennie would have curled up and died if we had invited her. I'll try to explain to Lance — he's usually a very understanding person.

He looked around at the crowd which relays of servants were serving wines and small cakes, and finally Conchita came through the side door and took his arm. Looking at her, Ross saw that she had been crying.

"What's the matter, little doll?" he said softly. "This is no time for tears."

"I know. But Jennie is so lovely in her gown of white, and everything is splendid and perfect and of such great happiness that I could not help it. I kept thinking that this should be ours, this wedding — that these people should have come to see you and me, and then I thought of all of the reasons it could not be — so — I cried. . . ."

"Those reasons will be removed," Ross told her. "In a little time, they will be removed."

"Yes," Conchita whispered; "yes, oh yes!"

Then the music started and Jennie was coming down the stately stairway, a vision in a cloud of white, on the arm of Doctor Benbow, who alone of the Natchez people had known her father, and as his friend volunteered to give the bride away. Then Rector McWilliams of the Episcopal Church came out and stood before the little altar and all the people gasped.

This was Jennie's doing. Privately, without Ross knowing it, she had argued Tom into joining the Episcopal congregation, telling him that since everybody who was of any importance belonged to it, they could not afford to shame Ross with the backwoods crudity of their own Baptist faith. The mere thought of how old Todd Blackwater would look presiding over the ceremony in such surroundings had been a telling point, even with Tom. Ross, early in his sojourn in England, had become an Anglican communicant; and throughout the

South, the Episcopal High Church was the church of the elect.

It was, of course, the final answer to the doubting. From this day forth, no one would question the Parys' standing in Natchez.

Jennie had a spray of lilies in her arms, and she was beautiful. Looking at her, Ross felt the old ache return, just a little. But he looked down at Conchita, seeing her green eyes misting over, and the feeling was gone.

Then the vows were said, and it was over. The guests poured into the great dining room, and Jennie cut the wedding cake with a saber lent her by an officer of the State militia. The dinner was talked about for months afterwards. Ross had borrowed one of the chefs from Antoine's in New Orleans to preside over his kitchen. People used to fine food exclaimed over unheard-of and outlandish delicacies: peacock roasted in the feathers, breast of guinea hen under glass, mountains of quail, golden brown, so small and delicate that a whole one was little more than a mouthful. The guests waded through such unaccustomed dishes as jambalaya aux crevettes, and ended with the matchless omelettée soufflée, that richest of all desserts. Even the coffee was not allowed to pass without drama; as the guests watched with puzzled expressions on their faces, servants extinguished all the candles. Then they came into the dining room bearing small metal bowls under which alcohol burned blue. As the bowls were placed before them, the guests inhaled the pungent smell of cognac, cloves, cinnamon, orange and lemon peels. Then the Negroes reached deftly at the side of each guest and stirred the mixture. It blazed up, throwing eerie blue shadows on each face, and the Negroes stood back watching. Then quickly they stepped forward once more and extinguished each bowl by pouring in the rich black coffee, afterwards transferring the whole mixture to regular coffee cups.

"Café Bûlot!" Doctor Benbow said; "I've never seen it done better!"

The guests sipped the heady mixture, the candles were relighted and afterwards the talk was free and gay. Conchita sat by Ross, holding his hand under the table and smiling into his eyes. Then the Negro orchestra struck up a gay dance tune, and the couples filed out into the great salon. The wedding, Ross reflected, had been a success. He whirled into the dance, feeling the good wine in his belly and the sense of warmth and comfort and certainty that to a man of his nature were the best of all possible feelings, when he became aware suddenly that Conchita had stiffened in his arms, and was staring toward the door.

He followed her gaze, and missed the beat entirely. Then he stopped dead. For Morgan Brittany stood in the doorway, clad in a dress that was a sheath of pure flame. No other woman in Natchez, Ross realized miserably, would have dared wear that striking shade of scarlet; and no one else he had ever known anywhere in the world would have looked like that in it. Above it, Morgan's black hair merged with the night behind her, and her warm red mouth repeated the color of the dress, smiling a little, the smile compounded of mockery and absolute self-confidence, and all the cruelty of the ages.

She came up to Jennie and said clearly, gaily: "So sorry I'm late, dear! How lovely you look —" Then, bending forward, she kissed Jennie's now entirely colorless cheek.

"And you, Tom," she said; "I congratulate you. I adore weddings — they are among the more interesting of masculine errors." She turned back to Jennie, smiling sweetly. "You won't mind, will you," she said easily, "if I kiss the groom?"

Jennie was beyond speech. Morgan went up on tiptoe and found Tom's mouth, caressing it with her own, her white arms making a circle about the dark stuff of his coat, dazzling under the light of the chandeliers. Then while all the matrons of Natchez stared open-mouthed, she clung her mouth to his for so long a time that all of those who from pure suspense had held their breath were forced at last to let it out again, making a rustle like a rising wind in the hall while Morgan kissed him still, his face above hers darkening slowly into beet-red and then into purple; but she kept kissing him until finally, convulsively he brought up his great arms and broke free of her.

"There!" she laughed gaily, "see that you do as well, my dear!"

"I'd kill her!" Conchita exclaimed fiercely. "Before God and His Virgin Mother, I'd kill her dead!"

"Somebody is going to," Ross said slowly, "one of these days. Come on, let's dance. It doesn't help matters for us to stand here and stare. It's much better to ignore her."

"I hate her," Conchita said. "She is enormously evil and absolutely without pity, and of a cruelty that is formidable. She can do things like that and get away with them because she doesn't care what people think. She is a law unto herself, and therefore she thinks herself able to break all other laws. . . . But there will be a time and a place and a day of reckoning. I wonder how she will face up to the punishment she has merited; or how well she will bear the castigation that will fall upon her?"

"She will bear it well," Ross said grimly, "her pride is as great as her cruelty."

They whirled away from the little group in the center and lost sight of Morgan. When they saw her again, she, too, was dancing, swinging lightly upon José Méndez' arm. Ross and Conchita whirled away from Morgan and José, and when they came back again, José was standing beside a pillar with a sulky look on his handsome face, and Morgan was gone.

"Poor Tom," Ross said.

"Yes," Conchita said "poor Tom! But better him than you, my own. And do not tell me that she has not smiled thus upon you, nor even that she has not kissed you so! But, *mi alma,* if for any reason I should learn that you have spent five little minutes alone with her, I shall scratch out both your eyes! And eat them!" she added.

"Conchita!" Ross laughed, "this jealousy does not become you. What man who could have you, would have Morgan instead?"

"Any man," Conchita said gravely, "since you are fools one and all, and such a woman to you is a thing wonderfully exciting. *Puta y fiera!* She should be lashed with many thongs!"

It was over finally, and the guests stood on the gallery and waved after the coach that bore

Tom and Jennie away toward the steamboat that would take them down to New Orleans.

"God grant them joy of each other," Conchita said tremulously, then, burying her face against the sleeve of Ross's coat, she wept.

"Why do you cry?" Ross whispered.

"I am thinking of them, and also of us. This night they will be safe in each other's arms, while you, *mi alma*, will sleep in your great master bedroom, and I will lie on my little bed next to my father's bed, because he needs much attention, and I will think of you and will not sleep. . . . And that, my Ross, will be a hard thing — to be so near you, and yet so far away. . . ."

"Yes, a hard thing," Ross muttered. "And I, even less, will be able to sleep."

"And should I," Conchita whispered, "walk in my sleep, he would awaken and call me. Perhaps he would even seek after me, and that would be a thing worse. . . ."

"Yes," Ross said, "much worse."

"Then we must have patience, must we not, my love? But I am so tired of having patience. I am so weary of being without you while my father spins his endless plots to free Cuba for which everything and all of my life must wait." She looked past him at the rain slanting endlessly down over the drive. "And not even the weather will help us. Tonight there might have been a moon so that we could have walked in the garden for a little while; but, instead there is only the rain weeping for us who are always kept from love. . . ."

"Not always, Conchita *mía,*" Ross said.

"Yes, yes — always! Other people marry and have sons. But you and I, my Ross, stand forever in the darkness, and listen to the rain. . . ." She whirled then and left him, running blindly through the doorway and up the wide stairs to the guest room where her father waited.

Lying sleeplessly in the darkness, Ross thought bitterly how right she had been. Twice during that night he put on his robe and stalked through the hall, only to see the glow of light coming from under her doorway, only to hear her father's voice, querulous and fretful, calling her name. It was, as Conchita had said, a hard thing. And when the morning came in gray-white and thin, he knew from the sound on the windowpanes that it was still raining.

At breakfast, he could see the look of determination on her face.

"José," Izquierdo complained, "where is he? Did he not come back last night at all?"

"That I cannot say," Ross told him; "no doubt he is visiting some of the nearby plantations. He told me he wanted to write about plantation life."

"So, so —" Eduardo said, "but we cannot remain here forever. There are things to be done."

"Those things can wait," Conchita said. "So many things have to wait." She turned to Ross, smiling a little. "My Ross, when are you going to show me the place as you promised? I would like to see all of it. You have a horse I can ride, do you not?"

"But, *muñeca mía,*" Eduardo Izquierdo protested, "it still rains, and —"

"And I can wrap up warmly. Besides I have a headache and the cool rain in my face would help much. Be patient, my father, it is a thing that I have wanted to do a long time, and Ross can have a manservant look after you during our absence."

"Of course I can," Ross said. "A little rain will not hurt Conchita. It is better that she gets used to it now, because here it rains much of the winter."

"I still think —" the old man began.

"Please, Father . . ."

"Oh, all right! But do not complain to me if you catch a grippe!"

"I'll be careful," Conchita said.

They rode away from the house in the light,

steady drizzle and neither of them said anything. Under his broad hat, Ross's face was frowning and thoughtful, and Conchita's green eyes were full of questioning. They went down the drive at a brisk canter and turned past the quarters toward the nearer fields. But, before they had reached them, Conchita stretched out her gloved hand and touched his arm.

"That house, what is it, my Ross?"

"That," Ross said, "is the house my brother occupied during the time that the big house was being built."

"Does no one live there now?" she said.

"No," Ross told her, his voice tightening while he spoke, "no one."

"It is very lonely, is it not? People do not often pass this way, do they, my Ross?"

"No," Ross said, "they don't."

"And there is, doubtless — a key?"

"There is — a key."

"Where is it, this key? You — you have not left it behind?"

"No," Ross said softly, "I have not left it behind."

A wood fire, Ross reflected, is a kind of magic. The oldest magic. There are shapes in it. The ghosts of the past, the ghosts, too, of what has not yet been. Look into it and you see things — the years ahead, the golden years, full of joy and peace. . . . And it sheds its magic, sending it flickering over everything it touches, spreading red and gold over everything, even over this little one now sleeping in my arms. . . .

How graceful she is. How cleanly, purely graceful now that there is no more shame between us. Even the scars are not ugly, now. The light takes the edges off them, and the rest of her is — beautiful. I'm glad they killed that man. I could not rest easy if he lived. I hope the others are dead, too, now; and if they are not, then I shall someday have a hand in their dying. For this is not a body for profaning — and those who thought it so have no further right to life. . . . Lord, I'm tired! But it is such a good tiredness. Don't know when I've felt so peaceful. . . . It could be like this for always. It must be like this — it must, it must!

So thinking, he bent down and kissed her mouth.

She stirred gracefully in his arms. The green eyes came open, endlessly deep, and the light was in them again.

"I slept! Oh, my Ross, how could I have! I have so little time with you and I spend part of that sleeping. That is a foolishness — a wicked foolishness. . . ."

"No, *muñecita mía,* that was a part of it, and a good part because it gave me time for thinking. . . ."

"And what have you thought, my Ross?"

"That this must never end. That you must marry me at once — whatever the objections, whatever the reasons against it, you must."

She sat up and looked at him gravely. Ross propped himself up on one elbow staring at her, as if to memorize her image. In the glow of the fire, she was bathed in light, little tremors of gold and shadow flickered on her, so that all of her was golden, soft-swelling curve, and deep-shadowed hollow, and he knew she could not pass out of his keeping.

"You have much right," she murmured. "Still it is a hard thing, that will require much managing. . . ."

"Your father asked us to wait a year. But too much can happen in a year. If it were done, we could wait that long before telling him, and afterwards he would come to accept it."

"I think so, yes. But what of the house — and the slaves?"

"We could go North. I have still my profession, and I could practice it there. Thus could we live."

She looked away from him, into the fire.

"La Señora Pary," she whispered. "Oh, my

Ross, how lovely it sounds! Yours, always and forever yours — Yes! You have right — it must be!"

"When?" Ross said.

"When I come back again. I shall find some excuse — before the spring has come I shall come back. And Ross —"

"Yes? Yes, *Chiquita Mía?*"

"I hope that it is raining then. For now always I shall love the rain."

Ross lay quite still listening to the sound of it against the windowpane.

"It is such a nice sound," Conchita said; "it makes the fire warmer, somehow — it makes it cozier here. . . . Now kiss me, my Ross. Take me again in your arms so that our bodies make the long kiss, all over from head to toe like fire. . . ."

"Yes," Ross whispered, "yes, yes, yes."

"I have much wickedness, no? But I have dreamed of this. Before that time when you were hurt I did not know it could be like this. . . ."

"But now that you know?" Ross prompted.

"It must be like this forever — all our lives, until we are tired and old and one day dead. And then I shall ask that we be laid together in one grave that we may sleep in each other's arms throughout eternity. And even when the trumpet of God shall blow and we shall rise again, I shall get up but slowly, unwilling to leave your embrace. But as God is good, He shall return me to it, I know. For in you is my heaven, soul of my delight, and I want no other! Now kiss me. I have talked long enough. . . ."

Yes, Ross thought, yes, it's no time for talking. . . .

The year of the half century went out in the whispering rains, and the new year came in with the winds still crying. Then late in January, 1851, Tom Pary came back to Moonrise, strutting like a peacock, and Jennie's face was radiant. Looking at them, Ross could not bear it. He was not an envious man, but the constant sight of so much happiness added bitter contrast to his loneliness.

Still, he dallied a long time before making the journey he had promised himself. Ross was not adventurous by nature, and the easygoing comfort of life at Moonrise seduced him into idleness. He had at the moment, no really pressing needs – the plantation provided him with actual abundance so that no longer did he have to seek for building contracts. He could, in fact, refuse those that did not particularly interest him. More than one ambitious planter, whose wealth outstripped his taste, found to his surprise, after he had stubbornly insisted upon grandiose ornamentation instead of simple beauty, that Ross Pary was quite capable of saying: "I'd suggest that you get somebody else. This isn't my kind of a house."

But when late in February, he did decide to go, his departure was delayed the better part of a whole day by Morgan Brittany. She gained entrance to his apartment by the simple method of pushing Wallace out of the way with her gloved hand and marching up the stairs.

Ross was tying his cravat when she came into the room. In his bedroom, his valises were piled up, waiting.

"Ross," Morgan laughed. "I was hoping I'd find you at home."

"Why?" Ross said bluntly.

"Because I'm lonely. You know how I hate being lonely. Mind if I come in for a while?"

"Yes," Ross said, "I do mind."

"Why, Ross?"

"Because Lance wouldn't like it. I wouldn't like it. This will only start more talk, and I prefer being guilty of what I'm accused of."

"Lance," Morgan said, "never listens to talk. Besides, he isn't here."

"Where is he?" Ross demanded.

"In Cincinnati. An uncle of his died up there

302

and left him a fortune. Funny isn't it, that fortunes seldom get left to people who need them."

"Yes," Ross said, "it is. How long will Lance be away, Morgan?"

"Oh — weeks. 'Til the estate is settled, at least."

"Why didn't he take you with him?"

"I didn't want to go. I hate Cincinnati. It's so dull."

"Duller than Natchez?"

"Much. Besides, Natchez isn't dull. I always manage to keep it from being so. . . ."

"You sure do," Ross grinned. "Well, since you're already here, sit down for a while. But not for long. I'll put you out when I'm ready to go."

Morgan made a face at him, and curled up on the sofa. She smiled at him, smoothing her face into that devilish counterfeit of innocence that Ross found so appalling in her.

"Please, darling," she begged, "let me stay. I'll be good — I promise you."

"Your promises," Ross told her, "are not worth the breath it takes to utter them, Morgan."

"Perhaps. But that's not the important thing. The important thing is that you, Ross Pary, are a coward. You're frightened to death of me."

"Yes," Ross said honestly. "I am. And also of myself. You're a very tempting baggage, Morgan."

"You know, Ross — that's the secret of your charm. Most men — even Lance who ought to know better, treat me with such diffidence. You have absolute contempt for me as a person and you don't mind showing it."

"Why should I? You're no damned good and you know it. I also happen to know it. Therefore, I haven't any excuse like all the others who read into you qualities you haven't got."

"And what qualities have I, darling?"

"Cruelty. Deceit. A certain coldbloodedness — a kind of self-command. For you aren't actually cold, though you pretend to be. That's another thing I know that most people don't seem to. . . ."

"You're right. If I ever turned loose, I could burn up the world. But I won't turn loose. To do that, I'd have to sacrifice what you call my self-command. And that's what gives me command over others. What other qualities do I have?"

"A kind of contempt for both the opinions and standards of other people. What you want is its own justification to you merely because you want it."

"I don't think that's odd. Most people feel the same way — only they haven't the nerve to maintain their own way in the face of opposition or the conventions. I don't give a fig for either. Life is too short. I mean to live."

"Yet," Ross observed, "in a way you hold to certain conventions. You've never been actually unfaithful to Lance, have you?"

"No — but not because the rightness or the wrongness of the matter bothered me. It's just that up till now, no man has interested me enough to make it seem worthwhile."

"Up until now. What do you mean by that, Morgan?"

"I mean that you might interest me enough — if you ever really tried. Your contempt for me is galling, I'll admit that. If I thought a pleasant evening — or a night with you would break down that contempt, I might try it. Only I'm not sure it would. It might even increase it. You called me a baggage. But a used and broken piece of baggage is never as interesting as a shiny new one. And virgin territory is far more fascinating than that which has been explored."

"That," Ross said drily, "is one journey I mean never to take."

"What journey, darling?"

"Into the unexplored territory of your

fascinating possibilities. Let's drop this subject, shall we?"

"Why? Does it bore you?"

"To distraction," Ross yawned.

"Damn you!" Morgan flared. "There are times when I could tear out both your eyes!"

"And eat them, no doubt. I've heard that before, too."

"Not from me," Morgan said, looking at him. "From whom, Ross? Tell me from whom?"

"That," Ross said evenly, "is none of your damned business, Morgan. Come on, get up now. I have to go."

Morgan didn't move. Instead she stared into the fire, peacefully.

"I just adore fire, don't you?" she said.

"You should," Ross told her; "playing with it seems to be your avocation."

"You're in rare form today," Morgan said. "Be a darling and play for me. I so seldom hear good music."

"No," Ross said; "I have to catch a boat."

"A boat?" Morgan said tensely. "A boat to where, Ross?"

"New Orleans. And before you ask me – yes, I'm going to see Conchita. Anything else you want to know?"

Morgan got up slowly.

"No," she said quietly; "but there's something you ought to know. You aren't going there. Not now – not ever. You're finished with her, Ross – finished."

Ross smiled at her calmly.

"Now," he said, "I'll tell you a funny one: I am going, Morgan. Right now."

He half turned to go into his bedroom, but out of the corner of his eye, he saw her tensing her body to spring, the fingers of her hands curving into talons, and he whirled and caught her by both wrists and pushed her ahead of him into the bedroom.

He paused a minute, then very quickly, he gripped both her wrists with his right hand and yanked open the closet door. Morgan saw her opportunity and took it; she tore free of him, and whirled out away from him, but not quite fast enough, for Ross's long arm came out, and his hand settled upon her shoulder and gripped it hard. Then, with one long shove, he pushed her into the closet and slammed the door shut.

"Now," he said pleasantly, "that should hold you for a while. I'll tell Wallace to let you out, after I'm gone." He slid the bolt closed.

As he turned to pick up his bags, she screamed just once – a high, animal scream, senseless and terrible. Then there was no more sound.

Ross picked up the bags. Then he put them

down again. The echo of that scream still grated along his nerves. Why didn't she cry out again? Why hadn't she hammered upon the door, and demanded to be freed? There was something wrong here; he could sense it. Yet, if he opened that door, he'd have his hands full, and maybe miss the boat and –

"I'm being a damned fool," he muttered, and drew back the bolt. He pulled the door open slowly, and stepped back, staring.

Morgan stood there, as rigid as a statue, every drop of color gone from her face, her lips white, too, only the shape of them distinguishing them from the rest of her countenance, the pupils of her eyes dilated, the eyes themselves unmoving as though staring at unimaginable horrors.

"Morgan," Ross whispered, "Morgan. . . ."

He put out his hand and touched her. The flesh of her arm was like ice. Then she bent forward, as though she would nod to him, and collapsed all over at once in a dead faint, straight into his arms.

"Sweet Infant Jesus!" Ross said.

He put her down gently on the bed, and got water from the kitchen and bathed her face. And when, finally, she came back again, she started to cry. Like a child. Like a whipped child – in hot, half strangled sobs.

Ross stared at her in breath-gone astonishment. He could imagine the end of time more easily than Morgan crying. Yet, here it was.

"I'm sorry, Morgan," he said; "I didn't know."

"I told you!" she said, shuddering; "I can't stand darkness! And I mustn't be shut in, Ross! I mustn't! I die when it happens! My breath stops, and I — I see things in the dark — awful things! They — they come very close and put their faces into mine and — and suck away my breath. . . . then I die . . . ."

"What kind of things, Morgan?" Ross said.

She looked at him sullenly.

"I don't know," she said, "I've forgotten. I never can remember afterwards. It was so long ago, Ross. The first time. My father was angry with me and — Oh, damn you! Let me out of here — I want to go home!"

"All right, Morgan," Ross said.

Standing on the deck, watching the high bluff fall away behind him through the white wake of the steamboat, Ross tried to understand it. If he could discover this thing — uncover the roots of the terror that had possessed Morgan this morning, he would comprehend her fully. In that terror, he was sure, was the very seed of her twisted being. From it, all her evil grew, making her the unwitting instrument of powers beyond her control.

If that were true, then Morgan Brittany was something other than he had imagined. If what he had seen a glimpse of was a part of her shaping, she was an object for pity—not for hatred. . . .

But he couldn't fathom it. The words that described it, the science that could explore it, did not exist. They would perhaps never exist – not fully.

It was no good to think about it. Deliberately he turned his mind away from Morgan. To think about her too much, was to slip over the boundaries into her world. And that way lay madness. No, better to think of Conchita now. He wondered how it would be in New Orleans – though, as a matter of fact, he did not plan to stay long. After he had seen Conchita, he meant to take a coastal steamer and push on to Georgia, where he would spend some time with the Lintons, before bringing Brutus back his Rachel and his son.

He remembered the miserable fiasco of his last trip to New Orleans. This time it would have to be better planned, far, far better arranged. He gave much thought to the matter all the way down the river. By the time they had docked at the foot of Toulouse Street in the morning, he had reached certain decisions.

He summoned a cab, and directed the driver to take him to a respectable boarding house. The driver took him to a large house far out on Ursuline Street, near Rampart. It was run by a handsome quadroon woman, who in her youth had been the *placée* of a wealthy planter. It was spotlessly clean, and very quiet. But, when he insisted upon an outside room, the quadroon smiled at him.

"If M'sieu wishes to have a lady visitor," she said discreetly; "it is, of course, against the rules of the house. But—" and the smile broadened, showing perfect white teeth; "I am no longer so young as I once was, and after ten o'clock I sleep very soundly, me."

Ross smiled back at her.

"You are all right, Madame Emilie!" Then he passed her a folded ten-dollar bill. To his vast astonishment she gave it back.

"No, M'sieu," she said; "now I know nothing, and can sleep soundly and with good conscience. To be paid would make me a part of some strange occurrence of which I know nothing. I prefer not to be a part. If M'sieu wishes, he can put the money in the little box for the poor inside the door of the Saint Louis Cathedral. The poor will not know from whence it comes, or why — and they will not be troubled. Now, if M'sieu wishes, I will prepare breakfast for him."

"M'sieu wishes," Ross said. Human ethics, he reflected, had a way of being as inexplicable as human sins.

He idled the day away, walking in Jackson Square, the old Place D'Armes, and browsing through the shops on Royal and Canal Streets. He bought a lovely antique necklace for Conchita, thinking all the time how much better it would have been if he could have bought a ring instead. Life flowed around him, the sights, the sounds, the smells — a bucket plummeting down on a rope from a third-story apartment to be filled by the grocer below; an old, black mamaloi, sitting in the shadows and making gris-gris for a wistful swain bent upon regaining his lost love, street venders crying their wares, two black urchins dancing for pennies. . . .

And himself alone in the midst of all this light and color and movement, himself starving for the simple joys of existence — joys which so far he had only been able to steal for an hour — while all about him was plenty.

Tired, he went back to his lodgings and lay down across the great four-poster bed, and watched the bright gold of the sun dim and begin to spill out of the air, and afterwards there was a star. He got up and dressed himself neatly and with care and went outside and hailed a cab.

All the way to Conchita's house he was wondering if José would be there, and about how he could overcome whatever difficulties might present themselves. But there were, astonishingly, none. Conchita was alone in the house except for the servants, her father having gone with José to a meeting of Cuban expatriates who were, as always, spinning plots to liberate their native land.

"My Ross!" Conchita said; "how wonderful that you came tonight when no one is at home. It will be after midnight before Father returns. We have hours and hours."

But Ross shook his head.

"It is better that you come with me," he said, "so that truly we can be alone without fear of being interrupted unexpectedly. You can leave a note for your father. Say that we have gone to the opera, and afterwards to a late supper. . . ."

"As you will, my Ross," she murmured.

He took her first to Antoine's, and they had supper, while Ross watched the clock impatiently, waiting for the hands to crawl past the hour of ten. When they had at last done so, he summoned a cab, and drove out to his lodgings. Conchita stared at him wonderingly when he opened the door with a key.

Then she stood in the middle of the room looking at it.

"This is very nice," she said, "I am glad that you have found it. . . ."

But afterwards, she lay propped up on one elbow, looking at him, and when he drew near again to kiss her, she drew her other hand back and slapped him hard, across the mouth.

Ross fell back, staring at her in astonishment.

"That," she said angrily, "is for coming to me from her — filled up with the ugly passion she gave you! I feel bruised — and unclean. I have the desire to go and wash myself! That you could come to me with your mouth still sticky with her kisses — oh Ross, Ross —" Then she buried her face in the pillow and shook all over with sobbing.

"Conchita." he whispered. "Conchita *mía*. . . ."

"No!" she raged; "not Conchita *tuya!* Never yours, now! Look at me! I am naked, am I not? And I have never before been naked with you — always I was clothed and covered with love! But this is not love — not this ugly thing! This is the thing you men buy — this is release merely from the bestial wanting that women like her give you. Why didn't you stay with her, Ross? She would have been glad of it! She must be accustomed to being bruised and torn, and then left naked and — and used. . . .”

Ross looked at her, pain moving in his eyes.

“Would you have wanted — that?”

Conchita whirled to face him, and the tears made great emeralds of her eyes.

“No,” she said, “no! Certainly not! And now I have much sorrow for my words. It is better that you came to me — even with this ugliness, than to have stayed with her. For then I should have lost you utterly. And this will not happen again. Tell me it will not, my Ross — even if you lie. . . .”

“It will not happen,” Ross said; “and I do not lie.”

“Darling, I am still one crazy little bird, no?”

“Neither crazy,” Ross said, “nor a bird. An angel, I think — sent from heaven to save me.” Then he drew her once more into his arms. Afterwards, he was very gentle with her, very gentle and very delicate, and their love was a kind of song sung in a minor key; then, again, finally it was fierce, but with a clean and tender fierceness peculiarly its own, so that there was no longer any question of giving or taking but the miracle of true union, of fusion when there is no longer any separation of spirit or of identity, and when Ross tenderly and sadly pointed out to her the lateness of the hour she clung to

315

him and wept and would not go.

"But your father. . . ." he began, patiently.

"This is no longer a thing of my father," she insisted, "but only of us. It is no more a thing over which I can have shame, or want to hide or need to have fear of. What can my father do or say that will outweigh the little dying of having to leave you? It has happened too much, this little dying — so that I have often the fear that it will grow into the big dying, and there will be no more — us. . . ."

"Conchita — listen to me."

"No! I will not listen to you. I cannot hear these ugly words, these eternal good-byes. I can only hear you when you say, I love you. Those are the only words worth saying, my Ross. This of the good-byes, no longer serves."

"You're right," Ross said. "They haven't served for a long time. And when you keep your promise to come to me, they will not exist any longer. When will that be, Conchita — tell me when?"

"Soon," she said softly. "Soon, *mi alma*, soon. . . ."

Then she put up her hands and let her slim fingers wander all over his face, then down his neck and over his broad shoulders. They rested there and tightened.

"No more good-byes," she said.

But, in the morning, when he told her of his proposed trip, she did not try to dissuade him.

"That is a good thing — an honorable thing," she said. "For I should not like to be separated from you. Yes, go and bring the black Brutus back his wife. For a thing like that I can wait. Then, when you are home again, I shall come to you — I shall come, and nothing on earth shall stop me."

For all that, as the steamer butted down the hundred and ten mile long channel to the sea, Ross was sick with worry. He wondered how she must have fared coming home in broad daylight from a night spent away from home in the company of a man. The Latins, he knew, did not forgive a thing like that easily. There was only one answer to the whole problem. Conchita must marry him — at once.

If, to have her, he must change his whole life, then he would change it. The things he had wanted, and now, finally had achieved, were nothing in comparison to her. Whatever the odds, Conchita must be his.

He reached Savannah after a quiet voyage of some days, and went straight to the hotel. It was late at night, so he went gratefully to bed, glad of the chance to sleep in a bed that had consideration enough for his weariness to keep still. The next morning, he woke up entirely rested, with a ravenous appetite. After a hearty breakfast, he started out to inquire after the Lintons. He returned to the hotel long after nightfall, completely discouraged. Nobody in Savannah, it seemed, had ever heard of a family by that name.

The next day produced the same lack of results. By the evening of the third day, Ross was ready to give it up and go home, when a dignified and portly gentleman of some sixty years came into the lobby and asked for him. When Ross had been summoned, the white-haired, goateed gentleman extended his hand.

"I'm Harry Linton," he boomed; "heard tell you've been asking for me about town."

"Thank God!" Ross said; "I've been looking all over Savannah for you. Now about the woman and the child, how much do you want?"

"What woman and what child?" Harry Linton said. "Just what are you talking about, Mister Pary?"

"Rachel," Ross said patiently, "and the boy — whatever his name is. The wife and son of my Brutus. He's pining away for them, so I thought as a matter of humanity I'd buy them and take them home. . . . But you know — I wrote you all about it."

"I have never had a letter from you in my life!"

"Well, I'll be damned," Ross said helplessly; "I'm sorry sir — there must be some mistake. There must be another Harry Linton hereabouts."

"There is," Harry Linton said. "My nephew — a fine boy, named for me. Owns the plantation, The Pines, out on one of the islands. I've just come from there. Come to think of it, I've been stupid. You wouldn't be asking for me, because I'm only visiting here. I've got a place of my own near Key West, Florida."

"Could you direct me to The Pines?" Ross said.

"I'll do better than that. First thing in the morning, I'll take you out there. But you'd better get up early, because it's a long trip."

"Thanks, I will," Ross said. "Now would you have a bourbon with me?"

"With pleasure," the first Harry Linton said.

Afterwards, over the bourbon, Ross found the talk interesting. Mister Linton was an importer by trade, and dealt largely in Cuban cigars and tobacco. He had made many trips to that unfortunate island, and what he said, dovetailed perfectly with Conchita's description of its hellish oppression at the hands of Spain.

"The thing that surprises an American," Linton said, "is the terrible hatred that the

Spaniards have for Negroes. We keep niggers enslaved, but we don't hate them. In fact, we're kind of fond of them — except for the poor whites, maybe. But the Dons hate them worse than they're supposed to hate Satan. Naturally, considering the way the niggers are treated, they rise up now and then and kill a few criollos or one or two Spaniards. . . .

"When the Dons catch 'em, they've one standard treatment — a nine-foot lash with fine wire buttons woven into the end. It lifts the flesh right off a man's bones.

"Another thing, a white woman, *criolla* or Spanish, is reasonably safe from the Dons — but only reasonably, because they have a remarkable appetite for the bed; but a good-looking mulatto wench, or a quadroon or an octoroon hasn't got a chance. While I was there they had a standard affair, from which all white women were excluded, but the colored wenches were forced to appear in the costume of Mother Eve. Believe me, Pary, there's absolutely nothing like a Don!"

"All the more reason," Ross said, "why Cuba should be freed."

"There are better reasons. With Cuba furnishing ten new slaveholding States, we'd beat the Abolitionists down every time they opened their mouths. Besides, it's Manifest Destiny.

These United States, boy, are going to be bounded on the North by the aurora borealis, on the South by the procession of the equinoxes, on the East by primeval chaos, and on the West by the day of judgment!"

"I don't agree," Ross laughed; "but I'll drink to the way you put it!"

Ross got up very early the next morning, but even so, he found the energetic old gentleman waiting for him.

"I won't be able to stay," Harry Linton boomed; "business, you know. But in a way that'll be an advantage. It gets damned confusing when people try to talk to me and my nephew at the same time. Speak to me, and he answers. Talk to him and half the time I'm butting in. I've often thought that one of us ought to change his name. But I can't change mine, and young Harry's too fond of me to change his. So there you have it: two Harry Lintons make a pretty kettle of fish."

"I think I could work out a system," Ross laughed. He found that he liked the elder Harry Linton very much. There was something genuine about the old man.

They took a hack down to the wharf, and there Harry Linton engaged a steam launch.

"Don't trust those sailboats," he explained; "we'd never get down there in one of them."

"Exactly where are we going?" Ross asked.

"Isle of Hope. Prettiest dad-burned spot this side of Paradise. De Soto explored it three hundred years ago, looking for gold. Didn't find any, so he left — the durned fool!"

"You left," Ross pointed out.

"Who says I'm smart? Besides I'm coming back one of these days — soon as I have enough money to put The Pines back in shape. . . . That fool brother of mine never could run anything right, and Harry's just like him. Cathy is the only person in the family with a lick of common sense."

"So I've heard," Ross said. "My Brutus told me to give her his kindest regards."

"Did he now? I ain't surprised; Cathy always did have a way with the niggers."

The little boat butted its way down the channel, its miniature sidewheels throwing a curtain of spray. Ahead of them the river sparkled in the morning sun. They meandered along under a high bluff, upon whose summit stood trees which were old when Columbus pushed his tiny caravels away from the shores of Spain. There were houses along the bluff, too, sitting placidly behind screens of oleanders and camellias, and occasionally bamboo.

In the little coves, the wild birds rose in clouds at the noise of their approach: plover and tern and wild ducks, and even the majestic white herons, standing motionless on one leg, staring at them.

They pushed on down the channel for nine miles, past Dutch Island, then as they swung inward past the sharp tip of Burntpot Island, Ross could see the little cove of the Isle of Hope, with its black wharves jutting out into the sparkling water. It lay peacefully before them in the sunlight. The prettiest spot this side of Paradise, Harry Linton had said. He was, Ross realized, very nearly right.

They slid into the landing, and the Negro pilot helped Harry Linton down.

"Wait for me," the old man said; "I'll be back in an hour."

He took Ross's arm and they walked under the great oaks until they came to a place where a little pony cart waited. It was made of wicker, and the shaggy, diminutive animal that drew it was scarcely bigger than a large dog. But once set in motion, he proved to have amazing strength.

The road wound under the trees from whose branches trailed festoons of moss longer than any Ross had ever seen before. On both sides of the road wild flowers grew, blooming although it was still winter. Neither of them spoke. Amid all that quiet and peace, the sound of voices would have been a kind of blasphemy.

They came out at last, quite unexpectedly, before the house. It was, Ross realized, one of the most beautiful old houses he had ever seen. Its style was not Greek Revival, but French West Indian: it was low and wide, and built mostly of gray cypress. Apparently it had never been painted, and the wood had weathered into a lovely pinkish-gray shade. A long gallery swept across it, its roof supported by slender cypress columns no bigger around than a sloop's mast. The roof was shingled, and green moss had colored it to a shade that was beyond the skill of man to duplicate. Coming closer, Ross saw that it was in a bad state of repair: panes were gone from many of the windows, shutters hung crazily upon one broken hinge; the door was warped so badly that it was impossible to shut out the weather, and troops of tiny green lizards gamboled on the porch.

In the trees about it cardinals darted from limb to limb, tracing a trajectory like bright flame. Bluejays scolded noisily, and mockingbirds imitated the sound in their sweeter tones. Fat, red-breasted robins hopped about tugging manfully at giant earthworms and turtle doves cooed peacefully from the higher trees.

A man, Ross thought, could get lost here. A

man could sink layers deep into all of this and forget to come up. . . .

As they walked toward the house, a tall young man came out of it. His clothing was as frayed and nondescript as the house, but he carried himself like a prince. He was very handsome, Ross saw. His skin had been burnt to the color of old teak by the sun, and his hair was as black as — as Morgan's the inevitable comparison flew into Ross's mind.

He had a corncob pipe stuck into one side of his mouth, and now he took out the pipe and smiled at them.

"Howdy," he said. "Back so soon, Uncle Harry? And who might this gentleman be?"

"Mister Pary," the elder Harry Linton said; "come to see about that wench you promised to sell him."

"Now do tell," the young man said; "you know, I'd plumb nigh forgotten that. Glad to see you, Mister Pary. Come in and set a spell."

His voice was rich and pleasant. Ross took the hand he offered him, then sank down into one of the comfortable wicker rockers.

"Downright peaceful here, ain't it?" young Harry Linton said.

"Very," Ross said.

"Planning to stay long?"

"No — I shouldn't like to inconvenience you."

"Be an inconvenience if you left too soon," the young man said pleasantly. "It's mighty lonesome way out here, and me'n' Cathy dote on having company."

"Then mind your manners and break out some corn likker," his uncle snapped; "I got to be pushing off right away, and I'll be damned if I want to do it on an empty stomach."

"Sorry," the young man said; "a man gets plumb lazy out here. Sary!" he called; "break out a jug and some glasses – and put a skillet on the fire. We've got company."

A few minutes later an old Negress, who could not have been many days under eighty, tottered out with a brown jug. For the first time in his life Ross Pary tasted corn liquor – the unrefined product from which the smooth, blended bourbon of Kentucky is made. It brought tears to his eyes; but he got it down after a fashion, and its results were immediate and pleasant.

Uncle Harry stood up and looked at his watch.

"Got to be going," he said, "or I'll miss the afternoon boat. Take good care of Mister Pary, boy."

"Don't worry," the young man said. "I will."

They had breakfast in the dining room. It consisted of mountains of pancakes drowned in butter and cane syrup, and cups of scalding coffee. After Sary had cleared away the dishes, Harry Linton put his feet on the table and rocked back with a contented sigh, sending up clouds of vile-smelling smoke from the corncob pipe.

"A man feels good when he's et," he said.

For the life of him, Ross could not keep from laughing.

"You're just about the most contented cuss I've ever seen," he said.

"And the laziest," Harry grinned. "Cathy does all the work around here."

"By the way," Ross said, "where is your sister? I'm very anxious to meet her."

"Now do tell," Harry grinned. "You'll be sorry when you do. She's a homely cuss — took after paw's side of the family — and what a temper! Bro — ther!"

"I've heard," Ross grinned, "that yours isn't so mild!"

"You been talking to that nigger, Brutus. Matter of fact, I seldom get riled. But Brutus ain't no ordinary nigger — he's too damned proud. I took a rawhide to that wench of his when she gave me some sass, and Brutus knocked me down. Naturally I had to give him a beating after that. Then he took to sulking and amuttering to himself, so I thought it was better to sell him than to have any more trouble. Reckon you've got your hands full with that big buck."

"No," Ross said, "strange as it may seem, Brutus and I get along famously. Best hand I have, in fact. I promised him that if he behaved himself I'd buy his Rachel and the boy — and he's been like a lamb ever since."

"Well, I'll be damned!" Harry said.

"By the way, how much do you want for them?"

"Oh — I don't know. Five hundred, I guess. . . ."

"Apiece?" Ross asked.

"No, for both of 'em. They ain't no good here always amourning after Brutus. Besides, I like you. I don't aim to cheat my friends."

Ross, who had been prepared to pay a cool thousand, stared at him.

"You beat me," he said. "I would have paid pretty nearly anything you asked. Doesn't money interest you at all?"

"Naw. Why should it? What could money buy that I ain't got?"

There is, Ross decided, absolutely nothing like contentment.

"Could I see them?" he asked.

"Sure thing. And afterwards, we'll ride out the east section so you can meet Cathy."

He swung his long legs down off the table and stood up, yawning.

"Come on," he said; "we'll have to saddle up ourselves. Ain't no niggers up here to do it for us."

Ross followed him out to the tumbled-down stables, and there they saddled two of the rangy little island horses. These animals were as hairy as goats, and so short that the stirrups almost trailed in the dust. Ross was aware of what a ridiculous figure he must cut, sitting astride the short horse; but Harry, who was even taller than he, apparently didn't mind.

They came after a short ride to the quarters. They were shacks of cypress, and the only words that described them was miserable. It was a good thing that the climate was so mild — after one hard winter any creature who attempted to live in these hovels would have died.

"Rachel!" Harry called.

There was the sound of motion in one of the cabins, and a woman came out, leading a little boy. She was as black as night and just as beautiful. It took Ross some minutes to realize this fact. For a man of Anglo-Saxon heritage and traditions to be able to see beauty in a black skin involves long and tortuous mental read-justments. That Ross was able to do so quickly was indicative of the sensitivity of his perceptions. Rachel was nearly as tall as himself, and she bore herself like a queen. Some obscure heritage of Arabic blood had refined her features from the indisputably ugly negroid heaviness, into a delicately-chiseled aquilinity that was doubly startling in one of her velvety, nightshade coloring. The boy was a fine, sturdy youngster — an exact replica of Brutus in miniature.

"Rachel," Harry said, "this is Mister Pary, your new owner. I just sold you and the boy to him. And I don't want to hear of you giving him no trouble!"

Rachel stared at Ross sullenly, and didn't open her mouth.

"I also own Brutus," Ross said gently. "I bought you and the boy so that you could be together."

The proud, sullen look dissolved slowly. Then it broke altogether and tears rained down Rachel's cheeks.

"God bless you, Marse Pary," she whispered; "God and all the Angels bless you!"

"Thank you, Rachel," Ross said. "What's the boy's name?"

"Numa," Rachel said. "That's African word. It mean lion."

Ross put out his hand and let it rest affectionately upon Numa's kinky head.

"You're going to be a good boy, aren't you, Numa?" he said. Then he brought a bag of candy out of his pocket and gave it to the boy.

Numa took the candy and stared at his new master with startled eyes.

"Say thankee, Numa!" Rachel commanded.

"Thankee, boss," the boy whispered.

"You good man, Marse Pary," Rachel said. "Be nice living on your place. When we going there?"

"In a few days," Ross told her. "Good-bye now. Good-bye, Numa."

"Good-bye boss," the boy said.

"Well, I'll be damned!" Harry Linton said as they rode away; "anybody would have thought they was white, the way you treated 'em!"

"They're human beings," Ross said curtly. "That's good enough for me."

"Never did believe in spoiling niggers," Harry mused; "but 'pears to me now, I may have been wrong. I'll bet your hands work like blazes for you."

"They do," Ross said. "You catch a heap more flies with honey than with vinegar, Harry."

"Reckon you're right at that," Harry Linton said.

They had left the quarters behind them now,

and came out into the fields. Far away, Ross could see a gang of blacks working under an overseer who sat on one of the little horses, lolling comfortably forward in the saddle. They rode toward them, and as they came closer, Ross was surprised at the youth and slenderness of the overseer.

"Cathy!" Harry called suddenly, and Ross looked around him in amazement. But there was no woman in sight. Then the overseer turned, and Ross saw the shirt strain tight across small breasts no bigger than seed oranges, and found himself looking into a pair of eyes as gray as woodsmoke.

"Well, I'll be a cross between a razorback sow and a bull 'gator!" he whispered, unconsciously repeating his brother's favorite expression.

"Cathy," Harry grinned; "this is Ross Pary, our guest. And from the looks of him, he's been thinking you're a boy!"

"Well, I'm not," Cathy said, and took off her broad-brimmed hat. Her lovely chestnut hair had been drawn back tight off her forehead, and tied in a loose braid that fell now almost to her waist. There was not a hint of curl anywhere in her hair, and she was as slim as a willow sapling. Her face and throat were covered all over with freckles, so many freckles that from a distance she appeared to be an even golden tan. Her cheekbones were as high and prominent as a Seminole's, and the line of her jaw firm and fine. Her cheeks were hollows in her thin face, but they were flushed with color, and her warm, red mouth was simply big – no other more kindly word would serve.

Harry had been right, Ross thought. Cathy is as homely as a hog in a gate; but, damn it all, I like her!

"Howdy, Ross Pary," she said and extended a hand that was as freckled as her face; then turning to her brother, added in that low musical drawl that was a delight to hear: "Gosh, Harry, where'd you get him? He's a sight too handsome to be real!"

Harry threw back his head and laughed.

"Cathy's like me," he chuckled; "when manners were passed out, she was hiding behind the door!"

"Oh, shush!" Cathy said. "You're going to be with us long, Mister Pary?"

"Only a few days," Ross said.

"Couldn't you stay longer?" Cathy asked; "we so seldom see folks out here."

Her nose, Ross saw, was as thin as an ax blade, with fine nostrils that flared with spirit. It was high-bridged, even a little hooked. Catherine Linton had not one good-looking feature, yet the whole of her was pleasing. You would, Ross mused, remember this face when many a prettier one would be forgotten. It had so much intelligence — so much spirit. And those wonderful gray eyes dominated it completely.

"Come on," Harry said, "ride back up to the house with us — so we can set and talk a spell."

"All right," Cathy said. "Reckon the niggers can get along without me."

Ross looked at her trim figure, perfectly revealed in the tight fitting linsey trousers she wore.

"Don't you," he asked, "ever wear dresses?"

"Sometimes," Cathy drawled, and reaching in her breast pocket, came out with a tiny Cuban cigar, as thin as a pencil, and half as long.

"You got a match, Harry?" she said.

"Sure, Cathy," Harry told her and brought one out and lit it.

Ross stared at her in astonishment as she inhaled deeply and with evident satisfaction, letting the fragrant smoke trail through her thin nostrils, like streamers. Looking up, Harry saw his face.

"That's right," he grinned, "ladies don't smoke — on the outside, do they? You'll just have to get used to us, Mister Pary; we sure Lord ain't gentlefolks!"

"It's all right," Ross murmured, but Cathy snatched the little cigar out of her mouth and threw it away.

"I'm sorry," she said; "I sure didn't mean to offend you, Mister Pary. Reckon we've sort of run wild — out here in the brush."

"No offense," Ross said evenly; "in fact, I'll be offended if you don't light another one. I find the sight of you smoking them fascinating."

"Then I'll smoke two dozen," Cathy said. "Lord knows I need something to make me fascinating."

"I don't think so," Ross said. "I think you'd be fascinating anywhere — in any company."

"You hear that, Harry," Cathy said triumphantly; "Mister Pary says I'm fascinating."

"Then," Harry grinned, "Mister Pary is tetched in the head!"

They came back to the pleasant old house, and at once Cathy dived into the interior of it and disappeared. Ross and Harry sat on the porch in the big rockers and savored excellent cigars.

"Uncle Harry brings 'em," Harry explained. "those little ones for Cathy, too. Best damned cigars in the world, I reckon."

"They sure are," Ross agreed.

They sat there very quietly without saying

anything much, and after a while, Cathy came out of the house. Harry stopped rocking and stared at her. She was wearing a dress and her straight hair had been wound into a bun on her neck, and had a red camellia pushed into it. She looked lovely. Ross tried to explain to himself the combination of circumstances that could make a girl as homely as Cathy look lovely, but he gave it up. The fact remained that she did.

"Well, I'll be damned!" Harry said helplessly.

"Don't use such language in front of Mister Pary," Cathy said.

Ross got up and steadied a rocker for her.

"He can cuss all he wants to," he said; "in fact I was just about to say the same thing."

"Do I look nice?" Cathy asked artlessly.

"Very. In fact you look lovely."

"Thank you, Mister Pary," Cathy said.

"Ross. That Mister Pary business makes me feel a thousand years old."

"How old are you, Ross?" Cathy said.

"Twenty-nine."

"That's a nice age," Cathy said; then: "I'm twenty-two, and Harry's thirty-one. . . ."

"Damn!" Harry said; "don't you know that ladies never tell their ages?"

"I'm no lady," Cathy said.

"Now the truth has been spoken!" Harry

laughed. "She's meaner'n a sidewinder!"

"I don't believe that," Ross said.

"It's true, though," Cathy said sadly; "I've got a temper that would scorch your sideburns."

"Then we'll have to do something about it." Ross said.

"Only thing that would do any good would be a nine-foot rawhide," Harry drawled. "Then you'd have to shoot her when you untied her. . . ."

"That wouldn't be my method," Ross laughed. "Any woman who's worth her salt is a good bit like a spirited filly. Beating them only ruins them. Gentle them a little and you'll have them eating out of your hand in no time at all."

"I wouldn't!" Cathy flared. "You men make me sick — all of you!"

"I don't doubt it," Ross said quietly, "I often make myself sick, Cathy."

Cathy stared at him.

"You're not proud, are you?" she said.

"No — nothing to be proud of as I can see."

"Lots of men with less — are," Cathy said seriously. "You're very handsome and you wear beautiful clothes, and your manners are so nice that they make me shamed enough to die. Makes me see what I've been missing out here in this Godforsaken place."

"No," Ross murmured, "not Godforsaken. This little Eden. This lovely little strip of Paradise. . . ."

"That's how it looks to you?" Cathy said in wonderment.

"Yes. The first time I saw this island I thought that a man could come here and forget to leave. That he could let all of life go by for the peace he'd find here. It's so old, Cathy — so peaceful and quiet. Out there, in the world you envy me, I have so little of that . . . ."

"Then stay!" Cathy said, suddenly, almost fiercely.

Ross stared at her, then cast a glance in Harry's direction. But the good breakfast and the liquor had had their way with him. Harry lay back against the rocker, fast asleep.

"It's quite impossible, little Cathy," Ross said gently. "I have a plantation more than three times the size of this one in Mississippi. And I have — other commitments."

"Committments in skirts," Cathy said bitterly.

Ross looked at her. This, he thought, is going very badly.

"Yes," he said honestly, "commitments in skirts."

"Thanks," Cathy said drily.

"Thanks for what?" Ross said.

"For being honest. Another man would have lied."

"I never lie," Ross told her, "if I can possibly avoid it."

"I believe you," Cathy said, and got up. "See you later," she said, and went back into the house.

That night, Harry dressed himself up, and rode off to visit one of the Barrow girls at Wormsloe, the biggest plantation on the island. He invited Ross to come along, but when Ross pleaded fatigue, he rode off without a backward look or an apparent qualm. It was, Ross felt, almost a left-handed insult to Cathy. This stupid oaf felt without a doubt that Cathy had so little attractiveness, that he could leave her alone in the house with a stranger.

Of course, Cathy was perfectly safe with him; but not for the reasons that Harry supposed. They were much better reasons: A girl named Conchita, and his own innate sense of honor.

He came out on the veranda and stood looking at the stars hanging like jewels between the branches of the oaks. The river was blue-silver in the night, and somewhere far off, a loon screamed terribly.

It was a warm, slumberous night, heavy-scented.

No, Ross thought, I shall not stay. It

wouldn't be good to stay. This is Circe's island — and Circe has a freckled face. . . .

He became aware slowly, that she was standing there beside him. But so silently had she come, that he was unable to determine how long she had been there. She didn't say anything, but stood there looking out over the mist-silver and blue surface of the water. Then she sighed.

"You're going," she said. "Tomorrow , you're going." It wasn't a question. It was a simple statement of fact.

"Yes," Ross said; "I'm going."

"I'm glad," she said, her voice flat, toneless, small; "it's much better that you go." Then she turned very quietly and went back into the house.

Ross stood there a long time staring at the river. Then he sat down on the steps and continued to look at it until a chill got into the air, and his knees ached dully. He got up then and went back into the room they had given him and lay down across the bed. But he could not sleep.

First thing in the morning, he heard Cathy's voice under his window. She was swearing like a trooper, using oaths that would have brought a look of envious admiration to a muleskinner's eyes. He raised up and looked out of the window. Cathy was already mounted, dressed in her boy's costume of yesterday, the stub of a cigar stuck in her teeth.

"Git along you lazy black bastards!" she snarled, "or I'll tan the rust from your hides!"

Whatever the softer emotion that had moved her last night, Ross knew, it was gone — and it would not come back. He felt a sense of regret that it was so. Then he got up from the bed and began to dress himself in preparation for his journey.

Chapter 10

Ross Pary stood at the bar in Connelly's Tavern in Natchez, holding the bottle of bourbon between his hands. He was dimly aware that he had probably wasted his money. In his present frame of mind he could have drunk wolfbane and hemlock without noticeable effect. Nothing had gone right, everything had gone badly.

In the first place, when he had stopped off in New Orleans to visit Conchita on his return from the Isle of Hope, he had found the door of her house barred in his face, and the servants armed with stern orders that under no circumstances was he to be admitted. The result, this — of Conchita's folly in refusing to return home at an hour that could support any reasonable explanation of their activities during his last visit. And since then, there had been no word from her — not even a note, nothing.

In the second place, he was no longer living at Moonrise, the house he had built, and which he loved as though it were a living thing. The reason for this was as simple as it was appalling. He had returned to Moonrise to find his new sister-in-law bathed in tears over evidence that had come her way which seemed to indicate that her husband of three months' standing was engaging in open, flagrant adultery with Morgan Brittany. . . .

No matter how Ross examined this evidence, he could find no flaw in it. It was exact and damning: Lance Brittany detained in Cincinnati by unexpected legal difficulties in connection with his inheritance; Tom and Morgan seen everywhere together — at all hours of the day and night; whispers along the Negro grapevine, that Marse Pary often left Finiterre when the sun was up, after spending the night. . . .

This, and his own private knowledge that Morgan's mood had reached a point of unprecedented recklessness when he, himself, had made discretion the better part of valor — all reinforced his reluctant belief that this time the rumors were true.

He had taken Tom to task about it, and the fury of the quarrel that ensued had left him white and shaking with rage and grief. Between any other two men not held in check by the memory of years of fraternal love, and generous cooperation, such a quarrel would have ended inevitably upon the sandbar in front of Vidalia, settled unalterably by the final arbitrament of pistol fire.

But Tom and Ross, were, after all, brothers; and in spite of their differences they loved each other still. But words were spoken that night which could never be forgiven; the close, warm relationship that had existed between them was broken once and for all. It was impossible for them to attempt to go on living together. One or the other of them had to go.

And in that matter, Ross had had no choice: He was unmarried, and Jennie was already with child. So he had packed his belongings and moved back into the apartment over his office. And from that day up to the present moment, his life had stood completely still.

He was able to salvage a crumb of comfort from two minor, irrelevant circumstances: Brutus' joy at his reunion with Rachel and little Numa, a reunion so tender and touching that Ross had wept unashamed tears at the sight of it; and a brief letter in a childish, misspelled scrawl from the hand of Cathy Linton. She missed him, she wrote. She hoped that someday they'd meet again. Harry was well. Her mare had foaled. And life went on much as usual. She was trying to stop smoking those little cigars, and to learn better manners; but both things were hard, since she'd smoked since she was ever so little, and there wasn't anybody around to teach her manners. She had signed it, "Love, Cathy."

Going home through the darkness, Ross felt a little better. The whiskey had warmed him, lifted him somewhat from his slough of despond. He would, he decided, write Conchita a letter. Perhaps she would never get it, but he was going to write it just the same.

He was surprised to notice, as he came up the stairs that the lamps were on in his parlor. Perhaps Wallace had lit them; but, if so, why? He pushed open the door, and saw the tall figure of Lance Brittany standing in the middle of the room, his back toward the entrance.

"Lance!" Ross said, "this is a surprise — it's about time you paid me a visit."

Lance turned.

"Yes," he said, "it is." But his voice was like ice.

Ross put his hand on the bell cord to summon Wallace; but Lance made a little gesture of protest.

"No," he said; "I haven't time. I'm here on

an unpleasant errand, Ross."

Ross let his hand fall away from the bell cord and stared at him.

"Very well," he said evenly, "state it."

"I've been pleased to think of you as a friend of mine," Lance began, heavily.

"And you've had cause to change your mind?" Ross asked.

"Yes. I was told that during my absence, you were seen constantly with — my wife. That's a mighty serious thing, Ross."

Ross put his hand back on the bell cord and gave it a tug.

"I agree," he said calmly, "if it were true. But it isn't, Lance. You should know me better than that."

"I thought I did. But I also know Morgan well — exceedingly well. And I know how little the best intentions serve against her once she makes up her mind. The point is, Ross, I've just realized that I'm an old man. Once killing people didn't particularly bother me. Now it does. Especially people whom I happen to like."

"Is this a challenge?" Ross said. "If it is, I won't accept it."

Lance stared at him.

"You won't accept it?" he began; but at that moment Wallace came into the room.

"Bourbon, Wallace," Ross said. "Some spring water — and some ice. Oh, yes — and you might bring a couple of lemons."

"Yassuh," Wallace said.

"You were saying that you wouldn't accept a challenge," Lance said.

"Oh, yes. I wouldn't accept any challenge, Lance — as a matter of principle. To me, dueling is an outmoded barbarism that proves nothing except perhaps that one man can shoot straighter than another. The man less given to nervousness, whose hand doesn't shake, always wins. But it hasn't the slightest connection with innocence or guilt. How many cuckolded husbands haven't you seen shot dead by their spouse's paramours, who then proceeded to crowd the mourners by repeating the offense?"

"You've got a point there," Lance admitted, "still . . ."

"Still, nothing. I especially wouldn't accept one from you because you happen to be the best friend I have in this world. I don't particularly relish the thought of dying. Unsatisfactory as my life is at the moment, the chance exists that things might better themselves. Then there is the remote possibility that I might accidentally kill you. I relish that even less. All the rest of my life guilt would haunt me — that I was fool enough, and coward enough, to bow to an archaic and obscene custom that has no valid place in modern life. I'm a civilized man, Lance. I don't fight duels. I wouldn't exchange shots or cross blades with a man who has always befriended me, who has gone out of his way to aid me — who has been endlessly kind. Not even if these malicious waggers of eternally forked tongues were telling the truth — which they aren't. At the risk of being redundant, I'll say it again: They're lying, Lance. What I want to know is — why?"

Wallace came in with the tray, and bowed before Lance. Lance took the decanter and poured bourbon for both of them.

"You sound almost convincing, Ross," he said tiredly. "Go on — I'd much rather be convinced than not. It would make things ever so much more pleasant all round."

"All right," Ross said, "though even having to vindicate myself is a kind of insult under the code you subscribe to — but let that pass. . . . It so happens that I left Natchez a day or two after you did, and that you were already here when I returned. I spent the entire time at the Linton Plantation, The Pines, on the Isle of Hope in Georgia, with the exception of a few days in New Orleans. If you want confirmation you can write Harry Linton — the owner. Wait — even that isn't necessary. I have a letter from

Miss Catherine Linton, the owner's sister, which mentions my visit."

He walked over to his secretary and took Cathy's letter out, and gave it to Lance. Lance glanced at the envelope then passed it back, unopened.

"No," he said; "I know the truth when I hear it. My humble apologies, Ross."

"Forget it," Ross said.

Lance stared at him thoughtfully, then asked the question Ross had dreaded.

"What," he drawled, "about your brother, Tom? It occurs to me now that all they said was Pary — not which Pary."

"Tom," Ross said easily, "was also away — on his honeymoon, for at least part of the time. After that, I don't know. But it doesn't appear to me to be likely that a man so recently wed would have developed a roving eye so soon."

"That's true," Lance sighed. "I guess I've made an ass of myself. I swore I wouldn't listen to talk, but I get so tired, sometimes. My brain gets tired. . . ."

"Why," Ross said gruffly, "don't you straighten Morgan out, Lance?"

Lance looked at him.

"You think I haven't tried? Every time I take her to task, she resorts to sarcasm so bitter that I can't bear listening to it. I'm afraid my temper might snap, and I'd kill her. Or she flies into rages that might be marvelously effective histrionics — or they might be actual insanity. I don't know which. If I knew, I could deal with them; either way I could deal with them. But I just don't know. . . ." His voice trailed off into silence.

Looking at him, Ross was filled with pity. Lance Brittany, he knew, could not be over fifty-one years old. At the moment he looked sixty, his dark, handsome face lined and sad. His hair had whitened so much in the single year that Ross had known him that the blackness had well-nigh disappeared from it. My God! Ross thought, she's killing him . . . she's slowly worrying him to death. . . .

"Why don't you get rid of her," he said harshly; "get an annulment — or a divorce?"

Lance raised his splendid, massive head.

"I love her," he said simply.

"I see. Sorry, Lance. I was way out of line that time. It's just that I hate to see you so troubled."

"Thanks," Lance whispered, and stared off into space, holding the bourbon untouched in his hands. "It's gotten to be damned lonely, Ross," he said quietly. "We give parties now — and nobody comes. They don't say Mrs. Brittany any more, now. It's 'that Brittany woman.'

You named our house better than you knew. Finiterre – land's end. The end of the world. . . ."

Ross got up and put a hand on Lance's shoulder.

"Buck up, old fellow," he said; "it'll work out all right. A little more time and . . ."

Lance stood up and drained the glass.

"No," he said; "it won't work out, Ross. Not ever." Then he picked up his hat and his crop.

"Sorry for the intrusion," he said grimly. "So long, Ross."

"So long," Ross echoed, and stood there watching him as he went down the stairs.

Chapter 11

Ross had slept late, a thing he rarely did, and which ordinarily would not have mattered at all. But on this July second of 1851, it had certain consequences. He was made aware of that at once. For, when he opened his eyes, he stared up into the face of Morgan Brittany.

He sat up in bed, staring at her. He rubbed his eyes and looked again, but Morgan was still there.

"What the devil are you doing here?" he said brusquely.

Morgan laughed. The sound of her laughter made him cold all over, despite the July heat. It was clear and limpid as spring water. Morgan, he thought miserably, achieves her most diabolical effects through contrast — a face as innocent as a Vestal's; a laugh like a schoolgirl's.

"Just a social call, darling," she said. "And at a most respectable hour at that. It's after eleven. Come on, you lazybones — get up!"

"No," Ross said.

"Then I'll join you," Morgan laughed. "You look so cosy there, and I'm tired. More over, won't you?"

"No," Ross groaned; "I'll get up. But go in the sitting room, won't you — and give me half a chance?"

"No," Morgan teased. "That nightshirt is such an adorable shade, and anyhow you have nice legs. I've seen them, you know; but only, I'm sorry to say inside that tight-fitting evening habit of yours. Come on, get up."

"Who let you in?" Ross demanded.

"Wallace. He couldn't help it, poor fellow. I threatened to take my crop to him."

"And I," Ross said morosely, "am going to take mine to him for doing it!"

Morgan threw back her head and laughed again.

"Poor Wallace! He really is caught between two fires, isn't he?"

"Will you go in the next room?" Ross said.

"No. You're too modest. You shouldn't be. You're a very handsome man, and such girlish sentiments don't become you."

"Morgan, for the love of God!"

"No."

Ross stared at her. You lovely little witch, he thought. By now, I could be lying on the sand-bar across the river with a bullet through my guts because of you, if I hadn't had sense enough to keep my temper.

"Where," he asked quietly, "is Lance right now?"

"Over in Louisiana — as usual. I told you, darling, he trusts me."

"He doesn't," Ross said flatly. "He was here not so long ago to challenge me to a duel because some damned, gossiping fool got me confused with Tom."

Morgan clapped her hands together, gleeful-ly like a child.

"How thrilling!" she laughed. "I would have liked to have seen that — two angry brutes ex-changing shots over me!"

"You disgust me," Ross said coldly. "You make me sick to the pit of my stomach."

"Do I, darling?" Morgan whispered, and got up from her chair. The old light was back in her eyes. Jesus God! Ross thought, will I never be free of her?

She started toward his bed, but at that mo-ment Wallace pushed his head into the room.

"Marse Ross, Marse Ross," he quavered,

"Missy Conchita's downstairs!"

All the color drained out of Ross's face. Morgan couldn't have done better if she had planned it. Conchita had the fiery temper of her Latin forebears, and a situation like this was impervious to any reasonable explanation. And of all the reasons that he could give Conchita for Morgan's presence, the truth was the most unbelievable.

"Send her up, Wallace!" Morgan laughed. "We'll be so glad to see her — won't we, dear?"

"Damn you!" Ross said fiercely; "damn you to hell and back again!"

"Now, dearest, don't be cross. I'm going to surprise you. I'm going to be self-sacrificing and gallant. I'm going out in the kitchen and down the back stairs — she'll never know I was here. Now, aren't I sweet?"

"Well, I'll be damned!" Ross said helplessly.

But Morgan was as good as her word. An instant before Conchita stepped into the room, the door closed quietly behind her.

"Ross," Conchita whispered, "my Ross —" and her words choked off. Ross could see the big tears in her eyes. She had been crying a long time — he saw that, too. Her eyes were swollen almost shut.

He was out of bed in an instant and gathered her into his arms.

"Conchita *mía*," he said, "what's wrong? Did your father . . . ?"

"Oh yes!" she wept; "my father — my father. . . . Oh, little father mine, how could you?"

"How could he what?" Ross said gruffly; "did he beat you?"

"Oh, no! My father was the soul of kindness. What he did was far worse! He — he left me, my Ross. . . ."

"Left you? But how — why?"

"There came a week ago a letter from Cuba, from the hand, I believe, of Joaquín de Aguero, my father's friend. Aguero plans the revolt upon which López counts so heavily. . . ."

"So there will be a revolt?" Ross asked incredulously.

"Oh, yes! A terrible revolt — many will die. In this letter, Don Joaquín must have asked my father's aid. I do not know — these things were kept from me. But there was much argument, loud and fierce, between Father and José. José kept telling Father that he was being a fool, and Father kept saying, 'I must go! I must!' "

"He went back to Cuba — old and crippled as he is?"

"Old and crippled as he is," Conchita said quietly; "my father is of the stuff of heroes. And now he will die — unless . . ."

"Unless what?" Ross asked.

"Someone goes to save him," Conchita said.

"You mean," Ross said harshly, "that I should join this new expedition of López'?"

"Yes," Conchita said.

"But, Conchita," Ross protested, "this thing is foredoomed to failure, and you know it. What would it serve if your father and I both died? Then you would be left absolutely alone."

Conchita looked at him, her green eyes very clear.

"Are you afraid, my Ross?" she murmured.

"Yes," Ross said frankly, "I am. This of dying is never a very pleasant thing; and now it is doubly unpleasant because it involves losing you."

"Letting my father die," Conchita said quietly, "also involves losing me, my Ross."

Ross stared at her.

"I see," he said at last. "In that case, I have no choice."

"You'll go!" Conchita breathed; "oh my darling, I knew that you would! It is not a thing of dying, my own, but of living — for with such a man as Don Joaquín to lead them, the people will rise; and when they do, their wrath will be terrible. They have so much to avenge — so many wrongs, so terribly many cruelties. . . ."

"Yes," Ross said; but all the time he was

thinking: Now there will be a new grave in Cuba, and nothing will be gained thereby. Now I am looking at you for the last time, you who are all my heart and my life and my hope of hereafter. You speak of cruelties, but this is the cruelest of all, that you send me out to my death, knowing I cannot refuse you. . . .

"Ross!" the voice called from the kitchen. "Darling – where are the towels?"

He felt Conchita stiffen in his arms.

"That perfume!" she whispered; "that scent I smelled when I came into the room! Her! Oh, Ross!"

Then Morgan was coming through the door, clad in Ross's green silk robe, and under that robe was only Morgan. She had tied it carelessly, so that the long sweep of her thigh showed each time she moved, and her black hair, under the turban she had made of the towel, dripped water.

Conchita stared at her wordlessly.

"How cosy!" Morgan said. "The minute my back was turned. Oh, darling, how could you!"

Conchita backed away from him, her eyes blazing.

"Thou!" she whispered. *"Puta y reina de las putas!"* She moved backward across the room until she came to Ross's little secretary. She put her hand back behind her and her fingers groped, closing finally over the paper knife. "Know you," she whispered, "that you have earned your death!" Then she sprang forward all at once, like a tigress.

Ross stepped between them, and his fingers closed over Conchita's wrist. He twisted cruelly and the knife clattered to the floor.

Conchita turned her face toward his, and the tears misted her eyes.

"Yes, yes!" she whispered, "you would save her! That follows, does it not? She also shares your bed. Then, oh faithless one, farewell! You may forget this of the expedition. My father is a proud man — he would not have his life at the hands of such a one as you!"

She jerked herself free of his grip in one convulsive motion, and ran toward the door. But in it, she turned, just for a moment.

"*Adios*, my Ross," she whispered; "Know thou that I have loved thee — much!" Then her high heels made a staccato clatter, going down the stairs.

Ross turned toward Morgan and his face was terrible.

"Get out," he said.

"Now, Ross," Morgan said; "don't be unnecessarily stupid. I had to save you from that. From what I could gather between the times you two were switching back and forth from

English to Spanish, she was sending you off on that asinine López expedition —"

"I said, get out." His voice was flat, calm, perfectly controlled; but Morgan, whose greatest talent was her ability to read men, knew what a limit he had reached. Why, she thought, he'd kill me! He really would!

"Like this?" she whispered.

"No," Ross said, coldly, "go dress yourself. Then go."

The minute she had left the room he flew into his clothes. If I hurry, he thought, there'll be time! The boat does not leave for twenty minutes yet — so there'll be time!

Five minutes later, he was pounding down the bluff toward the landing before which the steamboat waited. He saw Conchita standing on the deck and started up the plank toward her. But Conchita turned to the young officer at her side.

"That man," she said, "is pursuing me. Cannot a lady be protected from unwelcome attentions in your country, Señor?"

"You bet she can!" the officer said, and blew a little whistle. Two minutes later, Ross Pary was borne backward down the plank under a rush of four sailors. Be it admitted that he fought like a man berserk; but Ross, despite his height was slender; and, although he possessed considerable wiry strength, he was no match for four muscular sailors. He picked himself gingerly out of the dirt, and dusted off his clothing, staring at the steamboat as it moved majestically out into the channel.

Then, very slowly, he turned back to where Nancy waited, her reins trailing down over her well-shaped head, into the dust that was now the substance of his hopes.

When by the latter part of the month of July, 1851, no letter had come from Conchita, Ross Pary decided to go to New Orleans. He arrived in that city on the afternoon of July twenty-third, and debarked at the foot of Lafayette Street; both of which circumstances proved unfortunate, for the day was the one set for the great mass meeting in support of the second López expedition to free Cuba; and his route lay through Lafayette Square where it was being held. As a result, Ross found himself stopped by a cordon of policemen who absolutely forbade his passage into the city.

Swearing fiercely under his breath, Ross waited. López addressed the crowd, assuring them that this time his plans could not fail. To Ross's astonishment every one there appeared to believe him.

Ross looked at his watch. Goddammit to hell,

would they never get done with their speech-making? Two hours later he was still there.

On the other side of the crowd, separated from Ross by some thousands of people, Conchita Izquierdo also watched and listened. But she couldn't stay. The talk of Cuba only increased the gnawing fear she had for her father's safety, so, hours before the meeting was over, she left it and went back home, which she could easily do, for being on the side of the square that faced the city, her route was not blocked.

When she got back to her house, she found José Méndez waiting for her and with him a man, a young Cuban who looked so tired and ill that for a moment, Conchita forgot her grief.

"Bring him in, José," she said; "we must feed him and give him wine. You have come from Cuba, Señor? But that I have no need to ask; I can see that you have. Come in."

The two men followed her up the stairs. She moved with nervous speed through the rooms calling out to the servants, ordering food and wine; then she turned back to the stranger.

"Your name, Señor?" she asked.

"Alvárez, Miguel Alvárez, at your orders, Señorita. I — I have news for you."

Conchita stared at him; then she leaned forward, placing both her hands upon the table to steady herself.

"My father," she whispered; "is he — is he —"

"That I cannot say, Señorita," Miguel murmured; "I know only that when I left Nuevitas, he was in grave danger of being captured — or killed. . . ."

"I see," Conchita said, and sat down in the chair that José pushed forward.

"The news of glorious victories," José burst out passionately, "was spread abroad by Captain-General de la Concha's spies — and López believes them. Holy Virgin!"

"Tell me about my father," Conchita said.

"Of this I have much sorrow," Miguel began.

"Tell me!" Conchita spat.

"I have little to tell you. The few patriots that answered Don Joaquín de Aguero's call to arms were met everywhere by defeat, everywhere by death. When they sent me away to warn General López here, the last of our forces were fighting in Nuevitas, against Spanish armies equipped with artillery. I saw your father just before I left, Señorita. He was sitting in a wheelchair in the street, with a rifle in his hands and two revolvers in his lap. He was killing Spaniards with great neatness and accuracy. That's all I know, Dona Conchita. . . ."

"I see," Conchita gasped. Then: "Eat, Don

Miguel — you have need of strength."

José stared at her.

"They will not let him near López!" he said. "They swear he is a spy — Miguelito, here — the only man in New Orleans who knows the truth!"

"José —" Conchita said.

"Yes, Conchita?"

"When sails the mail steamer for Havana?"

"No, Conchita! No!"

"I asked you a question, José."

"Two hours from now. But you cannot go, Conchita! You are a woman, and the things that they do to women . . ."

"I know. You will purchase the ticket for me, José?"

"No! God and His Sacred Mother, no!"

"Then I will purchase it myself."

"I will go for you," José said; "this I cannot permit. . . ."

"It lies not in your power to permit or forbid, *amigo mío*. And you will not go. Your heart is not in this. And since he, whom I love, proved faithless, I care not if I live or die. Perhaps I can save my little father. If not, I shall avenge him."

"This is madness of a most formidable quality, and I will not have it!" José roared; "even if I have to bind you with ropes, I will not have it!"

"You cannot prevent me," Conchita said, standing up. "I go, my friends. Do not seek after me. I shall not return to this house."

José put his left hand upon the table, and lurched across it, seizing her arm in his right hand. Conchita whirled, and her hand came down upon the table and closed over the big fork that anchors the meat for the carving. She struck down hard and all at once so that the two tines went through his left hand, pinning it to the table. José turned her loose and hung there staring at the great dark drops oozing up around the two blades of metal that stood up from his hand.

"Mother of God!" Miguel groaned.

"I have much sorrow for this, José," Conchita said. "And now — I go."

So it was, that when Ross Pary finally reached the house late that evening, he found the serving maid in tears.

"M'amzelle Conchita ain't here no more, her!" the black girl sobbed; "She gone back to Cuba. And they going to kill her there! I just knows they is — just like they done killed her papa, them! Le Bon Dieu have mercy, M'sieu Ross — this here family is plumb ruined!"

Ross did not even answer her. He turned then, and started running — back toward Gravier Street, where Banks Arcade was, where a recruiting desk waited, and an expedition mustered its strength to set sail for the island of Cuba.

Chapter 12

Ross Pary lay in the bamboo thicket about twelve miles from Las Frices in Cuba. He put his left hand under the tattered mass of rags that was all that was left of his shirt and scratched tiredly. There wasn't, he reckoned, one square inch of his hide that the insects of Cuba hadn't been able to reach. They had even penetrated his curly blond beard; but even to scratch them, now, required too much effort.

He saw Narciso López speaking to one of the men. The man nodded grimly and moved off. After a time he came back, leading General López' horse. He led it up to the fire and took off its saddle; then, holding the bridle, he shot it.

The other men, one hundred and forty of them — all that were now left of the more than four hundred and fifty that had landed at Morillo on August eleventh, got up slowly, looking like a crew of dirty, ragged scarecrows, and moved over to where the animal lay. They went to work upon it with their knives, cutting off pieces of the flesh and thrusting them into the fire. When they had singed the meat a little they drew it out and ate it.

Ross didn't eat. He couldn't. López' horse had been a noble beast. He had ridden it himself on more than one occasion. To devour him now was almost like making a meal of Nancy, his own mare.

Ross looked toward López and saw that he was crying. There was enough to weep over. They had landed at Morillo and found the town deserted. They had fought at Las Pozas and won — but left Colonel Dorman, and Colonel Pragay, and Captain Ile de Fousse Overto dead upon the ground with fifty of their men, and a hundred more wounded. Since they could not replace their losses, this first victory of theirs had finished them. They had been separated from Colonel Crittenden's forces, and no man here knew if they'd ever see them alive again. Captain Kelly had brought back forty men whom Crittenden had left behind to guard his stores as he pushed on toward Pinar del Río. The Spaniards had attacked them, too, but they had escaped through the *manigua*, that spiny, subtropical Cuban jungle that ripped a man's flesh to pieces with thorns, and rejoined López's forces. They had fought again at Las Frices, and lost seventy more killed, and all their arms except sixty-nine muskets. Sixty-nine muskets for one hundred and forty men.

And some time during those two brief weeks, the Ross Pary who had been, died, and a new man was born out of the old. It started at Las Pozas, Ross thought, when he had had to climb out of the stream in which he had been bathing and fight the Spaniards with nothing but a revolver, lying naked in the dirt between two houses. Then he hadn't had time to be afraid, and afterwards it came to him that killing people who are bent upon killing you was a damnably easy thing to get used to.

And the second thing was the time that they had made a great circle after a friendly *hacendado* had taken them in and fed them and had come back to the place where they had left their wounded and the stragglers. They found them after the Spaniards had got through with them, spread-eagled upright between posts driven into the ground. The bones of their ribcages showed dull white where the skin of their backs had been. It had been taken off, inch by inch with a nine foot loaded lash — while they were yet alive, for the blood and pieces of flesh were spattered around them in a semicircle; and then the Spaniards had ripped open their bellies with their bayonets, so that the pink coils of their intestines trailed down into the dirt. And on the crosspieces and all around them in a circle the vultures perched, flapping their heavy wings and tearing at the bodies with their beaks. And when the wind shifted, there was the smell.

Ross had vomited up the good breakfast the *hacendado* had given him, but afterwards something had gone from him, too — something like gentleness, like compassion — and what had taken its place lay like a piece of iron at the core of his heart.

Yesterday, at Las Frices, he had discovered what it was like, this new thing that he had; he had made the acquaintance of the man he had become. He and the Metcalfes had stood under the mango trees and fired upon the charging Spaniards until finally they had no more ammunition. One of the Spaniards aimed a bayonet at Ross's belly, and Ross had turned aside like a bullfighter and brought the barrel of the Colt down across the man's arm, breaking it, and then he hit him across the head, and the Spaniard fell between him and the Metcalfes and all three of them smashed at his head with their gun butts until it didn't look like a head any more; then Henry Metcalfe spat on him. A month before, they had been civilized men.

And of Conchita Izquierdo — nothing — no word. The Spaniards had given him no time to search for her; and the people he had managed to ask stared at him blankly at the sound of her name. . . .

López got up now and raised his arms.

"Caballeros!" he said, "I want to ask your pardon — while we all are still alive."

Ross stared at him. Humility was not a trait that he had associated with Narciso López.

"I let my optimism blind me," López went on. "From talking to that good black, Pedro, who brought us back together, I've learned the magnitude of my errors. It seems that de la Concha had a group of fifty well trained agents in New Orleans, and fifteen in New York. Every report of victory that we received — every call for aid, came directly from his office. He wanted us to leave the States before General Gonzales and Governor Quitman were ready. He succeeded brilliantly — thanks to my stupidity. We came into Cuba expecting to be met by patriot armies. But those armies have been crushed and scattered, their leaders executed. Our mission has become hopeless.

Even the people are against us. The Captain-General has convinced them that we are Yankee Imperialistic pirates. . . ."

He bowed his massive head, his broad shoulders shaking.

"Upon my head," he whispered, "lies the guilt of all those who have died, and all those who will die — God forgive me!"

He stood still until he had mastered himself, then he faced them again.

"Now," he said, "we must try to reach the plain of San Cristóbal, and from there. . . ."

But a snarling mutter ran from man to man and cut him off.

"No!" they growled; "no gawddamned more marching. We've had a bellyful. It's safer here — out there, they'll shoot us down like rats!"

López looked at them.

"Caballeros," he said; "you have much right. I weep with you. You have borne yourselves like men and heroes, and now I cannot find it in my heart to blame you. Rest here, my children, and I will go down into the town and surrender myself, on condition that you be spared. *Adios, mis niños!* God be with you!"

He started off, but Ross Pary got up then and Henry Metcalfe got up with him and the two of them seized López' arms.

"No," Ross said; "not for us."

He turned toward the men to address them, but when he looked into their faces he saw that it was not necessary. They were all filled with shame, and some of them were crying.

"Hell," one Kentuckian growled, "who wants to die in bed, anyhow? We're with you, General."

The men roared a cheer, and they charged out of the wood and down into the plain where five hundred Spanish troops waited. They were like madmen, like demons — one hundred forty men without food and water, almost out of ammunition, with but sixty-nine muskets among them and no bayonets, charging an army.

The Spaniards broke under the first rush. Then they re-formed, deploying to the right and left, and opening up the middle, and through it came the cavalry. Ross and the others stood their ground screaming at the horsemen, but these were picked riders from Andalusia, and they came on with carbines and pistols and sabers, and thundered over the ragged little force in a cloud of red dust and came back again and after that there was nothing left for them to do. There were six men left alive, running for the hills: Narciso López, Henry Metcalfe, George Metcalfe, Lieutenant Van Vechten, Luis de Jiga Hernández, and Ross Pary.

They made it because the cavalrymen were too busy sabering the wounded. They pushed on until they came to the densest bamboo thicket they could find, and hid themselves in it. Nobody said anything. They lay on the ground and looked up at the sky through the leaves. The sky was very blue and clear and it was good to look at it. It reminded them of other skies over other places.

They rested for four hours and then went diagonally across the *manigua* and came out on the other side, but somehow in the darkness they had gradually turned so that instead of the sea only the plain lay before them, stretching out from the foothills of the sierras down toward the Southern Sea. They stood there looking at it, and a horseman came up to them and took off his sombrero and greeted them.

"I am Carlos Castenada," he said; "I would be honored if you would be my guests. I have no sympathy for our oppressors. Believe me, I shall hide you well."

"We have been betrayed before, Señor," López said tiredly, "by men who spoke as fair."

"Trust me, Caballero," Castenada said. "Within a week you shall reach the shore and a boat will be waiting. . . ."

López looked at the others. They shrugged. What difference did it make now?

They followed the Señor Castenada to his *hacienda*, and there they found a table spread before them. It was covered with rich foods and wines. All of the six started to eat at once — all except Ross Pary. He put his head down on the table and went to sleep at once without touching anything.

The servants stared at him.

"Señor —" they whispered; "the wine — he is not drinking the wine!"

"Señor General," Carlos Castenada protested; "the young blond one should be awakened. He has need of food — and wine."

"Let him sleep," López murmured; "he has more need of sleep."

Señor Castenada shrugged.

"Could he not be put to lie down?" Lieutenant Hernández asked.

"Assuredly," Castenada smiled. "Ramón and Rafael — put the young Señor *Rubio* to bed."

Ross did not awaken even when he was lifted in the strong arms of the two Negroes. They carried him into a large room, and laid him gently in one of the hammocks. Then they went away.

An hour later, the others came into the same room and saw him sleeping there.

"Poor fellow!" George Metcalfe yawned; "he's completely out."

"I could use some sleep myself," his brother muttered.

They lay down, then, all of them in the hammocks. Then, after some time, Ross heard dimly the sound of voices.

"Have care of the blond one," the voices whispered; "he did not drink the wine!"

He came awake at once, but he kept his eyes closed; gently he felt for his revolvers; but they were gone. Then he put his hand in his pocket, and it closed around the big pocketknife there. It was not too bad a weapon, considering the fact that its blade was eight inches long. Apparently the servants of the Señor Judas Iscariot Castenada had not considered it worth their while, or they had overlooked it. But how the devil was he going to get it open?

He opened his left eye a trifle on the side where the Negroes were. They had ropes and they were winding them around the unconscious forms in the hammocks. "Why in hellfire don't they wake up?" Ross thought; but then he knew. The wine. He alone had not drunk that wine. The others would not wake up. They couldn't.

Then Ramón and Rafael were coming toward him with the ropes. Ross held the knife open in his right hand. When they were close he lashed out all at once, and Rafael dropped the rope howling, and clapped his hands to a face that was slashed open from temple to the point of his chin. Ross rolled out of the hammock, and hit the floor on the side away from Ramón, landing on his hands and knees. Then he hurled himself under it and bore Ramón down; driving the knife into his belly the moment the black hit the floor. Then he was off, running through the door; but the moment he was outside he stopped. He had in the time he had been in Cuba developed a capacity for a kind of thinking he had never known existed before.

It was the natural thing for him to do to take to the woods. Castenada would expect that, and would seek for him there. So he wouldn't do the natural thing. Besides, what chance had he in the *manigua* armed with a pocketknife?

He doubled back at once, keeping his body flattened against the houses, until he had reached one of the stables. Inside it was cool and dark and smelled of wet hay and of horses. There was also a goodly supply of implements, including a row of *machetes* hanging along the wall in their scabbards. He took one down and felt its edge. He could have shaved with it. Then he went back deeper in the stable, and burrowed under some hay. There was a crack in the wall on that side, through which daylight showed. He inched over to it and looked out and then he saw the soldiers. They were bearing his friends away slung under poles like trussed pigs. There were more than a hundred men in the company. There was nothing he could do.

They moved off down the road and their commander came out of the house with Carlos Castenada. They walked straight toward the stable where Ross was, and a moment later he heard them enter.

"Here he is," Castenada said pleasantly; "the fastest horse ever foaled. I guarantee it, Cristóbal, he will come in ahead next Sunday by three full lengths."

"A noble beast," the Spanish captain said; "but about this *Americano* who escaped . . ."

"Do not preoccupy yourself, Cristóbal. He made for the bush — armed only with a knife. I would not preoccupy myself about him. In three days he will be dead of hunger, for he had not even the benefit of my excellent food today."

"Nor of your even more excellent wine," the captain grumbled. "Costa will be angry."

"That is your concern, Cristóbal. I care not for Costa who is a fat, obscene swine. Him and his music! The sexless dog fancies himself as an amateur of the arts — all of which he practices badly — except, perhaps, the art of breaking a man. But I have no interest in him. Now that this of the pirates and revolutionaries has been disposed of, I am interested only in Sunday's race. Come have another little *copa* of wine with me before you go."

"Gladly," Captain Cristóbal said, and they went out of the stable.

Ross lay very quietly under the hay until it was night. He was weak and sick with hunger; but he wouldn't give up. He had a score to settle first. He moved out of the stables and along the sides of the houses until he came to the *casa grande*. Through the window, he could see Castenada dining alone. He was being attended by a single aged Negro.

Ross circled around to the front of the house and pulled the door open. Castenada had no fears. He had not even locked the door. Ross walked very quietly into the salon and stood just behind the slim, elegant *hacendado*. Then the old Negro came out of the kitchen and saw him. The old black dropped the plate he was carrying with a terrible clatter, and fled with a speed astounding in one of his years.

Castenada turned in the big, high-backed chair, and his mouth came open, his jaw trembling foolishly. He put his hand down under his short Spanish waistcoat and came out with a pistol, but Ross brought the machete down sharply and the hand holding the pistol hung on to the rest of the arm by a single shred of flesh. Castenada stared at the blood pumping out from the stump of his arm, and his face grayed.

"Señor," he whispered, "Señor *Americano*, have mercy for the love of God!"

Then Ross cut him down.

He bent down and took the revolver and stuffed it into his belt. Then he sat down at the table.

"*Criado!*" he roared. "*Venga!*"

The old Negro came out of the kitchen, his face ashen with fear.

"Take this platter away, and bring another," Ross told him, "and bring me more wine!"

The old Negro did so, trembling.

Ross glanced down at Castenada's body.

"Drag this swine out of here, and mop the floor," he ordered. "He disturbs my appetite."

Half an hour later, full of good food and better wine, Ross Pary rode toward the *manigua* on the black stallion that was to have won the Sunday race. He was dressed in new trousers and boots, and was armed with a revolver, a carbine, and a *machete*. He could, he reckoned, hold out for a good, long time.

Chapter 13

The home of the González family was a pleasant place. It was on the outskirts of Havana, and was big and old-fashioned and comfortable under the shade of the ceiba trees, with the bougainvillaea bleeding dark purple over the sun-washed walls. It had a patio and fountains, and the sound of the fountains was like laughter. But to Conchita Izquierdo, sitting there on the patio, with María González, her friend, and holding the letter in her hand, there was no laughter.

"What says it — your letter?" María asked tensely.

"It says," Conchita said quietly, "that now I am twice damned."

"Twice?" María said. "This of your father's death — yes; but twice?"

"This letter," Conchita told her, her voice flat, calm, controlled, "was written by José the day after I left New Orleans. In it he tells me that the man I love, he without whom I have no more life — came to Cuba with the expedition — that perhaps now he is already one of the *damnificados* taken by the Spaniards. . . ."

"An *Americano*?"

"*Si,* an *Americano,*" Conchita breathed, "whom now I must seek even to the ends of Cuba. . . ."

"Conchita, you are mad!" María said. "Even to come back to Cuba was mad. And to seek one man, and he an *Americano* — *La Familia Santíssima!* You are mad!"

"*Si.* Yes, María, I am mad."

"Everyone knows the history of your father now. He is of the heroes, even of the Saints. But his daughter cannot live in Cuba. The Spaniards will take her and ravish her first, because she is beautiful, and afterwards they will torture her to death. My Conchita, dearest Conchita, heart of my heart, you must go!"

Conchita smiled.

"The mad," she said, "have not wit enough to flee."

"No," the deep male voice said from the doorway; "but I have wit enough to send her away before she brings disaster upon my house!"

Conchita turned and saw Enrique González standing there — a handsome mulatto. His dark face was flushed with passion.

"I do not know, Señorita," he said, "whether your father had right or wrong beliefs. It is sufficient that he has died for them. But I do know that I don't propose to die for harboring his daughter — nor to have my wife and child turned over to those beasts who walk upright in uniform. You have returned to Cuba; and that is your affair. But the safety of my own is my affair. I cannot permit you to place us in jeopardy, Señorita, for all that your father was my friend."

Conchita got up quietly, and picked up her shawl of white lace.

"At your orders, Señor González," she said.

"Oh, Papa," María began.

"Silence!" Enrique said. "I have much sorrow because of this, Señorita Izquierdo — and also much shame. But I cannot do otherwise. María and her mother are very dear to me. I think you understand that. . . ."

"I do," Conchita whispered; "oh, I do!"

"Therefore I have comprehension of the love your father bore you. For his sake Señorita — for his sainted memory — leave this land!"

"I cannot," Conchita said.

"I overheard my daughter say something of

an *Americano*. Doubtless this is a thing of love?"

"Yes," Conchita said. "Enormously."

"Then have I both pain and sorrow to tell you this: the Americans have all been captured. The Señor de Rey, Brigadier of the Plaza, has been ordered to shoot them — today."

Conchita stood still. María got up from where she sat and slipped an arm about her waist; but Conchita did not move.

"Conchita!" María cried; "Conchita *mía!*"

"You understand this which I have said?" Enrique asked gruffly.

María could feel her body loosening. It took a long time; but finally all of the stiffness went out of her, and after that she started to breathe again.

"Yes," she said; "I understand."

"You must go," Enrique said heavily.

"At what hour occurs the — the shooting?" Conchita shuddered.

"At noon. But you must not go there! It will be a very bad thing to watch and additionally there exists the danger that you might be recognized and . . ."

"What serves it now — this danger?" Conchita said.

"You are young," Enrique said; "there will be other loves."

"No," Conchita said, "there will be no other loves. This day I shall make sure of that."

"You'd die because of him?" María asked wonderingly. "Oh, Conchita — no!"

"Yes," Conchita said. "Or say rather that I would not live without him. I cannot, María *mía*."

"Then he must be — much," María said softly.

"Enormous, immense, formidable," Conchita said.

"Tell me about him," Maria said.

"He is a *rubio* — a blond, with hair like the sunlight on the *playa*, and eyes like the sea far out away from the shores. He is tall and thin and his face is serious. His eyes haunt you with sadness, and his voice is like music. He is very gentle and of all kindness and of a goodness so great that sometimes I have wished it were not so. I don't think he would knowingly hurt anything that lived. He came on this expedition to seek for me because of my madness in coming here. So, María *mía*, if he dies, I have killed him. You'd have me live on, knowing that?"

"You love him," Enrique said, "yet you could watch him die?"

"Yes. That I am certain of his death would be a relief. And then perhaps I could even save him. I could make a diversion that might enable him to escape."

"But you would die!" María wept. "You'd die – terribly!"

"So?" Conchita said.

"Father!" María cried; "You must not let her go! We must hide her – we must send her away. . . ."

"*Adios*," Conchita said, and slipped rapidly through the gate.

It was very hot in the Plaza and there was no wind. The people stood elbow to elbow, close-packed, sweating. The light was very hard and clear, and no cloud stood in the sky. And it came to Conchita then that she had always been happiest when it rained. She had the feeling that to die at all was a hard thing but to die on a day of great beauty under a crystalline sky in the full blaze of a noonday sun was a harder thing; but the bugles cried out all at once, and there was the roll of drums and she stopped thinking altogether.

Conchita saw them leading them out, fifty-two dirty, ragged men. She leaned forward, scrutinizing their faces carefully, until they had all marched past the place where she stood, and then she straightened up, for among the fifty-two men was no one who even resembled Ross Pary.

Then the officer of the day read the charges

against them, but Conchita did not listen. And the bugles cried once more and the drums rolled, and the sunlight pointed up the spotless uniforms. The Spaniards knew how to make a brave ceremony out of a man's helpless dying.

Conchita wandered through the streets of Havana until it was night. Then she went into a cemetery and lay down on a grave and slept. It was, considering the superstitious fears of the populace and the soldiery alike, the safest place for her to be.

The next day she went into a clothing store and purchased a riding habit for a quite mythical younger brother. She bought also a revolver and ammunition for it, and a small dagger, which she wore in a sheath next to her skin. Then she walked for five hours until she came to the *finca* of some friends of her father's, and there she hid in a canebrake until nightfall. After it was dark, she stripped herself and put on the riding habit, and the sombrero which she had also bought, and then she went into the stables and stole a horse, complete with saddle and bridle. To have asked for it, or to have tried to buy it would have been too dangerous.

She rode deep into the *manigua* and waited there until daylight in order to get her bearings. At daylight, she was off again, riding deep into the jungle until she came to a group of thatched *bohios* — the little houses of the poor. The people, who were all Negroes, came out of the houses, and stared at her, and then they were all around her, kissing her hands and crying; for these were the blacks that her father had liberated at the cost, finally, of his life.

Conchita got down from her horse and went with them into one of the houses and they brought her food and rum and water, and sat around her on the floor and watched her while she ate. She sat back after a time, sighing.

"The strangers who came to set Cuba free," she asked; "have you heard anything of them?"

A tall black named Pedro stood up.

"I guided them to safety near Las Pozas," he said; "but afterwards they were all taken or killed. Yesterday in Havana . . ."

"I know," Conchita said; "I was in Havana yesterday. I saw them killed. They died with enormous bravery. But not those — there were others. Know you, Pedro, anything of a young man with hair like gold? A tall man, thin, with a serious face that smiles but seldom. Know you of him?"

"*Si!*" Pedro said. "I spoke with him! Of them all he was the only one who spoke Spanish! He required of me proof of my truthfulness, and I showed him the scars upon my back."

Conchita leaned forward, her eyes filled with light.

"What of him, Pedro? What of him?"

"Dead or taken, I think. Tomorrow you can discover for yourself, Señorita. The last of them were captured upon the *finca* of that man of enormous evil, Señor Castenada, who gave them drugged wine. It is believed that one of them killed this *hacendado* before the drugs took hold. At any rate, they are to be brought into Havana tomorrow. If you like, Dona Conchita, I will go into Havana for you and discover whether —"

"No," Conchita said; "I shall go myself."

"But," one of the women protested, "what if they should recognize you? After that of Nuevitas, your life would not be worth a *centavo!*"

"I will wear one of your dresses," Conchita said, "and a turban upon my head, so that they see not the redness of my hair. I am nearly as dark as a mulatta now; and you shall stain my skin ever darker."

"What of your eyes, Señorita? Think you they will believe that any mulatta has eyes as green as shoal water?"

"Yes. I know some with blue eyes, even. The greenness of my eyes will not preoccupy them. Yes, yes — I shall go!"

"And afterwards?" Pedro said.

"If he is alive, we shall save him, and he shall be my husband, for I love him much. If he is dead, we shall avenge him — him and my father."

The Negroes looked at her wonderingly.

"But how, Señorita?" Pedro asked. "There are many and we are few. And they have guns — many guns. How could we harm the Spaniards?"

"We shall not fight them, Pedro. But in the night we will raid them while they sleep. We shall set many fires and burn their barracks. We will take from them the guns and bullets that we need. And we shall kill an officer here and another there — men like Don Juan Costa, and Percher and del Piso and Ballo. . . ."

"Good!" Pedro said and Conchita could see the other blacks nodding grimly as she mentioned the names of the most rabid Negro baiters among the Spanish officers.

"Perhaps we shall die," she said; "I do not know. Therefore I want only such men with me as are willing to come, and those who will fight for a free tomorrow for their children expecting nothing themselves."

"There is one thing more, Dona Conchita," Pedro said; "you must get a few white men to join us, and mulattoes, too, if they will. Else it will be said that this is a revolt of the blacks, merely, and all over Cuba our people will suffer. When we strike, we must strike as Cubans, not as black men or white men or mixed breeds. This is a very necessary thing, I think."

"Yes," Conchita said; "it is. I will try, Pedro. Now, if you will forgive me, I have much weariness, and must lie down. You have here an additional hammock, Isabella?"

"Yes," the woman said; "come with me, Señorita."

They brought Narciso López, and the two Metcalfes, and Lieutenant Hernández, and Lieutenant Van Vechten into Havana in the morning. They marched them along the Prado toward Morro Castle, and all the people who could reach them, struck at them with bamboo sticks, or kicked them, and spat into their faces and hurled rotten fruit and lumps of animal dung upon them. Their guards made no move to interfere. Long before they reached the Castle they were too tired to walk, and husky infantrymen flanked them on both sides and bore them up by the armpits, their bare toes dragging in the dust.

When they were within a hundred yards of the gate, a slim mulatta ran out of the crowd and slapped George Metcalfe across the face, hard. He reeled back and the guards turned him loose, grinning, while the mulatta slapped him right and left, and right again, and all the people laughed. Then the girl fastened her fingers about his throat and began to strangle him, her face contorted with fury. She thrust her face very close to his, swearing loudly in Spanish, but George realized suddenly that her fingers moved very lightly over his throat without really tightening and between the explosive Spanish oaths she was murmuring over and over again quick English words:

"Where is he, George? Where is my Ross? Tell me where? *Carramba! Hijo de la puta grande!* Where?"

Then George Metcalfe saw the green eyes staring at him out of the bronzed face, and a wisp of the reddish-brown hair that had escaped the turban, and with great control he kept his face impassive and murmured through lips that scarcely moved:

"Escaped – into the woods. Hit me again, Conchita."

She struck him with her closed fist against the mouth so hard that his lips cracked against his teeth, and the blood came out of the corner and trickled down his chin. He staggered from the impact, and no pretense was necessary. His guards took his arms again and grinned at Conchita, saying:

"A sufficiency, little one! Let us take care of him. And afterwards you can reward us – with kisses perhaps – or even something more. Where do you live, little *Morena?* We have much free time. . . ."

But Conchita was off, running through the crowds, and George Metcalfe had the questionable comfort of seeing, just before she went, that her green eyes were glazed with tears.

They marched Ross Pary through the brush toward the road, the ones who had captured him, and every time he stumbled, out of pure exhaustion, they prodded him with the bayonets. He was asleep on his feet. They had killed the horse a week ago, and from that time until now, he had not been able to lie down for more than five minutes. He had circled through the *manigua*, doubling back on his trail, never daring to stop, hearing the sound of his pursuers all around him in the darkness. His food had given out three days ago, and yesterday the last of his water. He had thrown away his carbine as a useless encumbrance.

They had taken him without a fight, finding him lying in a thicket unconscious from hunger and thirst and fatigue.

A Spanish soldier, Ross thought bitterly, can wake the dead when he puts his mind to it. . . .

It seemed that the march through the *manigua* would never end, and quite suddenly, he went down on his face and could not get up, and they were beating him, and then they stopped beating him and were shooting into the brush, and then the shooting stopped and they weren't there any more — that is, except the ones who were dead.

Then Ross felt his head being lifted very tenderly, and he turned his face sidewise, and great masses of red-brown hair tumbled down around him, and he was looking up into eyes as green as a tropic sea.

"Ross," Conchita murmured; "oh, Ross *mio* — *mi alma*, Oh Sacred Mother of God, I have no words!"

Then she bent down her head and kissed his mouth and all the blacks stood around them in a circle, grinning.

"Conchita," Ross said thickly, "my little Conchita. . . ." Then he felt himself going out, and strong hands came out of the darkness on both sides of him and lifted him upright and after a time his vision cleared.

Conchita was smiling at him, but at the same time, her face was wet with tears.

"Almost I have killed you, my own," she said, "with this madness of sending you here. But now I have you again and you are safe. . . ." She put both arms around his waist and clung to him, fiercely.

"I shall never send you away from me again," she said; "never, never, never!"

The Negroes held his arms and half led, half carried him over to the horse. He felt himself being lifted across the animal's back, then all the lights went out suddenly and stayed out for a long time.

When he awoke, he was in a little hut, and Conchita was bathing his face. Outside a fire had been made, and from simmering pots came a variety of good smells.

"How thin you are, my Ross," Conchita said gently. "You have starved and that too is my fault, because there are so many things I should have taught you. A man can live in the Cuban brush from the palm tree alone. The heart of the palm is both edible and good."

"I ate bananas," Ross said; "I'm sick of them."

Conchita kissed him quickly and got up and ran to the door. A few minutes later black Isabella came in with yucca, malanga, yams, oranges, squash, corn, fried plantains, and the milk of the cocoanut served in its own shell.

There was also a stew of a kind of meat that Ross had never tasted before. But it was very good and he ate it all.

"What is this?" he asked Conchita, as he put the bowl down empty.

"*Jutía,*" Conchita said.

"*Jutía?*" Ross echoed blankly.

"A kind of a rat," she said calmly. "It is good, no?"

Ross gulped; then he straightened up, grinning.

"Yes," he said; "it is good."

Then he started to eat the other things, but long before he had finished, he had fallen asleep again, his head bowed down upon the rude table. Conchita called two of the Negroes and they carried him over to the thick straw floor mat. Then they went out, smiling.

After they had gone, Conchita took off her boots and her jacket and lay down beside him, pillowing his bearded head upon her arm. She lay like that all night holding him gently, tenderly so as not to awaken him. Then in the morning she got up and went down and bathed in the stream and when she came back again, he was awake — really awake.

She knelt beside the mat and kissed him. She knelt there a long time holding his face between her two hands.

"My Ross," she said.

Ross smiled at her.

"We've got to go, Conchita," he said. "I have some money — maybe we could get one of the fishing boats to smuggle us over to Florida and. . . ."

"No," Conchita said.

"No?" Ross echoed wonderingly.

"Many Americans are alive and prisoners. We must try to save them. Yesterday they shot Colonel Crittenden and fifty-two others; but I don't think they dare shoot any more now. The American Consul in Havana has told de la Concha it might mean war. But they will imprison them. That is worse. Shooting would be much kinder."

"I see," Ross said.

"Your friends George and Henry Metcalfe are among the prisoners. George told me of your escape. Additionally there is the matter of the men who have lived too long now — like the fat one, Juan Costa, and del Piso, and Percher. It was the men of Costa who — who —"

"The scars?" Ross whispered.

"Yes."

"Then I'll stay," Ross said. "It's madness; but, as you say — those men have lived too long."

"Good," Conchita said. "Then afterwards,

we will go back to America — if we live."

"If we live," Ross said. "Conchita . . ."

"Yes, my own?"

"You were here last night, weren't you. Here in this *bohío* I mean."

"Yes," she said smiling, "and also in thy bed, my Ross. But you had greater need of sleep than of me."

"I'm sorry," Ross said. "I was so blamed tired that . . ."

"Do not preoccupy yourself, my heart; there will be other nights. Now, get up."

Ross looked at her, and a little light showed in his blue eyes.

"Instead of my getting up," he said, "suppose you —"

"No!" Conchita laughed.

"Why not?"

"There is no time. You and I, my soul, must go down to Havana today."

"Havana!" Ross said.

"Yes. There is a danger; but it is not great. You shall shave off that glorious yellow beard of yours, and the Negro women will stain your body brown with a kind of berry. We shall mingle oil and soot in your hair. Then we will go."

"But," Ross protested, "why must we go to Havana?"

"For news. It is said that they will dispose of General López today. It is necessary for us to know whether or not they will kill the Americans, too. If they do — then we must go to Florida at once and make such an outcry that there will be war. In such a fashion will Cuba be freed of Spain."

Ross stood up, smiling. He was surprised at how strong he felt.

"Very well," he said; "you can start to tarbrush me."

"I'll call the women," Conchita said.

"No!" Ross said — "Not unless my face and neck and arms and legs will be enough."

"Then I will do it. There is danger of your clothing being torn in the crowds, since we must dress very poorly. Additionally, should the Spaniards become suspicious, the disguise must be good and complete . . ."

"But, Conchita . . ."

"Silly one! There was a time once when you turned on a lamp, remember, because I had shame of my body. And I am ugly and scarred, while you are of surpassing handsomeness and very fine. Come! We shall go down to the stream and you will wash yourself, and afterwards we will come back here and make mulattoes of each other. It should be diverting, no?"

It should, Ross thought, be damned diverting.

It was. They came back to the hut and Isabella brought an earthen pot full of a thick brown liquid. They took off their clothing and smeared it all over each other, laughing like children. It was very amusing, and there in the clear morning sunlight that poured into the *bohío* through every crack, it was also curiously innocent. Ross had a feeling that he didn't want to spoil it. He turned to put on the ragged clothing that one of the Negroes had loaned him.

"No," Conchita said.

Ross turned back to her, and put out his arms.

"Nor that, my amorous one! It is only that it has not dried and will come off on the clothing. Also it will come off on me, and upon you, if you take me in your arms. Have patience — there will be a moon this big, tonight, and you will have no need of sleeping."

"I think," Ross said, "that I never want to sleep again."

The Spaniards strangled Narciso López in the public square opposite Morro Castle. And Ross and Conchita saw it. Narciso López died bravely; but it was not a pleasant thing to watch.

That night there was a moon that filled half the sky. It silvered the feathery leaves of the bamboo, and etched the royal palms blackly against the night. The little *bohíos* lay in the path of its whiteness, and between them, the Negro Pedro strummed a guitar and sang.

Conchita lay in Ross's arms, with her face pressed softly against the hollow of his throat. But Ross neither spoke nor moved.

"What ails thee, my Ross?" she whispered.

"I cannot," Ross said. "God help me, I can't. Not after today. I keep seeing him. It makes a sickness in me, little Conchita — it makes a debility of a most formidable nature."

"So?" she said. "I have much sorrow of that, my Ross. We have been too long apart. But do not preoccupy yourself. Come — let us go out and Pedro will sing to us. . . ."

They got up from the straw mat and went out into the darkness. Pedro saw them coming and smiled, showing his strong white teeth in the moonlight.

"Play, Pedro!" Conchita said. "Play us something gay!"

The lean, black fingers caressed the strings. Ross listened, frowning, Pedro was a natural musician — a master of his instrument. Ross sat down on the trunk of a fallen palm with Conchita by his side, and rested his chin on the palm of his hand, listening. Something in the music stirred him, a strange, half expressed theme. He kept waiting for Pedro to repeat it, but the Negro never did. It must have been, Ross decided, an accidental combination of notes improvised on the spur of the moment. How had it gone, now? He hummed the sounds over quietly, and excitement began to rise in him, sudden and strong. This was it — this was the thing he had wanted to do for Conchita.

"Conchita," he said; "get me something on which to write!"

"But, Ross," she said; "there is nothing, and besides why do you wish to write now?"

Ross didn't answer her. He got up from his seat and picked up a charred stick from out of the embers of the fire; then he went to a tree, and slashed off a strip of the bark with his knife. Swiftly he ruled in the lines, and then he wrote the notes, slowly, humming them to himself, erasing them with a bit of his ragged shirt, and writing them in again. Conchita leaned against his shoulder watching him with wondering eyes.

Ross studied the music he had written, then he gave it to Pedro.

"Here," he said, "play this."

Pedro stared at the music, blankly.

"I have sorrow, Señor," he said sadly; "but I cannot read."

Conchita took the piece of bark from his hand and studied it in the moonlight.

"But I can," she breathed; "I can — and this is beautiful!"

"It is for you," Ross said. "It is you — the way you are to me."

"Pedro, Pedro!" Conchita cried. "Listen — listen carefully!" Then she began to sing the notes, her voice flutelike and clear. She trilled them, birdlike, until the glissandos were like spring water running warm under a summer sun. She sang it all the way through, holding the last note, sending it soaring up high and clear and sweet.

"Now, Pedro," she said breathlessly, "play that!"

"Can't, Dona Conchita," Pedro groaned; "nobody could play that!"

"Yes, yes, yes! Play it! It goes so — listen, oh head of formidable thickness! Listen — hear it in your heart, like I hear it, oh, Pedro — please!"

She repeated the theme, singing the la-la-la's, so slowly that Pedro's fingers could follow them on the strings. Then after a time, he had them and began to play, his black face taut with the effort, then he loosened and the music came out free, warm with tropic sun, and the white wash of seas upon the silver *playa*, and the wind singing in the ceibas, and the smell of bougainvillaea and frangipani, above all the sun — it was drenched in sun, that music, Cuban sun of a clarity and brilliance unmatched anywhere else on earth.

Conchita scampered like a child halfway up the trunk of the fallen tree that lay inclined against two others. Then she soared out and up in a gigantic leap that was like flying, her skirt whirling out from her perfect legs. She touched the earth, weightlessly, and pirouetted, her arms and hands sculpturing the air. She had said she was a dancer, and Ross saw now what a dancer was.

Not like Morgan, whose dancing was a kind of somnolence, a subconscious expression of the dark forces within her. No, not like that. Conchita came alive when she danced. She was lifted out of herself, became more than herself. Even the crude cotton blouse and skirt she wore became things of beauty, shaping figures, brief arabesques in the moonlight, endowed with plasticity, fluidity, life. And her body, moving, stopped Ross's breath. Her small feet stamped the earth, flamenco fashion, her hands played *maracas*, so clearly that Ross could hear them. Her face was frowning, ecstatic, the music flowed around her, into her. Her body melted into the music, became one with it, so that there was no break between the warm flesh moving and the singing, rhythmic line.

Pedro grinned at her happily, his black fingers miracles upon the strings. And Ross Pary sat upon the palm trunk and looked at her, feeling her beauty stabbing into him so that even to watch her was the essence of exquisite pain.

She broke it at last with a grand *jeté* out of the classic ballet, and fell into his arms, breathless and sobbing. Ross lifted her into his arms and started back to the *bohío*.

"Good night, Pedro," he called; "many, many thanks!"

"Of nothing!" Pedro laughed. "God grant you a son!"

Ross shouldered open the door of the *bohío* and went inside into the dark. "This of the weakness," Conchita whispered; "it is gone now, is it not, my Ross?"

"Yes," Ross said, "all gone."

"Good! Now kiss me with all the kisses of your life of yesterday and today and tomorrow that I do not die now of too much feeling, Oh Ross, Ross, Ross!"

Outside in the clearing, black Pedro picked up his guitar and walked very close to the wall of the little *bohío*. Then he settled himself down comfortably on the earth and began to play the Dance of Conchita. He played it over and over again, inventing many piquant variations on the theme. He played it tirelessly, all night long.

And all night long they heard it, and blessed him in their hearts.

It went very well at first, before it started to go badly. For a time there was hope among patriots that Conchita Izquierdo and her blond *Americano* and their savage horde of black *machete* fighters would be able to accomplish what López had failed to. But when it started to go badly, it went all at once and in every direction at the same time. The Spaniards planted a treacherous black among them, and upon the very next raid, they lost all but ten of the Negroes and all three of the young Trigueños – wheat-colored ones, as the Cubans call white men – who had joined them.

And Juan Costa called Miguel de la Mancha, a favorite of his, a man without heart or fear or conscience, to direct the hunt.

Thereafter, they did not know a moment's rest. They moved through the *manigua* day and night, never daring to stop, until they dropped in their tracks from fatigue. The disguising stain had faded out, but that was the least of their troubles. When a man fell, they had to leave him, and afterwards they would find him spread-eagled between the posts furnishing food for the vultures.

They lay in a thorn thicket, Conchita and Ross and Pedro and three other blacks, all that were left now; and down below they could see a little church on the edge of the wood. Conchita gripped Ross's hand fiercely.

"Look at the *iglesia*," she whispered. "Ross —"

"Yes, Conchita?"

"We have had much joy of each other, which was a sin. I cannot regret it truly, but we are going to die now. I want to be your wife. It would sweeten the dying, knowing that I was yours in the sight of God and man."

"I have wanted that for a long time," Ross said.

"Then we will go down there. Padre Antonio Ferrer, the priest, is an old friend of my father's. . . ."

"Won't it be complicated?" Ross said. "After all, I'm not Catholic and —"

"Padre Antonio will understand that there is no time. We will do everything at once, the Instructions and the Baptism and the Sacrament of marriage. . . ."

"And Extreme Unction," Pedro said drily.

"That too," Conchita whispered; "but I do

not mind this of the dying any longer, as long as I die in your arms."

They got up out of the thicket and walked single file down to the church. The old priest greeted them with grave courtesy, and Conchita told him what they wanted of him.

"There is much that is irregular here," he mused; "how am I to know if the conversion is sincere?"

"A man about to die does not lie," Ross said tartly.

"That's true, but I have doubts that such a marriage as this would bear the scrutiny of my superiors."

"*Padre mío,*" Conchita burst out, "would you do the will of your superiors or of God? We have been in sin. If you refuse us we will live still in sin, and thus will we die. Have you no concern for our souls? Are the rules of the Church more important? What serves a mountain of dogma now to us who must die within a space of hours?"

The old priest stared at her.

"Irregular or not, it is right," he said half to himself. "Come, my son — we have much work to do."

Half an hour later, Ross had been baptized and confessed. It was, he thought wryly, an all-time record for such proceedings. Then

Conchita came out of the confessional box, her face radiant. They knelt before Padre Antonio, and he began the ceremony. But when he came to the rings, they both looked at each other, aghast. Neither of them possessed any.

But Pedro stepped forward, a handful of gold rings in his palm. Among this great selection they had no difficulty finding one that fitted each of them. And Padre Antonio was too wise and too kindly to ask Pedro where he had gotten them.

Then Ross Pary kissed his bride, and they came out of the church in the sunlight and saw the horsemen riding toward them with Miguel de la Mancha at their head.

They ran for the trees, firing, and Ross and Conchita and Pedro made it, but the other three Negroes had the good fortune to be killed instantly by the Spanish carbines.

Those Negroes, Ross thought, are better off than we. They died very quickly and without much pain. And I, God help me, am going to have to kill Conchita so that they don't get their filthy hands upon her again. Then it'll be my turn because I couldn't stand the tortures. That leaves Pedro. Poor devil, I wonder what'll happen to him?

They circled through the *manigua* all night, and all night long there was the sound of horses. But so far, the Spaniards had not brought the dogs up and until they did that, the three of them had a chance.

Just before morning they approached a clearing, and the wind brought over the smell of a fire. They crept close to the edge, and Ross saw a grossly fat man surrounded by five soldiers, eating heartily from a pot that hung over the fire.

Conchita's nails bit into the flesh of his arms.

Ross turned to her.

"Don Juan Costa," she whispered, "the cruelest of them all. And that way is the only way out of here. We cannot go back, because others of them are behind us. . . . This is the termination of it, my Ross. Now kiss me quickly and — and see that I am not taken — by them. . . ."

Ross made a sound in his throat that was like the growl of an animal.

"Here," he said to Pedro, "keep her here. I shall return."

"No!" Conchita begged. "No, my Ross, no!"

But Ross was down on his belly, crawling through the brush, the *machete* held in his teeth. When he was close enough, he sprang into the clearing, and brought his *machete* down the front of one of the soldiers, opening him from breast to navel, and whirling, he cut down two more in half a heartbeat, and met the others rising, and gave one of them the point in the belly and brought the blade sidewise across the throat of the other and rested there panting, watching the life pump out of them, ignoring Juan Costa, which was a mistake for that mountain of a man got ponderously to his feet and brought the barrel of a pistol crashing down upon Ross's head.

The blow did not land solidly but it was enough to stun Ross. He lay on the ground watching the tiny feet of the fat officer approaching. Then he lunged forward, catching Costa's knees, bringing him down.

Ross was off then, scurrying through the brush until he came to the place where he had left Conchita and Pedro. They were not there. The ground was torn with the hoof prints of many horses, and Pedro and Conchita were gone. Ross stared at the prints; then, slowly, his knees buckled under him, and he put his face down in the mud and cried.

He got up after a time and marched out of the *manigua*, straight for the town of Matanzas, which was closest to them, and where, doubtless, his wife and his comrade had been taken. He walked very slowly and tiredly under the guasima and algaroba trees, until he had almost reached the town. Then he saw the horsemen resting, and Miguel de la Mancha holding Conchita in his arms and laughing at her frenzied efforts to escape.

Ross got the revolver out and came forward firing, still walking at the same slow pace. One of the horsemen dropped and the Negro, Pedro, seeing his chance, dashed out and away from them and two of them started after him, and Ross dropped them both within three feet of each other. Then Don Miguel roared out an order, and the cavalrymen surged forward, and swarmed all over him, beating him with their gun butts and the flats of their sabers; because the last thing Miguel de la Mancha had said was:

"Take him alive!"

Through the rain of blows he could hear Conchita's voice screaming: "Do not kill him! Have mercy Caballeros, for the love of God!" Then a sunburst of lights exploded inside his head and he pitched headlong into absolute darkness.

De la Mancha stared at Conchita and smiled.

"You have much interest in this tawny one, don't you?" he said.

"He is my husband," Conchita said.

"So?" Miguel laughed; "I have always heard that widows make the most interesting of companions. Enough, Caballeros! We must not cheat the Señor *Rubio* of the opportunity for a heroic death."

"Beast!" Conchita spat. "Dog and offspring of a dog! Do you think to gain anything of me by killing him?"

"The Señora is then disposed to bargain?" Miguel suggested.

"No! Kill him and be damned. He would not have his life bargained for."

Miguel shrugged.

"As you will, little dove," he said. "It is scarcely likely that I could save his life in any event. The Señor Colonel Juan Costa has some interest in the matter. Besides, I return to Spain this week. It would give me much pleasure to take so beautiful and spirited a companion as you back with me. . . ."

"No!" Conchita said.

"There remains the fact that your husband will die. I might be able to persuade Don Juan to commit you to my tender care. It would be a better fate than being executed yourself — after having furnished some sport for the soldiery. . . ."

Conchita stared at him.

"Think you," she said scornfully, "that I care what happens to me after he is dead? Think you I'd even want to live?"

Miguel de la Mancha looked at Ross's unconscious figure.

"Strange," he said mockingly; "this thin, pale one with so little of manliness about him — and you have for him so great a love."

"He is a thousand times the man of any of you!" Conchita said.

"That will be seen," Miguel smiled. "Don Juan Costa has ways of testing the courage of any man."

Conchita looked at him and all the color drained slowly out of her face.

"No," she whispered. "Oh, no, no, no!"

"I think he will die quite badly," Miguel said. "These thin, aesthetic ones usually do. In ten minutes, I'll wager, he'll beg the Señor Colonel for his life. In twelve, for a more merciful death." Miguel shrugged his broad shoulders eloquently "But all that, of course, is up to the Señora."

"Up to me? How?"

"Men sometimes grow careless," de la Mancha said. "It is possible that the thin blond one might never reach the Señor Colonel. He might — escape."

"How? Unconscious as he is — beaten already half to death, how could he escape, Señor Captain?"

"He might revive. The soldiers might be pre-occupied with other matters on the edge of a wood, say. . . . These possibilities exist — if the so lovely Señora could find it in her heart to be a little more kindly disposed toward her humble admirer. . . ."

"I see," Conchita said.

"Of course, Don Juan will be terribly angry with me. But then I am already ordered back to Spain, so his wrath would serve him but little. And this poor devil of a husband of yours has so little flesh upon his back — it could be removed with so much facility. A few brief strokes and then. . . ."

"No!" Conchita shuddered. "Please, Señor Captain, no!"

"Then the Señora sees the reasonableness of my point of view?"

"Nor that. When he is dead and I am alone, what is to prevent the Señor Captain from summoning five soldiers — one to bind my skirts over my head, two to hold my feet apart, and two to hold my hands — arts at which Spanish caballeros are wondrously expert?"

Miguel stared at her.

"A certain repugnance at such methods," he said gently. "A faint hope that the Señora's gratitude toward me for saving her husband will ripen in time into something deeper and more lasting. The fact that the Señora's beauty and spirit have awakened in me a deeper emotion than I have ever felt before. . . . I want no weeping, ravished girl in my bed. Such are the methods of men who cannot prevail by the gifts the good God gave them. They dishonor a man. They are an admission of a certain lack, of a certain failure. . . ."

"I see," Conchita said; "your sentiments do you much honor, Señor Captain. But what proof have I that you will actually do what you say? Promises are such empty things."

De la Mancha whirled.

"José!" he barked; "Juan — Enrique! Take the *Americano* and place him gently in that thicket. Give him back his weapons and leave him there!"

The soldiers stared at him in astonishment.

"I gave you an order," Miguel de la Mancha said.

Conchita looked at him, and her green eyes misted over with tears.

"Very well, Caballero," she said brokenly; "I will go with you to Spain. . . ."

It was dark in the thicket, and the mosquitos came down in clouds. Ross sat there dully, not even trying to slap them away. His head ached damnably, and his body was one long bruise. He was trying to think, but his mind refused to work in orderly patterns. He was unsure of what was real any more, and what was imagined or dreamed.

He had come down the road under the algaroba trees, and had seen the Spanish soldiers. That much he remembered. But after that? He strained his mind, trying to force the mental picture into focus. One of the soldiers had had Conchita in his arms. She had been fighting him, and then he, Ross had started shooting.

That was all he remembered. There had been many of the Spanish horsemen — so many. Then what the devil was he doing here alive and free? Had they killed him? That wasn't possible, because no dead man's body could ache the way his did now. . . .

Snatches of it: Pedro running away, and the Spaniards falling. The men charging toward him. Then they had started hitting him and . . .

And they had thought him dead. That accounted for it. But why then hadn't they taken away his gun? And what was he doing here instead of out on the road where it had happened? His head ached so. . . .

But his mind was clearing. He didn't want it to clear. In a little while, he was going to be able to think, to remember something that he ought not to think about, dared not remember.

A moment later, he knew what it was: Conchita.

He hadn't been able to free her. By now she must be in the barracks of the cavalrymen. By now, by now — sweet Infant Jesus — now . . . He put his face down and vomited, but the sickness didn't leave him.

Why had they left him alive? Mother of God, why? What was it to live, remembering — this? His right hand, moving, brushed against the butt of his revolver. Without conscious thought, without any hesitation at all, he took it out, thrust the muzzle into his mouth and jerked the trigger. The hammer crashed against the empty chamber, and he remembered that he had emptied it, firing at the Spaniards.

He took the cartridges out of his belt and began to reload, but he never finished the task, for a company of Spanish infantrymen came through the brush with fat Juan Costa at their head.

"There he is!" one of them cried; "just where Captain de la Mancha said we'd find him!"

They started toward him at a rush, and Ross stood up quietly and waited, letting his revolver fall to the ground at his feet. Capture by the Spaniards was just as effective as a bullet through the brain. A little slower, perhaps, but just as effective.

"So," Juan Costa said, "the Señor *Americano* accepts our hospitality. That is good of him. I can assure him that he will not lack for entertainment."

Ross didn't answer. Words, now, were a luxury he couldn't afford.

They took him into their barracks, and through them toward a little building of stone. Don Juan unlocked the door, and strong arms propelled him inside, then four or five of them, including the fat Colonel, himself, came in with him. And the moment they were inside, it began.

They threw him down face forward on the floor, and Ross saw a big Spaniard uncoil the whip. I won't cry, Ross thought. I won't! I won't!

But he did. His head thrashed back and forth on the column of his neck and he lay there moaning and sobbing and retching with the terrible spasms of emptiness.

To occupy his mind, to hold himself against the surrender they wanted of him, he tried counting the strokes. But when they reached twenty, he fainted.

When he came back again, he was lying face upward on a table, and they were pouring water into his eyes and mouth.

"Ah!" Juan Costa murmured; "the Caballero

rejoins us! What a pretty boy he is!" Then he stretched out his fat hand and stroked Ross ever so gently upon the cheek.

"Dog!" Ross spat at him, "keep your filthy paws off me!"

"How discourteous," Juan Costa sighed. "I assure you, Caballero, my hands are quite clean. I take good care of them. The ointments which insure their smoothness come all the way from Arabia. . . ."

"Sexless dog!" Ross screamed at him. "Half woman!"

Juan Costa giggled, a high senseless sound.

"You speak Spanish well, Caballero," he said; "but your choice of words is — unfortunate. Now you have offended me. I don't like being offended. Ramón — get me a bayonet, please. Strip him, Caballeros. . . ."

They tore off Ross's rags, and, as they did so, a sheet of pliable bark, rolled up, fell out from under them. One of the soldiers picked it up and handed it to Juan Costa. He stood there studying it with pursed lips, and Ross's eyes came open again.

He was aware suddenly that Don Juan Costa was humming a tune — a very familiar tune, and after a moment he knew what it was: Conchita's dance. But how the devil —? Then, with an effort he looked up and saw that *El Gordo*, the fat one, was reading the notes from his bark manuscript. The sight amazed him. A man who had brains enough to read music, even, from the expression upon the round, greasy face, to enjoy music, and yet could remain a creature of such sick, obscene bestiality — it was beyond comprehension.

Don Juan stared at Ross.

"You wrote this?" he demanded.

"None of your Goddamned business!" Ross said.

"I asked you a civil question, Caballero. Please be so good as to answer me. You want more of the whip?"

"I wrote it," Ross said; "now leave me be. . . ."

"Give him his clothes back," Costa said quietly. "You, Ramón, help him to dress."

They stared at their commander.

"Do as I say!" Costa squeaked. "I do not kill artists! Not I, not Juan Costa, patron and amateur of the arts!"

"Well I'll be damned!" Ross murmured.

"Take him to my quarters," Costa directed. "Then send my personal physician to attend his hurts. When he has recovered sufficiently, he will play for us, Caballeros. We shall have a party. And there is need of a musician, no?"

They grinned at their commander then, and

put the filthy rags back upon Ross Pary. Afterwards they took him to a lavishly furnished suite and laid him down upon the floor beside the bed. After that, Juan Costa came in with a Negress who bathed Ross gently, and the doctor came a short time later and smeared him all over with a sweet-smelling salve that was wonderfully soothing. Afterwards Costa sent for an orderly who shaved away Ross's beard, and lifted him onto the couch that had been prepared for him.

Juan Costa settled his fat bulk into a chair, holding the bark before his pudgy nose and studying it. Then he turned to his desk and drew out several sheets of paper already ruled for music. He copied the manuscript carefully, in a tiny, delicate hand. Then he turned to Ross, frowning.

"There is much here I do not understand," he said; "but it is beautiful, I think. The contrapuntal arrangement is extremely interesting. Now tell me, Señor —"

"Pary," Ross supplied, "Ross Pary."

"Señor Pary, how came you by this theme? It is so typically Cuban!"

"It was inspired by my — wife," Ross said weakly. "My late wife, who was Cuban. . . ."

"The Señora is dead? How unfortunate."

"She was captured early this morning by a

group of cavalrymen," Ross said flatly.

"Then you have right," Costa sighed. "She is dead. Those cavalrymen are beasts!"

Ross stared at him in silent amazement.

Costa stood up.

"I leave you now, Señor Pary. In a few days you will play for us, no?"

"Yes," Ross said tiredly, "I will play."

"I have sorrow of the whipping. I did not know you were a composer. There will be no more of that. You will be sentenced to many years at hard labor, and then they will remand you to me — at my request. And the labor will consist merely of playing for me. Not of too much badness, no?"

"No," Ross said; "it's not too bad."

"Try to sleep, my son," Juan Costa murmured. "It will do you good."

It came to Ross just before he fell asleep that he was going to see the other side of slavery now. He, who had owned slaves, had become one. But it didn't bother him very much. Nothing did or could any more.

But it was fully eight days before he began to feel alive again. Juan Costa had taken very good care of him. Each afternoon, the Negress came in and fed him. The food was excellent, though at first he was able to eat only a mouthful or two. But now he was better. Things connected for him — made sense. The stripes on his back had healed enough so that they no longer stuck to the bandages. That was a good thing, for careful as *el médico* had been, changing the bandages had been very painful.

But on that evening of the eighth day since his capture, Ross was surprised to find out how much better he felt. The orderly had come with a message from Costa, requesting that Ross play for them that night. The doctor had expressed his belief that he was now well enough.

"Come," the orderly said. "The Caballeros await you. They have desires of hearing you play."

Ross followed the orderly until they reached a rude wooden hall. In one corner was a battered piano. He marched straight up to it without looking to the right or the left, and sat down, flexing his fingers.

Then he began to play. The music was the swift gypsy tunes from the district near Seville. In the very middle of the first one, the men stood up, cheering. Ross glanced over his shoulder to the place where Juan Costa sat. The fat one was flanked right and left by two very pretty boys, not yet out of their teens. He was stroking their dark curly hair and feeding them Cuban sweetmeats, pushing the sugary confections into their mouths with his pudgy fingers.

Ross turned back to the piano. It was no concern of his. But now Don Juan looked in his direction.

"Maestro!" he called; "please play for us your own composition. I have much anxiety to hear it."

Ross sat quite still. He couldn't do it. Whatever Conchita had been, whatever she had meant to him would be dirtied by this performance. He could not play Conchita's dance to entertain her murderers. Yet, if he refused there would be the whip again and other pleasant implements that the Spaniards doubtless had waiting. That they would kill him didn't matter. But how he died did matter. A man should be able to manage the final act of the long tragedy of his existence with dignity. And he couldn't manage to die well. Not the way the Spaniards ordered the business of dying.

Something had to be done. They were looking at him now, waiting. Then he had it. He put his long fingers on the keys and began to play Morgan's music. Juan Costa's hand stopped in mid air, holding the dripping sweet that he had been about to thrust into the mouth of one of his favorites.

The chatter of the soldiers stopped. They moved forward as though drawn by invisible cords until they stood in a group around the piano. They listened until Ross had finished it, then they cheered.

"Again, Maestro!" they said. "Play that voodoo music again!"

Don Juan got up and moved ponderously over to the piano.

"That is not the piece you wrote!" he said accusingly.

"It is another of the pieces I have written," Ross said; "and for tonight, I think a better one, Señor Costa. . . ."

"The Maestro has right, Colonel!" the men chorused. "Permit that he play it again . . ."

"Very well," Don Juan said and went back to his seat between the two boys.

But when he had finished Morgan's music, Juan Costa come back again.

"Now," he said, "play for me that Cuban Dance — which is ever so much better music than this savage thing."

Ross frowned. There were, after all, limits even to surrender. To preserve his life at the cost of profaning his grief for Conchita was a damnable thing. Very slowly, he shook his head.

"No," he said almost inaudibly, "that I cannot do. . . ."

Don Juan put his woman-soft hand upon Ross's shoulder.

"I understand your reluctance to play the piece you wrote for your lost wife in such company," he said; "but it is for me that you play it, not for these young swine. . . ."

Ross frowned. Don Juan Costa was a strange man. And yet, in his queer, twisted way, he had tried to be kind. Conchita now, wherever she was, would understand Ross's impulse to oblige this tender monster. Very softly, then, Ross began to play her dance.

But he could not finish it. In the middle, he caught sight of the drunken grins upon the faces of the soldiers, and remembered what they or others like them had done to her, and his stiffened fingers made a crashing discord upon the keys, and he whirled away from the piano and stood up.

"No!" he said; "I'll play no more!"

Instantly Ramón, the big Spaniard who had wielded the whip, was upon him.

"Remember last week?" he growled.

"I remember," Ross said quietly; "but understand this: if every man has his price, he has also some things beyond the purchasing. This music is such a thing, Don Ramón. I'll play no more."

Ramón drew back his hand and smashed his fist hard into Ross's face. The blow broke his nose in two places, and sent him down upon the floor, the blood pumping from his smashed mouth.

Instantly Don Juan Costa was at his side.

"Ramón!" he squeaked; "you are confined to quarters until I send for you! It seems to me you want a taste of your own medicine. Luis and Enrique, pick the Maestro up and take him to my rooms. The party is over!"

Lying on the couch, Ross realized finally how sick he was. The strength that had borne him up the first part of the evening was gone. He lay holding his throat hard against the black waves of nausea that rose in him, and the ceiling of the room moved above his head in slow and stately circles. For some minutes he burned furiously, then he was blue and shivering with cold. He had the idea he was dying and the thought was pleasant. So it was that when he first heard the knocking against the windowpane, he ignored it, attributing it to delirium.

But the knocking came again, stronger. Groaning, Ross raised himself and pushed at the casement, it opened outward, easily, and Pedro's black, grinning face was thrust through the opening.

"Come, Señor!" he whispered; "we must go now — quickly!"

"I can't," Ross groaned. "I cannot walk, Pedro."

Pedro pushed the sash up still further, and eased his lean body into the room. Then he picked Ross up as easily as though he were a child, and dumped him unceremoniously out the window.

Whatever remained unbroken inside his body was smashed now, Ross was sure; but Pedro came through the window and picked him up again, and started off at a trot, hugging the shadows. Just outside the sentry box two horses waited.

"Presents of the Spanish cavalry," Pedro grinned. Ross looked at the place where the sentry should have been. He was there all right, but he lay flat on his face, and one glance told Ross he would never rise again.

"What serves it, Pedro?" Ross said. "They will only hunt us down again, and this time they will kill us at once."

"I do not think they will seek for us in your country, Señor," Pedro said; "I do not think your countrymen would permit it."

"In my country?" Ross whispered.

"Sí. The boat of my Uncle Toloméo awaits us not one hour's ride from here. I beg of you to take me with you to your home in America, for after this Cuba is no longer a safe place for me to be."

"Gladly," Ross said. "Help me to mount, Pedro."

They came out upon the *playa* a few miles east of Matanzas, and there, as Pedro had said, the fishing boat was waiting. Uncle Toloméo hoisted all sail, and they moved out to sea.

Ross lay in the stern looking back at the island of Cuba. He kept looking at it until it dropped out of sight. All of his life lay buried there.

The next afternoon, Pedro carried the half conscious form of Ross Pary ashore at Key West. For most of the voyage, he had been raving; but now, at last, his mind was clear.

"There is a man called Harry Linton," he whispered through his swollen blackened lips. "Ask after him, Pedro. Just say the name. It will be sufficient. . . ."

An hour later, he lay upon the soft feather mattress in Harry Linton's guest room, and that courtly old gentleman stood staring down at his unconscious face.

"Those filthy beasts!" Harry Linton muttered to himself. "I told Pary what they were like. . . ." Then, more softly: "I'll send for Cathy — she'll know just what to do. . . ."

Chapter 14

"I like your face much better now," Cathy Linton said. "You're ugly, and a man should be ugly. You were much too handsome before. . . ."

Ross put the fingers of his right hand up and touched his broken nose. Cathy's right, he thought; I look like a pugilist!

"Don't worry about it," Cathy said; "It becomes you, Ross — it really does."

Ross smiled at her, looking into the pleasant face that now he liked better than any other living face in the world.

"I'll take your word for it, Cathy," he said; "though how a broken nose can become a man is more than I can see."

"It sure does, though," Cathy said. "It makes you look more — more rugged. Your face's got determination in it, now — and character. I like that. In fact I like you much better now than I did before."

"Thank you," Ross said and looked away from her toward the blue water shimmering in the sunlight. The Isle of Hope was a very pleasant place. He was going to hate to leave it.

And Cathy's pleasant, too, he thought. The first time I saw her again in Key West, I wondered what on earth I ever saw in her before. Now I know. It's just that Cathy's something kind of special and after a while that makes you forget how she looks. But that's only the first step. After that you start seeing how she looks again — all freckles and a mouth as wide as a cattle gate, and the sunlight in that chestnut hair, and eyes the color of woodsmoke, and a nose as thin as an ax blade, and a figure like a fence post, and I'll be damned if you don't start to like it. It's interesting, which is more than you can say for many a prettier girl. The modeling of the bones of her face is actually exquisite. If she'd only put on a little flesh, she really would be something. But she never will. She eats like a bird and she's never still long enough for her food to do her any good. . . .

"Ross," Cathy said, "why are you looking at me like that?"

Ross smiled at her.

"Because you're nice," he said; "I was thinking about how nice you are."

"I'd rather be pretty," Cathy said.

"Why? Put you in a room with half a dozen pretty girls, and every man present would go away remembering you, and forgetting the others. . . ."

"And holding his side and laughing fit to kill himself," Cathy said drily. "I'm not fishing for compliments, Ross."

"You don't have to. I've got a hunch that most of the world's really famous women have been interesting rather than pretty. You've got to learn to be proud, Cathy."

"Of what?" Cathy snorted.

"Of yourself. You're really something special. I don't think anyone who ever got to know you well would ever forget you."

"Fat lot of good that does me," Cathy said quietly, "with you."

Ross looked at her.

"Do you want it to?" he asked.

Cathy frowned and looked away from him out over the water.

"I don't know," she said seriously. "I knew that was the risk I took when I insisted on taking you from Uncle Harry's and bringing you here. I don't see any other men — except my brother. How do I know that it's not just lonesomeness?"

"I'm sorry, Cathy," Ross said.

"Don't be. It's not your fault. Besides, it's too soon after your — your wife's death, anyhow. . . ."

Ross's face suddenly took on a forlorn, aged look.

"Want to — to tell me about her, Ross?" Cathy said timidly.

"No, Cathy."

"I wish you would. It's terrible to sit and watch you sitting here eating your heart out day after day. Maybe I could help you, Ross. Perhaps I could even make you forget."

"Don't try it," Ross said gently. "It's no good to grow too fond of a man already dead. . . ."

"Let me be the judge of that," Cathy said. "Come, let's walk down by the water."

"All right," Ross said.

Cathy gave him her hand and they started out down the winding path that was so cool under the oaks. There was a little wind that blew against them and Cathy lifted up her face to it and her thin nostrils flared. The sun was dropping down toward the bluffs on the mainland, over Burntpot Island, and it caught in her straight chestnut hair and blazed. She moved in light, Ross thought, walking in an excess of illumination, wraith-thin, and fine. The freckles that covered her face and neck were golden in the sunlight, and her wide, generous mouth seemed to take on a warmer color. He could see the red mounting into her thin cheeks, and the ghost of excitement stirred in him.

This is two years too late, he thought, or a thousand years too soon. . . .

"When is Harry coming back?" he asked.

"I don't know," Cathy said. "What difference does it make? He won't get the money. . . ."

"Cathy, could I —?"

"No. Lending Harry money is like shoveling fleas in a barnyard. He'll lose the place sooner or later, and your money with it, if I were to let you lend him some. . . ."

"But what will you do once The Pines is gone?"

"Go to live with Uncle Harry, I reckon. He won't mind. Fact is, he'll be glad to have me. I'd be a lot of help to him in the business."

"That's true," Ross said thoughtfully. "Besides, down there you'd meet a lot of young fellows and . . ."

Cathy stopped. Then she turned and faced him.

"I don't want to meet any — now," she said.

"Why not?"

"I'd compare them with you. And that would finish 'em off so damn' quick that . . ."

"Cathy, please . . ."

"All right," Cathy said; "I'll stop now."

It would have been, Ross thought, a good time, one of the best times of all. He remembered the day that Cathy Linton had arrived in Key West. He was only half conscious at the time, but he remembered it. She had come into the room with a poke bonnet tied under her chin, and if he had been able, Ross would have laughed. She looked so thin and intense and countrified in her hopelessly old-fashioned dress. She had stood there, staring at him — and he must have been, Ross realized now, a sight. His lips were cracked and swollen, and both his eyes were black, and his nose was broken in two places, and then one of the Negroes turned him over so that she could see his back. And it was then that Cathy started to cry.

She didn't just stand there and cry. Instead she marched up and down the room crying and swearing at the same time and afterwards she took out one of the little cigars and lit it and strode back and forth with her jerky long-legged stride, sending up clouds of smoke that turned the air blue and saying words that turned it even bluer. Then, abruptly, she stopped swearing, threw the little cigar out of the window and began to dress his wounds.

And it was then that he started to get better.

Cathy had been very good with him. She had been expert and tender and very sure. But it came to Ross now that that hadn't been all of it, or even the most important part. The real thing that Cathy Linton had done for him was to make him want to get better. And that, come to think of it, was very curious, for nothing had changed. Conchita was dead. He must still live in voluntary exile from his beloved Moonrise. And there was still Morgan.

Morgan. That was the worst thing. He had been running away from Morgan Brittany almost since the day he had met her. He couldn't keep it up, now. He knew that. He had reached the stage in his life, in the growth of his spirit, when he had to stop running away from things. Why the devil did a man run anyhow? It was because, he answered himself, he was afraid that he would be confronted with a situation beyond his power to cope with, or to bear.

Such situations, being unknown, had all the added terror of the guessed at, of the imagined. But what was there now in his life that needed to be guessed at? He had journeyed to the limits of human endurance and beyond. He had eaten and slept with death. He had seen intimately the very ultimates of depravity. What was there left for him to run from now? What could Morgan do or say that would hold a feeble candle to what he had already seen and heard?

Besides, there remained one other unassailable fact: wherever a man fled, to whatever desert fastness, whatever impenetrable jungle, to whatever far island surrounded by terrible seas, he took himself with him. There was no escaping the seeds of destruction he bore within himself, no fleeing the image of his own damnation. . . .

"Ross," Cathy said softly, "what on earth are you thinking about?"

Ross looked at her.

"I was thinking about a woman called Morgan," he said.

"And this one isn't dead, is she?" Cathy said.

"No. Morgan is alive. Too much alive, I think sometimes. . . ."

"You — you're in love with her?" Cathy said.

"No. I hate her. But I can't help thinking about her sometimes."

"Why?" Cathy said.

"Because Morgan is your beautiful woman, Cathy. And the beauty that should exist to give comfort and pleasure to someone has always been used by her as a force of darkness, as a weapon of terrible evil. You reminded me of her when you kept harping on the subject of physical beauty. A black panther is a beautiful animal. Some species of snakes are beautiful. A tiger is beautiful. And they all — kill."

"This Morgan is like that? She kills people?"

"She hasn't yet. But I think she would without a qualm if it suited her purpose at the moment. But murder is not a subtle enough art for her. I think she'd enjoy much more having one man kill another over her — or driving a man to kill himself. . . ."

"You make her sound perfectly fascinating," Cathy said.

"She is. She's married to my best friend. It wouldn't surprise me in the least if trying to live with her doesn't drive him mad one of these days; that is, if he escaped being killed in a duel with one of her lovers."

"Are you one of her lovers, Ross?"

"Heaven forbid!" Ross said.

Cathy caught his hand and drew him down beside her on a log half buried in the drifting sand. The waves came in from the sea, blue and very quiet until they were close, then they broke upon the beach with a roar, eddying out in foamy whiteness.

"The sea," Cathy said, in that odd, dry voice of hers; "it goes everywhere, Ross. It touches all the shores. You throw a stone into it and the ripples wash up on the shores of China. I think sometimes that life is like that. . . ."

"Why, Cathy?" Ross said.

"There aren't any private acts. Everything we do makes ripples. The good and the evil. And they touch everybody finally — everybody in the whole damned world. . . ."

"That's true," Ross mused.

"Your niggerman, Brutus, only wanted his wife back — and that made a ripple that washed you to me. Your — your wife never heard of me, but she sent you down to Cuba and here you are again, thrown up, half wrecked, upon the beach of my life. I wonder about that, Ross — it's got a pattern, hasn't it? — these recurring ripples, I mean. And now this Morgan — what kind of a wave will she make that will touch my life? Maybe, the third time, if you're tossed up in my lap, you won't be able to leave. . . ."

"You'd like that?" Ross said.

"Yes," Cathy said; "I'd like it very much, Ross."

Ross sat there looking at her a long time. She has, he thought, the best and most honest eyes in the world. And that funny, freckled face, once you get used to it, is downright restful. If ever I began to feel again, she might mean something to me. If ever I dig up my heart again, it may very likely be hers. . . .

Cathy looked back at him; she didn't move or say anything, but sat very still looking at him. Then, very quietly, she moved closer, and raised her face to his, tilting her head back, closing her eyes.

Ross looked down at the warm, red mouth, full-lipped and generous. It wavered there, inches below his own.

"No, Cathy," he said gently. "Forgive me — but — no. . . ."

The gray eyes came open slowly, staring at him. Ross could see them searching his face, quick pain moving in their depths. Then the pain was gone as suddenly as it had come.

"You're right," she said, in that flat tone of hers, "it's too soon, isn't it? She hasn't been dead six months. I'm ashamed of myself, Ross. . . ." She looked at him, smiling a little now. "That was why you wouldn't kiss me, isn't it?"

"Yes," Ross said, "that was why."

"I don't think you dislike me. I think you may even be fond of me — kind of."

"I am very fond of you," Ross said.

"I'm glad," Cathy sighed. "Well, that's that. Come on, let's go back now."

Ross took her arm and they walked back to the lovely old house. They found young Harry Linton sitting on the veranda staring morosely into the gathering dusk.

"You didn't get the money, did you?" Cathy said.

"No," Harry said curtly.

"Harry," Ross began, "suppose I were to —"

"No!" Cathy said sharply; "I won't have it, Ross!"

Harry looked at her wonderingly.

"Why not, Sis?" he said. "If Ross could tide us over until I got in one good crop. . . ."

"No," Cathy said.

"I'll take the risk, Cathy," Ross said. "Besides I could never repay you for all you've done for me. . . ."

"I don't want to be paid. Besides, it's not a risk. It's a downright certainty. Harry's no planter and the soil's plumb worn out. It would cost damn near as much in guano as we'd get out of it. Another thing, say you made it possible for us to stay on here another year or two — would you really be doing us a favor, Ross? We've been cooped up here all our lives. Maybe Harry would make his mark in the world outside; maybe I'd be happier. . . ."

"That's so," Harry said. "Maybe I'll come out to Mississippi and take a look around. . . ."

"Do," Ross said. "Anything I can do to help you out, I'll be glad to."

"When does the bank plan to take over?" Cathy asked.

"Tomorrow. We'll all have to pack tonight. Sorry, Ross."

"It's all right," Ross told him; "it's time I was getting home anyhow."

"I wish you never had to go home," Cathy said; "never, never, never!"

"And I," Ross said, "wish I had a home to go to. . . ."

"Don't you have a home? I thought –"

"I have a house," Ross said. "A home's a different thing. Home is where the heart is. Good night, Cathy – I'll see you in the morning. Night, Harry."

"Good night, Ross," Harry said; but Cathy didn't answer him at all.

Nothing had changed about the city of Natchez, sitting high on the bluff, watching the river bend itself around the green and golden Louisiana shore. Nothing had changed, yet everything was different. It was quieter. It had taken on a certain serenity. And the wind moved through the oaks and the magnolias with a noise like sighing.

The roads radiated out from it like tunnels of green lace, the boughs of the oaks interwoven above them, shutting out the sky. The great houses sat under the trees, brooding and silent. And when Ross Pary came up Silver Street from the steamboat landing, no one greeted him at all.

He walked up past the Esplanade, and up Main Street toward the building in which he had both his apartment and his office, and just before he reached it, he saw Morgan Brittany coming toward him. Ross groaned. He had wanted more time to himself before risking an encounter with Morgan. But he was done with running away, so he waited quietly until she came up to him.

Morgan continued to walk until she was only a few feet away from him, then she stopped short.

"Ross!" she cried out; "Ross Pary! Oh, Ross – your face – your face!"

"Yes," Ross smiled; "it's a mess, isn't it?"

"Oh, no! It's – it's breathtaking! You look like a Roman gladiator emerging victorious from the battle. You look brutal – even a little cruel. But you still have your poet's eyes. Why, Ross Pary, I think you have just about the most exciting face in the world! Do you live up to it?"

"I have lived up to it," Ross said.

"Tom told me you escaped that bloody fiasco in Cuba. The Metcalfes are back, too. It seems that the Spanish Government didn't want to risk a war by killing any more Americans. Some are still prisoners, though. Colonel Wheat is in a dungeon in Spain. The State Department is moving heaven and earth to get them out. How I chatter! It's a sign that I'm getting old."

"You will never be old, Morgan," Ross said.

"Thank you. That's a very nice thing to say. If Cuba has made you like me a little better, then bless Cuba, I say."

Ross studied the serene little heart-shaped face before him. It hadn't changed.

"No," he said; "Cuba hasn't made me like you any better, Morgan. Only you could do that."

Morgan moved up to him until she was very close, and stood there with her head tilted to one side, watching him out of those black eyes.

"How?" she murmured; "how could I make you like me, Ross?"

"You might try being a little kinder," Ross drawled. "You could develop a little respect for people. Then I'd like you. That way I'd like you very much."

"I've always been kind to you, Ross."

"You've never been kind. You don't even understand what it means. Oh, yes, you can be very sweet when it suits your purpose — but only to gain your own ends. Ever tried a little disinterested kindness, Morgan? Ever thought of being decent for decency's own sake?"

Morgan threw back her head and laughed.

"What nonsense!" she said. "Of course not. And neither has anyone else — not even you, my saintly Ross. People are never good for goodness' sake. People are only good because they are afraid. That's where I differ. I'm not afraid."

"You are impossible, Morgan," Ross said.

"Now you've said something. I'm absolutely free of illusion and that is impossible. The world won't permit that. It kills such clear ones. It will kill me, finally. The cowardly dogs gather together in packs and hunt down the lone wolf. And men must kill the solitary tiger, because his very existence threatens their lives. Oh yes, one day I shall be killed. I know that."

"I don't doubt it," Ross said coldly.

Morgan smiled at him.

"Now," she said, "you're going to take me up to your apartment and tell me all about Cuba."

"No," Ross said. "You'd have me start my homecoming by running the risk of fighting a duel with Lance?"

"Why not? Then one of you would kill the other and I would be rid of one of the two men who trouble me more than anyone else on earth."

Ross smiled at her grimly.

"And which one of us died wouldn't make any difference to you, would it, Morgan?"

"Yes it would make a difference. Before you went away, it wouldn't have. But now it does. I'm sick of Lance, Ross. If you'd kill him I'd be ever so much obliged to you."

"Then you won't be obliged to me," Ross said. "I don't fight duels, Morgan. And I've killed enough men now to last me ten lifetimes. Besides, I'm very fond of Lance."

"The sickening old fool!" Morgan snapped. Then, just as suddenly, she smiled: "So you've been killing people, Ross? How exciting! Do tell me about it!"

"No," Ross said. "Look, Morgan – I can't stand here in the street any longer talking to you. I'm very tired, and everything you do makes a scandal. I'll ride out to Finiterre one day soon, and then we'll talk – all three of us: you and I, and Lance."

"You are going to talk to me today. I'm going upstairs with you right now."

"Morgan – please!"

"Don't try to appeal to my better nature, Ross," Morgan laughed. "You know well I haven't any." She hooked her arm through his. "Come on," she said.

Ross looked at her.

"All right," he said sullenly; "but don't try anything, Morgan."

"Vanity, thy name is man!" Morgan laughed. "I won't ravish you, darling. I don't think I could. You're very strong, despite your thinness. Besides, no matter how much you deny it, there's a bond between us. I don't want that bond broken. I'm not sure I could control you if I permitted you such liberties. Ross — my beautiful Ross with the battered face. You don't know how exciting it makes you look!"

"So I've been told," Ross said.

"Who told you? Oh, your little Cuban, of course. How is she, Ross? So far you haven't mentioned her name."

"She is dead, Morgan." Ross said flatly.

Morgan stopped still upon the second step.

"Oh!" she said. Then: "I'm sorry, Ross. Believe me I am."

Ross stared at her in pure astonishment.

"That," he said, "was the last thing on earth I expected you to say."

"I know. I'm unpredictable, aren't I? But I am sorry, Ross — truly."

"Why?" Ross said.

"Not because she's dead. I don't give a fig if any woman lives or dies. But because she was good for you. She had that air of fine bitchery that another woman can spot in a minute. And

448

that was what you needed, darling — to give your own ponderous solemnity a jolt once in a while. A man always sheds his dignity along with his trousers — thank God!"

"Don't be vulgar, Morgan," Ross said.

"Why not? Nearly everything of value in life is. But you'll find that out for yourself."

They came into the apartment, and Morgan put down her parasol and her bag and started moving about, taking the covers off the lamps and the furniture.

"I do have my feminine impulses," she said. "It's so ghostly in here with everything covered up."

The word caught Ross's attention. Ghostly. Yes, the apartment was haunted. It was filled with memories. The air was alive with them, whispering. Here, in the place it had begun. There — upon that bed. If he listened hard enough, Ross was sure he would hear the scamper of Conchita's quick moving feet. In the shadows, if his eyes could pierce the veil of mortality, he'd be able to see her smile. It came to him then, that he wouldn't be able to stay here any longer. He'd never be able to endure the nights when nothing would stop the thinking. There was no opiate against memory — no specific against anguished loss. . . .

"Tell me, Ross," Morgan said; "how did she die?"

Ross's head lifted slowly, and his broken face was ugly with pain.

"The Spaniards captured her," he said drily, "and tortured her to death. "We — we had been married an hour before. . . ."

"You couldn't save her?"

"I tried. They captured me, too."

Morgan stared at him in breathless fascination.

"And tortured you, too?" she whispered.

"Yes."

Morgan came up to him, and let her fingers stray over the rugged contours of his battered face.

"What did they do, Ross?" she moaned. "Tell me, what?"

Ross stared at her. The tone was — ecstasy.

"No," he said, brusquely.

"Please, Ross — please!"

"They smashed my face in with their fists and gun butts," Ross said evenly. "They threw me down and beat me with a whip."

Morgan put the palms of her hands over his ears and kissed his mouth slowly. There was, Ross realized, no one who could kiss like Morgan.

"My darling," she murmured; "my beautiful,

battered darling! There isn't any more softness in you, is there? They've taught you how to be cruel — haven't they?"

"Yes," Ross said grimly, "they have."

Morgan stood away from him, and looked up into his face.

"I think I'm going to marry you," she said. "You're my kind of a man now."

Ross frowned.

"Must I remind you that you already have a husband?" he said.

"I know. I'm sick of him. He's sick of me. Now you can kill him for me."

"Why do you want him killed?"

"Because I'm tired of him. He's gotten old and querulous — and he's no longer adequate. I've thought of taking a lover. But that's no good."

"The Morganian theory of ethics," Ross said wryly. "Why not, Morgan?"

"Because a lover would be too demanding. Having no real hold over me, he'd try to bind me to him. He'd be watchful and suspicious — and I couldn't stand that."

"But a husband — wouldn't?"

"My husband," Morgan said, "would have no need to."

"At the risk of being repetitious — may I ask why not, Morgan?"

"Because I'd only marry my kind of a man. Lance was, once. But he isn't any more. You are — you my darling with that face of yours that was excavated from the ruins of Pompeii! And I'd be absolutely faithful to you, as long as you knew how to treat me. You know that now — Ross, you know it!"

"Yes," Ross said quietly; "I do know how, Morgan. I reckon I've known how all along. Like a circus trainer with a tigress. Force. Cruelty greater than yours. Only I don't think I'd like it."

"Oh yes you would. The rewards would be adequate."

"Considering the fact that I have not the slightest intention of murdering your husband, I don't see. . . ."

"Don't concern yourself about it!" Morgan laughed. "I'll be rid of Lance, and you won't have to lift a finger." She went up on tiptoe and kissed him — hard. "There!" she said; "now we're engaged!"

"Well I'll be damned!" Ross said.

"Ross," Morgan said; "tell me something else — you said you killed some men. How did you kill them?"

"Why do you want to know that?"

"Just so. Oh, I'll tell you. I'm trying to find out something about you. Tell me, Ross — how did you kill them?"

"With a gun, mostly — in battle. Some of them with a *machete*. . . ."

"You mean those big cane knives?"

"Yes."

"Did you," Morgan asked eagerly, "did you enjoy it, Ross?"

Ross frowned. He thought about Castenada and the five soldiers of Juan Costa.

"Some of them — yes," he said quietly.

Morgan clapped her hands together gleefully like a child.

"Yes, yes!" she cried; "you have it — the kind of hardness a man should have! You'll do all right! Now, Ross — one more question and I'll let you be: Why did you enjoy killing them?"

"One of them," Ross said, "had betrayed my friends into the hands of the Spaniards. The others — threatened Conchita's life. It was a pleasure to kill them. As pleasant as I sometimes think it would be — to kill you."

Morgan caught the lapels of his coat.

"Yes," she said; "I shall marry you — Ross. Now you are capable of killing me. You weren't before. Ever noticed how everything close to death is heightened? The sword of Damocles, Ross. All pleasures are richer, when snatched under the very shadow of death."

Ross thought about black Pedro's night-long

serenade on the three-stringed guitar, and smiled a little sadly.

"That's true," he said; "that's very true. . . ."

"You're remembering her, aren't you, Ross?"

"As a matter of fact, I was. What difference does it make?"

"A lot. I don't give a fig about a living woman; but I won't play second fiddle to a ghost! You've got to forget her, Ross."

"And you," Ross said, "have got to learn right now that you don't tell me what I've got to do. My life is my own, Morgan. I do with it what I please."

"Right," Morgan said. "If I could make you do what I wanted you to, I'd hate you. But I'll keep on trying. That's the nature of a woman."

She went over to the table and picked up her parasol and her bag.

" 'Bye, darling," she said. "Look how peacefully I'm going this time. Won't it be nice when I don't have to go at all?"

"Yes," Ross mocked, "very. I shall wait very patiently. But now that you've confessed your great love for me, I expect anything to happen."

"Love?" Morgan said. "Who said anything about love, Ross? What's love got to do with it?"

"I don't know," Ross said. "You tell me."

"Love," Morgan said, "is an infantile emotion that afflicts fools. I'm quite incapable of loving anyone, Ross – even you."

"But," Ross drawled, "since, according to you, we're going to be married, once Lance has been safely disposed of – what sort of relationship can exist between us – if you don't believe in love?"

"This sort," Morgan said, and clung her mouth to his. " 'Bye, now, darling," she whispered; "you should be very useful – after dark. . . ."

Then she was gone, slipping easily through the half opened door.

The next afternoon, Ross rode out to Moonrise on a rented nag. Nancy, his blooded mare, was stabled out at the plantation. He'd have to retrieve her. Riding this bag of bones was pure misery.

When he came up the drive, the Negroes stared at him curiously as though they had never seen him before. But Simon, the butler, who had known him longer than any of them, recognized him at once.

"Marse Ross!" he quavered. "Thank the dear Lord, you's home again! Yassir, thank His Name!" He stopped, staring. "Marse Ross, what done happen to your face?"

"A mule kicked me," Ross grinned. "The folks at home?"

"Yassir — they's here all right. They and that gentleman from New Orleans — Mister O — O — doggone it, I never could say that name!"

Wallace came up behind him and stood there grinning at Ross.

"Bear," he said. "Oh Bear! Ain't that a funny name, Marse Ross?"

"That depends," Ross said. "What is this gentleman's business, Simon?"

"I don't know, sir. He comes up here to see Miss Annis."

Ross stood there a moment, frowning and thoughtful. So Annis has a suitor! Little Annis! Let me see — her birthday was last month and this is 1852 — my God! Annis is all of eighteen years old. . . .

"Tell them I'm here, Simon," he said.

"Yassir, Marse Ross! Right now!" Simon scurried away down the hall.

After a moment Ross heard him coming back, and after him a rush of many feet. Tom and Jennie came first, each of them carrying a child in their arms.

Twins! Ross gasped; "Holy Mother of God!"

Behind them Annis came shyly leading a tall young man by the hand. He was tall and dark, and exceedingly handsome. There was a Latin flavor to his looks, and all at once Ross understood the name the Negroes had been trying to say. Aubert — a Creole name, obviously. Pronounced French fashion, it did sound like Oh Bear.

Jennie drew a little ahead of the others, but when she was close enough to see Ross's face, she stopped dead. She peered at it a long moment, then, helplessly, she started to cry.

Ross could see Annis' face paling, and her fingers tightened convulsively around young Aubert's hand. Even Tom was silent then, his heavy brows drawn together in a frown.

"Good God!" he got out at last, "what happened to you, boy? You look like you smacked into a locomotive — head on!"

"Compliments of the Spanish garrison at Matanzas," Ross said quietly. "Don't cry, Jen — you'll get used to my face. I have."

"But you used to be so handsome!" Jennie sobbed. "And now you look like — like —"

"A bandit," young Aubert supplied. "One of the more romantic sort. How do you do, sir? I'm Danton Aubert. Annis has been telling me all about you. . . ."

Ross took the hand that Danton Aubert offered him.

"Not the truth, I hope," he said.

"Hardly," young Aubert laughed. "No man

could be as wonderful as your sister thinks you are."

I am going to like this one, Ross thought. He has poise and assurance and those things require something to back them up.

"Let me see the children, Jen," Ross said. "I didn't know a thing about them. Tom wrote me once or twice while I was in Georgia — but he never even mentioned the babies. . . ."

"They were born last September," Jennie said. "I called the boy Peter after my father. We named the girl after Annis — she does look like Annis a little, don't you think?"

Except that one of the babies was dark, and the other was blonde, they looked like babies to Ross. He couldn't even tell which was the boy and which the girl. But he sat there holding them both in his arms, looking from one of them to the other, thinking: These could be mine — if I were blessed with any luck. But whatever my destiny is, it certainly doesn't include happiness. . . . Then he gave the babies back to their mother.

"They're lovely," he said. "Which one is Peter?"

"Oh, Ross!" Jennie said.

"The little fellow with the black hair," Tom said. "Looks just like his pappy, don't you think?"

"Well," Ross grinned, "since we're reasonably sure of who his pappy is, I guess he does. . . ."

"Why Ross," Annis said, "what a perfectly outrageous thing to say!"

"Have you had anything to eat?" Jennie asked in some confusion. "You're so thin, Ross! We just finished dinner, but there are an awful lot of things left."

"I am hungry, come to think of it," Ross said. "Well, Tom — congratulations. They're a fine pair."

"Don't mention it, boy," Tom grinned. "Just wait until you see the next six or seven."

"You're looking at them right now," Jennie said. "That's all there're ever going to be."

Something in her tone caught Ross's attention. A note of grimness — even of suppressed fury. I wonder what Tom's done now, Ross mused. Oh well, it's none of my affair. . . .

He sat at the table and ate the good food, and Annis stood behind him and ruffled his hair.

"Ross," she said, "tell us about Cuba, won't you?"

Ross straightened up, frowning.

"All right," he sighed; "I'll get it over with. I'll have to sooner or later." Then he told them.

The silence afterwards had thickness and texture. It could be felt. Ross stood up, hearing the quick, rasping intake of the women's breaths, the first half-strangled sobs.

"I'm sorry," he said; "but you asked me." Then very quietly he walked down the long hall and out of the house. He stood on the gallery a long moment and Tom came out of the house and threw his big arm over Ross's shoulder.

"I'm sorry, boy," he muttered; "I'm mighty, Goddamed sorry. . . ."

"It's all right now," Ross said.

Chapter 15

Raoul Bergson, the great impresario, sat at his favorite table at Le Coq d'Or, a sidewalk café in the Montparnasse section of Paris. He always sat there at that particular table, under that particular chestnut tree, every day at the same time. He had done so for years, so that Le Coq d'Or had become a second office for him. Anyone who wanted to see him either on business or merely to enjoy the wit for which he was famous, knew precisely where to find him. In a very real sense, M. Bergson held court there, surrounded by a circle of admirers, his pudgy hands flashing diamonds from every finger, including his thumbs, a petite cognac resting untouched before him on the table. When he finally drank the cognac, that was a signal. His petitioners and friends knew that the interview was over.

But this spring day of the year 1853, only one man sat opposite M. Bergson, a seedy unimportant individual called Paul Dreyfus. This caused the great impresario a certain twinge of annoyance.

"Raoul," Dreyfus wheezed, "what of your new discovery? Aren't you going to tell me about her?"

"There's nothing to tell," Bergson said. "I haven't even seen her. André is quite excited over her, but you know André — everything excites him."

"Aren't you going to?" Paul Dreyfus asked.

"Yes, this afternoon. I have a feeling about this girl. I cannot define it, my old one, still — there is this feeling. A Spanish dancer — the times should be good for such a one, is it not so? If she has anything — any kind of esprit, any verve — name of a camel! I had no idea it was so late!"

"Tomorrow you will tell me about her, then?" Dreyfus asked.

Bergson shrugged, and drank a little cognac.

"If there's anything to tell," he said.

He got up then and proceeded along the sidewalk with his curious rolling gait, which, together with his short, fat figure made him easily recognizable all over Paris. Fifteen minutes later, he was sitting in the first row of a shabby hall watching the Spanish girl dance. She was a beautiful girl, with reddish-brown hair and green eyes. She was, M. Bergson decided, much too thin; but he suspected that her thinness was not usual with her; plainly she had fared very badly of late.

But before she was halfway through the first flamenco, Raoul Bergson knew she could dance.

Ma foi, he mused, I wonder if she knows how good she is? I hope not — for that would make a great difficulty over the question of pay.

The girl had finished the dance now, and stood there, waiting.

"Encore," Bergson said; "something different, this time."

The girl launched into a *baile gitano* — a gypsy dance, and Raoul Bergson felt the excitement rising in him.

Once every century — one like this one! He could see the marquees of the theatres now — here in Paris, in London, in New York — Raoul Bergson presents — oh well, he'd dream up a name for her.

He stood up, smiling.

"Enough, my little one. It is good. If you will come tomorrow to my office, we will discuss the terms of a contract. I cannot promise you much, still, I must confess that as a dancer you are not too bad. A few faults here and there, but with time and work they will eradicate themselves."

The girl stood there, unmoving, a sullen expression upon her face.

"M'sieur," she said, her French marked by a heavy Spanish accent, "could we not discuss it now, tonight? There are certain difficulties. . . ."

M. Bergson waved an imperious hand.

"That is an impossibility, child," he said. "Tomorrow we will talk. Till then, *au 'voir.*"

He had half turned, when he saw her sway. He turned back again, but he was too late. The girl had fallen full length upon the stage. The moment he reached her, Raoul Bergson saw that the faint was no counterfeit.

"André!" he bellowed; "Bring water – brandy – come quickly, *enfant* – Name of a name!"

His young assistant came flying from the wings, and together they carried her into one of the dressing rooms. One of the musicians came in carrying the cheap handbag she had brought with her. He stood there holding it and watching while M. Bergson got a stiff draught of brandy down her throat.

She blinked and opened her eyes. Raoul looked at her almost tenderly.

"How long has it been since you have eaten, little pigeon?" he said.

"Four days," the girl said weakly.

"André," Bergson barked, "go order a cab. For this little one the finest meal in all Paris. Your forgiveness, Mademoiselle — I was a dolt, not to have noticed."

"It is nothing," she said. Then she saw the musician holding her handbag. "My bag, please," she said.

The man started forward, but halfway across the room, he stumbled over Raoul Bergson's cane and dropped the bag. It burst open, strewing its contents over the floor. And the great impresario got down on his knees with the musician and a stagehand to gather up the girl's meager belongings.

He came up, holding a piece of a newspaper in his fat hands. Moving over to the light, he saw that it was from a provincial town in the Pyrenees, near the Spanish border.

"There is much excitement," he read, "touching the complete escape of the assailant who wounded the illustrious Captain Miguel de la Mancha of the Spanish Army. The captain had been spending a few days in France, accompanied by a beautiful woman. Police are searching for his charming companion, in the belief that she might shed some light on the mystery."

The impresario folded the newspaper clipping and passed it over to her.

She took it silently. Then André returned to announce that a cab awaited them.

"Come, my child," Raoul said, "let us go."

Raoul Bergson was, in his way, a diplomat. He waited until the girl had finished a meal as good – almost, as the ones he usually ate himself, before he pressed the matter.

He leaned forward across the table and smiled at her kindly.

"Well, little pigeon," he murmured; "why did you do it?"

The girl looked up fearfully at a passing gendarme.

Raoul put out his pudgy hand and took hers.

"This is not a matter for the police," he said. "In prison you are useless to me. Out of it – you could be very useful, I think. But if I am to protect you from the consequences of your folly, I have to know the details. I assure you, Mademoiselle, that this is not the idle curiosity of an old man. Have the goodness to tell me, please. . . ."

The girl studied the fat face before her. What she saw reassured her. Though Raoul Bergson thought of himself as a hard man, his kindness actually was a Parisian legend.

"He betrayed me," she whispered.

"Ah — so!" Raoul chuckled. *"Cherchez la femme.* Now there is a woman I'd like to meet, the one whom a man would betray some one as pretty as you for."

"There was no other woman," the girl said.

M. Bergson's face was genuinely puzzled.

"This," he said, "is a new kind of a marvel. There is no other woman and yet, your lover betrayed you?"

"He was not my lover," the girl said, "though in a way he was. I didn't love him — I — I hated him!"

"Name of a little pink sow! He was not your lover, yet he was your lover and you hated him. On top of all this he betrayed you in such a fashion that no other woman was involved. Please have the goodness to unravel all these mysteries!"

"He — he killed my husband — or had him killed, after promising me that he would spare his life. It is all very simple, M'sieur. We, my husband and I, were revolutionaries in Cuba. We were captured, and I bargained with Captain de la Mancha for my husband's life. My husband did not know this. For even though he faced torture, he would not have permitted it. . . ."

"The captain, doubtless, found you attractive?"

"Yes. I promised to come to Spain with him,

if he freed my husband. He did so, but afterwards, he gave the word to the soldiers where my husband, who was wounded and unconscious, might be found."

"There is only thing unclear in all this," Raoul said; "how did you discover the betrayal? It appears to me extremely unlikely that he would have told you."

"Yet he did tell me. In Spain we encountered a certain nobleman, who also thought that a mere captain should not be allowed to retain possession of a barbaric Cuban Señorita, whose savagery lent her a certain charm in his blasé eyes."

"So Captain de la Mancha brought you to France?"

"Yes. But he also asked me to marry him. As he would finally have to go back to Spain, his only hope of keeping me if this *hidalgo*, this Grandee of Spain, really put forth some effort – was to marry me. I pointed out to him that marriage was not possible since I was already married. It was then that he made the grave error of telling me that I was, in fact, a widow."

"Then?" Raoul prompted.

"Then I put several inches of knife blade into his carcass, and left. The rest, you know."

Raoul stared at her.

"Ma foi!" he murmured, "you *are* a savage creature!"

"Yes. We Habañeras often are."

"Habañeras? That is not your name?"

"No. I am called Conchita. Habañeras means the women of Havana."

"Habañera. . . ." Raoul mused; "La Habañera! That's it! Thank you for that, Mademoiselle."

"For what?" Conchita asked.

"For giving me your professional name — a name that will someday be known round the world."

"Then we do not remain in France?"

"But no! The discoveries of Raoul Bergson are known in every capital of Europe and in the New World as well."

"We go to America, then?"

"Yes — to New York and Chicago and San Francisco, and New Orleans."

"New Orleans," Conchita breathed; "I should like that. Yes, I should like it very much."

"Come, little pigeon," Raoul Bergson said.

By that same spring of 1853, Ross Pary had accomplished many things. He had risen to the very top of his profession, so that some of the public buildings in Jackson, Baton Rouge and New Orleans had been designed by him; he had established connections with architectural firms in New York, so that when the day came that he could leave Natchez, he would find a position waiting for him; he maintained a friendly correspondence with Cathy Linton, realizing that the attraction that he had felt toward her was merely the upsurge of his despair; and he managed the tightrope act of keeping up his friendship with Morgan Brittany without letting it develop into something more. Last of all, he had begun to educate his slaves with the view of freeing them as he had promised his lost Conchita.

It was the state of the nation that troubled him, rather than his personal life as he rode toward Finiterre that morning. The very air was big with destiny, and the feeling disturbed him. He had had enough of destiny; his part in the shaping of history had been sufficient, he felt, to last any man a lifetime; but the nagging fear persisted, dull like the ache of his old wounds in wet weather — that what was happening, what was going to happen would not leave him alone. The talk of secession was not yet ended; the interventionists mouthed their grandiose dream of a slaveholding empire stretching from the Mason and Dixon Line to the Amazon, which the Northern States, properly chastened, would be permitted to rejoin again — in their rightful place as junior partners — as culturally inferior domains. They talked glibly — almost gleefully, of war, if necessary; and Ross, who had seen war, grew cold and sick. . . .

He rode along on Nancy, his head bent forward on his chest, that face of his which had been that of a Phidian Apollo, and was now that of a battle-scarred Roman legionary, frowning and thoughtful. He paid little attention to the Negro who came limping up the drive, a bundle slung over his shoulder on a stick. Then the bundle itself attracted him. Runaway slaves commonly slung their few belongings into such a bundle. But surely no Negro was fool enough to keep to the highroads in broad daylight where the roving patrols were certain to capture him. He stared at the black curiously, and at the same moment the man threw down his bundle and raced toward him, his black face split in an enormous grin.

"Pedro!" Ross cried; "now what the devil . . ."

"Señor Ross!" Pedro laughed; "I found you! It has been a journey of formidable distances and of an immensity of trouble; but I have found you!"

The Cuban Spanish rolled off his tongue like gatling gun fire. Ross, who was out of practice, had some difficulty understanding him at first.

But the story was soon told. Pedro, ever restless, had tired of his work on the Linton estate in Key West. Key West was too much like Cuba — he wanted to see more of the world. So, armed with a letter from Harry Linton, and a few words of English, he had made his way to Mississippi. He had been arrested many times; but each time, his swift Spanish and Harry Linton's letter had been enough to convince the sheriffs that he was no fugitive.

He wanted to stay here with Ross. He would make the Señor a good bodyservant. As for wages, his needs were few; whatever the grand Señor Ross wished to pay him would be good and sufficient. All he asked was that he would not be enslaved. . . .

"Have no fear of that," Ross said grimly; and taking out a pencil, scrawled a note to Jennie telling her who Pedro was, and directing that he be fed and given a place to stay. Then he rode on, toward Finiterre.

As he rode through the gate, he saw his sister Annis riding toward him with Danton Aubert at her side. Even from that distance, Ross could see that her face was radiant. Love, he thought, is a wonderful thing — when well managed and accompanied by luck; but without luck, it is terrible. Even when you have good memories — it's terrible.

He rode up to them, and Annis looked at him, and lowered her head, then raised it again, covered with blushes and confusion.

"Ross," she whispered, "we — we . . ."

"We're going to be married, sir," Danton said; "with your permission, of course, and that of your brother."

Ross studied them gravely for a long moment. He had already taken the trouble to investigate the Auberts. They were sugar planters, and fabulously wealthy. Beyond that, they were gentlefolk, with generations of birth and breeding behind them; courtly Louisiana Creoles with all the old-world charm of manner. He admired, too, Danton's assurance, his completely unselfconscious ease. It was a trait that Ross could admire. His own had been so dearly bought.

"You have it," he said slowly, "and my wish for your happiness. . . ."

He put out his hand, and Danton took it in a firm grip. Then Annis kissed him, the happy tears wet upon her cheeks.

"You think Tom will agree?" she asked anxiously. "Oh Ross, I'm so afraid to ask him!"

"Don't be," Ross smiled; "he's already told me how pleased he was about the whole thing."

"That's good," Danton said. "It certainly takes a load off my mind. One other thing, sir

— could I persuade you to bring Annis down to New Orleans to meet my parents? Mistress Jennie is much too busy to act as chaperone, and it's something that has to be done. . . ."

"Gladly," Ross said; "When are you two planning to take the fatal step?"

"Oh, not until next year," Danton said. "My father insists that I take my Grand Tour first. He's old-fashioned in that regard. Of course I shall enjoy seeing London and Paris, but I'd rather do it on my honeymoon than alone . . ."

"We can go back again, dearest," Annis said teasingly. "Then you can show me all the places that you got into mischief in. I shan't speak to you for a month after you return. Then I'll forgive you, but only because I can't help it."

"I shan't get into mischief," Danton said stoutly.

"I have two brothers," Annis told him, "so I know men!"

"But neither of your brothers had the incentive I have to keep out of trouble. Quite the contrary. It seems to me that their romances have always led them into it. . . ."

"Right," Ross smiled; "see that you are wiser."

"Don't worry about that — Ross," Danton said. "I shall call you Ross now — that is

474

if you don't mind."

"I don't mind," Ross said. "Well, *au revoir* for now. I'll discuss our visit to New Orleans later. . . ."

"Very well, sir," Danton Aubert said.

When Ross reached Finiterre he saw Lance Brittany jumping his magnificent hunter, Prince, over the high gate. He did it once, and whirled the gray stallion about and came racing back toward it again. This time Prince stumbled the barest trifle on the take-off, and his left hoof caught the topmost bar high up and took a splinter out of it a yard long. But Lance hauled back on the reins and steadied him so that he came down on all four feet with just a little stagger. Then he rode up to Ross with a grin.

"There's life in the old man yet," he said. "I can still do it, Ross."

"That," Ross said angrily, "was a fool thing, Lance. What the devil are you trying to prove?"

"That I'm less than a thousand years old, I reckon," Lance said bitterly, "which is exactly the way I feel."

You look it, too, Ross thought, seeing the thick hair with no black left in it anywhere, and the lines about Lance's mouth and eyes that had not been there before. So this is what being married to Morgan does to a man. . . .

"Is Morgan at home?" he asked easily.

"Yes. Come on, we'll ride up there now and have a bourbon."

"No, thank you," Ross said. "I don't really want to see Morgan, Lance. You'll forgive me if I admit that I'm not too fond of your wife. Let's ride down into the city instead, and have our drinks there."

"All right," Lance said. "But first I have to see how Smithers is coming along with the planting. Come with me — if it isn't against your new-found abolitionist principles to watch slavery in operation."

"My principles," Ross said, "have received just about the same treatment as my face. With the same results. Neither of them has been improved."

"Your face has," Lance grinned. "That's one thing I agree with Morgan about. You were a mite too pretty before. Your features were so damned regular that they gave you a womanish cast. Now you look like a man — and one hell of a man at that. Bet the wenches look at you now and get the shivers thinking of how delightfully you'd manhandle them, given half a chance."

"They'd sure be disappointed, if it were put to the test," Ross said. "Well, come on — let's ride."

They rode down into Natchez an hour later, and stopped at Connelly's Tavern. All about them the talk rose hot and angry, the word "secession" being repeated over and over again.

"That Stowe woman ought to be tarred and feathered!" a man said. "Imagine her writing a book like that one. What the hell does she know about slavery anyhow? Heard tell she's never been out of Cincinnati in her life!"

"Too bad old Henry Clay had to croak. He was a good man. We're going to miss him. When he passed on I said to myself, there goes the last chance of settling this thing short of war. . . ."

"You would be in hot water," Lance smiled, "if they knew how you felt."

"But they don't," Ross said; "and I don't aim to tell them. When I'm ready, I'm going to put the Negroes on a boat bound for Liberia and get on another one myself headed for New York."

"We'll miss you," Lance said seriously. "You're the only friend I have left — that I can trust, I mean. I'm damned glad you aren't fond of Morgan."

Ross put his glass down.

"That reminds me," he said. "Lance, do you know why Morgan is so afraid of the dark and of being shut up?"

Lance glared at him.

"How the devil did you know that, Ross?" he said harshly.

"She told me. I ran into her downtown one day, and we got to talking. It came up some way, I don't remember how; but even talking about it made her look ill. . . ."

Lance sighed.

"I don't really," he said. "It has something to do with her father, I think. My guess is that he must have punished her as a child by locking her up in a closet. She's never said. I don't think she remembers it consciously, herself." He looked at Ross quizzically. "You're smart," he said. "Is that why you have so much patience with my bad temper?"

"Yes," Ross said.

"Thanks," Lance said drily. He stared away from Ross into the mirror over the bar. "Morgan's walking a mighty narrow line," he said, "between what is real and what isn't. Knowing that, I can't behave like an ordinary husband. More than half the time what I feel for her is — pity. I think that's what gets me more'n ordinarily riled at the men she gets mixed up with. Can't the fools see it isn't them — as people, as men — that interests her?"

"Then what is it, Lance?"

Lance stared at him.

"Power, vengeance — who knows?" he muttered. He looked about him at the angry, gesticulating drinkers at the bar, and his face took on an expression of distaste. "Bottoms up, boy," he said gruffly; "I have to go. . . ."

The rains came late that spring, after the blooming of the flowers. Ross had come back from taking Annis to New Orleans by the time they started. The Auberts had been all he had expected: fine, cultured folk. He had delighted them by speaking French to them. Everything was settled now; Danton had been packed off to Europe for his Grand Tour, and the wedding had been set for the week after his return.

But, once the rains started, it seemed that they would never stop. And rain always reminded Ross of Conchita. He remembered her with him before the fireplace, and outside the soft whispering of other rains. It had seemed so safe then — so safe and certain and enduring. And now, less than two years later, it was a lost thing, remaining only in memory. . . .

He studied the little daguerrreotype that Cathy Linton had sent him. The picture did nothing for Cathy — nothing at all. Her piquant coloring was absent from it; the picture showed only her thinness and her plainness, emphasizing certain unfavorable features — the size of her mouth, for instance. But Cathy's mouth, Ross remembered, was one of her good features: it was warm and generous. The picture didn't show that. Her head imprisoned in the photographer's wire rack, Cathy looked like a country schoolgirl, prim and plain, even a little grim. And Cathy, God knew, was none of these. . . .

He put the picture down and moved to the window. Outside was only rain and mud, oceans of mud, a gloomy landscape to contemplate. So he turned away from the window and took down a decanter of bourbon from the cabinet, and began to drink it. It had little effect upon him at first except to increase the painful somberness of his mood.

He had given it up when he heard the light sound of booted feet upon the stair. The tread was not heavy enough to be that of his brother, Tom – nor yet the girlish skipping of Annis. It sounded like – Morgan.

It was. She came into the apartment and tossed her hat and gloves carelessly on a chair, and moved toward him without a word and kissed him on the mouth. Then she turned away, humming, and picked up the decanter of bourbon. She poured herself a tall glassful and walked around the room sipping it, humming to herself all the while.

He saw her stop and stiffen. Then she put out her hand and picked up Cathy's picture from the table.

"And who the devil is this little witch?" she said.

Ross looked at her.

"Cathy Linton," he said; "a friend of mine."

"I didn't know you had any women friends — except me."

"Well you know now," Ross said.

"Yes," Morgan said, "I do. I don't like this wench, Ross. I don't like her at all."

"Why not?" Ross said.

"She's homely. Therefore she's dangerous."

"An ingenious conclusion. Why, Morgan?"

"Because she must be terribly interesting. You wouldn't have her picture if she weren't."

"Right," Ross said; "she is interesting, Morgan. She's one of the most delightful little creatures I've ever met. And she isn't homely — not really — not once you get used to her."

"That," Morgan drawled, "would take some doing!"

"It did. But the results were worth it."

"You say she's not homely. Prove it, my boy — prove it."

"I don't know if I can. You'd have to see her, and looks are a matter of opinion anyhow. It's her coloring, I think. Her eyes are as gray as woodsmoke, and her mouth's naturally red. . . ."

"There's enough of it," Morgan said.

"Yes, there is. She has lovely chestnut hair, and she's freckled all over like a setter pup. . . ."

"*All* over, Ross?" Morgan drawled.

"At least as far as I've seen," Ross said.

"All over," Morgan said drily. "Go on."

"She's as thin as she looks there, but most of the time she wears pants instead of a frock. The effect is very fetching. . . ."

"I can imagine. Tight pants, no doubt."

"Tight pants. And she smokes little cigars, and can outcuss any muleskinner you ever heard."

"Quite a girl. What else can she do well, Ross?"

"I wouldn't know."

"Gallant, aren't you? But you do know, don't you? Damn you to hell, you do!"

She was standing before his chair now and her face was twisted with rage. You'd think I'd betrayed her, Ross thought suddenly — that she were mine to betray. . . .

"If I did," he said drily, "I wouldn't tell you. It happens that I don't. I've never so much as kissed Cathy Linton. You can believe that or not as it pleases you; either way I don't give a damn."

Morgan straightened up, staring at him. Then, slowly, she smiled.

"They did something to you when they smashed your face, didn't they?" she said. "You used to defy me before, but never like this. Before you were always angry — and a little afraid. Now you sit there and tell me flatly that you don't give a damn what I think. And you don't, do you? You really don't."

"No," Ross said, smiling a little, "I really don't."

Morgan looked at him, the pupils of her eyes dilating in the dim light. Then she lifted her glass and drank it all, and set it down before him noiselessly, with exquisite, expressive control.

"Another," she said quietly.

Ross picked up the decanter and poured the glass brimful with a steady hand.

Morgan picked up the glass and stood there holding it and looking at him.

"You, too," she said.

Ross poured his own glass full.

Morgan drank half of hers and turned away from him, swaying a little. Then she turned back again.

"You — you frighten me," she said hoarsely. "Before you wouldn't have dared to do that. You would have refused to give me any more —

and you wouldn't have touched it yourself. You used to run away from me when things got a bit thick. But you wouldn't run, now – would you, Ross?"

"No," Ross said. "I've done all the running I'm ever going to do – all the hiding. I have to face up to things sooner or later. Now is as good a time as any to begin."

Morgan brought the rim of the glass up to her lips. She held it there, looking over it at Ross a long time. Then, very slowly, she drained it.

Ross drank his, too – all of it. He held the glass between his fingers then he threw it away from him into the fireplace. It broke, and the pieces lay upon the hearth, catching the light. The flame hissed briefly from the few drops left in the glass, and burned blue for a moment, then settled down again.

Morgan walked over to the fireplace. Standing above it, she opened her fingers and let her glass fall, adding to the shattered fragments and the little wetness. She stood there watching it, until the little whiskey she had had left in her glass began to smoke from the heat of the fire. Then it blazed, making flickering blue shadows on her face.

She turned back to Ross, watching him, catlike – her body drawn down and in a little, and Ross got up out of his chair and came to her. The fire made a cackling sound – like laughter. Morgan put her arms up about his neck and swung her weight from them and hung there staring up at his battered face until it blurred out of focus. Then she parted her lips and closed her eyes.

She tore away from him finally, and ran ahead of him into the bedroom, and Ross followed her and stood there watching her hands amid the swirl of skirt and petticoats and the long, clean good whiteness of her limbs. Then he looked beyond her at his little bed and the ghost of Conchita Izquierdo came into the room and stood between them staring at him with accusing eyes.

"No!" he said hoarsely. "No, Morgan – no!"

She stopped still.

"Why not?" she whispered.

"Not here," Ross said thickly. "Not here, Morgan!"

Morgan looked at his eyes and traced their line of vision past her to the little bed. Her hands came away from her clothing and anger flamed up in her.

"Not here," she said very quietly, "not here – not upon her bed. That would dishonor her memory, wouldn't it, Ross? Damn your soul to hell, I told you I wouldn't play second

485

fiddle to a ghost!"

Then she lunged forward all at once, and her hands moving were invisible with speed. Ross felt four white-hot streaks of fire move down his face, and Morgan's hand came away with bloody nails. He put his hand to his face and it came away dark with his own blood. Then he moved toward her and caught the front of her riding habit in his left hand and slapped her right and left and right again so that the sound of it was like small arms fire and her head jerked upon her neck and the tears jetted out of the corners of her eyes, arcing out and away from her face under the impact, leaving her cheeks dry. Then the rage was gone out of him leaving him nerveless and cold, and he opened his hand, and she crumpled bonelessly down upon the bed and lay there sobbing, making a hot, strangled sound like a whipped child.

"I'm sorry, Morgan," Ross said.

She pushed herself up on one elbow and lay there staring at him, the tears running down her face chasing one another down across the corner of her mouth and her face red and swollen, the finger marks livid upon it, and her mouth swollen too and bleeding from both corners; but she straightened up smiling, and put out her hands to him.

"You beast," she moaned. "You big, ugly,

savage beast! God, how long it took me to get you untamed!"

She came off the bed and put her mouth to his so that he could taste the hot, salt tang of blood. Then she pushed her nails into his back so hard that he could feel them through the stuff of his lounging robe. Bringing his hands up, he broke her grip.

"No," he said, "not here, Morgan. I told you, not here!"

She whirled away from him then and ran into the front room, and he came after her slowly, thinking: This is wrong, wrong, she is still Lance's and I, Oh, God, yes — I — But he was in the front room and she whirled against him and her hands ripped at the dressing robe and then at the remainder of her own clothing. He tried to draw back, but she locked her arms about his neck and hurled herself down backward and away from him, still holding on so that he was drawn down too and lost his balance at the last and fell heavily with her.

God help me, Ross Pary thought, while he could still think; God in His mercy help me!

Her face, when she left the apartment, had all the sweet innocence in the world.

Afterwards, as he rode away from Finiterre in the blackness of just before dawn — upon another night — so many other nights now — the rain drove needles of ice into his face. He rode bent forward in the saddle, his hat pulled down over his eyes so far that he did not see the man on the big gray horse until he was almost upon him. He put his hand under his coat to reach for his pistol; but it came away empty: the pistol was not there.

There is, he thought wryly, a kind of justice in my forgetting it. Then the man rode in close and Ross saw that it was not Lance Brittany after all, but his brother, Tom.

"What the devil are you doing out here?" he said.

Tom looked at him steadily, through the driving rain.

"The same thing as you," he said, "trying to see her."

"Then you don't any more?"

"Rarely," Tom said. "She has other interests now. Reckon you're one of 'em, boy. Maybe even the main one. Nothing to keep you from being. You're not all tied up."

"But she is," Ross said. "Come on."

They rode into the stableyard at Moonrise in the darkness, but inside the stable, Tom lit a match and put it to the wick on the oil lantern. He turned to open the gate to one of the stalls, and then he saw Ross's face.

"So you did see her! You look all in, boy — you look like a dead man!"

"I am a dead man, Tom," Ross said.

"Hell," Tom snorted; "don't talk like that, Ross. Tumbling a wench never killed anybody."

"No," Ross murmured. "Reckon you're right, Tom. I'm not dead. It's nothing so simple as that — and there are worse things. . . ."

Tom stared at him.

"Worse than being dead?" he said brusquely. "What kind of things, Ross?"

"Things like human bondage — like not being your own man any more. Like becoming a woman's creature — her toy. The thing upon which she satisfies her appetites. Something less than human, Tom. That's worse."

Tom Pary looked at his younger brother pityingly.

"You know," he said, "I kind of reckoned it would be like that."

"You were right," Ross said.

Then he turned and left the stable, walking slowly, tiredly, through the thinning dark.

Chapter 16

"That Cuban Negro of yours, Ross," Morgan said; "that Pedro — keep him away from here, won't you?"

She was walking about her room at Finiterre, holding a goblet of brandy in her hand.

"Didn't you hear me?" she said. "That Pedro —"

"I heard you," Ross said. "I'll keep him away. You — you're beautiful, Morgan."

"I know," Morgan said; "So I've been told —"

"Who told you?" Ross said.

"My husband, of course. And your brother, Tom."

Ross said, "Morgan, how did you get like this?"

"Like what, darling?" Morgan drawled.

"The way you are. You weren't born cruel."

Morgan looked at him, pausing momentarily in her savage pacing.

"I think I was," she said.

"No — something happened. Something twisted you. What was it, Morgan? Tell me — what?"

Morgan came over to where he was and sank to the floor beside his chair, as gracefully as a cat. She put both her elbows on his knees, and rested her chin upon her hands. Again, damnably, her face had that aspect of childlike innocence.

"I don't know," she said; "does it matter?"

"Yes," Ross said; "it matters very much."

"Why, Ross?"

"Because I've been trying to hate you, and I can't. That's a curious thing. Since I've known you I don't remember your ever having said or done a single thing that wasn't evil. I should hate you for that. I should despise you for what you've done to me. . . ."

"What have I done to you, darling? From the number of gallants hereabouts who've tried every trick they were capable of to achieve what you have without half trying, I can't see where you have cause for complaint."

"No," Ross said slowly; "you can't see it. I don't think I can even make you see it, you being what you are. . . ."

"Try," Morgan whispered.

"You've made me hate myself. Ever looked into your mirror and shuddered with self-loathing?"

"No. Why should I? I'm very nice to look at. Even I can see that."

"You are," Ross agreed. "But you're blind, Morgan. You can't look into your mirror and see the face of an adulterer staring out at you. Tarquin's face, ugly with sated lust. I see that. I say to myself, Lance was my friend, and I have betrayed him. That's bad. But what is really bad is to stand there and say: And I'm going to betray him again tonight and tomorrow, and every other time that he is absent from home. . . . That's worse than bad. That's terrible. I don't like being a slave, Morgan. Nobody's slave — not even yours."

"You aren't my slave. If you were, I should whip you. You're my lover, Ross. Such a wonderful lover, too! So strong and so tireless — so brutal, too — when I goad you into it. I like you best then. You should always be brutal. Tenderness is a kind of weakness."

"Or a kind of strength," Ross said tonelessly. "Who knows. I don't like what we're doing. A man like Lance shouldn't be made to wear horns. He has too much dignity to play the cuckold well. I don't like it, Morgan."

"Why not?" Morgan laughed; "hasn't it been – fun?"

"No it hasn't. I don't like going home with a tiredness like death in me. I am sick of being nail-ripped, teeth-torn. You call this wrestlers' duel to the death we engage in – love? Or me – your lover? You've made me something less than human, Morgan – an instrument to serve your pleasure; the toy of your quite fiendish appetites. There's no end to your hungers, is there? And they're all evil. . . . That brutality you insist upon – what kind of a sickness is that? No, don't answer. You can't, because you don't know. I think that's why I don't hate you – why I pity you, I can't hate you, because you haven't been born yet – you're not a person, not a living woman; you're evil incarnate, permitted for a little time to walk this earth – you said that yourself once, didn't you?"

"Yes," Morgan said unsteadily; "I did."

"I think that the day that you are born, you'll die. When you come out of darkness into light; out of that poisonous maze in which you wander, into reality, the recognition of yourself, of what you have been, will burn your heart to a cinder, and you'll die. You'll die mad – screeching. Oh yes, Morgan you'll die. . . ."

"You do hate me, don't you?" Morgan said.

"No. How can I? You don't exist. What I'd

like to know is how you managed to escape life? Tell me that, and I'll know why I cannot hate you."

Morgan turned away from him, stretching her long legs out before her. Then she lay back, her head resting upon his lap.

"I don't know, Ross. The things you say, don't mean anything, really. And yet they seem to mean something – a kind of meaning beyond meaning. If I could understand them, I'd enter into your world. Then, maybe I'd die – like you said. How did I escape life? The answer to that one, my battered darling, is I didn't. I was born into life. I was drowned in it so that it – all of it seeped into me through my very pores. More than other people ever know, more than they can feel . . . It used to wash over me in the darkness – like a wave. . . . "

She raised her head, staring away from him out the window.

"I used to lie upon my little bed when I was a child, and listen to the sounds of it in the darkness. Father wouldn't let me have a light. He wanted me to be brave. I've hated darkness ever since. The house we had was built above the Hudson. It was very big and very old. At night, it creaked, and the wind tugged at it, outside. . . . And sometimes I would wake up and hear my mother's voice. I never could make out what she said. But she seemed to be begging my father – imploring him. Then afterwards, she would scream. That scream is in my blood, Ross – it comes out sometimes, and I have to hit someone, hurt someone – see blood. . . . I was terrified of my father, as a child. And yet, I loved him. He was the most fascinating man you could ever meet. I told my mother once that when I grew up, I was going to marry him, too. I've never forgotten the look upon her face. It was death, and horror – and that's a part of life, too, Ross – one of the parts I didn't escape.

"When I grew up, I found out other things about my father. My mother loved him and hated him, but the love was stronger. I adored my mother, and when I found out about the other women – so many other women, Ross – I decided I'd kill my father, so that he couldn't make her suffer any more. But I couldn't. I loved him too much. . . . Does this makes sense to you?"

"Yes," Ross said curtly; "it does."

"When I was fifteen years old, one of the stableboys tried to rape me. I beat him, because I was terribly strong even then. I told my father about it, and he took his crop and beat that boy. I watched it. It made me feel wonderful to watch it – all soft and warm inside, and melting. . . . Father ordered him off the place but he couldn't go right then, because he couldn't walk. So Father let him stay until he was well enough. But in the meantime there was this French actress, and Father forgot the stableboy."

"But you — didn't?"

"No. I kept wondering what it would have been like if I hadn't beaten him off. So one night I crept up into the loft over the stable where he slept and told him to go ahead. Poor fellow, he was petrified with fright. In the end, I ravished him. He begged me for mercy, finally, and the next morning he disappeared."

"There were — others?"

"A few. But I soon found out that most damnable of masculine traits — the supreme ego of the human male. They started acting like they owned me, and lording it over me, and trying to tell me what to do. But I'd had enough of that from my father. Nobody tells me what to do; I'm my own mistress, Ross. After that there weren't any more lovers — except in the way I'd worked out. There's nothing more delightful than to watch them puff out their feathers, sure of a conquest, then stop them dead. Because men are all little boys — whistling in the dark, trying to keep up their courage — trying to delude themselves into believing they are lions instead of the wolves and jackals they really are. . . .

"After a while it seemed to me all men had one face and that face was the face of my father. I wanted to smash it — I wanted to destroy its insufferable conceit. That's why I avoided marriage. As soon as I'd known the man long enough his face became the face of my father. . . ."

"You married Lance," Ross pointed out.

"I had to. We were penniless, mother and I. Father had just died, after squandering the last of his money and Mother's. We didn't know until afterwards in what terrible shape our finances were. He died in precisely the fashion you'd have expected him to — in the arms of his latest actress. And Mother followed him a few weeks later, of a broken heart. I swore then, that I'd never have a heart to be broken — that I'd never be beaten by life. And I haven't been, Ross, I haven't been!"

"No," Ross murmured; "but what a price you paid for your Pyrrhic victory. Anyone as lovely as you would have had all life's bounties laid at your feet. But by this dehumanization of yours, you've cheated yourself; you've thrown away your birthright."

Morgan stood up, laughing.

"What nonsense!" she said.

"Perhaps," Ross murmured. "But there's one thing you haven't told me, Morgan."

"What's that?"

"Why you have such a horror of being shut in, and of darkness."

Morgan's face was suddenly sullen.

"I don't remember," she said.

"Now you're lying," Ross told her. "I can always tell when you are, now."

"Oh, all right! Though why you must know that is more than I can see. Father locked me in an upstairs closet once when I was a child – to punish me. I don't remember what I had done. Then he went away and met one of his little dillies and forgot all about me. He didn't come back until the following night. Mother thought he had taken me with him – he often did, you know – for days at a time. . . ."

"And you stayed in that closet all that time?"

"Yes – without light. Without too much air. It took them four hours to get me to speak after they got me out. Mother said I was rigid – like a statue. The strangest part about it is I don't remember it at all."

"You don't remember it," Ross said, "then how –"

"Only because mother told me about it. I had a nightmare once – after I was grown. I dreamed that I was locked in a kind of a ruined building. It had been destroyed — by fire I think, and I was caught in the ruins. Mother heard me screaming and came into my room and I told her. She said " 'You must have been remembering. . . .' "

"Perhaps you were," Ross said; "I must be going now. I'm not up to an encounter with Lance this morning."

"Nor any other morning when I've finished with you," Morgan laughed. " 'Bye darling. Kiss me good-bye, then go. I must have my beauty sleep, you know."

Ross kissed her lightly, standing away from her, and bending forward so that his lips merely brushed hers.

"You call that a kiss?" Morgan murmured. "No, you'll have to do better than that!" Then she arched her body upward against his so that it fitted from breast to toe-tip into every contour his leaning body made. Her head went backward and at an angle, and the hot, wet underflesh of lip and tongue-tip clung with their old accustomed expertness. Why was it that in this at least, Ross thought bitterly, that familiarity bred no contempt? That here, indeed, was only the added savor of anticipation?

Morgan whirled away from him, laughing.

" 'Bye, now," she said; "and remember, keep that Pedro away from my Bessie — he's giving her too many ideas."

How Pedro could give anyone ideas with that mangled English he had learned in the not quite a year he had been at Moonrise was more than Ross could see; but it was of little importance, anyhow.

"All right," he said; "I'll do that."

Riding away from Finiterre, Ross turned the whole thing over in his mind. How long had it been going on? Almost a year now. Let's see, he mused, it started just after Aubert left for Europe, and he will be home again in another month. Jennie and Annis are making preparations for the wedding now. And to think that I used to berate Tom about being a slave to the flesh. Well, who's the slave now? More than any black. We own their bodies and their labors, but their souls at least are free. I've made my Faustian bargain — for this woman, I've sold my immortal soul. . . .

Perhaps, he thought wryly, this "irrepressible conflict" that Senator Seward is accusing us of forcing, will free me of her. A minie ball severs all bonds. . . .

Back at Moonrise, where he could stay now, as often as he liked, since he had removed by his own actions the bone of contention between himself and Tom, he looked in for a moment upon Jennie and Annis. They were busy with their sewing; for though both he and Tom had offered to purchase Annis' trousseau from the finest shops in the land, the women had refused them, preferring to make it themselves. There was, Ross guessed, a certain satisfaction in being married in a gown you had made yourself.

"Well," he said; "how's it going, girls?"

"Oh, Ross," Annis wailed; "we'll never be done in time!"

"If," Ross smiled, "you wouldn't try to make enough things to clothe an army, you would be done. It's such a waste. You would look lovely even in a gunny sack, Annis. . . ."

"Thank you for saying so," Annis said, "even if it isn't true. Oh, dear! Jennie just look at this sheering — how awful!"

"Don't worry about it, darling," Jennie said.

Ross closed the door quietly behind him and went upstairs to his room. He lay down across the bed and stared at the ceiling, an unlit cigar stuck into the corner of his mouth. There was work to be done at the office but he didn't feel like going there; his assistants could take care of it without his being present. He had to do some thinking — now was the time that the decision had to be made. Most people went through life without knowing themselves; by dreams and evasions they magnified their better qualities, and pushed the things they were ashamed of out of sight and out of mind.

Ross would have little difficulty obtaining a position with one of the architectural firms in New York or Philadelphia or Boston. He had business connections in all three of those cities. Of course, to run away again was a confession of cowardice — an admission that he could not cope with Morgan Brittany or himself. But why not make the admission, since it was true? Wasn't it better to be a coward, to run, than it was to live here in shame? It was a weakness to fly, but if he stayed, would he have the strength to break with Morgan? He groaned, thinking of it. . . .

He got up from the bed and went into the bathroom. After he had bathed and shaved, he felt better. The decision actually was no decision at all — self-preservation was a law of life. If he remained in Natchez, Morgan would destroy him. If he fled, she would be forced to turn once more to Lance. Annis' future was taken care of. Jennie had once more the look of quiet happiness in her eyes. Only he hung whimpering upon the edge of life; in him only was existence all past and no future. . . .

In the North, he could start all over again. He was not old. At thirty-two he had vigor enough to start a great career; better still, he had wisdom and maturity enough to avoid repeating the errors that had wrecked so much of his life. There might even be the companionship of a gentle, understanding woman, though love was gone from him now — forever gone. Conchita and Morgan, between them, had managed to rid him of his capacity for love; Conchita, through remembered sorrow — Morgan with the fires of her strange, unholy passions. . . .

He dined alone in his room, pleading a headache. As usual, he scarcely touched his food. Then, after he was sure that the family had left the first floor of the house, he came down into the salon and seated himself at the piano. He tried to play Conchita's dance, but he could not; after the first line, the memory of her was so bright before his eyes that he could not go on. It seemed to him that her green eyes reproved him from the shadows — that wherever she was, she felt injured and betrayed. If he had loved again, if he had married, that, Ross felt, her wandering shade would have understood, could have forgiven; but this ugly, loveless passion for Morgan was quite another thing. It had to end — and now.

He got up from the piano and left the house. He walked down to the edge of the bluff overlooking the river. He sat down under an oak and smoked a cigar, looking out over the

Mississippi toward Louisiana. Lance was over there, busy with his plantations. Often he worked so late that he did not come home at all. He always told Morgan when he planned to be absent, which was a mistake, for it let her know exactly when she could safely send for Ross. Lance Brittany was a fine man, and Ross's friend. Under any given set of circumstances what had happened made no sense at all. It did Ross's conscience no good at all to remind himself that he had been driven to it. "He was my friend," Ross quoted bitterly, "faithful and just to me. . . ." And how have I repaid him? No — let Morgan rage all she cared to, he would never spend another night with her.

It grew dark slowly. A star hung in the pale dusk and winked at him. A little breeze stirred the moss on the oak trees. And the surface of the river darkened. Ross sat there until it was entirely dark. Then he got up stiffly, and went back up to the house. Early as it was, he undressed and went to bed, hoping that he would not be plagued by visions of Morgan. An hour later, he awoke to the realization that he had been dozing — that he actually was going to be able to sleep.

I've won, he thought, and burrowed contentedly into his pillow.

He came awake slowly in the blackness of

midnight, and lay in that curious state between sleep and wakefulness, listening to the shouting. It seemed to him that the voices were calling his name.

"Ross!" they called; "Ross Pary! Come on out – you and Tom!"

Hell of a kind of dream, Ross thought, and turned over. Then he saw that his window was red with the glare of torches. He was up at once, racing for the window. Down below, the yard was filled with more than a hundred men, mounted and armed. He pushed his head far out of the window. Among them he recognized George and Henry Metcalfe, Charles Dahlgren, Henry Montcliffe, and Levin Marshall.

"Come on down, Ross," Henry Montcliffe called; "there's trouble out at Finiterre! The niggers have revolted!"

Ross's face grayed. Ever since Nat Turner had led his revolt in August 1831, in which sixty whites had been killed, the South had lived in dread of what it grandiloquently called "servile insurrection."

He did not for one second doubt the report. With Morgan Brittany as mistress of Finiterre, the Negroes had by now, he was certain, excuse enough to rebel ten times over.

"Coming!" he called down and raced for his clothes.

As he reached the lower hall, he met Tom, pistol in hand, running for the door. Outside, a dozen eager hands helped them to saddle their horses, then the whole band rode off pounding through the night towards Finiterre.

"How'd you know about this?" Ross asked George Metcalfe as he rode by his side.

"A good nigger came out to Richmond and told Levin," George said.

And that, Ross thought bitterly, was always the history of the Negro in slavery. The good ones, the fawning, hat-in-hand ones, the ones who got the old boots and the cast-off garments and a kindly word from their masters, ran and told. It was a curious commentary on the state of Ross Pary's mind that he could not admire that kind of a black. It was always the proud ones like Brutus, the daring, like Pedro, who captured his sympathy. With his ready ability to put himself in the other man's place, Ross could well imagine what it was like to be held a slave. And he knew what he would do in such a circumstance — what, indeed, he had done: run away, fight, kill anyone who tried to place this monstrous indignity upon him. If that night, Ross rode with the pack, his heart was with the hunted.

They came up the drive to Finiterre, and before they reached it, they could see it burning. The fire, Ross was relieved to see, had not yet gained much headway. With a little luck, they'd be able to put it out.

Then as they reached the house itself, they heard the shooting. Lance Brittany stood at a window and fired very coolly and well. Three of the Negroes lay dead upon the ground, but the others stood behind the trees and shot back.

Where the devil had they got the guns? Ross wondered. But he didn't get a chance to think about it any more, for the horsemen thundered down upon the blacks, and the Negroes broke and ran for the woods. The men galloped after them, firing. But Ross and Tom and Henry Montcliffe stayed where they were.

Morgan again, Ross thought ironically, the legion of her lovers. . . .

Then the three of them rode down to the quarters, and commandeered the frightened blacks who cowered there, to put out the fire. Lance came out of the house with a musket in his hand and Morgan followed him with a carbine.

"Many thanks," he said quietly, and Ross saw the bleak misery in his eyes. "Have you captured them?"

"Not yet," Henry Montcliffe said; "but we will!"

Ross stood there, staring at Morgan. Her

small, heart-shaped face was alight with pleasure. It was, Ross knew, precisely the sort of thing that she would enjoy.

Then the men were coming out of the woods dragging the Negroes behind them.

"Had to shoot five more of the bastards before they'd give up," Charles Dahlgren growled. "Well, Lance — shall we get on with the hanging?"

"Well —" Lance began; but Morgan cut in sharply: "Yes! Yes! Hang them — the murderous beasts."

They made a fire in the clearing, and the men went down to the stables and came back with ropes.

"What about the rest of your niggers," Henry Metcalfe asked; "they weren't in on this, were they?"

"No," Lance said.

"I think," Morgan said sweetly, "maybe they'd all better be given a whipping to teach them a lesson, just in case . . ."

"Good idea," Dahlgren began; but Lance cut him off.

"No!" he roared; "I won't have a one of my good people touched! Do you realize, Charlie, that if they'd joined in this, we wouldn't have been alive when you got here."

"That's true," Dahlgren grumbled, "still . . ."

"Still," Lance said quietly, "I'll hold any man personally responsible who touches a hair of their kinky heads."

Ross turned away from Morgan, cold and sick with disgust. Then something in the appearance of one of the captured blacks caught his attention. Pedro! Mother of God, why did he have to get mixed up in this?

Then he saw the reason. One of the rebellious Negroes was Bessie.

Ross walked over to where Pedro lay, his hands tied behind him, his face bloody.

"Why did you do it?" he groaned; "Mother of God, Pedro – why?"

Pedro grinned at him.

"There was this of the beatings," he said. "Additionally, my little dove could not be kept a slave. *María Santíssima,* but the white woman is formidable!"

"I'll see what I can do," Ross said.

"And for my Bessie also?" Pedro begged; "for her even if not for me. . . ."

Ross walked over to Lance.

"One of those blacks," he said, "is a free Cuban Negro who once saved my life. I wonder if . . ."

"No!" Morgan said.

Lance looked at her tiredly.

"Sorry, Ross," he said slowly; "I wish I could.

But these men wouldn't understand. It might cost us both their friendship; and we're going to need that damned soon, or I miss my guess . . ."

"All right," Dahlgren said; "string them up."

Ross watched the hangings. The eleven Negroes died in different ways, most of them very badly, begging and praying for life. But Pedro and Bessie stood up proudly, waiting.

"Those two," Morgan said, "were the ringleaders. They were lovers. Hang them together, won't you?"

The men grinned at her. This wife of Brittany's sure Lord had spunk. Most of the women they knew would have been stretched out in a cold faint by now.

They pushed Bessie and Pedro under the tree and dropped the noose around their necks. Something in their bearing must have moved Lance. Turning to George, he muttered: "See if they've got anything to say. . . ."

"No, Señores, nothing," Pedro said easily when the question was put to him; but Bessie's dark eyes flashed in the firelight.

"Yes!" she cried; "sure Lord I is got something to say! Want to tell you gentlemens why I done it! Because of her — because of that wicked woman right there! Know I'm going to die — so I'm telling the truth. Never thought of fighting — never even thought of being free till she come! But she stuck a scissors through my hand 'cause I done her hair wrong. She kicked me down the stairs 'cause I was a little slow. And gentlemens — I ask you one favor — just you go up in the attic and see what you'll see. Even Marse Lance don't know about that — that place what she had made where she could chain us to the floor and beat us — not 'cause we done nothing, but 'cause it pleasured her to beat us! See the fancy door she made to lock us in!

"Go and look at that! And see the bloody stains on the floor. Go out behind the barn and dig up the bones of old Lucas what she done whipped to death one night when Marse Pary didn't come over to sleep with her while Marse Lance was gone. . . ."

Ross's breath stopped in his lungs, and in the little pause all sounds were curiously magnified. He thought he could pick out the note of each man's breathing.

"Yes, yes! Going to tell you 'bout that now, Marse Lance — 'cause I'm going to die. Dying folks speaks true. Going to swear on it, before the Living God — 'cause you been good to us — only she been meaner'n hell! Marse Lance — ever' time you spent any time out of this here house, she had some other man in it! Mostly it

511

were that Marse ʀary — ᴍᴏʀᴇ ᴍᴍ ᴛʜᴀɴ ᴀɴʏ-body else. But she done shamed you, Marse Lance — she done shamed you a thousand times!"

Ross, who was watching Morgan, recognized the precise instant she lost control. She jerked the carbine up and fired; but Lance's heavy hand caught the barrel so that the bullet plowed up a furrow of earth at Bessie's feet.

"Hang her!" Morgan shrieked; "hang the lying black bitch!"

"Yes," Bessie said contemptuously; "hang me now, gentlemens; I done had my say."

The ropes jerked, tightened, and the two dark figures kicked in the moonlight; then finally they were still, their toes swinging slowly through half the points of the compass; but nobody looked at them.

They were looking at Lance Brittany. They were watching the spectacle of a man's spirit crumpling quite visibly behind the walls of his flesh. Then, with an effort, Lance mastered himself.

This is it, Ross thought bitterly, here he comes now, and tomorrow I'll die my dishonored death. Tomorrow I'll exchange shots with a man who has always befriended me, who has gone to trouble and expense to aid me, who has trusted me implicitly — and I betrayed him. Maybe there is justice in the world, after all. How will it be tomorrow? How will it be when I fire my pistol into the air and stand there waiting?

But suddenly all the hard-held breath left his lungs with a rush, for Lance had turned away from him and was marching stiffly, straight up to his brother, Tom.

"Oh, no! God, no!" Ross whispered. But Lance's big hand came back, and struck Tom hard across his face.

Ross saw his brother stiffen. Then Tom straightened up, proudly.

"Before all these gentlemen present," he said in a deep voice, "and before the God I serve, I want to declare that I'm innocent of these charges. But I'll meet you, Mister Brittany — any time or place you say."

"The sandbar," Lance got out; "in front of Vidalia. The choice of weapons is yours, Mister Pary."

"Pistols," Tom Pary said.

Ross broke out of the trance in which he had held. He ran over to where Tom and Lance stood.

"Lance," he said; "You've got the wrong Pary. I'm the guilty party, Lance — and I'm as guilty as hell."

Lance stared at him with dull eyes. There

was so much fatigue in his face.

"Gallant as usual, eh Ross?" he said tiredly. "I understand how you feel. After all, he is your brother. . . ."

"No!" Ross cried; "I'm not lying, Lance — I'm the guilty one, not Tom!"

"Sorry, Ross," Lance said heavily; "I won't fight you. I know what kind of relationship existed between you and Morgan. I have the right man all right."

"All she said was Pary!" Ross wept; "she didn't say which Pary."

"She didn't need to," Lance said.

"You'll have to meet me!" Ross raged; "if you kill Tom, I'll challenge you. Oh you stupid jackass, can't you see I'm not lying?"

"No," Lance said; "I can't see it. And if you issue a challenge, I'll refuse to accept it." He turned slowly, and with massive dignity, to the other men.

"Gentlemen," he said gravely; "my heartfelt thanks for your aid. Also my humblest apologies for the disgraceful scene that has transpired here. I assure you, that after this — the Brittanys will trouble Natchez no more. I would not have you reminded of the shame of my dishonored house, or have your ladies disturbed by the presence of one who has disgraced all Southern womanhood. And now, gentlemen — good night!"

Only a few of them answered him. In a way, they shared his shame. For a while hereafter the wives of Natchez would be troubled by much suspicious questioning.

Henry Montcliffe moved over to Lance, his face filled with concern.

"Go light on her, won't you, Lance?" he whispered.

Lance glared at him.

"Go light!" he said; "If she's alive tomorrow — it will be because my arm has grown too tired. Good night, sir!"

Morgan turned her gaze in Ross's direction. Her black eyes were filled with terror.

"Ross!" she gasped; "don't let him! Ross, please . . ."

Ross looked at her.

"God give his arm strength!" he said.

The river, moving, made a little peaceful sound as it washed against the sandbar. Ross Pary turned his head toward Natchez, already bright with sun because of the height upon which it sat. But here upon the sandbar before Vidalia, the light was still gray with morning mist.

Doctor Benbow knelt a little apart, examining his instruments. A little distance apart,

Lance Brittany stood silently beside Charles Dahlgren, his second. Both banks were lined with spectators, armed with telescopes; and the river was filled with skiffs, loaded to the gunwales with men come to see the slaughter.

The Judge stood up now, beckoning to the two men to come together. Ross heard his instructions only vaguely:

"Thirty paces – fire upon the count of three – any man firing prematurely to be shot by his seconds – duel can be terminated now by an apology given – or by mutual agreement. It can be ended later after an exchange of shots under the same conditions if no one is wounded. In the case of a non-fatal wound, the victor can declare his honor satisifed upon first blood. If he does not so declare, the duel must continue. Now shake hands and go to your places. And may God have mercy on your souls!"

Ross's eyes were red from lack of sleep. He had spent all of the remaining hours of the previous night, arguing with Tom, begging him to refuse to fight, pointing out that he had a wife and children, and that he was innocent.

"In a way I am," Tom had drawled. "In another I ain't. I never had nothing serious to do with her, but it sure Lord wasn't because I didn't try. Besides, Lance slapped my face in front of all those men. You want me to play the coward?"

Against such invincible stupidity, Ross was helpless. There was nothing more he could do. If his brother insisted upon dying for a sin he had not committed, Ross could only avenge him; that was all. Even that was not so simple as it looked. Avenge him against whom? Certainly Morgan was much more at fault in this matter than Lance – and he, himself, was perhaps the most at fault of all. If Tom died, who among them had murdered him? The hand that pulled the trigger? The woman who had tempted him with her body until he found himself standing almost guiltless in this fatal place? Or Ross Pary, his brother, who had done the thing for which now, he must die?

The two men were standing facing each other now. The judge began his counting.

"One!"

Ross's hand tightened upon the butt of his own pistol. What if he were to fire? As a second, he could shoot only under a violation of the conditions laid down. They would hang him for murder – but what mattered that if he saved Tom?

"Two!"

But Lance was his friend. And he had betrayed him. He couldn't kill Lance – he couldn't. . . .

"Thr –"

The two shots made one sound. Ross saw Lance reel. A patch of red blossomed high upon his left shoulder. Tom still stood there, unmoving. Ross raced over to him; but while he was still yards away, Tom's knees buckled very slowly, and he pitched forward on his face in the sand.

Ross threw himself down beside him and lifted his head into his lap. Tom opened his mouth to say something, but he never got it out, for his words were drowned in a rush of blood. The ball had gone through his lungs, and he was drowning. He lay upon Ross's lap, coughing up blood in clots, his big, handsome face turning blue. It took him a long time to die, for he was a man of great strength.

Ross eased his inert head back down upon the sand and stood up. His own clothing was drenched with his brother's blood. My soul is covered with it, too, he thought; and I shall never be clean. . . . Then in one wild rush, he started toward Lance.

But Dahlgren and Doctor Benbow bore him down. He struggled with them so fiercely, shrieking with rage, that Charles Dahlgren finally brought the barrel of his pistol down across his head.

Lance stood there staring at his inert form.

"Poor devil," he murmured. "He was my

friend. But this finishes that. In a way it finishes me, too. . . .”

He looked past Ross to where Tom lay, sprawled out in one of those postures that have no counterpart in life, and shuddered.

“Well, gentlemen,” he said quietly, “shall we go?”

When Ross regained consciousness he found himself on his own bed at Moonrise, and someone was bathing his face. Then his eyes cleared and he saw his sister, Annis, sitting there beside him, bathing his face and crying.

“Jennie?” he whispered.

“Upstairs in her room,” Annis said.

“How is she taking it?” Ross said.

“Hard. She hasn’t cried. Oh, Ross, what an awful thing it is not to be able to cry.”

Ross struggled to sit up. But the room reeled drunkenly, and sledge hammers started pounding inside his head. He kept trying it until at last he was upright, and then Jennie came into the room and put her hand on his chest and pushed him down again.

“No,” she said; “no more killing, Ross.”

“But —” Ross began.

“The only one who should die for this,” Jennie said in a low voice, “is Morgan, Ross. And she will die — but not by your hand. I won’t have that. She’ll die in the fullness of time — by the hand of God. . . ." She stared past him, out the window. "And it will be terrible dying. She will die very slowly and in such a fashion that she will beg for death long before it comes to her. But you mustn't challenge Lance. Promise me that, Ross. Promise me!"

"All right," Ross said. "I promise."

"Try to rest, Ross. Doctor Benbow thinks you might have a slight concussion."

"So?" Ross said; "you think I should care about that?"

"Yes. You're not a coward. Death is so easy, Ross. It would be ever so much easier for me. But there are the children. So I must live. And you, too, Ross – for they're your flesh and blood, too. They must have some future."

"Yes," Ross whispered; "they must."

He lay upon the bed looking at her, and he saw that her eyes were dead and her face was terrible. She got up very quietly and left the room. Ross turned to Annis.

"Go to her, Annis," he said; "don't leave her alone. I'll be all right."

After Annis had gone, he lay upon the bed and tried to think. But his head ached damnably. He slipped after a time into a curious somnolence – a state halfway between sleep and wakefulness. When he roused himself again, it was night.

He sat up in the bed. His head ached dully, but the room no longer reeled. When he tried it, he found that he could stand. He dressed quickly and went down the back stairs and out into the stable and saddled Nancy. Then he started riding toward Finiterre.

She has lived long enough, he thought. Jennie is right — not Lance. Lance was the tool of circumstances; the unwitting instrument of the fates. But Morgan did this thing — with my help. With the help of my weakness, my cowardice, my lack of will. My part in it won't go unpunished, because it will take its end from this. But she cannot be permitted to go on sowing destruction to the winds and reaping her deadly harvests. Lance won't be here tonight. After this morning he will be in need of comforting. He'll go to Connelly's. Only I will be here — and Morgan. And that will be enough.

As he rode through the high gate, he noticed that the splintered top bar had neither been repaired or replaced. That was indicative of something. When a man like Lance began to neglect his home, something had gone out of him.

He got down from the horse and tied her to the hitching rail. Then he went up the curving stairs to the gallery and into the house where no servant waited and there was no sound. He moved surely up the stairway to Morgan's bedroom, and just before he reached it, he heard her whimpering.

He pushed open the door, and looked into her eyes. They were the eyes of an animal, senseless and glaring. She had a lock of her thick, black hair pulled down into her mouth and she was chewing it, slowly.

Ross moved over to where she lay across the bed, and when he was close he saw that the back of her dress was lashed into ribbons and sticking to her. But she didn't say anything. She lay there chewing the lock of her hair, and whimpering.

Ross backed away from her, toward the door. The Hand of God, Jennie had said. This was a strange thing. God was seldom so prompt in dealing with the affairs of men. . . .

As he went down the stairs again he was conscious of a feeling of relief. What he had meant to do, he would have done more in sorrow than in anger — neither out of hatred nor of vengefulness; but because he was convinced of its necessity and now it seemed no longer necessary.

The next three days were the ones that he tried afterwards not to remember. They were days of silence and of sad preparations. But they were over finally, and the burial ground at Moonrise held its first Pary.

They were moving back up to the house, with David Martin and Ross supporting Jennie between them, when they saw a Negro riding toward them at a hard gallop. Ross didn't know the man; but he did know the horse he rode; it was Satana, Morgan's black mare.

The man pulled the mare up as he came up to them and took off his ragged hat.

"Marse Ross," he quavered; "Miz Morgan say you come right now! There's been an accident . . ."

They all stood still, staring at the black. Even Jennie stopped her helpless crying.

"An accident?" Ross had a premonition. "What kind of an accident?"

"Marse Lance, suh. He tried to jump that there high gate agin — and Prince didn't make it. Reckon he dead, suh."

Jennie's fingers tightened convulsively upon Ross's arm.

"She killed him!" she moaned. "Oh, Ross — she's killed him too!"

"No, Jen," Ross said. "Lance was always jumping Prince over that gate. And it was too high. I saw him miss breaking his neck by inches not so long ago, myself. Reckon Lance got careless — or he was overwrought. All right," he said to the Negro, "tell your Mistress I'm coming."

He did not push Nancy on the way. There was no hurry now. Whether he arrived late or soon would not help Lance Brittany. He wondered if subconsciously Lance had not pulled Prince up too soon, or held him back a little too hard. After the duel, there had been a death wish in Lance's eyes. A man like Lance did not kill himself knowingly; but he might easily become dangerously careless when life no longer mattered. . . .

He rode through the broken gate without half looking at it. The top bar was shattered and the one below that was splintered a little; he saw that without looking at the gate but these details were meaningless to him. Some of the Negroes were hitching a team of mules to Prince's broken carcass, getting ready to drag it away.

He went up the stairs and into the hall. The doors of the dining room were open and he could see Morgan standing there, beside a blanket-wrapped object on the table. She was neatly dressed and her hair was combed and her eyes were cool and steady and absolutely griefless. Ross came into the dining room and walked past her and stood looking down at the covered body of Lance Brittany. Then he put out his hand and drew the blanket off his face and looked at it. Lance's face was serene and quiet. He looked singularly peaceful. Even his eyes were closed. Were it not for the dreadful angle that his head tilted toward his left shoulder, it might have been possible to believe he slept.

Ross turned toward Morgan, his gaze filled with speculation.

Her eyes, he saw, were utterly peaceful, and on her face was a deep and quiet smile.

"Now," she said; "now we are rid of him, Ross. Now you will marry me and we'll live here at Finiterre and be the happiest two people in the world. . . ."

Then going up on tiptoe, she kissed his mouth.

His hands came up and gripped her shoulders and hurled her away from him. She struck the table so hard that only the weight of Lance's massive body prevented it from turning over.

She lay back against it and the trapped animal look was back in her eyes. But only for a moment. Then they cleared.

"Ross," she whispered, "Ross . . ."

Ross stared at her. He was trembling. He had felt like this only once before and that was the time they had come upon the bodies of their companions in Cuba, spread-eagled upright between posts with their bellies ripped open. The sickness was down inside of him so deep that he regretted momentarily that he could not die of it.

He opened his mouth to scream at her, to call her — what? And it came to him that no epithet existed that was not pale and colorless against the actuality of Morgan.

She came up from against the table and stood there looking at him, and Ross could see that her mouth was moist and parted, and that she was beginning to pant a little like a feline she-thing, and the sickness curled itself into a knot at the pit of his stomach and stopped his breath. But he rammed his will downward out of the core of his heart into the nerves and muscles of his limbs and whirled away from her silently and marched out of the room and did not stop until he came to the place where his mare waited. He mounted her and rode away from the house toward the twelve-barred gate that had cost Lance Brittany his life.

He did not know what made him stop and look at it. He had the feeling that something was wrong with it, something he could discover if he used his eyes. But he could not see it. The top bar was broken on the left, precisely in the place that the forefoot that Prince always carried low in jumping would have struck it. Beneath it, on the bar below the top one, a yard-long splinter had been gouged out. That was all. But he couldn't shake the feeling that something was wrong with that gate; something he knew, something he had seen before.

He turned Nancy away from it and headed back toward Moonrise. And when he had ridden five hundred yards, it came to him. He yanked the mare around and came back toward the gate at a gallop. Just before he reached it, he pulled her up, hard.

The splintered planking of the topmost bar had the bright, clean yellow coloring of freshly broken wood. But the piece gouged out of the second bar was old. The broken place had weathered and turned brown from months of exposure to sun and rain. It had been knocked out of the bar months ago, almost a year ago, for he, himself, had seen it when it happened. Why, in the name of all that was holy, had the Negroes used the old planking when they repaired the gate? What sense was there in shifting this board downward to a lower position, when the bar below it had been untouched? His mind worked slowly, raggedly.

To do that, they would have had to throw away a perfectly good bar, or change the places of the two bars so that the top one was intact

527

while the second one was broken. Even so, it didn't make sense; and Lance wouldn't have permitted it. There was enough already cut and seasoned lumber on the grounds to build a house, let alone replace a broken gate bar.

Then quite suddenly, and with dreadful certainty, he knew what the Negroes had done — and at whose orders they had done it. All he had to do now to prove his thought was to count the bars. But he couldn't bring himself to do it. The broken place on the second bar was old. And Prince had carried his left forefoot low in jumping, but not low enough to break through two bars at once. The second bar had been the top bar, and looking at it now, Ross Pary could see that the nails that held it in place were rusted. They had not been removed. The broken top bar had not been removed. All they had done was to — He started counting:

"One, two, three, four, five —" It must be; it would be like her to think of this.

"Six, seven, eight, nine, ten —" I can't. It would be too much — enormously too much.

"Eleven, twelve — thirteen." Thirteen bars on a twelve-barred gate. Another bar — eight inches higher than the space that Prince had been able to clear at the top of his jumping form. Coming up to the gate at a gallop, Lance Brittany hadn't had time to count the bars.

There was no reason why he should have thought of counting the bars since he was not the one who had given the orders to make the gate higher. There it was. It was out now. Thirteen bars on a twelve-barred gate. And Morgan Brittany had murdered her husband.

He sat there on Nancy, cold and sick with helpless rage. There it was, and there was absolutely nothing he could do about it. He knew that he should go to the authorities, though the chance of their believing him in a case like this was slight. He, himself, with his brother dead at Lance's hands, would have a much better motive in their eyes for killing Lance than Morgan did. But it was not that which deterred him. It was rather, the belief that he should have disposed of Morgan himself, long ago — that as the unwilling partner in her crimes, he should have been the agent of just retribution. And he had muffed the chance. Now he would not do it — because he could not. . . .

He rode back toward Moonrise through a world turned gray, gone dead, where even the branches of the trees had a sinister life of their own. They seemed to pluck at him with ghostly hands. And the rising wind mocked him.

"Coward!" it shrieked. "Fool and coward!"

When he got back to Moonrise, he called Simon and Wallace and ordered them to pack his things — all his things — enough for a long journey. Annis came into his room before they had finished, and stood there watching them.

"You're going away," she said.

"Yes."

"For how long, Ross?"

"I don't know," Ross said. "Maybe a year — maybe forever."

Annis looked at him, and her blue eyes misted over.

"What will we do, Ross?" she said tremulously; "what will we do without you?"

"David can take care of the place," Ross said; "and you'll be married to your Danton in another month."

"No," Annis said; "not in another month, Ross. I'm going to wait a year now — out of respect for Tom. Danton won't like it; but I can't marry him now — I can't!"

"I see," Ross murmured. "I think he'll understand. He appears to be the right sort."

"You'll write us, Ross?"

"No," Ross said.

"No?" Annis echoed. "Why not?"

Ross looked at her.

"I want to forget this place," he said heavily; "at least for a while. I want to make my heart whole again with other places — other scenes. Time dulls the edge of everything, Annis.

When I can — if I can, I shall come back again. When I've made up my mind about that — whether I shall return or not, I'll write you. Don't worry, Annis — I'm going to be all right."

"I think you will," Annis said tensely, "as long as you're away from her."

So it was that once again Ross Pary left the land of his fathers. He wandered for a year. He lived for varied periods of time in New York, Philadelphia, and Boston. By the end of that year, some of the pain had gone out of him; the twisted skeins of terror and shame and hurt had loosened their tentacles from around the walls of his heart, leaving him free to breathe again, to feel. . . .

But what was left was emptiness, and a loneliness so great it filled his world. He endured it for some months longer; then he embarked upon a coastal steamer and got off a few days later at Key West.

Cathy Linton saw him coming up the path to her uncle's house and waited breathlessly for his approach. Then, when he was close, and she could see his face, certainty burst upon her like a great light, and she ran down the stairs, straight into his arms.

Chapter 17

They rode in the cabriolet along the Champs-Élysées in Paris until they came to the Place de la Concorde. Then they swung halfway around the square and turned into the Rue de Rivoli by the Tuileries. The Louvre lay some distance beyond, shaped like the letter Y with an arch between the prongs.

"Let's get out here," Cathy said; "I want to walk under the trees."

"All right," Ross said.

He paid the driver and they got down. Then they started to walk under the chestnut trees in the Tuileries. It was late in the fall of 1857, and the air was silver gray. An old man sat on one of the benches, feeding the squirrels. The pigeons arched far out over the Place de la Concorde, banking together in the same smooth circle above the spire and across the Seine, then back over the Tuileries again.

"I can get tickets for the Opéra tonight," Ross said. "Would you like to go there?"

"No," Cathy said miserably. "I want to go home!"

"Home?" Ross said. "To Key West?"

"No! To your Moonrise, silly! I'm sick of all this. . . ."

"Don't you like Paris?" Ross said.

"No — everybody speaks French to me. Even you forget and do it sometimes. It's been a nice long honeymoon, darling — but it's lasted too long to my way of thinking. I'm tired of being a bride, Ross. I'd like to start being a wife. I'd like to manage your house and — and have a baby. Why haven't we had a baby, Ross? We've been married almost two years now. In three more months it will be two years. Why haven't we?"

"God knows," Ross said.

He looked at Cathy. She was dressed in a black plush pelisse with beaver fur at the cuffs and around the hem. The fur went straight across the bodice above the breasts and over the shoulders and down the back to the waist, where it met in a vee. Cathy's little black hat had ostrich tips, and was tied under her chin with a bow of green ribbon. Her dress was of green silk with lingerie collar and cuffs. On Cathy, the whole effect was very fetching. She was one of those women designed by nature to wear handsome clothes. The couturiéres delighted to see her enter their shops. Not only was Ross generous with her to a fault; she was a walking advertisement for their wares. Many another wealthy English or American woman was moved to ask her where she bought her clothes. Any shop that Cathy Pary frequented was sure to notice thereafter, a considerable increase in trade.

There were many women in Paris much more beautiful than Cathy; but their very beauty tended to divert attention from the clothes they wore. Cathy's stark, exciting face, and the thin figure that the matchless cuisine of Paris had been able to add only a few pounds to, caught the eye and made it linger. Beauty, in itself, Ross mused, is after all commonplace — but you never forget a face like Cathy's. It's not pretty; but it's anything but plain. It's so damned alive.

Cathy smiled at him, and let her gloved hand rest lightly upon his arm. When she smiled, the freckles on her nose crinkled delightfully.

"Can't we go home, Ross?" she teased; "can't we?"

Ross frowned.

Go home. Back to Moonrise standing on the bluff above the river under the oaks. Back to the smell of the camellias, and the roads that were like tunnels of green lace under the overhanging boughs. Back to the sweep of blue sky and rolling field, and the dark voices singing in the sun.

Back to where Finiterre brooded white and ghostly above the river. Back to where Morgan is — Morgan the terrible, who can twist a man's soul between the palms of her hands. . . .

He felt something moving just below his heart — something like pain. He hadn't realized just how much he missed his home — how much he wanted and needed to be there. Besides, there was a job to be done: now that Tom was dead, he could free his slaves. He could move the burden of that particular guilt from his vastly overburdened soul. Hang Morgan, anyhow! Ever since that day nearly eight years ago that she had stood there laughing in the sunlight while the river rats beat him to a bloody hulk, she had had entirely too much influence upon his life — all of it bad. He smiled suddenly, joyously.

"Yes, Cathy," he said; "yes — we'll go home!"

Then Cathy kissed him.

They dined that night at a café in Montmartre, savoring their last night in Paris.

Across the street from where they sat under the elms on the sidewalk, facing each other across the little table, there was a theatre. Ross could read the signs on the billboards from where he sat.

"La Habañera!" they proclaimed, "the foremost Spanish Dancer of the World!" There was even a painting of La Habañera. In the dim glow of the street lights, it looked vaguely familiar.

Cathy followed his gaze.

"Would you like to see her?" she asked.

"No," Ross said quickly. "No, Cathy, I wouldn't."

"All right," Cathy said. "Let's just sit here. It's ever so much nicer to sit here alone together."

"Yes," Ross said; "it is."

He was glad that Cathy did not ask him why he didn't want to see the Spanish dancer. The memory of Conchita was a dull ache now, buried under the passing years. He didn't want it awakened. It would do no good to revive it now. If they went into that theatre there would be the swift, fiery beat of Spanish music again; there would be the patterned thunder of flamencos, and it would all come back again — the sight of her scampering up the fallen palm; the memory of the perfect legs in the swirl of

536

skirts launching the classic grand *jeté* in a wild Cuban clearing; the sound of Pedro's serenade on the three-stringed guitar. No, it was far better like this.

They sat there a long time after supper, holding hands across the table and looking into each other's eyes. And after a while the doors of the theatre across the street opened and the crowd poured out of it.

"My God, it's late!" Ross said; "we'd better get back to the hotel and get some sleep — we're catching the early train for Cherbourg."

"A little longer, Ross," Cathy said softly; "it's so nice here. . . ."

They sat there a little longer, and the street grew quiet again. Finally, regretfully, Ross stood up, and touched Cathy's arm. She stood up too and they walked to the edge of the sidewalk, and Ross lifted his cane to summon a cab. One of them turned toward them, the ancient horse slow-clopping toward the curb. Ross opened the door and took Cathy's arm. And it was at that moment that the Spanish dancer, la Habañera, came out of the theatre on the arm of Raoul Bergson, her manager and saw him.

She stopped dead, her long fingers gripping his arm.

"What ails you, darling?" the manager said.

537

"Have you gone mad?"

"That man! That man! Oh Raoul! I could swear. . . ."

"You could swear what?" Bergson said gruffly.

Across the street Ross Pary lifted his head.

"No," she whispered; "the face is different. There is an immense difference about the nose. Still in spite of that he looks like him. Enormously!"

"Like whom?" Bergson said tiredly.

"Like a man I knew once – in Cuba. A man I was once in love with. The only man in truth that I have ever really loved. . . ."

"There have been enough of them since, darling," Bergson said. "Come on – you must rest. Tomorrow we go to Marseilles. . . ."

The cabriolet bearing Ross Pary and his bride clopped off in the direction of the right bank. The dancer stood there staring after it.

"Could we not follow them, Raoul?" she said insistently; "perhaps they go to a hotel and I could discover . . ."

"No," Bergson was brusque. "This is a great folly. *Ma foi,* but you have strange whims. . . ."

Ross and Cathy reached New York City in January of 1858, and lingered there for two months while Ross talked to the heads of various architectural firms.

"What do you want to talk to all these men for?" Cathy complained; "I want to go home."

"Business," Ross said.

"But you have your own business, and your plantation. I don't see . . ."

"Don't worry your little head about it," Ross said.

"But I have to," Cathy said, the color flaming in her cheeks. "What concerns you concerns me. The way it looks to me is that you're planning to move up here!"

"I am," Ross said.

Cathy's gray eyes opened wide. She stared at her husband and a little tremble started at the corner of her mouth.

"You — you'd live up here among all these Yankees — after all that's happened?" she asked in astonishment.

"I'm afraid we're going to have to, Cathy," Ross said gravely. "I'm going to be mighty unpopular in Natchez when I get through freeing my slaves . . ."

Cathy's breath came out in a rush, audibly.

"You're going to turn your niggers loose?" she said.

"Yes, Cathy."

"I'm afraid I don't understand. . . ."

Ross came over to her and took her hands.

He looked into her eyes sadly.

"Twice in Cuba," he said, "black men saved my life. While I was there, I was captured and beaten with a whip — the way we sometimes beat Negroes. I was held like a slave — kept in order to furnish music for my — owners. So I know the other side of it, Cathy, honey. I know in my heart that no man has any right to own another man, like a horse."

Cathy snatched her hands downward and away from his grip.

"You do this, and I'll leave you!" she said; "I won't be married to a man who's a traitor to the South!"

"Look, Cathy," Ross said gently; "I'm an American. I don't belong to any section — North, South, East, or West. And I think that slaveholding shames our whole nation. I think it's an outmoded barbarism without any moral justification whatsoever."

Cathy looked at him. Then, suddenly, she began to cry.

"I thought I knew you!" she sobbed; "But I didn't! You're as bad as that old John Brown who killed all those people out in Missouri!"

"We gentlemanly Southerners killed a few ourselves," Ross said drily. "It was way back in 'fifty-five that five thousand Southerners invaded Kansas and took over the polls. And, if I remember correctly, it was May twenty-fifth of 'fifty-six that John Brown and his men killed those five slavery men at Pottawatomie Creek — four days after we chivalrous Southerners had burned the free soil capitol of Lawrence to the ground — the same day that another Southern gentleman beat a small and frail Massachusetts Congressman almost to death with a gutta percha cane. Or maybe you approve of Bully Brooks?"

"Oh, I hate you!" Cathy sobbed. "Damn your ornery hide, I hate you!"

Ross came up to her and put his arms around her.

"It's not our quarrel, Cathy," he murmured. "I love you — and things will work out. . . ."

"No, they won't! And there's going to be a war. Then which side will you be on, Ross Pary?"

Ross sighed heavily.

"I'm sorry you asked me that," he said. "Truthfully, Cathy, I'll be on the side that holds all men free and equal under God. I hope I can get you to see things my way before that happens. God knows I hope so. . . ."

"Never!" Cathy said.

They reached Natchez in June after a lengthy stay with Harry Linton in Key West, and two full weeks in New Orleans. Ross had been in no real hurry to get home.

He started walking with Cathy up Silver Street, hoping to find a public conveyance to take them out to Moonrise once they had reached the upper town. But, before he was able to find any kind of a hack, he saw Henry Montcliffe driving toward them in a smart, two-handed rig.

"Ross!" Henry cried. "Look at the prodigal! Bless my soul, but you look fine!" He turned his gaze upon Cathy, and his dark eyes sparkled.

Cathy looked at him and in spite of herself, she smiled. This one sure is handsome, she thought. Good-looking as Ross used to be before his nose was broken – no, better-looking. Good bit of the devil in those eyes, too. . . .

"Who's the lady, Ross?" Henry said.

"My wife," Ross told him. "Cathy, may I present my friend, Henry Montcliffe?"

"Mighty proud to make your acquaintance, ma'am," Henry said. His voice at the moment, had a certain warmth to it. Nice little creature, he was thinking. Sort of homely – but nice. Slim – lines like a racing filly's. The only trouble with the whole damned thing is that Ross hangs around home too much. But the smile upon his face when he turned to Ross was

542

candid and clear.

"Can I give you folks a lift, Ross?" he said.

"We'd be mighty obliged," Ross said; "but we're going way out to Moonrise, and that's a pretty fair sized trip."

"Think I'd let a little thing like that spot me?" Henry grinned. "Where are your valises? You must have some."

"I left them at the sawmill," Ross told him. "Figured they'd be safe there. It was a mite too hot to lug them all the way up Silver Street."

"All right, then," Henry said; "we'll drive down there and pick them up first."

"Don't bother," Ross said. "You're doing enough for us now, Henry. Besides, there are trunks, too — so I have to send a wagon out from Moonrise for them anyhow."

"Tell you what," Henry said; "we'll pick up the valises — you'll need them right away. Then when we pass Laurel Hill on the way to Moonrise, I'll send some of my niggers after your trunks. That way, they'll be at Moonrise a heck of a lot quicker."

"Now really, Henry . . ."

"Don't mention it, Ross; don't you say a word. Glad to do it."

He's nice, Cathy thought. He really is nice. And so handsome, too. I hope he comes to visit us sometime.

"Do you ever come out to Moonrise, Mister Montcliffe?" she asked him.

"Well, I haven't very much before," Henry laughed; "but I'm going to now. Got to solve the mystery. . . ."

"What mystery?" Cathy asked.

"How come a sweet little girl like you went and married this mashed-faced scoundrel," Henry said.

"And when you've solved it?" Ross asked lightly.

"I don't know," Henry said. "Reckon I'll try to steal her for myself — if she can be persuaded. What about it, ma'am? Could I persuade you to leave old broken nose?"

Cathy looked at Ross, and a dangerous glint showed in her gray eyes.

"Reckon maybe I could," she said quietly, "if he doesn't behave better than he has these last few months. . . ."

"Fine!" Henry laughed; "I'll start working at it right away!"

There was, Ross thought, an undertone in all this jesting that he didn't like. It cut perilously close to truth. And if ordinarily he held husbandly jealousy an unworthy trait, insulting to his wife, and demeaning to himself, he could not deny that the relationship between himself and Cathy had been showing signs of strain for a long time. The root of it was the fact that he did not love Cathy — a state of affairs difficult to conceal from any woman, and quite impossible to hide from anyone as intelligent as Cathy. More than one accidental remark of his, he suspected, had already sowed the seed of disaffection between them. He'd have to walk carefully. . . .

It came to him then that this, too, hadn't worked out right — that so little in a man's life ever did work out right. Who was to blame for that? Men who marshaled their affairs so stupidly or the God who withheld from them the wit to arrange things better?

"What on earth are you thinking about?" Cathy said. "You haven't said a word for miles."

"God," Ross said.

Henry Montcliffe lifted his hand, and pointed his index finger at his temple, moving it about in a circle in the age-old symbol for insanity. Cathy smiled at him.

"Sometimes I agree with you," she said.

Then they were rolling up the drive toward Moonrise and Jennie was standing on the gallery waiting for them.

Ross was surprised and pleased at how well kept the plantation looked. Apparently David Martin, the overseer, had done his work with uncommon thoroughness. They came to a stop before the house, and the Negroes swarmed about the rig, crying greetings and reaching up to take the baggage.

Ross kissed the cheek Jennie offered him, and turned to Cathy.

"This is Jennie, Cathy," he said.

"Welcome home, Cathy," Jennie said softly, and took the slim girl in her arms.

"Where are the twins?" Cathy said; "I'm just dying to see them!"

"Upstairs. Come on in. You, too, Henry – if you like."

"No'm," Henry smiled. "Reckon I'll be getting along back to Laurel Hill. Be seeing y'all. . . ."

" 'Bye," Cathy said, and put out her small, freckled hand. "It was nice meeting you. . . ."

"The pleasure was all mine, ma'am," Henry said. "So long, Ross. I'll be out to see you – some night when you ain't at home!"

Then he turned the pair away from the house and moved off down the drive.

"He's charming," Jennie said.

"Yes, he is," Cathy agreed.

"He's going to make a charming corpse," Ross said grimly, "if he isn't careful."

"Oh, you!" Cathy laughed, and gave his arm an affectionate squeeze.

They moved upstairs to the bedroom. Inside, little Peter and Annis were playing cheerfully upon the floor. It came as a shock to Ross to realize they were now almost seven years old.

Cathy picked up little Annis, a blonde cherub, with chubby pink cheeks. She sat down, holding the child on her lap, and little Peter stopped his game of toy soldiers and climbed up beside her. Suddenly, helplessly, Cathy started to cry.

"What's the matter, dear?" Jennie said.

"I — I want a baby so much!" Cathy sobbed; "and it looks like we'll never have any!"

"That's the will of God," Jennie said gently. "But you can help me with these all you want to — and believe me, you'll have your hands full!"

Ross turned sadly away from his wife, and, as he did so his gaze fell upon the night table beside Jennie's bed. There was a pipe upon it — half full of tobacco ash. Jennie saw his astonished look and smiled.

"David and I have been married a month," she said. "It was better that way. The children needed a father. And with their uncle forever away from home they were getting a little undisciplined. I — I hope you approve, Ross."

"I do," Ross said heavily. "Dave's a fine man. There's only one question in my mind, Jen —

do you love him?"

"I respect him," Jennie said. "It's a great comfort to be married to a man who always comes home at night. . . ."

"Still thinking of that, eh? By the way, how're Annis and Danton making out?"

Jennie's face was very still.

"They aren't," she said.

"They aren't?" Ross echoed blankly. "Why not, Jen?"

"They were never married. After you left — Morgan started coming here asking after you. I told her I had no news of you, but she kept coming — I'm sorry, Cathy — you have no cause for concern. Ross never loved Morgan; it was the other way around. . . ."

"Thanks, Jen," Ross said.

"And I thank you, too," Cathy said impishly. "I don't think he'd look very pretty with his eyes scratched out on top of that broken nose!"

"Don't mind her," Ross said brusquely. "Tell me what happened. . . ."

"She met Danton, of course. And you know Morgan. Danton is a very handsome boy; she just had to have him on her string."

"And she got him, " Ross said grimly.

"The funny part about it is I don't think so. Danton came here afterwards and begged me to intercede for him with Annis. He swore by the

Virgin and on the honor of his mother that he was innocent. I believed him, Ross; but Annis — didn't. She gave him back his ring and broke the engagement. He pleaded with her. He wrote her — he came back again and again; but Annis simply said: 'That woman killed my brother. She's poisonous. I don't want anything her lips have touched.' "

"She compromised him," Ross said; "she arranged something — something that would look worse than it was . . . ."

"Yes," Jennie said. "Out of spite. Out of pure wickedness — because she wanted to hurt you, I reckon."

"And Annis?" Ross said.

"She's upstairs in her room. She vowed she'd never leave this house again. She hasn't, Ross — and it's been over two years. . . ."

"You'll excuse me, Cathy?" Ross said; and started for the door.

"No," Cathy said; "I'm coming with you. The poor thing! What she needs is a woman to talk some sense into her head."

"It won't do any good, Cathy," Jennie warned. "I've tried it myself."

The face of his sister shocked him. Annis had always been a very pretty girl, and now she was lovely. But the loveliness was not of this world. It was wan, dreamlike, ethereal. It was a spiritual loveliness, born of resignation – of acceptance.

"Annis –" Ross said.

"Oh!" Annis said, Then: "Ross – you're back. I'm glad."

But there was no gladness in her voice, nor surprise either. There was nothing in her voice. It was dead.

By his side, Cathy stared at her sister-in-law pityingly.

"Poor thing!" she murmured.

"Look, Annis," Ross began.

"I know," Annis said quickly; "you're going to tell me I'm very foolish to stay here like this. You're right. I am."

"Then why in the name of heaven –"

"Because I can't help it," Annis said.

"Why can't you help it?" Cathy said. "Why can't you, Annis?"

Annis stared at her.

"Who are you?" she said.

"Your sister-in-law. Ross's wife. My name is Cathy."

"Cathy?" Annis said. "Cathy. I like that. It's a pretty name."

"Oh, God!" Ross groaned.

Annis smiled at him gently.

"You think I'm mad, don't you, Ross? You're right. I am – a little."

"You can't do this, Annis!" Ross said; "You can't stay here like this! You're young and lovely and . . . ."

"I have to, Ross," Annis said. "You see, he was never here. In this room, I mean. He was everywhere else. We rode together all over the plantation and all through Natchez and most everywhere else around here. When I go out it reminds me. The trees remind me – the flowers, the river. Everything reminds me – so I can't go out. You see?"

"No," Ross said gruffly; "I don't see."

"Oh, Ross," Cathy whispered; "take me out of here! I'm going to cry and I don't want her to see it. . . ."

"All right," Ross said. "I'll come back later to talk to you, Annis."

"Do," Annis said. " 'Bye, Cathy."

" 'Bye!" Cathy choked. Outside in the hall, she fell against Ross, sobbing.

"Oh, Ross," she wept; "how could she? What a terrible thing!"

"The woman who did this," Ross said, "is terrible. Come now, we'd better go down again."

They came down into the dining room where Jennie was fixing supper for them with the aid of several slaves.

Just after they had sat down to supper, David Martin came into the house. He saw Ross sitting there, and his clean-cut face reddened with embarrassment. But Jennie got up and kissed him quickly.

"It's all right, dear," she said; "Ross knows —"

"And approves," Ross added, and put out his hand.

David took it, grinning boyishly.

"Thank you, sir!" he said; "I'm mighty glad — that worried me a whole lot. Kind of reckoned you'd think I'd aimed too high. . . ."

"The man who doesn't aim high is the one who's not worth his salt," Ross said. "Cathy, I want you to meet David Martin, formerly my associate — and now a member of the family. . . . David, this is Cathy, my wife."

"Mighty happy to make your acquaintance, ma'am," David said. "Your husband's a fine man. Everybody hereabouts respects him."

"They won't any more," Cathy said tartly, "if he doesn't give up some of his foolish ideas. . . ."

They all looked at Ross inquiringly.

"I didn't mean to bring it up so soon," he said; "but now that Cathy's mentioned it, I might as well. Look David, would you and Jennie consider selling me the Negroes that Tom left you?"

Jennie looked at her husband then back at Ross.

"He didn't leave us any, Ross," she said. "He left everything to you with the provision that you'd keep me and the children here as long as you were able to. . . ."

"I see," Ross said. "In a way that simplifies things — and in another way, it doesn't. . . ."

"You're planning to sell the place, sir?" David asked. "If you are, I've got a good idea. Last year the lumber mill made more money than the plantation. It's going great guns. Now if you'd let me buy into that, I'd be mighty beholden to you."

"That does it!" Ross said. "Heck, Dave — I'll sign the mill over to you and Jen. And you can stay here at Moonrise — without working the place. I'm going to sell most of the land except that right around the house anyhow."

Jennie stared at him.

"Why, Ross?"

"Because," Cathy said flatly, "he plans to set the niggers free."

Oddly enough, it was David who recovered first.

"Well, sir," he said, "you're within your rights; but you sure picked the wrong time to do it!"

"He's not within his rights," Cathy said hotly; "not now. To do such a thing would be giving aid and comfort to the enemy!"

Jennie looked at her and her mouth tightened.

"A lot of great men have agreed with Ross about slavery, honey," she drawled, "Thomas Jefferson, for one. He called it an 'insufferable crime,' and freed his Negroes. George Washington directed that his be freed at the death of his wife or his daughter, I don't remember which. . . ."

"I don't believe it!" Cathy said.

"That's always the refuge of those who don't like to face facts, Cathy," Ross said gently.

Cathy stood up, her fingers gripping the tablecloth.

"I don't care!" she cried. "Niggers were meant by God to be slaves! And until He comes down to earth and tells me different, Himself, I won't believe it!" Then she whirled and ran away from them, up the stairs.

"You have got something on your hands, Ross!" Jennie remarked drily.

"I have," Ross admitted ruefully, "I really have."

In a matter of weeks, he discovered exactly how much he did have on his hands; for, when he applied to the courts for permission to free his blacks and transport them to Liberia, the storm that broke about his head was of a ferocity that even he had not anticipated.

Men called at his house to argue, to threaten.

His friends tried to point out to him the folly of the whole thing; strangers, and mere acquaintances were openly abusive. Within the space of three weeks he received twenty-one challenges. He refused them all.

The worst of it was the fact that Cathy would not speak to him at all — not even to make the simplest request. She added to his burdens by refusing to wear the riding dress he had bought her, and galloping about in one of his own habits which she had cut down and made over, riding astride like a man, with a little cigar stuck in her teeth to the great scandal of the whole countryside.

The lower courts denied permission. The State law, they declared, clearly denied a man the right to free his Negroes under any conditions whatsoever.

Ross called his Negroes up to the gallery of the house and told them the bad news.

"What you gonna do now, Marse Ross?" Brutus rumbled. "Gonna let them folks lick you — or you gonna fight?"

"I'm gonna fight, Brutus," Ross said quietly. "This is the right thing — I'm going to fight."

He took the case to the higher courts down in Jackson. And this, of course, had certain consequences. For while he was absent, Morgan returned after a long absence from Finiterre.

She rode like a queen out to the house. And one of her first visitors was Henry Montcliffe.

"Heard about Ross Pary?" he said. "Damn fool is fighting like hell to free his niggers. The whole neighborhood is up in arms over it. Me'n' Henry Metcalfe and Levin Marshall talked some of the boys out of riding over there and burning his house — pointed out to them that Tom's wife and kids had nothing to do with it, and they'd be the ones to suffer most."

"That was sweet of you," Morgan drawled; "no, I hadn't heard. I didn't even know he was back."

"Yep. Came back all right. Brought the cutest little filly with him I ever did see. Got the funniest-looking little face, freckled all over like a setter pup —"

"Big mouth. Chestnut hair. Thin. . . ."

"How the devil did you know, Morg?"

"Cathy —" Morgan whispered; "Cathy Linton! So he married her!" And the fury was there now, in her black eyes.

"Yep," Henry grinned, "sure Lord did. It aggravates me, Morg. 'Cause that lil' gal's done given me the itch so bad. . . ."

"The itch?" Morgan said, looking at him narrowly, "what kind of an itch, Henry?"

"I want her," Henry said huskily. "Goddamn my black soul to hell, I want her!"

"So?" Morgan mused. "So little Cathy's interesting, eh?"

"I'll say she is! You should see her — rides astride like a man, and can take jumps that nobody in his right mind would even attempt. She does it standing up in the stirrups with a little cigar stuck between her teeth. Brother! I'll bet she'd burn a man up! Damn her skinny little soul, she fair sets me wild. . . ."

"Hmmmn," Morgan said. Then suddenly, startlingly, she started to laugh. And the whole room rang with her laughter.

Henry stared at her.

"What's got into you, Morg?" he said morosely.

"Nothing! Nothing much, anyhow. It's just that I have a wonderful idea. Come here, Henry darling, and give me a kiss."

Henry grinned at her.

"Sure thing, honey child!" he said.

"That," Morgan said a few moments later, "was payment in advance."

"For what?" Henry said.

"For Ross Pary's wife. I'm going to give her to you," Morgan said.

Cathy woke up that morning, and stared at the empty place beside her. For Ross, as usual, was away at Jackson, fighting his case.

557

"Damn him!" she said aloud; "Oh, damn him, damn him, damn him!"

Looking out of the window, she saw that it was late — much later than she usually awakened, so she dressed hurriedly and went downstairs into the dining room. She ate her skimpy breakfast alone, for the Martins had long since had theirs. Then she went out on the gallery, wondering what on earth she was going to do.

"Oh, heck!" she said fretfully, "reckon I'll go riding again . . ." But as she turned to go back into the house and change into her mannish riding habit, she saw someone coming up the drive. She waited quietly, and when the rider was close, she saw that it was a woman. The most beautiful woman, she was certain, that she had ever seen in all her life.

"How do you do?" the woman said. Her voice, Cathy noted, was low, rich, thrilling. "You must be Cathy. . . ."

"I am," Cathy said. "Who are you?"

"Morgan."

"Oh!" Cathy said.

"I can see you've heard of me," Morgan laughed. Her laugh was as clear as spring water, as unsullied as a child's. "Terrible things, no doubt?"

"Yes," Cathy said; "terrible things. They aren't true, are they?"

Morgan swung down from Satana.

"Why do you ask that?" she murmured.

"Because looking at you, I don't believe them," Cathy said. "You don't look like a wicked woman."

Morgan slipped a firm arm about Cathy's waist and leaning forward, kissed her cheek.

"Thank you for that, Cathy, dear," she said. "It's sweet of you."

"Are they?"

"Why, yes," Morgan smiled, "as a matter of fact, they are. I'm just as wicked as people say I am. No – wickeder."

"Well, I'll be damned!" Cathy said helplessly.

"You're a charming girl," Morgan said. "We're going to be great friends, aren't we, Cathy?"

Suddenly, impulsively, Cathy smiled at her.

"Why, yes we are," she said. "Damned if I don't like you, Morgan. Come on in the house."

"I can't," Morgan said; "I have only a minute. I rode over to invite you over to my place tonight. I know Ross isn't here and you must get lonely."

"I do," Cathy said.

"Then you'll come?"

"Yes," Cathy said, "I'll come."

"Don't tell Jennie. She doesn't approve of

me. Just say you're going riding. 'Bye now."

" 'Bye, Morgan," Cathy said.

That night, out at Finiterre, Cato admitted her with a profound bow.

"Miz Morgan say you come upstairs," he said; "she in her bedroom."

Cathy climbed the stairs, and stood looking at the doors; then Morgan came out of one of them and took her arm.

"Come in, Cathy!" she said. "Oh, I'm so glad to see you. Sit down — have a glass with me."

The goblets were huge, bell-shaped affairs. They'd hold a mighty heap, Cathy reckoned; but a mood of recklessness was upon her.

"Don't mind if I do," she said.

Morgan poured the goblets full of ancient, potent brandy — a liquor that Cathy had never tasted before in her life. Before she had it half down the room was beginning to swing about her head in circles.

"Another?" Morgan said softly.

"God, no!" Cathy gasped; "I feel awful!"

"Excuse me a moment," Morgan said; "I'll get you something for that."

She was gone a long time. Then the door opened again, and Cathy looked up. But it was not Morgan who stood there. It was a man. A tall man — Henry Montcliffe.

"Cathy . . ." he whispered thickly, "my

little Cathy. . . ."

"What do you want?" Cathy said.

"You," Henry Montcliffe said.

Then he was bending above her, searching for her mouth. His breath was heavy with liquor, and Cathy turned her head away from him. His hands came down upon her shoulders. Cathy felt herself being borne over backward, then lifted, and thrown down across the bed, hard. His big hand was among her skirts, hot upon the flesh of her thigh. And it came to Cathy then that she had been tricked. Then the rage rose in her and beat about her temples. It cleared away the fumes of the brandy.

She brought her knees up until they crowded against her small breasts, and kicked out with both feet. They caught Henry Montcliffe full in the belly and sent him over backward. Then she came up off the bed, fast, and picked up the lamp from the night table. Fortunately for Henry it was not lit. She lifted it in both hands and brought it down upon his head. It broke into pieces, being made of china, and the blood and the kerosene mingled in curious streams on his face.

When Morgan, attracted by the noise, came back into the room she was already gone, scurrying down the stairs and out into the moonlight.

Morgan stood there looking down at Henry Montcliffe, groaning on the floor. Then clearly, delightedly, she began to laugh.

"That Cathy!" she said. "A girl after my own heart!"

Chapter 18

"Ready, Brutus?" Ross said.

"Yassuh, Marse Ross, we's ready."

Ross looked at the boy, Numa, a proud stripling now — almost as tall as his father, and at black Rachel, grown a little heavier with the years, which made her look all the more like a queen. They were the last. All the other Negroes were gone. He felt a momentary anger at the method he had had to use to free them, finally — slipping them off by twos and threes to the wild, wooded country north of Finiterre. But after tonight he could breathe, for Brutus and his family were the last.

He had won his case in the Supreme Court finally, won it months ago. Through the uproar of men cursing and waving their canes and threatening to lynch Ross Pary, the Judge had handed down the decision that although the State law forbade the freeing of Negroes, it had been designed to prevent the increase of free blacks within the borders of the state, and since the plaintiff Ross Pary had declared his intention of removing the Negroes to Africa, the law hardly applied in this case.

That should have been all of it, but it wasn't. For, when in the fall of 1859, Ross Pary returned to Moonrise, determined to carry out his own wishes in the matter, he found himself faced with the threat of physical violence at the hands of men who had been his neighbors and friends.

He and Cathy got down from the carriage to find the front yard filled with a crowd of more than a hundred men. The men parted and let them through until they reached the gallery. Then Ross turned and faced them.

"Well, gentlemen?" Ross said.

A heavy set man, whom Ross recognized as Anthony Niven, an upriver planter, stepped forward.

"Pary," he said, "we're here to tell you that if you set those niggers free, we're going to stop you. We'll stop you peacefully if we can, 'cause we haven't a thing against you personally. You've been a good planter, and a good neighbor.

"But, right now, the future of the South's at stake. Them black Republicans are gaining power every day. Let them seat a man in the White House and it'll mean war. Things like this only help them out. So, Pary, if we have to, we'll use force. . . ."

He paused, looking around him at the other men.

"We're prepared," he said heavily, "to hang or shoot every nigger what attempts to leave this place — and you with 'em, if you offer resistance. That's all Pary; I've had my say. You've been warned."

Cathy could see Ross stiffen, and she laid a restraining hand upon his arm. But he took a step forward, his blue eyes cold as ice, and just as hard.

"All right, Niven," he said; "you've had your say, now I'll have mine. I see before me a fine example of Southern chivalry, and of Southern courage. It took an immense amount of bravery, didn't it, for a hundred of you to ride up here to tell one man what he must do.

"I've always wondered why dogs and jackals travel in packs; now I know . . ."

Cathy could see the rage flaming in their eyes, but Ross went on unperturbed.

"You say you'll kill my blacks, and kill me, too, if I persist. Very well. I've always been prepared to die for what I believe in. That's not the question. The question is – are you? For, my dear Niven, if you force me to it, I shall arm my Negroes and meet fire with fire. And I make you my solemn promise before the God I serve, that I shall make sure that you and the other five or six ringleaders in this business do not leave the field alive. Now if you want to prevent me from doing what the courts of this State and the laws of the land have given me a perfect right to do, go ahead; but damn your filthy souls to hell, be prepared to take the consequences!"

He turned then, and marched with Cathy on his arm into the house. And Cathy and Jennie waited anxiously for half an hour while the men milled about outside and muttered threats. Then, finally, they rode away.

On the first of October, Ross began removing the Negroes from the place. At Jennie's plea, he did so secretly, to avoid conflict. A wagon load of small faggots moved northward in broad daylight; but under the twigs and small branches, ten Negroes lay. The blacks slipped by twos and threes every night, and hid in the woods north of Finiterre. Many bales of cotton, each containing a man, were carried down to Ross's steamboat landing, and a vessel took them away, landing them about fifty miles below New Orleans.

The few Negroes left sang and talked loudly in the quarters, and round about Moonrise, the men watching at the fires got tired of waiting.

"He's given up," they said; "we've got him licked."

And now, finally, upon this October night, 1859, Ross Pary and Brutus and Rachel and the boy, Numa, climbed down the bluffs before Moonrise and got into a skiff. The men watching around the plantation had not thought of this.

Brutus and Numa took up the oars, and the skiff moved northward, against the current. There, four miles above Finiterre, the steamboat waited, commanded by a man who had expressed his willingness to sail pine knots into hell, if paid enough.

He already had steam up. Ross and the last of his slaves came aboard, and the sternwheels threw white water. The smoke stood up from the stacks, blacker than the night itself, and the Mississippi shore slid backward slowly.

At Biloxi, a vinegary Maine captain, who had decided ideas upon the subject of human slavery, waited with his ship. He had already taken on a consignment, bound for the Mediterranean; but he was willing to make a detour of some hundreds of miles to land the blacks on the West African Coast. When, six months before, the case had already become a national *cause célèbre,* Captain Benton had written Ross and offered his services. Through the mail and in the strictest privacy, the arrangements had been made.

So it was that now Ross Pary stood on the deck of the *Augusta* with his people clustered about him. The younger children were laughing and playing, but most of the older blacks were in tears. They all knelt upon the deck while Ross said a prayer for their safety. Then he started down the ladder to the little boat that would take him ashore, and they crowded about him crying and kissing his hands. Ross wept too, and he was not ashamed of it. Then as he moved off from the ship, Rachel started to sing something. It was a spiritual, but Ross had never heard it before. And one by one the other voices took it up until they were all singing it. The words rolled out over the water, thunderously deep on the basses of the men, and angel-sweet in the women's high soprano tones.

Straining his ears through the splashing of the oars that bore him toward Biloxi, Ross could just make out some of the words.

"Before I'll be a slave," the Negroes sang;

"I'll be buried in my grave,
and go home to my Lord, and be free!"

"Amen," Ross whispered, watching the smoke come up from the *Augusta's* single stack, amid the forest of her masts and cording, "Amen!"

And the *Augusta* stood out to sea.

He got back to Natchez on the afternoon of October 16th, 1859 — the very worst day he could have chosen to come home. David and Jennie and Cathy were at the landing waiting for him in a landau with a pile of lap robes on the floor between the seats.

"Quick," Cathy said urgently; "lie down on the floor! Get under the robes!"

Ross stared at her.

"Why?" he said; "what's all this foolishness about, Cathy?"

"Do as I say!" she snapped. "They'll kill you!"

"Who'll kill me?" Ross asked patiently. "Whom do you want to hide me from?"

"The people," Jennie said. "Ross, today that old fool John Brown raided Harpers Ferry in Virginia in order to start a nationwide slave uprising. The people are pretty excited — and they know you've freed your blacks by now. That man Niven came back yesterday and found the quarters empty and you gone. Oh, Ross, they might kill you! They really might!"

"I see," Ross said. Then, "Dave, take the girls home."

"Look, Ross," David began.

"Do as I say!" Ross thundered; "I don't sneak into town under a blanket – not even to save my life."

"I knew he'd say that!" Cathy wept. "Oh, you big, stupid jackass – I don't want you killed!"

"And I thought so too," David said, "that's why I had a nigger I borrowed from Finiterre follow us on Nancy. He's waiting over there. You got a gun, Ross?"

"Yes," Ross said; "I have a gun."

"Then you better ride like hell," David said.

"Thanks, Dave," Ross said.

"Oh, you fool!" Cathy sobbed; "you damned stupid fool – haven't you brought me enough sorrow already?"

"Reckon I have," Ross smiled. "Maybe, now, you'll be rid of me. . . ."

"But I don't want to be rid of you, darling!" Cathy wept; "I don't wan –" But Ross stopped her protests with his mouth. Then he was off, running toward where the black waited with Nancy. He mounted up and started up Silver Street; but, to their astonishment, he rode very slowly.

"Oh, my God!" Cathy said; "he's too damned stubborn to even run!"

David Martin pulled at the reins and they started off after him.

"Maybe he's right, Cathy," he said; "to come pounding through Main at a gallop might attract too much attention."

Ross had thought of that, so he rode slowly, quietly through the crowds. Nobody noticed him until he was almost out of town. Then Tony Niven reared up his great bulk and thundered:

"There's one of the same kind! There's that damned nigger-loving Pary right now!"

The men started forward at a rush, and Ross pulled his revolver out and sat on Nancy waiting.

"I'm not running, men," he said quietly; "I don't want to kill any of you; but, by heaven, I will if I have to."

They hesitated. Tony Niven danced up and down with fury.

"Don't let him buffalo you, men!" he bellowed; "he can't kill us all!"

Instead of answering, Ross brought the revolver up and sent a shot crashing into the earth exactly between Niven's wide-spread feet. The bullet plowed up the earth, splattering it over his boots.

"No," Ross said pleasantly, reining Nancy to one side as he spoke until she moved in upon Niven; "but I can kill you, Niven. And it would be a pleasure, believe me. Now tell your friends to move aside and let me through, or you'll get it right where it'll do you the most good. I can scarcely miss from here."

Anthony Niven stared at him, his beet-red face paling.

"You win, this time," he said; "but I demand satisfaction. You'll meet me at Vidalia tomorrow!"

"Gladly," Ross smiled. "I have the choice of weapons, of course?"

Niven hesitated. Suppose the damned fool chooses rapiers, he thought. Anthony Niven was notorious for his clumsiness.

"What's the matter, Tony?" some one in the crowd called "Scairt?"

"You have your choice," he said huskily.

Ross smiled at him.

"Bowie knives." he said gently; "over a handkerchief at three paces, our left arms to be bound together. Good day, gentlemen."

Tony Niven stood there, sweating. He could see those flashing blades now, feel the rope biting into his left wrist. And this Pary, damn him, he thought, is thin as a sidewinder and just as quick. Hell, he'd slash me to ribbons while I was getting set. . . .

So thinking, he jerked his revolver out, and sent a bullet whining a scant half inch above Ross's head. Then Ross turned in the saddle and shot him. The ball caught Niven in the fleshy part of the right arm, breaking the bone. But out of pure terror, he spun and fell so convincingly that all the others thought him dead.

They started shooting at Ross; he flattened himself out along Nancy's neck, and rode like hell, while the men in the street scattered, bolting toward their horses, and a moment later they were pounding through Main Street after him, slashing their horse's flanks with whip and spur, leaning forward, standing in the stirrups.

Ross came out of the town on the road that led toward Moonrise and Finiterre. But that was a bad thing, for to take refuge in his own house would only endanger it and those who lived in it. Those men riding hell for leather behind him meant business. They were not wasting their ammunition by trying the difficult feat of trying to shoot him from the saddle at a gallop. No, they meant to corner him like a rat, and deal with him at their leisure. . . .

He'd have to turn off the road, make a break for it through the brush, lose himself among the trees. Here, a good chance of that existed;

but he wanted to put a bend of the road between himself and them before he turned off, hoping to confuse them even momentarily.

But as he rounded the curve leaning far over toward the inside sweep of it so as not to upset Nancy's balance, he almost crashed headlong into a rider coming from the opposite direction. He had barely time enough to yank Nancy's head savagely into a tighter turn, and leap her over the ditch into the high brush. But as her feet came down, he turned in the saddle and saw that the rider was Morgan Brittany, mounted upon Satana.

That does it, he thought; she'll tell them sure as hell, and curl her little pink toes inside her boots from joy watching them string me up. . . . But the oak grove was to his left, thick and dark, so he pounded into it, and drew Nancy up waiting.

He saw the men come boiling around the curve in a cloud of dust, and then they were pulling up, milling around Morgan, and Ross could see her pointing — away from him, into the swampy morass on the other side of the road, away from him, with a slight, negligent gesture giving him back his life.

They went over the ditch in rows, and disappeared among the further trees. Ross sat there waiting, and as he expected, Morgan turned

Satana off the road and came riding in the direction he had taken. When she was close, he rode out and met her.

"You're in a mess," she said, smiling. "Why, Ross?"

"Those boys got a mite riled up over my bad timing. I turned my Negroes loose the day before John Brown raided Harpers Ferry. I came back into town shortly after the news came from Virginia. And if I'm not exactly John Brown, they thought I'd make a mighty good substitute!"

"Come on," Morgan laughed, "let's ride."

"Where?"

"Finiterre. I'll hide you until this blows over."

"It won't blow over, Morgan," Ross said quietly; "I'm afraid I've killed a man in the bargain."

Morgan looked at him, and Ross could see the fire leaping behind her black eyes.

"Then you'll have to leave Natchez for good!"

"Yes," Ross said sadly; "I was planning to anyhow; but not so damned fast. Reckon I'll go up to New York, and send for Cathy. . . ."

"Just where," Morgan asked sweetly, "are you going to catch a boat or a train?"

"Oh, damn!'" Ross groaned; "I hadn't

thought of that!"

"But I have. Come on darling, we'll ride back to Finiterre — and I'll buy the tickets."

Ross stared at her, hard. He couldn't believe this. As long as he had known her, Morgan had never stepped out of character for an instant. Now, in one day, she had saved his life, and was preparing to help him escape — him and Cathy. Tickets, she had said, I'll buy the tickets.

"Oh, come on!"

They rode northward through the brush, and came out near the high gate that had cost Lance Brittany his life. Morgan saw Ross looking at it, and reached over and touched his hand.

"Don't think about that, now," she whispered.

When the Negroes came to take the reins, she bent down and said to them.

"Take Mister Pary's mare around to the stables, and saddle a horse for him. This animal," she added to Ross, "is completely blown. . . ."

"You think I'll have to ride again?" Ross said.

"I don't know. I just want to be prepared. I'm going to get on the upriver boat and pay the Captain to stop here, at the foot of the bluff. You can come aboard there. Then we'll go to Cincinnati and —"

"We?" Ross stared at her; "we!"

"Of course, darling! You didn't think I was going to purchase passage for that freckled wench you married? Oh, Ross, how stupid of you! I'm going North with you, dearest — that's the price you have to pay for your freedom."

"And when we get there?" Ross said coldly.

"I'll be your sweet little helpmeet," Morgan mocked, "and your devoted slave."

"No," Ross said quietly, "no, Morgan."

Morgan smiled at him.

"Help me down, darling," she said.

Ross put up his arms and lifted her down, but she put her two hands on his shoulders and stiffened her elbows so that she slid down slowly along all his length. Then she stood before him, serene, secret-smiling.

"Kiss me, Ross," she said.

"I salute you," Ross said bitterly, "the murderess of my brother; the killer of your husband. . . ." Then he kissed her.

Morgan drew her little, heart-shaped face away from his and stared at him.

"I didn't make the error that caused Tom's death," she said; "I avenged it. And I ridded myself of a man I hated, in order to have the man I love. You'd blame me for that, Ross? You, who were the cause of it all?"

"No," Ross said; "you are beyond blame or praise or any other consideration that affects the lives of men. The rules you live by were made for angels or for devils — I don't know which. . . ."

"Come into the house, Ross," Morgan said eagerly. "I'm going to hide you. I'm going to get those tickets. Once we get to New York, you can still send for your Cathy — if you still want to. My guess is that you won't want to — since you don't love her, never have loved her, and never will. . . ."

"I'll still send for her, Morgan," Ross warned.

"Up here," Morgan said, "there's a room in the attic, that they don't know about. You'll be safe there. So you think that you'll send for Cathy. Yes, come to think of it — you would. You've always gotten your feet entangled in your precious conceptions of honor and decency and all such rot. But the one fly in the whole ointment is — I don't believe your little Cathy would come."

"Why not?" Ross growled.

"Henry Montcliffe," Morgan said.

"You're lying!" Ross spat.

Morgan turned upon the landing of the last flight of stairs before the attic and caught at his lapels.

"I'm not lying, Ross," she said. "I only lie to stupid men. But what good would it do me to tell you a lie that you could disprove so easily? For instance, if I told you they'd cuckolded you, I would be lying. They haven't — yet. All they've done is to see each other constantly here at Finiterre, with my assistance."

Ross looked at her.

"With your assistance," he said. "That figures, doesn't it?"

"Yes. I wanted her to run off with him. Then you'd be left — for me. I said once that love was a lot of foolishness, didn't I? I was right — it is. Only — after you left me, I found out that there're worse things than being foolish. . . ." She looked up at him, and tears were there suddenly, bright in her eyes. "All right," she said bitterly; "you can be proud, Ross Pary — because you're looking at a fool!"

"Go get those tickets, Morgan," Ross said.

But afterwards, sitting there in the darkness, in the attic, he had time to think about it. His thoughts ran around in circles, getting him nowhere. There was the shape of betrayal in them, the black of treachery. There was the ugliness of anger, and of jealousy and of grief. He walked up and down rubbing his hands together until he came to the door.

He stopped short, looking at that door in the

gloom. It was of heavy timbers, hung with strap iron hinges. It was — or had been, counterweighted, so that when anyone left the room into which it led, all he had to do was to pull up a small brass stop attached to the bottom of it, and it would swing closed behind him. But now the counterweight was missing from the cords that ran over the pulleys. Ross looked around until he found the weight sitting in the corner. He attached it to the cords and tried the door. It worked perfectly, swinging shut the instant he took the pressure of his hand away from it.

Funny that Morgan didn't have that fixed, he thought. Then it came to him that it was equally strange that he had fixed it. It's the idleness, he mused, and the waiting. . . . Why the devil don't those beggars come?

He tried the door and this time it swung open wider, and he caught a glimpse of some objects on the floor. In the dim light, filtering in from a tiny barred ventilator under the peak of the roof, he couldn't make out what they were. So he pushed the door open, and went in. The moment he turned it loose, it started to swing shut, and he had to leap and catch it. As he set the brass stop, he looked at it. There was no handle on the inside of it, no knob, nothing.

Whoever had built that door, hadn't meant

for it to be opened from the inside. And the moment Ross lit a match, he saw why. There were manacles attached to the floor by lengths of chain. On the walls were hung whips as cruel as the one he'd felt in Cuba. Ross put out his hand to take one of them, but then he drew it back. He didn't need to pick up one of the damnable things. Bessie, before she had been hanged that night, hadn't lied. Not even about this had she lied.

He backed out of the room, and released the stop so that the door swung shut. As he started down the stairs, it came to him how near a thing it all had been, how much better it was after all merely to lose his life. With Morgan a man could lose more. Much more.

He came out into the sunlight, and mounted the horse the Negroes had brought around to the hitching post before the house. He started riding northward, towards Vicksburg, thinking: Damn them, they've had all the time in the world!

And they had had. But for the two hours they had spent pulling one of their number and his horse out of the sticky black mud of the swamp into which Morgan Brittany had directed them, they would have reached Finiterre long ago.

When they did reach it, they circled the place

and one of them went into the stable and found Nancy standing there, still saddled.

"She did trick us, boys," he growled. "The bastard's here all right — his nag's out in the stable."

They surrounded the house then and started shooting into it, and the two or three Negroes inside of it ran out waving sheets and tablecloths and anything else they could get their hands on. The townsmen let them pass. At the moment, they weren't interested in killing Negroes.

One of them stood up, and called:

"Come on out, Pary! We know you're in there."

There was no answer.

"Reckon we'll have to smoke him out," another one said.

"Well — now — it ain't his house."

"It's hern! And she damn near got us all drowned in that black-gum swamp!"

"Damned right. Burn it, I say."

The leader stepped forward again.

"Come on out, Pary," he said, "or we'll burn that shack around you!"

But, when they did start to fire Finiterre, they found it difficult. It had been a wet fall, and the twigs and moss they gathered refused to do more than smolder, sending up great puffs of smoke. Even when the rugs and curtains caught at last, there was more smoke than fire.

Riding northward, Ross Pary saw the smoke, and whirled his horse around. At the landing, below the house, Morgan saw it, and started running down the plank before it had touched ground, and up the path that wound up the bluff. She came up on the terrace, panting, and slashed open the face of the man who tried to stop her with her riding crop, and dashed into the house. All the way up the stairs she was screaming his name. The smoke boiled into her lungs, but she kept on, falling and getting up, and crawling up the last flight until she came to the room where she had left him. She groped around it from side to side, running her hands over the walls, the floor. Then she remembered the other room, and pushed with all her strength against the heavy door. It came open and she fell through it, and lay on the floor sobbing and gasping for breath and the door swung shut behind her.

Pounding down the road toward Finiterre with Henry Montcliffe and the Metcalfe brothers, and Charles Dahlgren, and Levin Marshall and two dozen others of the real aristocracy of Natchez, men deeply opposed to the methods of such men as Anthony Niven and his followers, Cathy saw the smoke, too. Only, by the time they reached Finiterre, there was flame in it, too.

They poured through the high gate, sending up great clods of mud from their horses' hoofs and the men who had burnt it, turned and ran for their horses, and hurtled away northward into the thick woods above Finiterre. And not a shot was fired in anger.

The men dismounted and formed a bucket brigade from the big house down to the spring and fought the fire stubbornly for half an hour, with Cathy taking her place in the line next to Henry Montcliffe and working as hard as any of them. Twenty minutes later, Ross Pary rode back into the courtyard and took up a bucket with the rest, and they kept the buckets moving down the line to the spring house and back again full, and the men at the head of the line splashed them upon the fire. They won finally, after two hours of back-breaking labor. That they won, that the fire was put out, was due as much to the three-week siege of rains that had preceded this day as to their efforts.

And Ross Pary walked away from the line to the bluff and stood there looking at the beautiful house he had built, blackened by smoke and ruined on the ground floor by fire, but not beyond repair. He sighed, and half turned, and then he saw the upriver steamboat waiting quietly at the landing. And he realized then, that some of the men in that line, the ones he didn't know, must have been passengers and crew members from the boat, and last of all, more slowly — that Morgan must have got here after all.

He started for the house then, running, but before he reached it, Cathy put out her hand and caught his arm.

"Ross!" she said, "now what the devil—"

"Morgan!" Ross cried and tore free of her.

Henry Montcliffe heard him and he and some of the others started up the stairs after Ross. The house was still filled with smoke, and smelled of burnt wood and cloth. They found Ross Pary in the attic, in that strange room, leaning weakly back against the wall staring at the inert figure on the floor. One of them went down to the third floor and came back with an oil lamp.

Morgan was lying on her side, with her face turned toward the door. Her face was smudged with smoke, through which her tears had made white streaks. Otherwise, there was not a mark upon her. But — she was dead.

"Holy Jesus!" George Metcalfe said, "look at her fingernails!"

Ross looked at her hands. The nails were broken off down to the quicks and the ends of her fingers were bloody. And on the door were long, deeply gouged furrows. She hadn't been unconscious, Ross realized. Then, walking around the other side of her in the direction her face was turned, he saw that she hadn't. Morgan's eyes were wide open, staring upon unimaginable horrors.

"Smoke, I reckon," Henry Montcliffe muttered.

Ross stared at him. Then quietly he bent down and picked Morgan up in his arms.

He came down the stairs with her and placed her tenderly in a swing on the gallery, and put up his hand and closed her eyes and took off his frock coat and covered her with it. When he turned, Cathy saw his face.

She didn't say anything to him. She merely turned and walked away from him toward her horse, and mounted and rode away through the high gate toward Moonrise.

Ross mounted then, and rode after her. She drew up her mount and waited for him and they rode down the road together without saying anything. Finally, just before they reached Moonrise, Cathy turned to him.

"What are you going to do now?" she said.

"We're going North, Cathy," Ross said,

and Cathy stiffened.

"You're going North, Ross," she said; "I'm staying."

Ross looked at her, pain moving in his eyes.

"You'd leave me over this?" he said.

"I," Cathy said, in that flat voice of hers, "am tired of living with the ghosts of your old loves, Ross. Yes — I'd leave you over this."

They came back to Moonrise, silently, sadly.

Ross began to pack slowly, with Cathy sitting there watching him, her elbows resting upon her knees, and her chin upon the palms of her hands.

"Cathy," Ross said, "I'm asking you to come with me."

"No," Cathy said.

Chapter 19

In the late fall of 1860, Jennie Martin received a letter. At first she thought it was from Ross, because it came from New York; but then she saw it was sent by someone who knew nothing of her more recent history, for it was addressed to Mrs. Thomas Pary. But for the fact that it was also addressed to Moonrise, and the postmaster in Natchez knew Jennie well, she might not have gotten it at all.

She opened it and read:

"Dearest Jennie,

"I have the happiness to be back in America after so many years of absence. Yet I have also sadness, because everything reminds me of my beloved Ross — who died in my behalf so long ago."

Jennie straightened up. Who died? Is she

mad? Then she went back to the letter.

"It was originally planned that I should come to New Orleans — but since the election of that strange, wonderful Abraham Lincoln, there is so much talk of war, that my manager, M. Bergson, thought it wiser to cancel them. I am a dancer now, called, extravagantly, I think, 'La Habeñera.' I wanted so much to come to New Orleans, for then it would have been possible for me to visit Moonrise, to see once more the house of him who became my husband — did you know that, Jennie? But how could you — since he died in Cuba.

"I don't think that I shall ever stop loving him, or forget the smallest gesture of his. He was so wonderful, my Ross. I can write no more. The memory is insupportable. Please, if you can, write me, Jennie *mía* — I shall never forget your wedding.

Adios,
Conchita"

Jennie looked at the letter just once more and that was to mark the address of the theatre from which it was written. Then she dashed down the stairs and mounted her horse, and set off for Natchez at a hard gallop.